THE FANDOM

THE
FANDOM

ANNA DAY

Chicken House

SCHOLASTIC INC. / NEW YORK

First published in the United Kingdom in 2017 by Chicken House, 2 Palmer Street,
Frome, Somerset BA11 1DS.

The publisher does not have any control over and does not assume any responsibility for
author or third-party websites or their content.

Library of Congress Cataloging-in-Publication Data available

ISBN 978-1-338-23270-7
10 9 8 7 6 5 4 3 2 1   18 19 20 21 22
Printed in the U.S.A.   23
First edition, May 2018
Book design by Elizabeth Parisi

For Ellie and Charlie

PROLOGUE

Exactly one week from today, I will hang.

I will hang for my friends, my family, and, above all else, love. A thought that offers surprisingly little comfort when I think about the noose closing around my neck, my feet searching for solid ground, my legs flailing . . . dancing in midair.

This morning I was clueless. This morning I was at Comic-Con, inhaling the scent of hot dogs and sweat and perfume, taking in the brightly colored costumes, the flash of the cameras, the bass drums and the violins. And yesterday I was in school, stressing over some stupid English presentation and wishing I were in another world.

Be careful what you wish for, because sometimes the reality truly blows.

CHAPTER 1

I BEGIN TO STAND, realize my maxi skirt has stuck to my thighs, and subtly unpeel the cotton from my skin.

"Go for it," Katie whispers.

I don't reply. Why did I volunteer to do this stupid presentation? Public speaking: not my strong point. Let's be honest, public *anything*: not my strong point.

"Whenever you're ready, Violet," Miss Thompson says.

I give the fabric one final tug and make my way to the front of the class. I suddenly feel very small, like my classmates have shrink rays attached to their eyes. Shrinking Violet. This makes me laugh—now I look unhinged as well as nervous.

Miss Thompson smiles at me from her crumbling desk. "So, Violet, tell us about your favorite novel, which is . . . ?"

"*The Gallows Dance* by Sally King," I reply.

A collective groan from the boys in the back row. But they're only faking disappointment. I saw them at the cinema less than a year ago when the film version came out and, as I recall, they all left with suspiciously red eyes.

I take a deep breath and begin to talk.

"*Once upon a time, there lived a race known as the humans.*

"The humans were smart and ambitious, but they were also greedy, a greed that extended to their ever-increasing obsession with perfection—the perfect body, mind, and life. At the turn of the twenty-second century, this obsession led to the first wave of genetically enhanced humans."

I leave a dramatic pause and glance around the room. I'd hoped they'd look enthralled, wide-eyed, but instead they look half-asleep.

"The Gems. Genetically Enhanced Man. Tall, strong, good-looking, Intelligence Quotients above 130. It wasn't long before the Gems moved to beautiful areas of countryside called the Pastures, free from disease and crime."

I shift my weight between my feet, sweep my hair from my eyes, and push that nagging thought that I'm making a giant fool of myself into the dark, unused part of my brain.

"But what of the non-genetically enhanced humans? Normal men and woman like you and me. They became known as the Imperfects. The Imps. Sealed inside the old cities—London, Manchester, Paris, Moscow—rife with disease and crime, locked behind miles of snaking city walls and bombed into submission. Only the stronger and more able Imps were permitted to enter the Pastures, to serve the Gems as slaves.

"The word human *became unspoken . . . forbidden.*

"There were only Gems and Imps—"

"So, I'm an Imp," Ryan Bell interrupts from the back of the class. "Is that what you're saying?"

Great. Just what I need—a heckler. And I wish I had the balls to point out that he must already know this, having sat through two hours of the film, Kleenex firmly clamped to nose.

"Shut it, jerkhead," Katie says. Her red bob whips in a perfect arc as she spins around to face him. I can't see her features, but I know she's giving him *that* look. The one where she narrows her pea-green eyes and presses her lips together.

"There ain't nothing imperfect about me," Ryan says.

Katie makes this strange noise, halfway between a laugh and a cough.

Miss Thompson frowns. "I think what Violet is trying to say is that we're all Imps, Ryan. Unless you're a superhuman from the future—which I highly doubt."

Deep breath. Ignore the numb lips.

"To ensure the continued subjugation of the Imps, the Gems gathered every week in great Coliseums and watched the Imps hang, an event known as the Gallows Dance. But some of the Imps refused to accept their fate, forming a group of rebels, determined to reinstate basic Imp rights. The rebel leader was called Thorn."

I fumble with my papers and locate his picture. A printout from the film. Miss Thompson slides it from my clammy fingers and pins it to the wall. Thorn's image completely fails to capture his power, his drive. This small, he just looks like a bondage-pirate-action-man, head to toe in black leather, eye patch slung across his chiseled face.

"Thorn hatched an elaborate plan to obtain Gem government secrets and asked his two most trusted rebels to recruit a young, female Imp.

"They recruited Rose."

Rose. The heroine of this tale. Passionate, impulsive, courageous. Every day, without fail, I wish I were her. And so far, here's how I measure up . . .

Passionate: My nickname is Violet the Virgin.

Impulsive: I spent two days planning this presentation.

Courageous: My face has started to sweat.

In fact, the only thing we share is our pale skin and our taste in men.

I nod to Miss Thompson, who takes her cue and crosses to the interactive whiteboard. A YouTube clip launches into action—the opening scene of the film. The camera zooms in on Rose as she scales the outer stone wall of the Coliseum. She looks awesome, her long dark hair tumbling down her back. She reaches the crest of the wall, accompanied by a swell of violins.

The camera switches to the spectators inside the Coliseum. A crowd of Gems—their beautiful faces baying for Imp blood. Nine condemned Imps are led onto a wooden stage, the nooses placed around their necks. I know they're only moments from being freed, yet I still feel this twist of anxiety in my stomach. I steal a quick look at my classmates. They actually look concerned, absorbed. A smile pulls at the corners of my mouth.

The Gem president appears on a giant screen behind the stage and introduces the condemned Imps by their alleged crimes: theft, rape, murder. The camera swings back to Rose, her dark hair whipping before her eyes—she knows the condemned Imps are guilty only of poverty and hunger. She pulls a grenade from her belt, touches it to her lips, and then hurls it over the crowd below.

The clip ends just before the bomb goes off.

I turn back to the class, bolstered by their sudden interest.

"While the Gems were distracted by the bomb, the rebels launched a rescue mission and saved the condemned Imps from the gallows. Rose slipped down the outer wall undetected, her worth as a rebel secured.

"So Thorn sent Rose on the most dangerous rebel mission to date: the Harper mission. Rose infiltrated the Harper estate deep in the Pastures and posed as a slave for the master of the house—Jeremy

Harper, a powerful Gem official. Rose quickly befriended Jeremy's son so she could discover classified Gem information.

"Jeremy's son was a Gem named Willow."

Willow. The main reason I wish I were Rose. And even though my hands still tremble, the residue of adrenaline moving through my veins, I keep gripping his picture, holding it up for the class to see. I just can't bear the thought of a thumbtack jabbing a hole in his perfect face. I've gazed at this poster for hours, memorized every contour of those features—all caramel skin and cheekbones. I hear a couple of sighs from the girls, a couple of "hubba-hubba" noises followed by a cluster of giggles. I tuck his image back into my pile of notes, a sense of possession gnawing at me.

"Spying and relations with a Gem: two crimes punishable by death for any Imp unfortunate enough to get caught. But Willow was kind and beautiful, and Rose soon realized that her greatest threat was the strength of her feelings for him. Unable to betray him, she fled the manor without ever revealing her true identity as a rebel. She returned to the Imp city, informing Thorn that the Harper mission was a failure—"

"Boring," Ryan says.

"Ryan, seriously," Miss Thompson snaps. "Stop interrupting, you're seventeen now and I expect better." She turns to me and smiles. "And I think we've just reached the midway twist, the turning point, is that right, Violet?"

I nod. "Rose fled the manor to protect him, she prioritized Willow over the rebels. She chose love."

"Yes. An example of how popular, modern novels still follow the traditional plot structure . . . Carry on."

"Willow disguised himself as an Imp and followed Rose across the city, desperate to win her back. But he was captured by the rebels and,

finally, he learned of Rose's initial plan to betray him. Heartbroken, held captive, all hope seemed lost.

"*But Rose told him she truly loved him, and together they escaped from the rebels, determined to forge a new life together.*

"*Sometimes, however, love cannot conquer all.*

"*The Gem authorities tracked them down and Rose was taken to the Gallows Dance, accused of seducing an innocent Gem boy.*"

Another YouTube clip. Rose at the Gallows Dance, but this time, she stands on the wooden stage at the front of the Coliseum with a noose around her neck, the crowd of Gems chanting for her blood.

"*STOP!*" Willow vaults onto the stage. "*My name is Willow Harper. And the Imp you're about to hang has a name. Rose. And she is the bravest, kindest person I've ever known. Imp or Gem, she is a human being. She isn't a temptress or a criminal. She is my best friend. And I love her with all my heart.*" He gazes into her determined face. "*I love you, Rose.*"

"*I love you, too,*" she cries back.

I know what's going to happen, of course I do, but I still feel the weight of tears on my lower lashes, this overwhelming urge to reach into that 2-D image and snip the rope.

The trapdoor beneath Rose's feet flies open. Her body drops, her legs twisting and kicking as she dances her final dance.

The clip ends. Nobody speaks.

Finally, Miss Thompson breaks the silence. "What a wonderful black moment the author created. But surely there's some sort of resolution?"

I nod, and shuffle to my last page of crumpled notes.

"*Willow cradled Rose's lifeless body, his tears falling onto her face. He berated the Gems for allowing government-sanctioned murder to*

continue, he begged them to join him. So moved were the Gems by this
tragic scene, they ripped the gallows to the ground.

"*The Gallows Dance was finally banned.*

"*Rose's death sparked a revolution.*

"*And the Imps and Gems called themselves humans once again.*"

The walls seem to absorb my final words, and I somehow
manage to swallow even though I have no saliva in my mouth.
Another silence. I wish Alice were here; she would clap and cheer
and shout, "Encore," and everyone else would join in.

I catch Katie's eye for a moment. She winks. Not quite the
public display of support I'd hoped for, but it makes me feel better
all the same.

"Thank you, Violet." Miss Thompson peers at me from over
her glasses. "What a wonderful presentation."

"Thanks, I wanted to do the book justice."

Miss Thompson smiles. "I can tell from the amount of color
you put into it. We'll make a writer of you yet."

I flush with pleasure. Writing has always been Alice's thing—I've
never dared touch it, until now. "Thanks, Miss Thompson."

Kiss ass. Teacher's pet. Hisses from the back of the class.

I slide back into my chair. Katie nudges me and whispers, "That
went really well." But I can still hear Ryan and his accomplices snig-
gering, the edges of their words blurring together, and my cheeks
begin to feel hot and itchy again and the bastard notes won't stop
sticking to my palms. Rose wouldn't have fallen to pieces like this.
I let my hair fall in front of my face, providing a dark, wavy shield.

"So there we have it," Miss Thompson says. "We've heard the
plots of three very different novels, yet seen how they all follow
roughly the same structure."

The bell rings, accompanied by the scrabbling of books and pens and backpacks.

Katie helps peel the paper from my clammy hands. "God, you really love that bloody book."

"Yeah."

"You should have seen your face when you mentioned Willow."

"That's just my face."

She bats her eyelashes. "But Willow was kind and beautiful, and Violet—sorry, I mean Rose—soon realized that her greatest threat was the strength of her raging hormones." She puckers up her lips, making the freckles on her nose elongate.

"Piss off." I laugh. Katie always makes me laugh. The tension drains from my body and I finally manage to stuff the disintegrating notes into my bag. Katie moved from Liverpool to London only last summer, so I haven't known her long, but we had this instant connection. She's got this dry sense of humor and she uses all these hilarious swearwords like *cockwomble* and *knobjockey*, and she talks with a gentle Liverpudlian accent that always makes her seem grounded—"salt of the earth," my dad once called her. Yet she looks like something from a Jane Austen novel, with her doll-like features and light-red hair . . . She actually plays the cello. The only thing I play is the Xbox.

"Don't worry about Dickhead, he just fancies you," she says.

"Yeah, right. He's embarrassed 'cause me and Alice caught him blubbering in the cinema last year."

She shoves her chair back. "Come on, you know you're hot."

I laugh. "Yeah, I'm sweating like a pig after that car crash."

"Just because you're not six foot and blonde like *some* people."

She means Alice. I don't reply. It's hard when your best friend looks like Britain's Next Top Model. A little kernel of envy lodges in my chest and I hate myself for it. We join the throng of students in the corridor, all hurrying to get home.

I change the subject. "I can't believe you still haven't read *The Gallows Dance*, it's a rite of passage." The crowd snatches my voice away, and I'm left feeling very small once again.

"Well, I don't need to now. You should come with a spoiler alert."

"You haven't even seen the film."

"Again. Spoiler alert."

We elbow through a group of fourteen-year-old girls who don't seem to know the unspoken rule of moving out of the way for upperclassmen.

I accidentally-on-purpose tread on a blonde girl's toe. "Yeah, but Russell's seriously fit." I'm talking about Russell Jones, the actor who plays Willow in the film.

"Really? You've never mentioned it. Here comes Alice." The smile never leaves Katie's mouth, but it slips completely from her eyes. Like me, she's learned to tell when Alice approaches by reading other people. Every male glances over his shoulder, every girl falls silent, brow knitted in a tight frown.

Sure enough, the crowd parts like the Red Sea, but this Moses has long, bronzed legs that swallow up the tiled floor as she strides toward us. A smile lights up her perfect oval face. She's always had that smile, ever since I met her on our first day at primary school—the kind of smile that makes you forgive her for being so beautiful.

She stops dead in the middle of the corridor, confident she won't get jostled. "So how did it go?"

"It was a bag of crap," I say.

Katie pats my back. "No, it wasn't, it was great."

"Yeah, a great big bag of crap," I reply.

Alice flips her pale hair over one shoulder. "Don't worry, Vi, they clearly don't get the beauty that is *The Gallows Dance*— philistines." She shoots a meaningful look at Katie.

"It's hardly Shakespeare," Katie mutters.

Alice sighs. "I wish I was in old Thompson's class, you get loads better stuff to do than us. Plot structure, I could have really contributed to that." She loves reminding us she's a rising fanfic star. She writes all this new material based on *The Gallows Dance*, messing with the plot, making the characters bend to her will. It's ironic she feels the need to do this when she's so accomplished at getting people to do what she wants in real life—perhaps writing is where she hones her art. I swallow down that little kernel of envy again.

"Miss Thompson said Violet could be a writer, didn't she, Vi?" Katie says.

Alice looks at me and winks an inky-blue eye. "Bullshit. You haven't got the imagination, you'd just rewrite *The Gallows Dance* again and again." She loops her arm around my shoulder and gives me a squeeze. "Which is a good thing, obviously." The scent of her hair—cherry blossom and lemongrass—fills my nostrils. I suddenly feel very special, Alice hugging me in public.

Katie glances at her watch. "Look, guys, I've got to go. I've got a cello lesson in five, but I'll see you tomorrow, yeah?"

"Comic-Con," Alice and I say in unison. We look at each other and smile. We've been waiting for this for months; we get to meet Russell. *Willow.* The dry mouth returns and I get this tremor of excitement in my belly, this feeling like my skin's been briskly toweled.

"We're going as characters from *The Gallows Dance*, agreed?" Alice says.

"Yeah, Nate's been planning his costume for days," I reply. Nate's my little brother, he loves *The Gallows Dance* more than me if that's possible, and Mum insisted he tag along. Thanks, Mum.

Katie begins to walk away. "See you tomorrow, fangirls," she calls over her shoulder.

CHAPTER 2

WHEN I PULLED on my costume this morning, I suddenly understood how Clark Kent could fly, how
Peter Parker could scale walls with his sticky palms.
It's that feeling like you can be anyone . . . do anything. I imagined
somehow absorbing Rose's strength and beauty, simply by wearing
her clothes—that burlap fabric knitting into my skin and becoming part of me.

I'd really embraced cosplay this year. Brown tunic, green leggings, army boots, my dark hair allowed to curl and frizz. I'd even
smudged my cheeks with olive eyeshadow in an attempt to look
battle-ready. My only nod to vanity was the red sash I'd tied around
my middle, emphasizing the narrowness of my waist. I *felt* battle-
ready, Comic-Con ready, bring-down-the-Gems ready.

But now, swaying to the rhythm of the Underground, I just
feel like an idiot.

The tunnels change from cast iron to brick as we hurtle toward
Kensington Olympia. I feel the pressure of sixty-odd eyes on my
back, and my fingers grip the cool of the handrail a little tighter.
But when I finally stop staring at the grubby train floor, I notice

most passengers are gawking at either Katie—who looks even more stupid than me—or Alice.

Granted, people always stare at Alice, but today, dressed in an electric-blue minidress and propped against a vertical yellow pole like she may just launch into a routine, she commands even more attention than usual. Her hair is hanging down her back and, I notice with a burst of pride, she's wearing her split-heart necklace. My fingers toy with the other half, the jagged edge cutting into my fingertips. She studies her ghostlike reflection in the window, biting a painted lip as though something isn't quite right. That's the thing when you're gorgeous; you've got something to lose.

I touch her hand, a habit from childhood. "You look amazing."

"As do you." She flashes her perfect smile.

"I look like an urchin."

"I thought that was the point. Rose *is* an urchin, all Imps are."

Katie groans, appraising her boyish frame. She's wearing a black catsuit with a series of multicolored stockings slung diagonally across her middle—strange vines hugging a tree. "At least your tights don't keep falling down." She repositions a neon-yellow stocking beneath her armpit and attempts to fasten it with a safety pin.

Nate throws her a sideways glance. "You do know what a DNA helix looks like, don't you, Katie? You look more like a human helter-skelter." He's fourteen, but he looks about twelve and sometimes talks like Sheldon Cooper from *The Big Bang Theory*. And he looks so silly dressed as his hero, Thorn. His eye patch swamps his angular face, and his narrow body barely fills his leather coat. He doesn't look old enough to deliver a pizza, let alone Imp emancipation.

Katie eyes the outline of his jacket. Her lips press together as she prevents an insult from popping out, instead muttering, "I know, I know" before the motion of the train makes her fumble the pin. "She must have pricked" her finger, because she grumbles, "Crap" and sucks the blood before turning back to Nate. "But I didn't want to come as an Imp. Everyone will come as an Imp—" She glances at me, guilt flickering beneath her dainty features. "Sorry, Vi. And I couldn't very well go as a Gem, not like Alice the Amazon here . . . I'm only five foot two."

Alice strokes her hair, as though coaxing an idea from her brain. "There are loads of attractive midgets . . . Tinkerbell . . . Smurfette."

"Who'd fancy a Smurf?" Katie says.

"Another Smurf," I say.

The Tube hits a smooth patch and Katie finally secures the clasp. "Well, I'm not a bloody Smurf, am I? I'm a helix and I'm proud."

"You should be flattered," Nate says. "Who'd want to look like the human Barbie over there?" He gestures to Alice.

"Aw, thanks, Nate," Alice says, her cheeks filling with color.

He snaps up his eye patch and gives her a long, hard stare. "It wasn't a compliment. Filthy, Frankenstein Gem."

"That's brilliant . . . Filthy, Frankenstein Gem . . . and it isn't from the original . . . not canon?" She always refers to *The Gallows Dance* as *canon*, once again reminding us of her status as a fanfic writer. She's even started calling her own work *the current*, as if the original novel is totally old-school in comparison. She has no idea how arrogant it makes her sound. She whips her iPhone from her Michael Kors bag and begins typing in the insult, her azure nails clicking against the screen. "Filthy, Frankenstein Gem—I'm totally going to use that in my next piece."

Nate exhales sharply. "Write your own material."

The Tube slows and we hear the pop of the metal doors opening. The Scooby-Doo gang pile in, shining like multicolored tiddledywinks against the gray backdrop of the Underground. I realize we're nearly there. *Comic-Con.* I inhale a shaky breath. In only a few hours, I will meet Russell Jones, *Willow*, and I'm dressed as the object of his desire—Rose. The Juliet to his Romeo, the Scarlett O'Hara to his Rhett Butler. I feel like stamping my over-size Imp boots in a happy little dance.

"You know he's going to meet hundreds of Roses today, don't you, sis?"

I hate the way Nate can read my mind.

The washed-out symmetry of Olympia seems completely at odds with the brilliance of the May sky and the cartoonlike figures weaving toward the entrance. We join the back of the queue.

"I suddenly feel very overdressed," I say, unable to avert my eyes from the acres of exposed flesh. Princess Leia, Wonder Woman, Daenerys Targaryen—all thighs and cleavage and fake bake. I study my pale forearms and suppress a sigh. "And by overdressed, I mean not nearly naked enough."

". . . Are the words no little brother should ever have to hear," Nate says.

Katie laughs. "Aw, poor Violet. How do you think I feel?"

"Like you should have come as Lara Croft," Alice says. "Seriously, girls—and boy—how am I the only one who owns a Wonderbra?" She puffs out her impressive chest and winks.

"I own a bra," Nate says. "Sophie Wainright's . . . and it's red." He must see the look of horror on my face, because he quickly adds, "Nothing weird. I swiped it off her clothesline as a dare."

He flicks his sandy hair from his forehead. He looks more like a pixie than a boy.

The queue moves slowly. *Time* moves slowly. I examine every stitch of Indiana Jones's waistcoat, every crimson brushstroke of Iron Man's chest. I imagine Russell Jones's face, the bow of his upper lip, the way his hand will skim mine as we pose side by side for the camera. By the time I reach the entrance, my ticket's pretty much dissolved in my sweaty hands.

I visited Olympia a few months ago on a school trip. Katie and Alice came, too, looking slightly more normal and slightly less excited. I still remember the way the sun slanted through the wall of glass, the dust motes dancing all the way to the domed ceiling, the white lattice of the metal beams. It looked beautiful, like a vast, forgotten ballroom. Today, crammed with the vivid and slightly disorienting world of cosplay, it feels like stepping onto a film set or a different world.

"This is awesome," Katie says. It's the first time I've ever heard her excited about anything *Gallows Dance* related.

I nod. "Finally, she gets it."

That tremor of excitement returns as I struggle to take it all in. Cosplayers and plain-clothed fans spill from the balcony and pack the ground floor. They talk and laugh and pose for photos—just the sheer number of them makes me feel so insignificant. Banners fall from the ceiling like great, colorful sails, boasting slogans and Photoshopped faces. *Game of Thrones*, *Star Wars*, *The Gallows Dance*. And the air feels almost humid on my skin, laced with the scent of hot dogs and sweat and perfume. The flash of cameras surrounds me, and it feels like I'm standing in a massive disco ball.

"There's Willow." Alice clasps my arm, her fingers curling into my flesh like talons. For a moment, I think she can actually see *him*—Russell Jones—and my stomach spasms. But then I realize she's pointing to the banner overhead, his face staring down on us like some giant, St. Tropez–ed angel.

"Come on, let's check out *The Gallows Dance* stall." Alice strides ahead and the crowd parts, as per usual.

I can feel Nate, pushing his arm into mine like he's scared he might lose me. And I suddenly feel the overwhelming weight of parental responsibility, Mum's words thumping in my head: *You must look after your little brother, Violet.* I link my arm through his and push after Alice, elbowing several Spocks in the ribs and hopping over Captain America's toes. I dodge another Rose, who scowls at me, and nudge past Boba Fett. He carries his helmet beneath his arm, the dark of his hair plastered to his forehead with gel. He winks at me—I mean, actually winks, like he doesn't look like an oversize silver crustacean. Secretly, I feel pleased he winked at me and not Alice. Maybe I *can* be anyone . . . do anything. A smile tugs at my lips.

"Will you stop thinking about Russell," Katie says, studying my face.

I glance at my watch. "Less than an hour now."

"There'll be a queue, mind," Alice says. "Willow's the hottest guy ever to exist in a dystopian future."

"Surely it's utopian, then, if Willow's there," I reply.

Alice snorts. "Gale . . . Four . . . Men that hot would make anywhere a utopia in my mind."

"Stupid names, though," Nate says, dodging Spider-Man. "It's one of the unwritten rules of all dystopian novels—love interests must have stupid names."

Katie laughs. "And everything starts with a capital letter, even if it's just a normal word, just to make it sound *scary.*"

"That's so true," Nate says.

"And the government is always the baddie," Katie says. "Without fail. It's so predictable. No wonder I haven't read *The Gallows Dance*. I bet it's like all the others."

"You're so ignorant," Alice snaps.

"Anyway, Willow isn't a stupid name," I say, a little hurt by the remark. "It's natural . . . earthy. It even sounds like leaves, sweeping the grass, bumping up against each other, trailing in the water."

"Amen to that," Alice says.

Nate pulls my arm into the thinness of his ribs. "God, you're pathetic."

I scoff, but he's kind of got a point. I am pathetic when it comes to Willow, even though I know he's make-believe—a figment of some dead author's imagination. I also know that Russell Jones is an arrogant actor-drunkard who beds models and snorts cocaine . . . but in the absence of Willow, I will pose with his avatar.

Speaking of which, an Avatar walks by. Tall, broad, even-featured. He looks like he may be attractive under all that blue.

"OMG," Katie squeals. "A sexy Smurf."

CHAPTER 3

WE WAIT TO meet Russell in a long, darkened room. The queue's shorter than I expected—only a couple of teenage girls scrolling through selfies on their phones.

A lady with a clipboard takes our names and collects our crumpled ten-spots. "Right, we're doing well for time. I'll be with you again shortly."

She leads the selfie girls through a door at the back. I crane my neck to see if I can catch my first glimpse of Russell, but they're too damn quick.

Alice grips my hand. "I can't believe this is about to happen."

"I know," I reply.

"Do I look OK?" she asks.

I don't even bother studying her. "Yeah, 'course."

"Do you think Russell will have heard of me?"

Nate laughs. "No way. He's a megastar, he's not going to be reading some random fanfic by some wannabe Sally King."

"Thanks, but I wasn't asking you," Alice replies, her voice sour. "And FYI, who'd want to be Sally King? Poor cow killed herself after one novel. I'm going to write a trilogy."

"Wow, you're all heart," Nate says. "RIP, the lovely Sally King."

"Who invited you anyway, squirt?" Alice pokes him in the ribs and he squeals like he's five. Anyone would think *they* were the siblings, the way they carry on.

Clipboard Lady reappears. "Right, you guys are next."

Alice pushes past us, her heels clacking against the floor. We follow and enter another dimly lit room. I can see Russell Jones standing at the back, his toned body squeezed between the selfie girls, his strong fingers wrapped around their waists. He smiles as a camera flashes, lighting up the network of scaffolds overhead and the canvas behind him. The theme tune fills my head, all violins and drums, and I feel a sudden surge of adrenaline.

Julia Starling—the actress who plays Rose—perches on a desk and talks to some security guards. Cast in the emerald glow of the stage lights, she looks even more ethereal than usual. Her thin hands flutter before her face as she laughs her bell-like laugh, and her hair cascades down her back in dark, glossy waves, no frizz in sight. I notice she wears blue jeans and a white blouse. I suddenly feel like a fraud, standing in my tunic, pretending to be Rose. I know I'm pretty, in a quirky, pale way (at least, people tell me I'm pretty, in a quirky, pale way) but I could never match Julia's grace, the delicacy of her features.

The selfie girls leave. I watch Russell take a swig of water. I can just make out the shape of his Adam's apple moving down his throat like the tip of a blade.

"Enjoy," says Clipboard Lady, ushering us toward him.

He nods at us, and his gaze immediately fixes on Alice. That little kernel of envy expands to fill my entire body.

A smile creeps across his face, his teeth so white they almost glow. "A fellow Gem. An unpopular choice, but if you can pull it off, why the hell not?"

Alice laughs—a nervous trill. "I know, right."

He swishes his caramel hair from his eyes and turns his attention to me. "Ah . . . Rose, my love, you've found me at last." His eyes look just like Willow's—amber flecks radiating from his pupils, like sunshine escaping from a black sphere, a solar eclipse. But they lack some of Willow's kindness.

"Jules," he calls. "Hey, Jules, this is the best Rose we've seen all day."

Julia glances over her shoulder and grins. "You want my job, girlie?"

I open my mouth to reply, but no noise escapes.

She laughs. "I'm just screwing with you . . . You look great, really. I love the sash."

"Thanks." My smile threatens to split my face in two.

Russell extends his hand toward Nate. "And you must be Thorn."

Nate shakes his hand, a little too excitedly. "Big fan, big fan, big, big fan . . ."

Russell gestures at the brooch on Nate's tunic: a thistle head carved from oak. "Nice badge—the symbol of Imp rebels."

"Cut us down and we come back stronger." Nate's face lights up. "You know, like weeds."

Russell slaps him on the back, I think to shut him up, and then turns to Katie. "And . . . you are?"

"A DNA helix," Katie says.

"Clever, I like it."

I notice Alice scowling, the foundation cracking on her usually flawless skin.

Something creaks overhead. The emerald light wobbles, sending a giant shadow scudding across Russell's seamless features. "So how do you want to do this, guys? Group or individually?"

"Group," Katie and I say in stereo.

But Alice doesn't hear, because she says, "Individually, please."

I hear it again. My eyes scan the scaffolding; it looks sturdy enough. The violins must be messing with my head.

"Come on then, superhuman." Russell loops an arm around Alice's waist, but I don't feel jealous, I just feel dizzy—like I've downed a vodka and Red Bull.

I hadn't noticed the photographer until now. He seems to emerge from nowhere, as though cut from the dark itself. I hear that creak again, another shift of emerald light.

"So, what's your name?" Russell says.

"Alice."

"Well, you really are in Wonderland now."

Willow would never say that. Disappointment surges up my throat, making my lips tingle. The camera flashes, bleaching out their faces, sending another shadow jutting up the canvas, all spikes and dips. I blink several times.

Alice giggles. "Anime Alice, that's my pen name. I write loads of *Gallows Dance* fanfic, you may have heard of me?"

Russell looks impressed. "So you're Anime Alice? *The* Anime Alice. Sure, I've heard of you. You're becoming quite the internet sensation. Hey, Julia, get a photo of me with Alice here, it'll look great on Instagram."

Alice can't resist a flick of her eyebrow for Nate's benefit, right before that infectious smile bursts across her face.

Julia fishes her iPhone from her pocket. "I hope he's paying you for this, Alice, was it?" She takes the photo. "Hey, next Comic-Con you should come along, sit on the fanfic panel. You've got a great face for publicity."

Alice opens her mouth to respond, but the drums seem to

swell, drowning out the rest of her words, and this strange smell fills my nostrils—medicine and burning fabric. I clasp my hands to my temples, my pulse ramping up a gear.

"Violet?" Katie says.

The creaking is back, louder this time—it definitely isn't the violins. And that emerald light begins to flicker, like a bulb's about to blow or a thousand moths have gotten stuck behind the glass casing.

"Violet? Are you OK?" Katie says. Her face turns from green to white, white to green.

The floor seems to swing a foot to the left, and I start to feel like I've stepped off a carousel—this morning's porridge hot and thick at the base of my throat. I think I hear someone scream my name. I turn to see Nate's mouth pulled open in a yawn, his brown eyes wide. Instinctively, my eyes flick up. And that's when I see it. The emerald light spinning from a cable, the scaffolding lurching forward. I barely have time to cover my face as the entire metal structure hurtles toward us.

CHAPTER 4

WAKING FEELS LIKE crawling out of a bog. Every time I see the surface, feel the fresh air on my skin, some dark phantom pulls me under again. It's so tempting to just keep on sinking, but the thought of the scaffolding pinning me down, imprisoning Nate, Alice, Katie . . . even Russell and Julia . . . drives me on. Somehow, I drag my body from the mud, force my eyes to open, compel my brain to engage.

The light from the fire door casts the room in a ghostly glow. I can just pick out the metal rods of the scaffold, spearing the floor like a bizarre postmodern sculpture. That smell—medicine and burning fabric—grows in my nostrils, causing my eyes to smart.

"Nate?" I pull myself onto my elbows. Pain shoots through my skull.

"Violet?" I hear his voice, wavering at the edges, soaring above the muffled theme tune and the chime of metal against metal.

I extend my fingers like I can somehow draw him to my body. "Nate, are you OK?"

I see his face, etched with fear, pitching toward me in the gloom. "Violet, you're bleeding." He slips his hands beneath my armpits and pulls me into a half-standing position. My head feels like it may explode.

"Alice? Katie?" I push my hands into the wet flesh of my forehead.

"I'm OK . . . I think." Alice kind of reels toward us, her dress and thighs streaked with ash. "What the hell happened?"

But I don't answer, I need to find Katie. I drop onto all fours and begin to pat the ground. She was standing right next to me, she can't have gone far. "Katie? Katie?"

I hear a groan to my right. My head pivots—pain slamming into the backs of my eyes—and I see her neon tights, luminous in the black. Nate reaches her first. They wobble into a kneeling position.

"I'm fine, I'm fine," she mutters, almost to herself.

That alien scent grows, and we hear another creak, louder this time.

"The fire door . . ." Alice says, her voice stretched with panic.

And somehow, a unit of four, we stagger toward the exit sign, stumbling over metal and equipment. We burst through the door, hacking and spitting and clinging to one another. The daylight stings my eyes, and I feel like some kind of ghoul, squinting and recoiling. I can't help but notice how cold it's become, my skin growing coarse with goose bumps. We slide onto the tiles, backs pressed against the cool of the stone walls.

"Where the hell are we?" I say. At least, my mouth forms the words, but I hear only this deafening noise, like I'm standing in a tunnel with a train storming past—rumbling and groaning and kicking up dust. At first, I think it's a bad case of tinnitus, my brain objecting to the movement, but my eyes slowly make sense of the colors and shapes. People. Thousands of people. All tall and slim and dressed in tailored clothes. Fists pumping the air, voices raised, the vibrations of stamping feet traveling through the backs of my thighs.

"We need to get help," Nate shouts, pulling his phone from his pocket. His eye patch must have fallen off at some point, because I notice both his eyes glisten with tears. "No signal," he says.

I nod, which I immediately regret, the pain kind of sloshing around my skull like toxic goop. "Russell and Julia are still in there . . ." *And the security guards, and Clipboard Lady . . .* I try to say, but my voice sinks beneath a fanfare of trumpets.

"Is this some kind of cosplay event?" Alice shouts.

I wipe the blood from my face with my sleeve and blink quickly. I recognize the scene now. We're in the Coliseum from *The Gallows Dance*, ground level, right at the back. The sloped auditorium, filled with perfect, symmetrical faces, surrounds us on all sides, leading the eye upward to the crest of the circular stone wall, dotted with armed Gem guards. Before us, an angry crowd pushes forward with a life of its own, perfect bodies topped with thick, glossy hair. I can't see, but I know the stage and the gallows rest at the front, hidden by the throng.

"It's like the best role play ever." Alice removes her broken heels and stands to get a better view.

She's right—they've even got the smell right. The Coliseum rests on the border between the Imp city and the Pastures, and I can smell the sweetness of the Pastures battling the filth of the city. Pollen and freshly mown grass colliding with dead meat and vinegar.

"Screw role play," Katie shouts. "We need to find security." She leaves the safety of the fire exit and dashes toward the back of the crowd.

"Screw security," Alice says. "We need to make sure Russell posts that photo."

Nate helps me stand, and even though my head feels like it may dissolve, the thought of Russell and Julia trapped and wounded forces my limbs into action. I grab a tall, broad shoulder, briefly noticing the blood on my fingers as they splay before me. A man turns to look at me. The symmetry of his features makes my words jar in my throat.

"We need help." My voice comes out scratched and damaged like an old analogue recording.

He looks confused for a moment. "Get lost, Imp, or I'll call the guards."

"Look, I know you're in role," Nate says, "but there's been an accident. The blood's real."

The man easily shoves Nate to the ground. "I said, get lost, Imp."

"Jesus, Nate, are you OK?" I drop beside him, brushing the dirt from his hands.

"And I thought *I* was a *Gallows Dance* fanatic," he says. "This fandom is hard-core."

I jump to my feet and grab another person. This time a woman in her forties, maybe even older, it's hard to tell. She's still beautiful, her skin kind of smoothed over her face like a veil, her auburn hair curling to one side. She looks at me and her almond eyes narrow with disgust. "Don't touch me, you . . . you filthy Imp . . . you ape. Guards!" She begins to shout. "Guards!" But her voice gets swamped by the crowd and the fanfare and the stamping feet.

"Forget it," Nate says, pulling at my arm.

We loop around the back of the crowd, eyes darting from side to side, trying to find someone . . . anyone . . . who looks like they may be vaguely official. Katie doesn't seem to be having any more luck, her mouth drawn tight with confusion as a slender blonde woman shouts in her face. But a group of concerned cosplayers gather around Alice, nursing the small cut on her forearm, smoothing her golden hair from her face. For once, Alice actually blends in. They must have contacted every modeling agency in London . . . Britain . . . to make this role play seem so real.

I climb the bottom few steps that lead to the sloped seating at the back of the Coliseum, Nate beside me. We can just about see over the crowd. Sure enough, at the front, I can see the stage. A rickety, wooden construction topped with a broad beam. Nine loops of rope dangle, surrounding the necks of the nine condemned Imps. Their faces flash on a giant screen behind. I can make out every imperfection. The slight crookedness of their features, the odd gray whisker, the mishmash of yellow teeth. But their imperfection stands out even from a distance. Their physiques aren't quite right—too skinny, slightly stooped, broad in the wrong places. I actually feel a little relieved, just seeing their humanity staring back at me.

"It's the first scene," Nate says, excitedly. "God, they've pulled out all the stops. The condemned Imps look just like the actors from the film."

He's right. I know every freckle and every line on those nine faces. The woman with bloodshot eyes who repetitively touches her ear as though the action brings her some kind of comfort. The man with bruises on his forearms who keeps his eyes closed for most of the proceedings. And a girl, who can't be much older than sixteen, yet grits her teeth with such tenacity her jaw looks like it may fuse together. I can tell you about each Imp in detail—I've watched the film forty-six times.

I swallow, hard. "Nate. Focus. We need to find help."

The giant screen behind the stage fills with the face of the Gem president: President Stoneback. He looks so unnatural, like a drum—skin drawn over perfect features and fastened with invisible pins. And this big, his eyes look like huge glass orbs, completely hollow and incapable of holding any warmth or kindness. He addresses the crowd with his reedy tone, just like he did in the film.

"Fellow Gems, we are gathered here today to witness the death of these Imps. Guilty of theft, rape, and murder." The crowd cheers. *"Because in order to keep our world perfect, we must eliminate these imperfect beings . . . these vermin."*

The drumroll begins to build. The hangman, a figure in black, moves toward the lever. I know it's only for show, but this feeling of unease spreads through my abdomen . . . something isn't quite right. I'm about to pull Nate from the steps when Katie runs toward us, swinging her hands above her head and mouthing the word *Julia*.

We look up and see Julia Starling, standing high on the crest of the wall, hands on hips, dark hair flailing in the wind. Framed against the gray of the sky, she looks truly awesome. Terrifying. That feeling of unease begins to morph into panic, my heart throwing itself against my ribs like it's some kind of trapped animal. Something definitely isn't right. She's escaped completely unharmed and has somehow managed to dress as Rose. Tunic, leggings, army boots. I watch as she touches her fist to her lips. She says something to herself, and then hoists her arm above her head, pummeling it down in a graceful arc.

I know what it is before I see it. A grenade. But not one that wreaks death and destruction. No. A thistle-bomb. Designed to release the rebels' symbol of hope. And of course a handy distraction.

It launches over the crowd, hovering for a moment like a black bird of prey before filling the Coliseum with a loud *clack*. Hundreds of white thistle seeds disperse into the air, floating upward and outward like scraps of down. I hear the odd gasp, the crowd pointing, tracking the seeds through the sky.

"This is amazing," Nate shouts above the drums. "A thistlebomb, just like in canon."

"A little too amazing," I reply. The smell, the actors, the sheer scale of the set. It's all too real. I begin to feel woozy and the drumroll grows to fill every space in my head.

Suddenly, the drums stop. Peace. The crowd remains captivated, statue-like, their flawless chins lifted skyward. This is the moment in the film when the Imp rebels appeared, releasing their smoke bombs and storming the stage, liberating the condemned Imps from the gallows. And Rose slipped away unseen, just melted back into the gray of the Imp city, having proved her worth as an Imp rebel.

I hold my breath, awaiting the battle cry of the rebels.

But, instead, I hear Katie, screaming at the top of her lungs. "Julia! Julia! Are you OK?"

The last thing we need is to draw attention to ourselves.

"Katie, no!" I shout.

She runs toward the stands, waving her arms above her head. "Julia, be careful, you might fall."

"Katie, stop," I shout.

But it's too late. The guards swivel in their podiums, alerted to Julia's presence, guns cocked and aimed. Julia turns and a strange expression grips her face, a hybrid of acceptance and determination. The sound of gunfire ruptures my skull and a series of red dots spreads across her tunic, merging into one large splotch. It forms a belt of blood, reminiscent of my own sash. She glances at her abdomen—a bemused smile gripping her rosebud mouth—and begins to topple. Her slender hands whirl before her, grasping for an invisible man, but she falls between the stalls like a doll, her hair a black cape streaming behind her. She smacks the pavement, inhuman and lifeless. A sack of grit. I watch as the life leaks from her, two ruby butterfly wings unfolding across the concrete.

This can't be real.

I'm about to jump from the steps, about to run to her, when another sound grabs my attention. The sound of nine trapdoors flying open. Nate grabs my hand with his, so hard it hurts. And I know what I'm about to see, I know I should just look away. But I can't. I can't. Nine bodies fall, nine pieces of rope snap straight and taut, and nine sets of legs kick and twirl. The man with the bruised forearms, the woman with the bloodshot eyes, the girl with the fused jaw—all of them—dancing their final dance.

Instinctively, I look to Katie. She stands, frozen, her knuckles bleached and ragged as she clutches her face. Next, I find Alice, her painted mouth ajar, her eyes loaded with tears. And I can still feel Nate, crushing my hand, tugging at the fabric of my tunic like he's five.

And I know we share only one thought:

We're not in cosplay anymore.

CHAPTER 5

A MAN PUSHES FREE of the crowd and runs toward Julia's twisted body. He wears the regulation gray overalls of the Imp slaves—the Imps who work in the Pastures for the Gems. I can't help but notice how uncomfortable they look in real life, the fabric coarse and poorly stitched. He drops to his knees as he enters her blood pool, and kind of scoops her into his great chest in one easy motion. Her hand flops away from her and begins to twitch, like she rests on the edge of a dream. The twitch becomes more pronounced, and I begin to wonder if she's still alive, then I realize her small frame has been swallowed up by the movement of the Imp as he convulses with grief. I suddenly feel like I should look away, like I'm somehow intruding.

The ground around him begins to explode as the guards open fire. I want to shout to him, *Run, run away*, but my lips won't move. He looks up, and for some reason, his eyes find mine. We stare at each other and I absorb his face. Mahogany skin, dirt rammed into every crack, a nose that has stopped too many fists. I recognize him from the film. Matthew. One of Thorn's most trusted rebels, and responsible—at least in part—for recruiting Rose. The tendons on his neck stand out like rods; he thinks I'm intruding, too.

The gunfire causes a few of the Gems to turn, their beautiful faces changing from joy to horror as they clasp their cheeks. Panic breaks out at the back of the crowd. A few of the Gems dash toward the great metal gates at the side of the Coliseum that lead to the Pastures.

The bullets stop, guards afraid of piercing the wrong belly, just long enough for a woman, also dressed in gray overalls, to fall onto the man. She pulls at the clothes on his back, her thin mouth shouting orders, her raven, gray-streaked hair fanning around her face. Saskia, the other rebel responsible for recruiting Rose. She has the same hard face as the actress in the film, yet she looks kind of different.

Matthew stands, clasping Julia to him as though she's a sleeping child. He pauses and, again, catches my eye. He then looks to Nate, and I see a shift in his dark eyes as some impulse shoots through him. He lays Julia back in her own blood, whispering something meant for her only, and then runs toward us, arms extended. I don't flinch, shielded by disbelief, but I notice the blood on his hands as he grasps a handful of my tunic.

"Quickly," he roars. "Come with me."

I look to Nate, expecting a nonchalant shrug, but his face remains frozen with anxiety. *We are in The Gallows Dance,* his eyes say. I almost start to laugh. *We are in The Gallows Dance.*

Matthew seizes my shoulders. "For God's sake, you won't last a second with all these Gems." He pulls me forward so my nose almost touches his.

He's the same height as me, which strikes me as odd—he seemed so big on the silver screen. Then I remember, I'm still standing on the steps. But I don't move, caught between shock and laughter. This close I see he also looks slightly different from his film counterpart—the structure of his face looks more robust, his eyes an even deeper brown.

He pushes me back, frustrated, and grabs my cheeks with slippery, warm fingers. "Look." He forces me to contemplate the stage. Nine bodies hang limp from their ropes, their necks arched almost like a swan's, their feet no longer dancing but pointing toward the earth.

Saskia runs up behind him. "Leave 'em, Matthew. Bloody leave 'em."

But Matthew doesn't budge. "You want to end up like them?" He squeezes my cheeks, causing my lips to pop out. "'Cause that's what will happen if you don't shift your arses, right now."

His words obviously rouse Nate, who tugs at my tunic. "Come on, Violet."

And it's this motion that finally unlocks my legs. If we truly are in *The Gallows Dance*, then we are in the most dangerous place imaginable . . . the place where they hang non-genetically enhanced humans. Me. Nate. I pull my face from Matthew's grip and clasp his hand, wrapping my free arm around my brother. We begin to run around the back of the crowd, crouched low, anticipating more bullets.

"Where are we going?" Katie shouts, catching up to us.

Only when I see Katie do I remember with a burst of guilt that four of us entered this nightmare.

"Alice," I scream. "Alice."

But I can't see her anywhere. Panic winds around my chest. Matthew begins to drag us through the Gems, I bash into perfect figure after perfect figure, they look at us, disgust registering on their faces, but the disgust keeps us safe, causing them to recoil like we have some contagious disease. I hear a couple of cries. *Apes, filthy apes.* But still no Alice. I slow for a moment, trying to catch sight of her blonde hair, gleaming at least a head above the rest of the crowd. But what normally sets her apart instead makes her impossible to spot.

"Guards," a Gem shouts. "Guards, there's some rogue Imps in the Coliseum."

"Come on," Matthew says, his grip tightening.

"Alice." My voice soars above the crowd.

Saskia runs up behind us. "Shut your face, you little idiot. You'll get us all killed."

Then, faintly, I hear a voice. I want to say that familiarity draws me to it, something deep-rooted that recognizes the timbre, the pitch, but it's the fact that she calls my name. *Violet. Violet.* She wobbles toward us, standing out only because of the soot and terror that mark her face.

She lunges into me. "Where the hell are we? What the hell's going on?"

"We need to leave," I reply.

I don't think she can hear me above the crowd, but she must read my urgent expression and, without another word, begins to follow us—crouched low—as we weave through the crowd.

We reach a small wooden door that must lead to the Imp city. The dead meat smell intensifies and my stomach turns. We're right next to the Imp-pen, a wooden cage that holds the relatives of the condemned Imps, allowing them to witness the death of their loved ones. They watch us through the gaps in the bars with stony, tear-lined faces.

Matthew ushers us toward the small wooden door, pulling a gun from his belt, anticipating the guards' arrival. "Hurry."

My trembling, ghostly hands reach before me, scratching at the wood surrounding the doorknob. And just as my fingers encompass the globe, I hear the rounded vowels of a Gem guard. *Don't let them escape.* I imagine I can feel the red spots of the lasers tremoring just above my neck, a swarm of angry fireflies. A fresh wave of panic surges through me.

But I don't look. I just focus on the metal grating beneath my hands. I rattle the handle—nearly dislodging my arms from their sockets—but the door remains firmly shut. Saskia pushes me to one side and maneuvers the knob with deft fingers, her hands surprisingly steady. Finally, the door opens and we tumble into the city.

CHAPTER 6

MATTHEW PULLS THE door shut behind him.

"We're in *The Gallows Dance*," Nate says, his voice trembling.

"Not anymore, you're not," Saskia says. "We just got you out of there."

He shakes his head, like Saskia doesn't quite get it. "No, no, we're in the *world* of *The Gallows Dance*."

Saskia doesn't even acknowledge he's spoken. "Hurry, before the guards follow."

I work out why she looks different. She has a port wine stain the shape of Africa just above her left eye. Come to think of it, Rose didn't look quite like Julia Starling, and I don't just mean because of the blood pool and the broken limbs—her hair was curlier, her physique more childlike. It's as though these characters have stepped directly from the author's imagination. But I don't have time to figure it out, not with the guards so close. I follow Saskia and Matthew down an alley, my legs struggling to keep up, my friends panting in my ears.

I know the Imp city from the book, and then again from the film—"atmospheric and disturbing," as one critic said. London, centuries in the future, bombed to its foundations and robbed of all color and grace. The camera showed a sweeping panorama of the collapsed rooftops, the toppled lampposts, mist snaking around rubbish heaps like smoke. And Nate and I shouted out when we saw the dilapidated landmarks: the remnants of Tower Bridge; the fallen London Eye, rusted and cracked like a giant hamster wheel; half of Big Ben, the clock face long gone. I recall watching it on my squishy sofa, cushion hugged to my chest, and thinking: *God, future London really sucks, I'm glad I don't live in future London.* But as I follow the two Imps through a maze of alleyways, my feet burning, it's the stench that hits me above all.

It reminds me of the time Nate and I found an injured thrush. Rolling eyes, broken wing, crumpled feathers, blood smudged across the kitchen window where it had smashed into the pane. Nate was only four and he just wouldn't stop crying. So I scooped it up and laid it in an old shoebox, placed a wad of cotton under its head, a handkerchief over its body, and a strip of berries at its feet for when it woke hungry. We punched holes in the lid with a pencil and hid it in my closet so Mum wouldn't find it. Of course we forgot about it. A week or so later, I noticed this smell coming from my closet, a strange smell like pickle and burned toast. Only when I removed the lid did the full stench hit me.

Rotting bird. Just like the city.

"Keep up," Saskia shouts over her shoulder. "Unless you want them bastard soldiers to catch you."

We tear around the corner into another maze of alleyways, and eventually we enter a narrow lane. A line of laundry hangs above us and quivers like neglected bunting in the wind. I briefly wonder why anyone would bother washing clothes just to hang them in such foul air. Saskia pauses to catch her breath, and we all stop. I put my hands on my knees, a stitch gathering in my side.

Out of nowhere, Saskia spins around and slams Katie into the wall. I hear her spine crack against the brickwork, followed by a sharp expulsion of breath.

"What the hell were you playing at, you little brat?" Saskia spits the words into Katie's face.

I move to try and pull Saskia away, but Matthew steps between us. "She got Rose killed," he says, holding out his hands and turning them like he's seeing her blood for the first time, already transformed from vivid scarlet to a layer of brown flakes.

I look from Matthew to Saskia. They both look wrecked, damaged, but in a different way; Matthew looks like he may buckle with grief, and I can almost see the cracks of rage forming across Saskia's skin. In canon, they had this long backstory with Rose, having met her a few months prior to the thistle-bomb mission. Thorn had asked them to find a beautiful Imp girl capable of infiltrating the Harper estate, capable of seducing a beautiful Gem boy. When Saskia and Matthew pulled Rose from a street fight, they immediately recognized her irresistible mix of fragility and courage, and she became the obvious choice for the Harper mission. And they really took her under their wing, training her night and day. They grew to think of her as a friend, a daughter, as much as a fellow rebel. It's not surprising her death has hit them hard.

A great tear rolls down Matthew's face and hangs from his chin. He pulls his hands into his chest like he holds her ghost to his body.

"For God's sake, Matthew, stop crying, will you?" Saskia throws the words over her shoulder without loosening her grip on

Katie. "Rose wouldn't want us to fall apart. She would want us to figure out who the hell these Imps are."

Alice looks at me, her eyes wide as if to say, *Now what?*

"I'm so sorry," Katie says. "I don't know what happened, really I don't. I thought she was Julia . . ."

"That wasn't Julia," I say. "That was Rose. *The* Rose."

She's never seen the film—no wonder she's so confused.

"Julia? Who the hell is Julia?" Saskia shoves Katie into the wall again.

"Get off me." Katie bucks and rears, but she's no match for Saskia.

"What she means is, she looked like a friend of ours," I say. "Katie was just trying to warn her."

"Warn her!" Saskia shouts. "She didn't need warning. She would have been fine if it weren't for you. And all of them condemned Imps, we could have saved 'em. We were *meant* to save 'em." Her voice wavers. "They all hanged 'cause of you."

"You don't know that," Alice says, her face struggling to hide the lie.

Saskia looks at Alice as if seeing her for the first time. She releases Katie and sidles over to her, lifting a piece of her golden hair. Slowly, she turns it in her fingers. "You look like one of *them*." She says the word *them* like it tastes bad.

Alice stands, statue-like and rigid. Only her nostrils move, flaring slightly as she takes a trembling breath.

"I said . . . you look like one of *them*." Saskia yanks the lock of hair and I hear it tear from Alice's scalp.

Alice yelps, her hand flying to the site of pain. "One of who?" she says, her voice indignant, pretending like she doesn't know.

But she just looks foolish, leaning against the crumbling wall in her minidress like a model in an urban photo shoot. We watch the strands of golden hair drift through the air and settle on the paving slabs.

"Tell me why I shouldn't kill you. Right now." Saskia taps her belt, and for the first time, I notice the rusted handle of a knife protruding from beneath the leather. "Just stick you in the belly and watch the Gem blood drain out of you."

Alice turns this chalky-white color.

I try to speak, try to intervene, but my mouth feels like it's gummed up and my legs won't move.

"I think there's been enough blood today." Matthew lays a hand on Saskia's arm.

She flinches as though unused to touch. "Gem blood don't count."

"I'm not a Gem," Alice says.

"Oh, yeah?" Saskia grabs Alice's silver bag and empties the contents on the floor. A lip gloss, a stick of gum, a designer change-purse, a compact with a picture of a dragonfly on the back, and an iPhone. Saskia scoops up the phone and turns it in her fingers. The screen illuminates as she catches it with her thumb. "What the hell is this, then? You think Imps have crap like this?"

"It's just a phone." Alice raises her hand like she may try to grab it but changes her mind at the last minute.

Saskia frowns. "Any more crap like this? Or do I need to strip-search the lot of you?"

Reluctantly, we dig into our pockets and hand over our possessions. Wallets, phones, lip balms. I didn't think I could feel any more vulnerable, but without my phone, my emergency taxi money, and my family photograph, I feel completely naked. I think we all do, our arms folding across our chests, protecting our organs— our hearts.

But Saskia doesn't seem to care. She rams them into Alice's bag, the stitches pulled tight at the seams. "This looks like Gem stuff to me."

"I'm not a Gem," Alice repeats.

"She's not," Nate says. He uses his *I've just had an idea* voice, and it comes out strong. His arms unfold and his chest seems to rise.

Saskia turns to him, raising her knife so quickly that I barely register the movement. "Shut it, young 'un."

Nate watches the blade, but his voice stays strong. "She's a spy, for the Imps. We use her 'cause she looks like a Gem."

I can't help feeling a little put out. I'm the older sibling, I should have the ideas and the strong voice. Alice was right, I *am* lacking in the imagination department.

Saskia starts to laugh. "Bullshit!"

Matthew looks at Nate, his eyes large with sympathy. "There ain't no spies we don't know about."

"That's not true," Nate says. "Ask Thorn."

Saskia's brow furrows. "Here, how do you know about Thorn?"

Nate doesn't even pause. "I work for him. We all do."

"Nate," I hiss. But Katie silences me with a look that says, *Trust him.*

"Why else would she run after us?" he says. "She ain't stupid, you know, she knew running into the city was suicide, but she had to get back to Rebel Headquarters."

I notice with a pang of pride that Nate has flattened his vowels to sound more Imp-like. And I'm ashamed to admit I never thought of using my knowledge of the canon to our advantage. We know many rebel secrets—we've watched them and read them and discussed them in detail for the past two years. I have to remind myself sometimes he's only fourteen.

"Yeah?" Saskia looks unnerved now, her purple birthmark crinkling around the corners. "So where's Rebel Headquarters, then, smartarse?"

"Don't tell them." Katie cuts in, clearly enjoying the shift in power. "They may not be rebels, they may just be trying to find out."

Saskia and Matthew throw their heads back and laugh, revealing their grimy throats and the brown of their molars. It's the first time I've seen them smile, and it's like only their mouths remember how.

"Oh, now you're just kidding," Matthew says, the smile gone as quick as it came.

I look at Alice, her fists clenched and trembling slightly. I take a deep breath. "I'll tell you if you leave us alone. Deal?"

Saskia moves toward me, slow and almost seductive. "Go on."

"The headquarters are in the bombed-out church."

Saskia's features draw together. "OK." Her voice changes, suddenly guarded, like she's scared of giving anything away. But she knows I'm right.

"Saskia?" Matthew says.

"Shut up. I'm thinking." She pushes her fingers into her eyes like she can reach into her brain and arrange her thoughts. "OK, but that don't mean your Gem friend 'ere is a spy. What can *you* tell us, princess?"

Alice looks nervous, her voice pinched. "It's by the broken bridge. Down by the River Thames." She cringes as she realizes her mistake; they don't call it that anymore.

"The river what?" Saskia says.

"The river, down by the river," Alice garbles.

Saskia raises her eyebrows. "OK, you know too much. We're going to see Thorn. Then *he* can stick you all in the belly." Her fingers play with the fabric resting just above her collarbone. I remember this backstory—Thorn slashed her a few years ago when she botched a mission. And it's as though she's remembering, too, tracing the ridges of the scar through her overalls. She laughs, unexpectedly. "We was meant to be introducing him to Rose today, the newest member of our rebel family. But he gets to meet you instead. Lucky bastard."

"But you said you'd let us go," I say.

"Never trust an Imp." Saskia smiles again, and this time it extends to the rest of her face. Her sapphire eyes flash.

Nate knocks me with his hand, low down so nobody sees. "It's OK, Violet. We need to see him, anyway. We can all go together."

I don't know why Nate wants to see Thorn. He would string us up in a second if he thought he couldn't trust us. Maybe we can dupe Saskia and Matthew, but there'll be no duping Thorn.

Matthew takes a sharp breath over his teeth, like he's testing the air. "What we gonna do about . . . *that*?" He gestures to Alice. I can't tell if the cold or the anxiety makes her shiver.

"He's right," Saskia says. "Two minutes on the main street and the Gem look-alike will get lynched for sure. And you'll be no good to Thorn if you're dead."

Alice's tremor becomes more apparent. I want to wrap my arms around her, but I'm afraid I'll make her look weak.

Saskia wriggles her arms into her overalls and somehow unzips the front from the inside. It drops to the floor and wrinkles around her feet like she's a python shedding an extra skin. Beneath it, she wears gray burlap trousers and a cream shirt, stained with brown. I hadn't realized how thin she is under all that material; the sharpness of her shoulders and hips juts from beneath the cloth. I can't help wondering when she last ate.

She uses the toe of her boot to flick the overalls across the floor to Alice. "'Ere, put these on, try and blend in a bit." She turns away and mumbles into the cold, "And you look like you're freezing your tits off."

I suppress a little smile. It's the first glimpse of kindness I've seen in her since we arrived. She was much nicer to Rose.

Katie and I help Alice into the overalls, and I notice her feet remain shoeless and slightly bloodied from the mad dash through the city.

"Christ, Alice, your feet," I say.

"Oh, yeah, I hadn't noticed." Her voice sounds a little numb, and she pokes at a sole like it belongs to someone else, a mannequin perhaps. The overalls are far too small for her, and the material pulls around her crotch as she tries to inch her shoulders in. "I think I'm too tall."

Saskia kneels in front of her and rips the fabric between Alice's legs. Alice looks slightly horrified at the indignity of the situation, but she keeps quiet and manages to wriggle her shoulders in. The fabric yawns a little between her legs, revealing a flash of electric blue.

Nate laughs. "You look like a giant baby, you know, with the opening so you can get to the diaper?"

Alice looks like she's going to cry.

"Shut it," Saskia snaps at Nate. "Or I'll throw you over my knee and smack your arse, then we'll see who looks like the baby."

Matthew nudges Saskia. "And what's this all about?" He gestures to Katie, who is still wearing her helix outfit.

They start to laugh again.

Katie wrinkles her nose. "It's a long story."

"And you talk funny. Which city you from?" Matthew asks.

Her eyes flick to mine, slightly panicked.

"Liverpool," I say. I'm sure Liverpool is one of the Imp cities still standing in canon. I look to Nate, who nods a confirmation.

"Figures." Matthew yanks on the tights twisted into the sort-of helix.

"Hey," she says—a token objection at best. The safety pins buckle and give way, and the tights flop to the ground. She looks less conspicuous all in black.

Matthew grunts from the movement and lets his shoulder slump forward. Blood drips from his fingers and spots the floor. He grimaces, clasping his hand to his shoulder. His shirt sleeve is soaked with blood, fresh blood—one of those bullets must have nicked him. He never even winced. "At least she's clearly an Imp." His words slur a little from the pain.

"We gotta get that shoulder looked at," Saskia says.

"I'm fine," he says. "Let's just get to headquarters, they'll look at it there."

"Nah, you'll pass out before we get there. And you're too heavy to carry. We can get it patched on the way. Come on, I know who can fix it up." Saskia turns to us, her face dark. "You follow us, got it? You make a run for it and I'll squeal that princess 'ere is a Gem, top of me lungs, then let's see how well you last."

We all nod.

"And try to blend in." Matthew shakes his head in despair. "Worst bloody spies I've ever seen."

"Spies my arse," Saskia grumbles.

We begin to walk down an old arterial road, completely pedestrianized simply due to the lack of vehicles. I recognize the large expanse of tarmac stretching before us from the film.

"This place is truly grim," Katie whispers.

I nod. Skeletal beams peak through the carcasses of buildings. Plastic or rags are stretched across doorframes, and dark stains left by abandoned fires mark the middle of the streets. But the lack of green strikes me above all, more so than in the film. Trees are emaciated and pale, and grass sits in faded yellow clumps. I see no flowers, no color. Just a world of gray.

"Why's it so quiet?" Nate whispers.

He's right. It's eerily silent. In the film there was this hustle and bustle, malnourished Imps exchanging greetings and insults. I look around and see that all the Imps stand still, glowering at us. More specifically, at Alice.

"Tuck your hair in your overalls," I whisper to her.

She does it quickly and without argument, her eyes locked on her bare feet as they slap the tarmac, like she can't bring herself to look up and acknowledge the danger. Nate, Katie, and I walk around her, surrounding her so the Imps have to see through us to get a proper look. Gradually, the noise picks up and the Imps lose interest. We watch Saskia and Matthew walking in front of us.

"What's going on?" Katie says. "Where the hell are we?"

"We're in *The Gallows Dance*," I say.

"Well, I kind of figured that out, eventually. What I mean is, how are we in a film or a book or whatever the hell it is?"

Nate snorts. "There must have been some sort of temporal shift in reality when the set collapsed at Comic-Con. We've entered an alternate universe, *The Gallows Dance* universe."

"In English?" Katie replies.

"I don't bloody know, do I?" Nate replies. He laughs a little manically.

I rest a hand on his arm. "I think you're right. It's some sort of alternate universe—if we were in the film things wouldn't look so different." I realize just how ridiculous it sounds saying it out loud, yet here we are, surrounded by Imps and broken-down buildings, breathing in eau de rotting bird.

"I think I'm dreaming," Alice mumbles to her feet. "It's just a bad dream, and when I wake up I'll be in bed in my pajamas."

"You're so self-obsessed," Nate says. "This could be *my* dream. It's not all about you."

"This isn't helping," I say. "Let's just keep quiet and try not to get killed."

"I don't think it's a dream," Katie says, her voice a little hollow.

Alice sighs. "Me neither. My feet hurt too much for it to be a dream."

"How's Thorn going to help?" I ask Nate. "I know he's your hero, but in case you've forgotten, he's kind of a psycho."

He smiles. "Thorn isn't going to help."

"Stop talking in bloody riddles," Alice says.

Katie nods. "Yeah, seriously, if you've got a plan, you need to tell us."

"Not Thorn," Nate says. "Baba. She'll tell us how to get home."

"Nate! That's brilliant," I say.

"Er, I'm almost afraid to ask," Katie says, "but who's Baba?"

Nate glances at Saskia and Matthew to make sure they aren't listening, but they're too engrossed in their own conversation. They're unaware of Baba's existence—I know this from canon—and I guess Nate wants to keep it that way. Baba's precognitive powers are Thorn's greatest weapon in the fight against the Gems—the fewer people who know about her the better. And Thorn would be beyond pissed off if Nate spilled the beans.

Nate turns to Katie, his voice dipped but his face animated. "She's a total gross-out. She looks like a granny-turned-zombie with all this long gray hair, and her skin covers up her eyes and nostrils, and she has a slit for a mouth and no teeth, and she's all hunched over like this . . ." He stoops and screws up his face in an attempt to look like Baba.

"Yes, but who is she?" Katie whispers, a little impatient.

I can't help butting in. I love Baba, she's one of my favorite characters; she looks terrifying, but she's always so enigmatic. "She was one of the first-ever Gems to exist, and the only Gem to survive the first wave of experiments, back when humans were refining the art of genetic enhancement. They over-enhanced her empathy and her immortality, so she can read minds and see the future and she's survived for centuries. She remembers the world before all the city walls were built and the Gems dropped their bombs."

Nate grins. "She does this really cool thing called a mind blend, where she places her hands on your head and sucks your thoughts from your brain, like a Slushee."

"And this psychic zombie is at Rebel Headquarters?" Katie asks.

I nod. "Thorn keeps her hidden in an underground chamber."

"But she's a Gem," Katie says. "Is she a prisoner or something?"

Alice scoffs. "Keep up. She's on Team Imp. They created her, they looked after her—she hates the Gems."

"And this zombie will tell us how to get home?" Katie asks.

"That's the plan," Nate says.

"She's our best shot?" Katie says. "Our best shot at going home? A really, really old woman called Baby?"

I glance at Nate and Alice, who both offer stilted nods and mutter, "It's Baba."

Katie laughs—a sad titter. "We are so screwed."

CHAPTER 7

W E PAUSE IN front of a sagging building. I recognize it from the film: Zula's Tavern. Saskia and Matthew took Rose there after she released the thistle-bomb to celebrate her first successful mission, and to give her some courage before meeting Thorn. At least, I think it's the same tavern; it looks dirtier and ready to collapse—the door is riddled with woodworm, and a sap-like substance oozes from the brickwork. It actually looks more like I imagined when I read the book, before it got the old Hollywood makeover. I notice the poster of President Stoneback hangs from the wall, softened by rainwater and torn by the wind, same as the film. But this president has horns drawn on his head and a noose scribbled around his throat; detail that didn't make it into the book, or the film, or my own mental image. Detail that makes it all seem scarily real.

"Zula will fix up that arm of yours," Saskia says to Matthew.

This confirms my suspicion, and I realize I stand exactly where Rose stood, just left of the door. I get this creepy feeling like I'm retracing the footsteps of a ghost.

Matthew nods at Alice. "You think it's wise, flaunting a Gem look-alike under their noses? There's a bad crowd in there some days, and even in them overalls, I don't think she was fooling anyone out on the street."

"You got any better ideas?" Saskia replies. "You're not going to make it across the city bleeding like that." She looks Alice up and down. "He's right, though. You still look like a Gem."

"Not with this thing on, surely." Alice scans the overalls, her nose wrinkling with disgust.

"We could knock a couple of your teeth out," Saskia says.

Alice's hand flies to her mouth, partly from shock, partly to protect it.

"That's a bit extreme, isn't it?" I say.

Saskia grins. "You won't be saying that if the Imps think she's a Gem. You'll be wishing I'd knocked her teeth out."

"Steady, Saskia," Matthew says. "If you bloody up her mouth now she'll attract more attention." He places his hands on Alice's shoulders. "You can slouch, yeah?"

Alice adjusts her posture so she's an inch or so shorter.

Saskia laughs. "Well, that did a lot of bloody good, she's practically a midget now." She sidesteps Matthew so she can inspect Alice more closely. "That hair's gotta go, tucking it into your overalls like that . . . it just looks like you're hiding summit."

I think Alice may whimper. "Not my hair."

"Blondes are unusual in the city, hair dye's pretty low down the list of necessities, but we can hack it off." She pulls a knife from her belt and begins to wipe it on her shirttail.

All the color drains from Alice's face, leaving only two streaks of blush that stare from her cheeks like war paint. "You can't be serious."

"It's only hair," Katie says. "It's better than the alternative."

"Yeah, come on, Barbie," Nate says. "Let's see you work a bowl cut." But even he sounds a little afraid.

Saskia approaches Alice with the knife, and this time Matthew doesn't intervene, obviously considering this a sensible idea.

I see Alice's coral lips quiver, her whole body fold in on itself. And suddenly I'm seven years old, sitting behind her, braiding her hair, the scent of cherry blossom and lemongrass, the strands slipping through my fingers and catching the sun like threads of gold. I want to grab that knife and throw it into the mud, but something stops me. Fear, I think—the way those Imps looked at her on the street. The hate in their eyes.

"Hold still." Saskia bundles up the ends of Alice's hair and pulls her head back.

Alice starts to struggle, pawing at the air before her. "No, no, please."

"Bloody hell," Saskia says. "Grab her, will you, Matthew, and make her shut it."

But before Matthew can move, I've clasped Alice's arm and begun whispering into her ear. "You always wanted short hair, remember? Like Audrey Hepburn in *Funny Face*. It will show off your bone structure and that lovely long neck of yours. And when we get home, I'll take you to Toni & Guy and get it tidied up. You'll look amazing, I promise." I feel her body relax a little. "It's for the best—you need to blend in right now."

Tears sparkle in her inky eyes, but she stops struggling and squeezes my hand. "OK, OK, I get it. I'm just too beautiful for this dump." She kneels, demonstrating her cooperation.

Saskia pulls the sheet of gold taut and begins to lop off great chunks. They float toward the ground like yellow feathers. When

Saskia's done, Alice runs her fingers through her cropped hair, her face rigid. She then puts her hands over her face and begins to weep.

"Oh, for God's sake," Saskia says, tucking the knife back into her belt. "You keep crying like that and you'll wash away the dirt. Then I'll have to rub your face in the mud."

Katie and I help Alice up. It's as though she's wounded on the inside, as though she's Samson from the Bible. Even Nate must understand how hard this is for her, 'cause he smiles and says, "You look great, Alice, honest." Though he can't resist adding, "And if the career in writing fails, you can always get a part in the next Lego movie."

"It suits you," Matthew says.

Saskia frowns and plunks her hands on her hips. "Right, keep quiet, all of you. If you make a break for it, you know what I'll do, yeah?" She knots her long, streaked hair into a loose bun like she's getting ready for business. She did this in the film, and it strikes me as odd that in spite of the changes caused by our arrival—Rose's death, the hanging of the nine Imps—we still seem to be in sync with canon. My thoughts topple like dominoes: In canon, a controller lurked behind that tavern door. I know the passage from the novel backwards. *Controllers—self-appointed enforcers of Imp-city law. Of course there is no law, only their greed and their twisted desires.* They took a shine to Rose, got a little too friendly, and she had to use her last thistle-bomb as a decoy so she, Saskia, and Matthew could make their escape. They ended up hiding in a bricked-up doorway down some alley to avoid being lynched. At least Rose isn't here to catch the controller's eye—only Alice. My heart sinks.

Saskia's about to lean into the door.

"Wait," I say.

Nate's eyes widen and I can tell he's connected the dots, too.

"What now?" Saskia pauses, half in, half out.

"We don't know who's inside . . . they may be dangerous," I say.

Saskia's scowl deepens, causing her stain to halve in size. "Stop talking crap or I'll chop more than just your locks off."

Before I can object, Matthew's hustled us through the door.

A wall of stench hits me—that smell Dad gets when he drinks the night before. Stale beer. But mingled with other odors: cabbage and onions and something else, I think it might be urine. Certainly, the room looks like it should smell of urine. The sawdust on the floor, the mildew on the walls, the tattered cushions, all discolored and mustard yellow. It looks like an older, jaded version of the film set.

Several Imps stare at us from their stools. Most of them wear gray overalls to signify their slave status, but some wear plain clothes—faded jeans and threadbare shirts. Their chatter drops as we follow Matthew and Saskia to the bar. I've been in a few pubs before, clutching my fake ID, but the anxiety I felt when illegally ordering vodka and Coke was nothing compared to this—my heart feels like it's going to hammer a hole in my chest.

I search for the controller, but I see no sign of him. My muscles begin to loosen.

The Imp behind the bar wrings out a cloth with nicotine-stained fingers. Zula. She has skin so lined it swallows up her expression so I can't tell if she smiles or frowns. I swear she was never *that* wrinkled in the film.

"What happened to you?" she asks Matthew.

"War wound," he replies.

She nods and leans forward on the bar, allowing the tops of her breasts to sag over her corset. "And who are your friends?"

I open my mouth to reply, but Saskia cuts over me, her voice deceptively light.

"They're just some new Night-Imps, Zula. They work in the Pastures with me and Matthew."

Zula studies our faces. "Oh, yeah?"

I fidget with my hair. "Yeah."

She looks at Alice and narrows her eyes. "I don't want no trouble, yeah?"

"We've had a long shift," Saskia says. "We just need to get Matthew bandaged up, then we'll be on our way."

Zula smiles, a matrix of wrinkles swamping her eyes. "You wanna pop 'round the back, honey? I can sort that out for you."

Matthew grins like it had never occurred to him. "Thanks, you're the best."

"I ain't doing it for you . . . you're dripping on my floor."

He lifts his hand so the blood leaches into the front of his shirt, and follows her into a back room.

Saskia leads us to a counter at the rear of the bar, putting as much distance between us and the other Imps as possible. She leans in. "When Matthew's fixed up, we leave—we've got quite a hike to headquarters."

I recall the bombed-out church from the film. Home to Thorn and Baba, general meeting place for the rebels. I feel this pull in my stomach as I swing between excitement and fear. I can't believe we're going to the actual, real-life headquarters, that we're going to meet the actual, real-life Thorn and Baba. It's like finding out dragons are real. You run outside and watch them circling the sky—awe-inspiring, mind-blowing—until they set you on fire and swallow you whole.

"Our pretty friend is attracting a little too much attention," Saskia says, glancing at the other Imps. Even wearing overalls and with her newly chopped hair, Alice draws the gaze of several Imps.

"Get used to it," Katie says.

I kick her under the table.

"You was right, girl." Saskia's eyes move to a figure slinking toward us. The controller from canon. Only this version of the controller has so many freckles that they can't quite fit on his cheeks, spilling onto his forehead, his eyelids, and lips. And he looks more defined, his features whittled away so only the sharp bits remain, his face filed into a weasel's. My stomach tightens.

He stands over Alice. "Well, what have we got here? A pretty girl on the wrong side of the city walls, always a pleasure."

"Give it a rest," Saskia says. "She's just finished a long shift. We all have."

He taps his star-shaped badge, just like in the film. "*This* demands a little more respect, woman." He turns his attention back to Alice. "So how come I haven't seen you around before?"

Alice looks at Saskia.

The controller smiles. "You can talk for yourself, I reckon, pretty mouth like that."

I begin to wish Saskia had knocked a couple of Alice's teeth out.

"Look, we were just going, OK?" Saskia says.

"You just got here."

"And now we're leaving. I'll get my friend, he's 'round the back with Zula. He got shot by some Gem soldiers." She's trying to win brownie points, but she just sounds desperate.

The controller laughs. I notice how pink his tongue is, like he's been sucking on a jawbreaker. "Well, aren't you the heroes?"

Saskia hurries toward the bar, but the controller doesn't leave. He drags up a chair, shoves Nate out of the way, and sits beside Alice. "What, she your mum or summit?"

Alice giggles nervously.

"Aunty." I flatten my vowels so I sound more like him, but my voice comes out a little shaky.

"Yeah, she's a real pain," Katie says, unable to mask the lilt of her Liverpudlian accent.

The controller drapes an arm around Alice's shoulder. "Well, maybe you should ditch your aunty and come sit with us."

Alice looks rigid as a board. "I don't think she'd approve." But she changes her voice a little, sounding more Imp, and manages to hold his eye like she isn't shitting a brick. For a moment, I think she's going to pull it off.

"You're shaking," the freckly controller says. He leans into her and I imagine how foul his breath must smell. "It ain't cold in 'ere, you know? Why are you shaking?" He sticks out his bottom lip like he's worried about her. "Am I making you nervous, sweet'eart?"

She opens her mouth, I think to answer, but the controller doesn't give her the chance. "'Ere, Terry."

Another Imp sidles over, star-shaped badge pinned to his lapel. He has receding gray hair, and his stocky build suggests he has no problems finding food in the starving city.

The freckly controller smiles. "I got a trembling, pretty girl over 'ere. And while I would like to think it's down to my good looks, I suspect it's because she's a stinking Gem."

Everything seems to slow. Nate grabs my hand under the table, his palm slathered with sweat. I wish I had Rose's last thistle-bomb right now. We could sure use a decoy.

Terry studies Alice's face for a moment and looks a little perplexed. "She hasn't even tried to look like an Imp. No wig, no fake scars, she's just rubbed a bit of dirt in her face and hacked off her locks. It's a poor show, really, a tad insulting p'raps. I mean, I know we Imps are thick, but still . . ."

The freckly controller shakes his head and tuts like he's disappointed. "Gem spies are really slipping."

"She's not a Gem," I say. My voice sounds tinny and unreal.

"Yeah, leave her alone," Katie says.

The freckly controller looks at me, then Nate, then Katie. "I guess traveling with Imps is good thinking, helps her to blend in."

"She's not a Gem," Nate repeats, all the strength stripped away.

"Pipe down, young 'un. You may be an Imp, but if you're helping a Gem, that makes you as bad as them."

"What about this one?" Terry thrusts a finger into my sternum. "She's verging on Gem material—she's pretty enough."

The freckly controller looks at me long and hard. "No cheekbone enhancements, her lips are too thin, they would have plumped those, and she has a mole on her cheek, they would have sliced that off."

I don't know whether to feel offended or relieved.

He leans into me. "Don't look so miserable, who'd want to be a stinking Gem?" His breath smells like damp wood and gin. Suddenly, he grabs my hair and yanks my head back—it feels like my scalp is going to rip away from my skull. My mouth automatically lolls open and he runs a finger over my teeth—it feels like a slug and can't taste much better. I hear my friends shout their objections, but the controller ignores them.

He shakes his head. "Clean but wonky—definitely Imp."

Terry does the same to Alice so she can move only her eyes, which swivel in their sockets, large and engorged with fear.

More Imps wander over. A couple stand behind Katie and Nate, their hands pushing down on their shoulders.

Terry cups Alice's chin, almost tenderly. "Her teeth are perfect."

They exchange a knowing nod and haul us from our chairs. I only reach the freckly controller's chest. He bursts out laughing. "I think we can be confident this one's Imp, gotta love a midget." He lets me drop to the floor. I land awkwardly, knocking my chair so it clatters across the floor. Pain shoots up my tailbone. Nate tries to help me, but a burly Imp still leans on his shoulders.

I turn to see Alice, taller than Terry even without her heels.

Terry smiles this long, sick smile, like he knows he's won. "Well, well, almost six foot, I'd say. Do you know how rare that is without the help of a little genetic tweaking?"

There's an awful pause. I think Alice opens her mouth to say something, but the words never emerge, because in a sudden burst of movement the two controllers tear her overalls away from her body, revealing her slender limbs and her Comic-Con outfit. A piece of dress gets ripped and hangs from the sphere of her shoulder like a long blue tongue.

"Leave her alone, you bastards!" Katie shouts.

Alice tries to lift the tongue back into position, a look of horror contorting her features.

"The final test," Terry says, gripping her arms. "You wear overalls, you reckon you're a slave, then you should be numbered."

All Imps who work in the Pastures have a slave tattoo, a number on their backs that denotes their place of work. It also means only Imps who've been vetted for strength and health are allowed into the Pastures. And of course it means the Gems don't need to use their names—what better way to deny their humanity. I hold Alice's gaze for a second. We both know she's in for it now. The controller lunges toward her and rips down the back of the dress, revealing the blank canvas of skin where her tattoo should rest.

I try to stand, try to reach her, but my arms knock awkwardly against the fallen chair. I hear a loud *bang* as a door flies open and smacks the wall. Matthew comes storming from behind the bar, a bandage crisscrossing his shoulder, blood already seeping through. "Get off 'em, you shits." He thumps and kicks his way toward us.

The Imps block his path and I just see a blur of fists and shoes. Everyone in the bar seems to wade in—an explosion of sound and movement. Hands pulling, voices shouting, knees jabbing. I feel a clap across my back, pain wraps around me like a pair of hot arms. I scrabble to my hands and knees and start to crawl toward Alice. Something hard plows into my ear, a boot, I think. Everything goes blurry and it feels like I'm crawling through water. But I don't stop. I reach Alice's ankles and pull on her calves with all my might. She crouches next to me and quickly, almost desperately, rests her cheek against mine.

"We have to get you out of here." I deliver the words straight into her ear.

She doesn't reply, but we start to crawl toward the door. An Imp falls in front of me, nose caved in. He tries to shout, but I shove my hand in his face, dump my knee on his rib, and just climb straight over him. And somehow, through the confusion, I clamber to my feet and blunder toward the door, Alice beside me.

"Stop them," someone shouts.

"Nate!" I scream. "Katie!"

"I'm here." Katie emerges from a blur of limbs and flounders toward us, her red bob now just a pile of mats stuck to her head.

I grab her hand. "Nate?" I ask, pulling her toward me.

She shakes her head, her eyes wide and startled.

"Nate," I scream, trying to peer through the movement. "Nate." But I see only angry faces storming toward us.

Alice grabs my shoulder. "We've got to run."

I feel torn, straight down the middle. Nate or my friends. But something in Katie's eyes and the rip in Alice's dress forces me to prioritize them. We burst into daylight and run and run and run. My ear burns and my back screams, but my legs know what to do. One foot in front of the other. And all I can think—arms pumping, fists clenched, lungs stinging—is, *I left Nate behind.*

CHAPTER 8

We PAUSE FOR a moment, around the back of some terraced houses, gulping the air and wiping the sweat from our eyes.

"She went that way."

The boot must have damaged my ear because the words kind of slosh together, but I recognize the controller's nasal tone all the same. We start to run, ducking beneath clotheslines, jumping over mounds of rubbish. Alice's long legs carry her farther ahead, and for a moment I think she may leave us behind.

"Alice," I manage to say.

She slows and we reach her side.

"We can't get too far from Nate," I say.

"We won't, don't worry, Vi," Katie says. "We'll go back for him in a sec."

I hear the controller's voice again. "Come on, lads, let's flush 'em out." He's louder, closer.

I frantically scan the alleyway for a hiding place. That's when I see it—the bricked-up doorway from canon, the one Rose, Saskia, and Matthew hid in, a mess of crumbling bricks and pitted mortar. I catch Alice's eye and we share an unspoken moment of understanding. We begin to pull away the bricks, disturbing a nest of wood lice. Katie drops to her knees and begins to help.

"They came down here," someone shouts.

I hear Alice gasp, but we don't stop, panic driving us on.

Terry's voice sails over the rising stamp of boots. "Come on, you useless bunch of cretins."

We cram our bodies into the hole, pulling back the bricks with frantic, urgent movements.

I hold my breath and pull my knees toward my body with trembling, sticky hands. The ground vibrates as the Imps pass. The air stirs against my cheek, and I watch my hands turn pink to black to pink as their shadows block out the light. Only when my hands stay pink for a while do I start to breathe again.

"They've gone," Alice whispers. "Just like in canon."

"What do you mean?" Katie asks.

"Rose, Saskia, and Matthew hid in this very doorway to avoid the same lynch mob," I say.

"That's weird," Katie says.

I nod. "You're right. It's like the original plot seems to be . . ." I pause, searching for the right words. "Haunting us."

Alice lets her head slump back against the wall. "How the hell did we end up in this place?" In the shadow of the bricked-up doorway, I can just make out the tears glistening on her cheeks.

"It's insane." I shift my weight so our knees knock together.

"I want to go home," Alice says.

"Me, too," Katie says.

I wish we could just stay in this doorway forever, huddled and warm and safe.

Alice wipes her nose with the back of her hand, something I've never seen her do. "It's funny, you know," she says. "I used to wish and wish I could be inside *The Gallows Dance* . . . but now we're actually here and"—her voice breaks from the weight of the emotion—"it really sucks." She makes this soft, rhythmic noise, halfway between a laugh and a sob.

"At least you've read the book and seen the film," Katie says. "Why couldn't we be in Narnia or Neverland or . . . or . . . or *A Midsummer Night's Dream*? At least then I'd know what was going on."

I don't reply. I focus instead on the pain—my head, my ear, my back. It kind of distracts me. We listen to something drip nearby, a distant sound of chatter, the mew of a cat.

"We need to find Nate," I finally say. I know we probably lured every angry Imp away from the tavern, but all the same, I won't feel happy until I've seen him alive and well.

Alice nods. "Give it a second longer, though, yeah? Make sure those bastards have definitely gone. I think Rose waited for an hour or so."

I shake my head. "He's only fourteen . . ."

Katie squeezes my leg. "But he's super-smart, he can think his way out of anything."

We share a sad smile and begin to push the bricks away. We emerge from the doorway, stubbing our toes on the rubble, upsetting the brick dust. It catches in my throat and I stifle a cough.

Maybe we didn't wait long enough, maybe it was the cough, but somebody spots us.

"There they are," an Imp shouts. "I told you they came this way."

My stomach flips. But we don't pause, we don't even turn to look, we just start running again. We skid around the corner to see more Imps; an angry, ugly wall. They close in on us, pinning us in, rounding us up, and I spin faster and faster as I realize walls surround us, of both flesh and brick. I grab Alice and Katie by the hands and balance my weight on my toes, ready to move at any opportunity.

The freckly controller smiles—long and slow—like he knows how scared we must be. "Well, look what we have here."

I don't respond, too scared to speak. Beneath my tunic, my skin bristles.

"A Gem and her friends—two Imp traitors."

I open my mouth, but only a whimper escapes.

"For God's sake," Katie shouts, "she's not a Gem."

The controller ignores her. "You know what we do to Gems and traitors?"

Another Imp cries from the back of the group, "String 'em up."

In the film and the book, the Imps are the goodies, the ones you root for, so it's strange to be at the receiving end of their hatred. I wish I could explain this to them, sit them all down and show them the film, *their* film, make them see that this isn't real. None of this is real.

And suddenly I don't feel the heat in my ear or the pain in my back, I don't think about my friends' hands, slicked with sweat and cold in my own. I just feel my whole body melt on the spot. My legs cave, my lungs stop gasping, and my heart stops squeezing. I hit the ground like a dead weight.

"She's beaten us to it."

"Can you hang a traitor if they're already dead?"

"You can never kill a traitor too many times."

I hear Alice's voice, like she's talking through cloth. "Violet, wake up, Violet."

Colors dissipate, shapes fragment, sounds ebb to nothing.

I sail toward the clouds, toes pointed, legs stretched. I reach the peak of an invisible arc and glance down—the trampoline oscillates like a magenta sheet pulled between the trees. Mum laughs and Nate claps his hands. *Jump, Violet, jump. We won't let you fall.* And then I hear a voice, muffled, like it's moving through water. It belongs to Dad. *That's it, Violet, come on, baby girl. Wake up, wake up.* My eyelids flicker, the effort of opening them feels like lifting a massive weight. And I can smell something clean, a lack of rotten bird, something crisp and medicinal. But the trees dissolve, the rotten bird returns, and Dad's voice turns to a scream. Alice's scream.

The grogginess lifts, and I realize I'm sailing toward the clouds not because of a trampoline, but because of the hands that have seized my limbs, heaving me upright. The earth vanishes, and I momentarily hang in the air like a doll. Then, my heels smack the ground and bounce off the cobbles as the Imps drag me down an alley. The strip of sky above opens into an expanse of washed-out blue. I'm back on a main street again.

I turn my head and catch a glimpse of Alice, hoisted high above the heads of several Imps, her face twisted with fear. I hear shouts and jeers. Judging from the increase in volume, quite a crowd is gathering. Hands grab at my skin. *We've caught us a Gem. We've caught us a traitor. String 'em up. Make 'em pay.* They flip me onto my stomach and I lose sight of her.

"Alice!" I scream to the cobbles.

The Imps ignore me and lug me toward a barrel. Alice has already been dumped on one; she stands tall, her chin stretched high, probably because she's afraid of falling, but I can't help thinking how she looks like the tiny fairy from my music box. I half expect her to start spinning. And then I realize, with a bolt of horror, that she stands so tall because of the noose around her neck.

Before I can shout or scream or cry, I feel a rope slip over my own head and tighten beneath my chin. I try to lift my hands—to pull, to claw, to break free—but at some point the Imps must have bound my wrists together. This sends another shot of panic through me, as though the use of my hands could somehow save me.

The Imps plant my feet onto a barrel next to Alice and pivot me into an upright position. The other end of the rope whistles past my ear like a bullet, arcing over a battered streetlamp and whacking the ground. Then it's Katie's turn. I watch them jostle her onto another barrel, her rope sailing after mine. I look down on the hateful faces and lock my legs, trying desperately to stand—I know that slumping will be the death of me. But the rope tightens against my throat, cutting off my air supply, and can only get tighter. I close my eyes and wonder if the noose will prevent the vomit rising any farther. I wish my hands weren't bound, just so I could hold my friends' hands one last time.

An Imp with a hooked nose steps forward and raises his voice. "Silence, fellow Gems, this is your president talking."

The crowd laughs and claps.

The president slices his hands through the air. The crowd falls silent.

"Welcome to the Gallows Dance." He purposefully rounds his vowels, inflating his chest like a cockerel ready to crow. "We are here to witness the hanging of these . . . Imps."

"What are their crimes?" someone shouts.

He looks to the sky as though communicating with a higher power. "Their crimes are scraping an existence, feeding their families, contending with your disgust, your persecution, your sexual advances."

The crowd makes jeering noises. One Imp lunges forward and tugs at my tunic. The barrel wobbles and I feel my body lurch against the rope.

The president laughs. "Their crime is poverty."

I try to breathe, but the air is thin. My legs weaken with every passing second.

"Their crime is disease."

It's strange what goes through your mind when you're about to die. But my final thought goes something like this: *What a shame to come all this way and not meet Willow.*

"Their crime is starvation." The president sweeps his hands in a giant circle. "Their crime is . . . holding up a mirror to the ugliness within."

The crowd bursts into life, laughing and braying.

The president raises his hands in surrender. "But wait. These are no Imps. They are wolves in sheep's clothing." He points an accusatory finger at Alice. "This one is a stinking Gem." He turns his attention to me and Katie. "And these two . . . God knows what they are. Imp by birth, but Gem by allegiance. Traitors through and through."

"She's not a Gem," Katie rasps. "She got a C on her math exam and she had a cold last week."

"Shut it, traitor," the president says.

I stare into his eyes, searching for a morsel of compassion. The compassion that shines from the eyes of the Imps in the film. But I see only loathing.

He sneers. "So what should we do with our stinking Gem and her stinking sidekicks?"

A chant begins, soft at first, but gathering strength with every word. *Make 'em dance. Make 'em dance. Make 'em dance.*

The president bows and the chanting stops. This is it. We're about to die. The Imps remove their hands from my body and I teeter on the edge of the barrel. Somehow, I manage to squeeze some words past the rope. "We just want to go home."

The controller laughs. "Tell someone who cares." He looks at the barrel and pulls back his boot.

"STOP!" This voice doesn't travel through water. It's strong and clear and hangs in the air like thistledown.

I squint into the crowd and see an Imp pushing his way to the front, his strong face set with determination. A shock of black hair spills onto his porcelain skin, and even from afar, blurred by movement, I can tell he owns the palest blue eyes I've ever seen.

"For God's sake." He strides right up to us, his strong nose raised high. "What the hell do you think you're doing? I know these girls, they're Imps. All of 'em. You're about to hang three Imps."

The freckly controller runs an anxious hand across his brow. "The little ones are, but the tall one, she's Gem, for sure."

"She's definitely Imp, I grew up across the street from her. She's always been bloody gorgeous. I keep telling her, you need to break your nose or summit, or one day you're gonna end up flipping on a barrel like a fish."

There's this awkward pause. A tense silence from the crowd.

Terry moves first, slapping the black-haired Imp on the back. "It's OK. I know this kid—he's all right, I tell you. He's Ma's boy, and if he says she's an Imp, she's an Imp."

"So where's her tattoo, and why was she hiding a dress under her overalls?" the freckly controller asks, his voice laced with disappointment.

Alice manages to croak a few key words. "I'm working for the rebels."

"Of course," the black-haired Imp says, catching on quickly. "She's pretending to be a Gem so she can get us some secrets." His eyes flash an amazing pastel blue. "She deserves a goddamn medal, risking her life to save you idiots, and what do you do? String her up like she's a monster."

The crowd begins to murmur, exchanging confused, sideways glances. The president circles his hands again, keen to watch the finale to his show. "Since when did innocence matter?"

But several hands have already sliced the ropes and helped us from the barrels. The black-haired Imp pushes his body under my arm and supports my weight, looping his spare arm around Alice's waist. Katie's fared better and manages to walk behind us, her hand resting on my shoulder like she's lost her sight.

I can't help but notice how strong the black-haired Imp is, in spite of the knots of bone that push through his shirt and into my flesh. I can barely walk, yet he sweeps us along with ease. We begin to weave our way between the baffled spectators.

"Just keep moving," he says.

Alice groans in response.

"Nate. I need to go back." My words merge together, but the boy seems to understand.

He hoists me a little higher and shakes his head. "Do you have a death wish? Just keep moving before they change their mind."

"We'll find him, Vi," Katie whispers from behind.

"Who are you?" I ask the black-haired Imp.

"Your hero by the looks of it," he replies.

CHAPTER 9

WE VANISH INTO a side street, and after several confusing turns, he pulls us through a doorway.

"You're safe here."

Upon hearing those words, I sink to the ground and adopt the fetal position. I think I must retch because bile fills my mouth, and I guess I've started to cry, because I hear the sobs of a terrified girl. My hands flit between clawing at my neck and shoving away imaginary demons—a colony of ants crawling all over me, biting, nipping, burrowing down. Katie sits beside me and strokes my hand, and the black-haired Imp holds my hair from my face in case I puke. These kind gestures pull me from my pit. I struggle into a sitting position and lean against the wall beside Alice. I turn and take in her face, pale and drawn and streaked with mascara.

"Are you OK?" she asks.

I shake my head and register a new pain; the burning ring of fire encompassing my neck. I run my fingers across it and feel something warm and moist oozing onto my split-heart necklace.

"Violet's noose was really tight," Katie says. "I could see it cutting into her skin." She's trying really hard to speak in her normal, practical tone, but I catch the waver at the end of her sentence.

The Imp passes me a cup of steaming liquid. "Here, try and drink something."

I take it with quavering hands and let my chest just rise and fall of its own accord. I take small, broken sips and the pain around my neck subsides. It tastes a bit like black tea. He passes one to Katie and Alice, and I hear them muttering *thank you*. Alice sniffs it and places it on the floor.

I gradually grow aware of my surroundings—a small room, sparse and uncarpeted, boxes instead of chairs, a small sink in one corner and an open fire in the other. The Imp lifts a quilt from a nearby box and throws it around my shoulders. Only now do I notice how cold I feel.

"So, what's your story?" the Imp asks.

A single word spears the bleariness: *Nate*. I recall the last time I saw his face, tight with anxiety. "I need to find my little brother." I try to raise my body up, but my arms buckle, the world rotates, and I end up slumping back against the wall, tea slopping onto my lap.

The Imp takes the cup from me, his fingers grazing mine. "You're not going anywhere for a little while. You're in shock, and those bastard controllers may still be out there." His voice sounds warm, like he's known me for years, and I feel my muscles unwind a little.

"He's right," Alice says.

Katie nods. "Nate will be fine, he's with Saskia and she's a right old battle-ax."

I bite my bottom lip, pinning it in position, trying to stop it from trembling. Silence spreads between the bare walls.

"I'm Ash," he finally says, touching my arm.

I feel my head jerk upright. "Ash?"

He looks a little bemused. "That's what I said—Ash."

"Ash from canon?"

He shakes his head like I'm mad. "From what?"

"Now you know how I feel," Katie mutters.

"Do you work at the Harper estate?" Alice asks him.

He nods. "Yeah, I'm a Night-Imp."

Alice and I look at each other for a moment.

"It's Ash from canon," Alice says, and then laughs.

Canon-Ash was one of the Imps who looked after Rose at the Harper estate, though he had no idea she was a rebel. He showed her around, helped her with her chores, and stared at her a lot. I always felt a little sorry for Ash; he was like Jacob from *Twilight*, traipsing after Bella like a lost puppy. Ash from the film even *looked* like a puppy—big blue eyes, floppy black hair. But current-Ash looks more like I imagined him after reading the book, more feline than canine—sleeker and prouder and just more attractive. I can't help wondering if Russell Jones didn't want the on-screen competition. I bet R-Patz's heart sank when he saw Taylor Lautner for the first time.

"But you look so . . . so different," I say.

"Stop drooling, Vi," Katie whispers.

Either Ash doesn't hear or he ignores her. "Have we met before?"

I shake my head, a little too vigorously, and the pain intensifies. "No . . . no . . . My mistake."

He smiles. "And you are?"

"Violet," I say.

"The color or the flower?"

"Both."

He looks at the wound on my neck. "Do you mind if I take a look?"

"Go for it."

He reaches beneath my hair. The sharpness of his nail catches my collarbone and something warm and fluttery grows in my stomach.

"That's gotta hurt." He smiles this wonky smile and cocks his head to the side. I realize he feels a little awkward touching me— he's only eighteen, a year older than me. He wipes my blood on his overalls and scowls. "I can't stand those nasty controllers, deciding who lives and who dies." He moves across the room to the sink and runs a cloth under the tap, which flows straight from the sink into a drain cover on the floor, no pipe or anything. Even from a distance, I can see flecks of brown in it. The reek of raw sewage wafts toward me.

Alice wrinkles up her nose.

Ash pretends he doesn't see. "They're just power-hungry idiots. No better than the Gems, if you ask me." His eyes flick to Alice. "Sorry."

"I'm not a Gem." Her newly cropped hair reveals her neck, which remains smooth and unblemished. Katie was right; my noose was particularly tight. This thought sends another wave of nausea through me.

He arches a dark eyebrow (current-Ash has way better brows than canon-Ash, not a unibrow in sight). "Seriously? You just look like that?" he asks.

She smiles. "Yeah, I guess."

"Oh, please," Katie says. "Her head's quite big enough already."

"Hang on," I say to Ash. "If you thought she was a Gem, why did you save her?"

He wrings out the cloth and shrugs. "We're all just animals."

"So you . . . don't hate Gems?" I ask.

"'Course I do, but I wouldn't kill 'em." He moves toward me, and I notice the stark line where the darkness of his hair meets the white of his skin. "We should probably clean that up."

I let him dab at my neck. I can't help but notice how his skin looks almost translucent in the dimness of the room, lending him a vulnerability completely at odds with the breadth of his chest.

"So, where are you from?" His breath skims my ear.

I falter on my words. "We're from a different universe."

He laughs. "Let me guess, one where Imps rule the world."

Now it's my turn to laugh. "Would that be so weird?"

"Not really. We used to, didn't we? Before genetic enhancement was discovered."

Ever so gently, he tilts my chin. I look straight into his eyes. The cool expanse of blue reminds me of winter. He slides the cloth around the back of my neck, under my hair, and I catch his scent— sweat and soap.

"So maybe we're from the past," I say.

"Time travelers, the plot thickens." He pauses for a moment and we smile at each other. His smile takes up his whole face; even his proud nose has to fight for space.

Katie turns to Alice. "I'm suddenly feeling invisible."

"Hello." Alice waves her hand. "We still exist, you know. When do *we* get our own personal sponge bath?"

Ash and I laugh, a little nervously, and our breath mingles in the space between us.

He rocks back onto his haunches. "You must be hungry?"

My stomach growls of its own accord. I haven't eaten anything since breakfast.

He moves across the room to a cauldron and stokes the fire. "Ma put a stew on before she left."

"Who's Ma?" I recall the controller's words: *He's Ma's boy, and if he says she's an Imp, she's an Imp.* Obviously, Ma demands respect.

He stirs the pot. The heat and movement release an aroma of stewing meat, overpowering the sewage smell and making my mouth water.

"She's the local Imp midwife," he says. "Everyone loves her, and the Imps need her, you know."

"I guess there's no hospital, then?" Katie says.

Ash grins. "You really are from another universe, aren't you?"

I can't imagine what the women must go through, giving birth in these conditions, walls caked with muck, water flecked with brown.

He keeps on stirring, and I let the melody of his voice lull me into a trancelike state. "She's the reason that mob let you go; I get a lot of respect being her son, even the controllers value her, 'cause it's their mistresses and babies she's saved. She loses the odd one, baby or mother, and then she cries in her sleep for a week." He pauses, staring into the stew like he can see something he once lost and can never retrieve.

"She sounds amazing," I say.

But what strikes me as even more amazing is the amount of backstory that wasn't in the book or the film. It's as if this universe extends beyond the edges of the canon. I want to discuss it with Alice and Katie, but I'm afraid Ash will think I'm mad.

He pulls himself from his thoughts and starts ladling the stew into bowls. Brown lumps suspended in discolored water. "Yeah, Ma's amazing, all right." He hands us each a bowl.

It smells even better up close.

"Violet," Alice hisses, placing the bowl next to her cup. "You know what this is, don't you?"

My mind reels back to the film, the scenes of the hungry Imps catching and skinning rats, interspersed with clips of Gems stuffing their pretty faces with gourmet food.

"Is it rat?" I ask him.

"Rat?" Katie says. "For real?"

He looks a little confused. "What else could it be?"

The thought of eating rat makes my stomach turn, of course it does. I remember this scandal in Shepherd's Bush a year or so back, when a restaurant was closed down for serving rat instead of chicken. I didn't eat meat for a week, and when I finally did, Dad and Nate hid this plastic mouse in my turkey sandwich. I screamed at them. I mean, *really* screamed. And then I didn't eat meat for another week.

But I look at Ash, the way he cocks his head to the side, watching me watching him. I force a smile. "Yeah, 'course. Thanks." I rest the bowl on the floor and use my hands to shovel the glop into my mouth.

Alice and Katie watch me eat in silence, still holding their bowls with suspicious hands.

When I've finished, Alice and Katie start to giggle.

"You've just eaten a rat," Alice says.

"An actual rat," Katie says.

I start to laugh, too. "It tasted OK."

"It's the best rat this side of the broken bridge," Ash says.

Something clicks in my brain. "We need to get to the broken bridge."

"You sure about that?" Ash says. "There's only trouble down by the river."

I nod. "Yeah, Nate will be there."

Ash looks confused again. "I can take you so far, but I've got to get back to the city gates before the buses leave. I'm heading to the Pastures tonight."

I notice his regulation gray overalls for the first time, taut across his chest.

Alice sits bolt upright. "The *Pastures*?" She emphasizes the word *Pastures* like she did the word *Hawaii* after her big family holiday last year. She returned even blonder, even more sun-kissed, and just a touch smug. She leans in. "Of course you work in the Pastures, don't you."

"Yeah, I'm a Night-Imp, I thought we cleared that up."

"What are they like?" she asks.

I can almost hear a ukulele and the swish of a grass skirt.

"What, Night-Imps?" He frowns. "Sun-starved, kinda pasty, vitamin D deficient."

Alice laughs like she can't hear the sadness behind the sarcasm. "No, no. What are the *Pastures* like?"

"OK . . . you know . . . readily available food and clean water, all those luxuries." He scans her face for a moment, but distrust rather than adoration flickers beneath his features. "Why are you so interested?"

Her hands fidget around her mouth and she stifles a nervous laugh. "Oh, you know, just trying to make conversation and be a good houseguest."

He glances at her untouched bowl of stew. "A good houseguest would have eaten the rat."

This makes me laugh and he turns his gaze to me. "You sure you want to go to the bridge?" he says. "It's just . . . I really can't come with you, not that far. If I lose my post my family won't survive."

I get this burst of sympathy and a lie forms on my lips. "Don't worry, we're not going to go all the way, just in the general direction. We'll be fine. We've got friends waiting."

"It's just, I won't be able to protect you, not this time." He lowers his dark lashes, and I notice how long they are, grazing the crown of each cheekbone.

"And I thought you were our hero," Alice says.

He ignores her coquettish look and raises his gaze so it meets mine, the warmth of his smile tempering the ice of his eyes. He then picks up Alice's and Katie's bowls and slops the contents back into the cauldron. "Yes, but the Imp-bus waits for no one, not even us heroes." He dashes from the room for a moment.

Katie turns to me. "How do you know where Nate is?"

"Saskia and Matthew were taking us to Rebel Headquarters, remember?" I say.

"And headquarters are by the broken bridge?"

"That's right," I say.

"I don't remember Ash being that cute," Alice interrupts.

"He most definitely wasn't," I reply.

"Who's Ash?" Katie says, the frustration rising in her voice.

"Think Jacob from *Twilight*," I reply.

She shrugs. "You think I've read *Twilight*? Do you know me at all?"

"Oh, for God's sake," Alice says. "Even my gran's read *Twilight*."

"OK, think Buttons from *Cinderella*," I say. "Ash followed Rose around like a lost puppy."

Katie's face lights up. "Ooh, like Silvius from *As You Like It*."

Alice rolls her eyes. "Or Geeky McGeekyson from *Attack of the Nerds*."

Ash returns with a pair of tattered leather shoes dangling from his hands, one of which has a hole in the bottom, plugged with some sort of dried straw. He hands them to Alice, who holds them between her thumb and her forefinger like she's avoiding touching them.

Katie can't stop grinning. "Not quite Jimmy Choos, are they?"

Poor Ash looks thoroughly confused again—he looks really cute with his forehead all creased up. "They're not Jimmy's, they're mine." He points at Alice's feet. "But they should fit you OK, you've got massive man feet for a girl."

I catch Katie's eye as we try not to laugh.

"We'd better get going, then, find that little brother of yours." Ash grins at me, and that warm, fluttery feeling stretches to every extremity of my body.

CHAPTER 10

I DIDN'T THINK IT possible, but the city disintegrates even more the deeper we go. Buildings without walls, streets ripped in two, huts built from scraps of metal and plastic. It's so much worse than in the film. Even worse than how I pictured it from the book. And the stench just grows and grows. I raise my sleeve to my nose, hoping to filter the air, and notice that Katie and Alice do the same.

I peer into the shelters and catch the odd glimpse of movement; mothers feeding their babies, fathers hacking at salvaged bits of wood. It occurs to me that all these Imps have a backstory, a life, which Sally King didn't write about. Just like Ash. How is this even possible? Did King write about each Imp in detail before she died? Or has this world sprung directly from King's imagination?

"So, what's your story?" Ash asks me. "Why's your little brother at the broken bridge?"

The words *little brother* ignite guilt inside me. Already I've forgotten why I left him in the tavern, why I failed to prioritize him.

"Violet?" The concern in Ash's voice makes me a little teary.

"If I tell you, I'll have to kill you," I say.

He laughs. "Ah, now your story just gets more and more intriguing, doesn't it? Time traveler, assassin . . ."

Our upper arms nudge against each other. He seems happy not to pry, to walk beside me, his arm resting against mine like we belong.

We see fewer and fewer overalls. The plain-clothed Imps look lean and desperate, even for Imps. Recessed eyes, angular cheekbones, fingers like twigs. I remember this from canon. The Imps who work in the Pastures live nearest to the gates and are the rulers of the city. The ones who are fed and clothed and given a small allowance. But the Imps nearer the river look close to death, their lips tinged blue.

I watch as the sun slips down the sky. Back home, it's springtime—the air tastes balmy and sits easy in your lungs. Here, it's early autumn, and the cold begins to worm its way beneath my tunic and into my bones. I briefly wonder what time it is back home, whether Mum and Dad have set the table for tea, waiting for me and Nate to return from Comic-Con. I imagine their anxious faces as time ticks by, and I get this lump in my throat like I've swallowed a piece of shrapnel.

The air changes and the wind picks up, delivering a pungent odor of fish and sewage.

"We're getting nearer to the river," Ash says. "I need to get back to the city gates. If I run, I can still make the last bus." He cups my elbow with his hand—a spot of hot sun. "I hate leaving you here, you nearly got hung in the *nice* part of town."

"That was *nice*?" Alice says.

He smiles his crooked smile. "Just keep heading south and you'll hit the river soon enough. Just stay away from the rebels, yeah? They're bad news. I know it's a worthy cause, Imp emancipation and all that, but they're a bunch of ruthless bastards—they'd kill their granny if they thought she was a Gem." He gestures briefly to Alice. "And you'll have trouble convincing them that Bigfoot here hasn't had her helixes tampered with."

Alice sighs. "Jesus, will everyone stop going on about how hot I am?"

He turns to leave and catches my cheek with his lips. A weird feeling gathers in my stomach; a twist of longing.

"Thanks," I say.

He cocks his head to the side and holds me for a moment with those amazing frosted-blue eyes. Then he turns and jogs back up the street.

"I need a hero," Katie sings, just loud enough for me to hear.

"Oh, piss off," I say.

Alice joins in. *"I'm holding out for a hero till the end of the night—"*

"Guys, seriously!" I say.

Katie clutches her heart and throws her head back. *"And he's gotta be strong and he's got a big dong . . ."*

We start laughing, really loudly, like we're back home, the three of us lined up on my sofa, watching horrible television and throwing popcorn and insults at Simon Cowell. But something about our laughter sounds so out of place in this strange, concrete world—like birdsong in a war zone—and gradually it tapers into silence.

"I guess we keep on walking," Alice says.

I reply by moving my feet, the monotony of the tarmac bedding into the soles of my boots.

"Alice?" I ask.

She grunts.

"When you wrote all your fanfic, did you give all the Imps backstories?"

"What are you getting at?"

I struggle to order my thoughts. "It's just, Ash's got this rich history that is completely new to me, and most of the Imps we've seen aren't from the film or the novel . . ." I trail off.

"That *is* weird," Katie says.

Alice nods. "I know what you mean. I don't think fanfic has the answer, though. I think maybe Nate's right."

"Alternate universe?" I say.

Alice laughs a breathy laugh. "This is mental."

"So what happens next?" Katie asks.

Alice pulls at her ragged hair as if trying to make it grow. "Bet you wish you'd listened to Violet's presentation now."

"I did," Katie says, looking at me, concern registering on her neat features. "Honest I did, Vi. It's just everything here is such a mind mush it's hard to remember it all. And you said something about the canon haunting us, so it might help hearing it again."

"Then try reading something other than Dickens," Alice says.

I step in. "So Saskia and Matthew took Rose to meet Thorn at Rebel Headquarters. Which is where we're going now, to find Nate. Then Thorn took Rose to see Baba."

"The psychic zombie?" Katie says.

I nod. "Baba read Rose's mind, and told Thorn that Rose would be the one to save the Imps."

"Through self-sacrifice and love," Alice says, unable to resist butting in.

I push on. "So Thorn trusted Rose to take the lead in the biggest rebel mission to date—the Harper mission."

"And that's where she met Willow?" Katie says.

Alice nods and sighs. "Ah, Willow. To think we're breathing the same air, standing beneath the same sky."

I get that same tremor of excitement, like we're back at Comic-Con thinking about Russell Jones. With all the commotion, all the worry about Nate, I'd completely forgotten about Willow.

Eventually, the road opens up. Bombed-out buildings sit on either side, the shadows of their foundations remaining. Weeds push through the cracks in the tarmac and, for a brief moment, I feel relieved just seeing the green. And then I notice them. Thistles. Hundreds and hundreds of thistles. Forcing their way between the paving slabs, nestling between bricks, peering from mounds of rubble.

"The symbol of the rebels," I say.

"Cut us down and we come back stronger," Alice replies, a little dreamy, like we're back at the cinema watching the film.

I nod. "We're nearly there."

Rose walked this very path with Saskia and Matthew on her way to meet Thorn for the first time. The thrill of her first successful mission was fading and nerves were setting in. I recall how she saw the thistles and said, *"Is he as spiky as his favorite weed?"* And Saskia smiled and replied, *"Even spikier."*

Now it just seems ridiculous that Rose felt nervous. She hadn't destroyed the thistle-bomb mission, and she hadn't lost her little brother, and she hadn't been transported to a different universe. That piece of shrapnel is back and I start to feel sick again.

Alice must be thinking the same, 'cause she squeezes my hand. "He's not *that* spiky. Remember, he loved Ruth, didn't he?"

"Who's Ruth?" Katie asks.

Alice turns to me. "You tell her, before I scream."

"She was a main part of Thorn's backstory," I say. "She was the love of his life years ago, when he was our age, but she was hanged at the Gallows Dance before they could elope. Thorn never recovered."

Katie gasps. "That's tragic. Poor Thorn."

"Yeah," I say. "And watching the love of his life hang at the hands of the Gems did wonders for his anger issues. He's a ruthless psycho."

Alice cackles. "*Ruth*-less, get it?"

Katie manages a half smile. "That would be funny if we were still talking about a book."

But I can't even force a half smile. All I can think about is the fact my little brother may already be at headquarters with Thorn.

"Yeah, sorry," Alice grumbles.

We continue to head south, keeping the ever-fading sun to our right. The bunches of thistles increase, the stench of rotting fish overpowers us, and, finally, my eyes fall upon the church. It stands among the devastation, ragged and tired yet mostly intact. Proof of divine intervention, the book said.

"Nate." I start to run toward the church.

The tarmac blisters and curls as the road reaches an abrupt end. I come to a halt. The term *broken bridge* is an understatement. The bridge isn't broken, it's gone. Bombed into nothingness. Seeing it for real and not behind the pane of a television screen—encircled by creature comforts—really knocks the air from my lungs. I look along the river; not a single bridge, the city carved in two by water. No evenly proportioned buildings illuminating the skyline, their lights reflecting off the water like lanterns on a lake. Just the jagged remnants of what used to be. I can't help feeling this sense of loss for the city I know and love.

Katie and Alice reach my side.

"Jesus," Katie whispers.

I feel an overwhelming urge to sink to my knees and sob. But I think of Nate, possibly with Thorn at this very moment, and my strength returns. I swallow down a mouthful of fish-tainted air and continue running toward the church.

"Violet, slow down," Alice yells.

I don't stop. The smell of fish and sewage gain strength, filling my lungs as I leap over stones and cracks and thistles.

I step into the shadow of the church and the air temperature dips a degree or two. I'm there—Rebel Headquarters. Without the thumping drums and violins blaring in my ears, it looks kind of serene. It's based on the church of St. Magnus the Martyr, a real church that Alice and I visited after we'd watched the film. The porthole windows have been replaced by plastic and rags, and part of the roof is missing, but without the surrounding high-rises and the bluish glint of The Shard in the backdrop, the church seems bigger, more imposing.

The wooden doors stand before me, sturdy and closed. I try the iron handle. Locked. I slam my fists into the wood and begin to shout. "Nate!"

Alice grabs my hands and tries to silence me. "Violet! Are you mad? You can't be hammering down the rebels' door. They'll kill you."

I bash the wood harder. "Nate? Are you in there?"

Katie and Alice try to drag me away, but the adrenaline fills me with strength.

"Stop it, you nutter," Alice says. "Do you even remember Thorn? The way he scalped that Gem for insulting his dead girlfriend?"

"Yeah, let's not piss off the psycho," Katie says.

Panic winds around me again, a serpent constricting my chest, crushing my heart. "What if that psycho's got my little brother?" I lay my palms against the wood, close my eyes, and try to sense

Nate. It feels like my body gives up—throat closes, lungs freeze, mind empties. Finally, my arms dissolve beneath my weight, allowing my cheek to press against the door. Cool and coarse and real. I wish I could just sink into it. But the door has other ideas. It creaks and falls away from me. I see a woman's face peering through the gap, an unmistakable stain on her forehead.

Saskia.

"You found us," she whispers.

Before I can jam my foot in the gap, she darts outside and pulls the door shut. I try to move around her, but she clasps my body in an awkward embrace. I feel so surprised, so desperate, I just let my arms hang limply by my sides.

"We've been worried about you," she says.

"Is Nate OK?" I attempt to sidestep her, but she won't budge.

"Yeah, 'course. He's fine."

I feel like I've been tossed high into the air, like I hover at the point where I can't go any higher—the peak of my arc, magenta trampoline below—just waiting for gravity to kick in. Suspended, weightless, free.

"Really?" I whisper.

"Yeah, he's fine. He's just meeting the rebels. Come on, I'll show you in."

"I don't like this," Alice says. "You've never been nice to us before."

Saskia throws her a stern look. "Shut it, princess."

"Alice is right," Katie says. "Something weird's going on."

I wipe my eyes on the back of my sleeve and laugh. A strange, shaky warble that doesn't belong to me.

Saskia steps aside and gestures to the door. "Just go on in," she says, smiling.

I feel strange, like my feet no longer connect with the ground. But I command my body to move. I heave open the door and step forward. Katie stands beside me, her hand clutching mine, and I barely notice Alice hanging back, her trembling voice begging us not to enter.

The church is a vast, open space. Elegant pillars reach toward a pale, scalloped ceiling, and the late-afternoon sun trickles through the portholes, worming through the gaps in the rags, softened and marbled by the plastic. I see no pews, only rows upon rows of desks. It looks so similar to the film version, yet certain details make it alien and new—the smell of stone infused with incense, the way the dust hangs in the air like specks of gold, the stone flags pushing into my feet. My skin pricks with sweat.

"Violet!" I hear Nate's voice. He runs to me, arms outstretched, and almost knocks me over with the strength of his embrace.

He repeats my name, but he doesn't sound happy—he sounds terrified.

That's when I see the other Imps. Standing in the shadows. Smiling and holding out their arms like they carry presents. But they don't carry presents. They carry firearms. And every flash of metal is aimed at my head.

A tower of a man steps from behind the rebels. Thorn. He wears his signature eye patch; perhaps because his remaining eye is so intense, so piercing, it appears to do the work of two. He smiles this perfect, grid-like smile, catching me off guard with his beauty. He's even more striking than the actor from the film, even more formidable. His skin the color of Demerara sugar; his hair so black it almost looks blue. And he wears different clothes—the leather trousers and trench coat have been replaced with a tattered gray blazer and black jeans, making him seem less pantomime.

Katie grips my hand. "That has to be Thorn."

I nod. He walks toward us, his step as lazy as his smile. "Well, well. What have we got here? Two more so-called spies. You have a lot of explaining to do."

He looks from me to Katie, and something crosses his face, something tender and vulnerable and fearful all at once. He lifts a hand, and for an awful moment, I think he's going to strike her. But instead he touches the backs of his fingers to her cheek. Katie pulls back, heaving in a mouthful of air like his skin's poker-hot.

Nate tugs at my sash and opens his mouth like he wants to speak, but the sound of Alice screaming silences him. An Imp forces her through the arched doorway.

Thorn reclaims his lazy smile. "And here she is. The Gem who thinks she's an Imp spy."

Alice tries to say something—my name, I think—but the Imps smother her words, teeming around her, wrenching her slender arms behind her back and forcing her to her knees.

"Alice." I try desperately to reach her, but the Imps shove me against the slabs.

"Stop it, stop it," Katie screams, pulling at their shirts, trying to heave them off me. But Thorn wraps his giant arms around her, and I'm left pressed into the stone, my eyes trained on Alice. I writhe and twist and scream like I'm possessed, but it's no use. And just before an Imp cracks me across the head and everything melts to black, I hear Saskia's voice.

"I told you they were worth waiting for."

CHAPTER 11

I WAKE IN A small ocher room. The floorboards feel hard and unyielding beneath my body, cords bind my wrists and ankles, and a rag that tastes of alcohol plugs my mouth. I manage to ease myself into a sitting position so I face the door—my back pressed into the peeling wall—and I feel a little less defenseless. There's a large window to my right, so caked in grime it may as well be bricked up, but the odd splinter of dying afternoon light pushes through, suggesting our prison is not underground. This makes me feel a little better.

Alice sits beside me, the imprint of her body warm against mine. Nate sits opposite; a gag contorts his mouth into an eerie, fixed grin, and he holds his body as though his left side aches. I look into his eyes—sore and inflamed—and we blink a slow, teary greeting. At least we're both alive. Next, my eyes find Katie—same gag, same eerie grin. She winks. But a tear rolls down her cheek, magnifying her freckles and soaking into her gag. I bet she's wishing she never moved to London, never laid eyes on me, never even heard of *The Gallows Dance*. I feel a pang of guilt and let my head fall back against the wall. A reassuring *thud*. I hear this constant drone like a swarm of bees, and a tar-like substance clogs my left eye—my own blood, I suspect.

I don't know how long we sit in that room. We stare at the walls, our feet, exchange the odd sympathetic glance. And of course I start to deliberate how we got into this mess. It started with the accident at Comic-Con. An earthquake? A bomb? An experiment gone wrong? I press my eyelids shut, my thoughts knotting together. I desperately want to be able to talk it through with the others, but I can't quite spit the rags out.

I turn my thoughts to the canon instead. Although we can change it, we still seem to keep crossing back into it. We're like two pieces of thread, running side by side, then twisting into each other only to separate again. So, at this point in canon, Rose had entered the church and was talking to Thorn about how she released the thistle-bomb at the Gallows Dance earlier in the day. I've watched the scene so many times; the main body of the church filled with night-lights as the sky darkened and the other rebels left. Thorn tried to work out whether she was the right Imp for the Harper mission, and he was much nicer to her than to me—he didn't crack her over the head and lock her in a room, for a start. "Spiky" was definitely an understatement.

Eventually, I fall asleep. I know this because I have a strange, muddled dream of the city—not *my* London, but future Imp London. Broken walls, crumbling buildings, a bleak sky imprinted with battered rooflines. I scream and waver on the edge of a barrel. The freckly controller stands beneath me, pointing, laughing, pulling back his boot. Ash cries out and wraps his arms around my thighs. He lays me on the ground like I might crack and leans over, I think to kiss my forehead. His eyes look the exact same color as the sky behind, giving the impression he has two holes in his head. And suddenly, it isn't Ash anymore, it's Nate. A dark chasm opens across his chest.

You did this to me, Violet, he says.

I push my palms into the black hole, but I can't stem the flow. Blood streams down my arms and spots my face. *I'm sorry.*

He rests his lips on my skin and whispers, his breath as cold as snow. *If only you'd looked after me better, none of this would have happened.* He sits back and his eyelids flicker.

Nate, stay with me, I say.

His body dissolves into a red mist, hovers for a moment—a piece of gossamer cut into the shape of a boy—and disperses into the atmosphere like ashes. Like thistledown. I reach out, pawing helplessly at the air. But I feel only a smattering of droplets and the ever-increasing spaces in between.

And that's when I hear a familiar voice, pushing through layers of time and love and warmth. Mum. *Violet, stay with me.* I can smell that clean, medicinal smell again, and the faint scent of her favorite perfume, star anise and jasmine. *Violet, stay with me.*

The creak of the door wakes me. Two dark shapes slip into the room, gaining detail only when they flick on the overhead light. My eyes quickly adjust. It's Thorn and another Imp, striding across the boards toward me.

Thorn pauses beside Katie for a moment, watching as a dream causes her lashes to tremble. He then kneels beside me and removes the cords from my ankles and wrists. "They tell me you look just like her."

I wait for the rush of blood to my feet and hands, but they feel completely dead, and when I try to pull the rags from my mouth, my fingers just bang awkwardly into my face.

"Here." He leans forward and pulls the gag free, his gloved fingers surprisingly tender.

"Who?" I manage to say. "Who do I look like?"

"Like Rose," he replies. "I never met her, but Saskia and Matthew swear you're her double."

Alice mumbles something through her gag. He turns to her. "It'll be your turn shortly, princess, don't you worry."

She falls silent. I briefly let my palm settle on her knee.

Thorn extends his hand toward me. I don't know what to do, so I take it. For a moment, I feel thankful he wears a glove, sure that his flesh would otherwise sear my own, like it seemed to Katie's. He pulls me into a standing position, and I force myself to look into that single eye. It holds me like a spotlight.

"I apologize for the rough treatment of you and your friends." Again, his gaze settles on a sleeping Katie. "I fear years of oppression have dulled our humanity somewhat. It's something we hope to reinstate. And the death of Rose, the failure of the thistle-bomb mission, have left the rebels rather shaken and confused. I'm hopeful you can answer some of our questions."

He looks at me again—he's terrifying. His size, his power. But I refuse to appear weak, so I just stare defiantly into that single, piercing spotlight.

He smiles. "Come, I'll show you around our humble abode."

I can't help wondering why he's singling me out. I guess it's because I look so like Rose, or perhaps it's the canon, dragging me along again. I follow him from the room, casting a quick glance over my shoulder to Nate, whose mouth remains fixed but whose eyes blink firmly, reassuring me, lending me strength.

Thorn leads me down a dark staircase. The Imp with a rifle follows me, so close I can hear the rattle of phlegm in his chest.

We step into the main body of the church. Just like I remembered, hundreds of night-lights bathe the stone in a warm glow—a glow that never reaches the ceiling, giving the appearance that the roof is missing and we stand beneath a dark, empty sky. Most of the rebels have returned to their nearby shelters to rest. I suddenly feel very small, except for my heart, which feels all swollen and ready to split my chest in two.

Thorn stares at a boarded-up window, and I imagine how it once looked, filled with stained glass, a kaleidoscope of color. But the Gem bombs put an end to that. A plaque rests beneath the window, roughly engraved with the words: *Apes became Imps, Imps became rebels—the pinnacle of human revolution*. I recall this from the book, a play on the old Gem motto: "Apes became Imps, Imps became Gems—the pinnacle of human evolution."

"You like our motto?" Thorn asks. He asked Rose this exact same question. The threads are twisting together again.

"It's very clever," I reply, just like Rose did. It makes me feel safer, knowing the lines.

"And what about our cause? Imp emancipation, equal rights," he says, again, straight from canon.

"Your cause is the same as mine." I know it's optimistic, but I can't help hoping that if I just keep saying what Rose said everything will be OK. He'll invite me to meet Baba, and I'll say yes—just like Rose—and then I can ask Baba how we get home.

Thorn continues to stare at the boarded-up window. Slowly, he pulls my smartphone from his blazer pocket. "What's this?"

Damn. Those threads have just diverged, big time.

"My phone," I answer numbly.

"Saskia thought it was Gem technology. But it isn't, is it?"

"No."

"It's old technology. Very old. And I'm guessing it's Imp."

I nod.

"Care to enlighten me how you and your little friends have ancient Imp technology in your possession?"

I swallow. "You wouldn't believe me if I told you."

"Try me."

"We're ancient Imps." It must sound so ridiculous, but I can't think of anything else to say.

He scowls and taps the phone against his chin. "A comedian, hey?" He slips it into his blazer pocket. "So why kill Rose?"

This sudden change in conversation throws me, and I have to replay the words in my head several times before I can extract their meaning. My hands start shaking, my nails bite against my palms. "We didn't kill Rose," I reply.

"Not directly, I agree. But your presence got her killed. Saskia told me. Your pretty red-haired friend alerted the guards."

"I know. I'm sorry . . . We never meant for it to happen."

"So what were you doing at the Coliseum?"

I stare, transfixed by that single eye. In canon it was gray, like a piece of broken slate, like the city itself festered inside him. But current-Thorn's eye is lavender blue . . . and full of hate.

"Well?" he asks.

I try to formulate some clever response, something that will keep us alive if not get him on our side. But it's like the rags sucked all the words from my mouth. "I don't know."

He moves toward me. A candelabrum sends an angular shadow scudding across his face, making him all the more terrifying. He holds my face with his gloved hands, the leather cool against my skin. "Saskia swears you could be Rose's sister. Are you?"

"No," I whisper.

His voice hardens. "Were you sent by the Gems to replace her and infiltrate the rebels?"

"God, no. I was at Comic-Con."

His hand drops from my face and it's like he's pulled the rags out all over again because the words start tumbling out of me. "I'm from the past, well, not the past, from a different reality, which is *your* past. That's how we've got the phones—the Imp technology. You see, in my world, Rose is a character from a book, which they made into a film. She's this really cool heroine—she's brave and strong and beautiful and everything I'm not. That's why I'm dressed like her, so I could pretend to be her, just for one day."

He chuckles. "You don't think you're beautiful?"

I shake my head, and my eyes drop to his boots.

My vulnerability must rile him—he grabs me by the shoulders and pulls me forward. The sudden movement extinguishes several night-lights; their thin lines of smoke escape toward the ceiling. I find myself envying that smoke.

"Stop playing games," he shouts. "Tell me the truth or I'll bring your little friends downstairs and slit their throats, one by one, as you watch."

"No!" I feel a stabbing pain in my head. A layer of sweat coats my skin and the rat meat churns in my stomach like it still has claws and teeth and attitude. I must look a little peaked because Thorn slips his hands beneath my elbows, taking my weight.

"Darren," he shouts over his shoulder. "Go and fetch the boy."

He sounds like he's far, far away, and I suddenly feel strangely detached, like I really am about to watch a scene from a film.

"No, not Nate," I manage to say.

But Thorn doesn't even look at me. "You heard me, Darren. Bring me the boy."

Darren darts back up the stairs. I watch him go and this shape-less, horrible emotion rises up my throat. "No, no please. I'll do anything."

Thorn clasps my hands to his chest as if forcing me to pray. "Tell me the truth."

The emotion takes form: fear. "I am telling you the truth, I swear it. I don't know what else to tell you. In my world, you're a character from a book set in the future, a dystopian one, you're this . . . this flawed hero."

He throws his head back and laughs, revealing the ridges of his palate. "A flawed hero?"

I know I'm babbling, but the adrenaline seems to have dulled my brain and roused my vocal cords. "Yes, a flawed hero. You're brave and strong, but you're also mean and blinded by revenge."

I hear Nate before I see him; a muffled cry followed by a series of thumps as Darren hauls him down the stairs. Nate looks so young, so helpless, his eyes revolving in their sockets like a hunted animal's. Darren shoves him to the ground. Nate trips on his own feet, and with his hands still bound behind his back he's unable to break his fall. I rush to catch him, but Darren pulls me back, dig-ging the nose of the rifle between my shoulder blades.

"It's OK, Nate, I can fix this, I promise." I feel my tears, cold against my skin.

Thorn moves behind Nate, swamping his torso with a heavily muscled forearm. With his spare hand, Thorn pulls a switchblade from his belt and presses it against the smooth stretch of Nate's throat.

"Please, don't!" A high-pitched wail I barely recognize as my own.

"The truth," Thorn says.

I can see the slight dent in Nate's neck where the knife pushes in, a peach about to be sliced, the skin only just protecting the soft tissue beneath. I think I may be sick. "Please don't hurt him, I'll tell you anything."

Nate keeps his eyes on me, and I get a strange wrench of sadness. *Thorn was your hero, and now you're going to die at his hand.* But Nate doesn't look sad, he looks determined, clear-headed, his light-brown eyes desperately trying to tell me something. *I need to think like Nate. I need to be smart.*

"What do you mean?" Thorn shouts. "Tell me or I'll slice him like a pig."

Something falls into place and I don't feel scared anymore. Because I am a diehard *Gallows Dance* fan, I don't just know things about Thorn, I know what makes him tick. If anyone can talk their way out of this, it's me. "Ruth . . . you want revenge because of what they did to Ruth. The Imp girl who you fell in love with when you were young. The Gems hanged her at the Gallows Dance because she had a relationship with a Gem—you." I watch Thorn's grip loosen a little, the blade easing against Nate's skin. But I don't stop. "You see, I know things I shouldn't, don't I? Because I've read them and I've watched them—you're a Gem. And underneath that eye patch is another working eye. You just wear the patch to break up the evenness of your features, because you're ashamed that you're one of *them*. And every time you punch a Gem, or scalp a Gem, or kill a Gem, you're actually trying to kill that part of yourself that you loathe—the Gem part. Because deep down you blame yourself for her death, because if you hadn't loved her, she would still be alive."

My words echo around the vast stone chamber, simply refusing to fade.

"Shit," Darren says, the pressure from his rifle easing against my back.

Thorn releases this guttural noise like I've punched him in the stomach. He stares at me, his face caught between disbelief and sorrow, tears spilling from his uncovered eye and seeping beneath his eye patch. He raises his hand, blade glinting in the candlelight. For a heart-stopping moment, I think he's going to stab Nate in the head.

But instead, he pulls the gag free.

"Baba!" Nate screams, like the word was corked up inside him. "We need to see Baba."

Thorn nods. "I think perhaps you do."

CHAPTER 12

I RECOGNIZE THE CORRIDOR from the film, stone and tight and sloping downward, taking us deep into the bowels of the church. Thorn leads the way, stooping slightly to avoid knocking his head on the domed ceiling. Rose walked this very corridor, but unlike me, she had no idea what waited for her behind that wooden door. A faceless precog. Sometimes, ignorance really is bliss.

"This is so cool." Nate pulses his hands in a quick rhythmic motion, his wrists still red and sore from the recently removed binds. "We're going to meet Baba."

I silence him with a glare. The way he's talking, all excited, anyone would think we're about to meet a celebrity. We follow Thorn into the chamber. It's just like the film set, but there's this sense of oppression, the air almost sticky with something sweet and fresh—lily pollen perhaps. And it strikes me as odd that I can smell flowers in a place so lacking in vegetation. I imagine I can see the ghost of Rose walking beside me, about to meet Baba for the first time. I suddenly feel this sense of loss. Rose is dead.

"Rose is dead?" a voice says, as though echoing my thoughts.

I know exactly where to find Baba, hunched in the corner like

a pile of rags. She lifts her head and I see her. The book described
her as having an extra piece of skin stretched across her face, seal-
ing in her eyes and nostrils, and a mouth that is no more than a
thin opening, as though long ago a surgeon's knife wished to hear
her words. In the film, she was even worse, like some kind of grue-
some, featureless monster. But the woman before me just looks
asleep, her heavy lids resting shut. She doesn't even look that old,
maybe the age of my grandma, and her skin looks soft and doughy,
like it would retain the indentation of a fingertip if touched. The
only real peculiarity is her lack of nostrils, but I only notice that
when she tilts her head back.

I hear Nate exhale slowly, clearly disappointed by her more
approachable appearance.

"Such a shame. I liked Rose," Baba says.

"You never met her," Thorn says.

She shrugs. "OK, well, I was going to like her."

Thorn plumps a cushion and slips it behind her back. "Would
you like me to see to the fire?" It's strange seeing Thorn so atten-
tive only minutes after he held Nate at knifepoint, and it's this
unpredictability that makes him so scary. He's all smiles and
cushion-plumpings one minute, only to swing into psycho mode the
next. He's the same in canon, only now of course the knife is real.

And I think Baba must feel the same; unable to trust his kindness. She waves him away. "No, thank you. I can manage myself."
She turns to me, as though she can somehow make out my shape
through her eyelids. Perhaps she can—they're so paper-thin. "Who
have you brought me instead, Thorn?"

"God knows," he replies.

She laughs and her eyeballs shift beneath their lids like baby
birds wriggling inside their eggs. She reaches a trembling hand

toward me, and without thought, I take it. I brace myself for the bolt of pain, the shot of fire transferring through her palm into mine . . . but it never comes.

She smiles, revealing a pair of toothless gums. "This flower is little, but she has other qualities. Her name is Violet. Always shrinking, am I right?"

"You're right." My exact thought as I stood at the front of the class.

Thorn steps forward, and for a moment, I think he may pull my hand from hers, but he settles for clenching his fists. "She knows things she couldn't possibly know. It's like she's in my head or something. Is she like you, Baba?"

"Do you have precognitive abilities? Can you mind blend?" she asks me.

I shake my head, then realize she can't see, so I say, "No," then realize she can probably read my thoughts, so I blush and feel a little silly.

"And what about you, Nate, any precog talents?" she asks.

He claps his hands together and uses this fast, excited voice, as though she just gave him a permission slip to speak. "Oh my God, you know my name, that's so cool. And you're nowhere near as scary as you are in the film, they really got you all wrong."

Thorn clips him round the back of the head. "That's what the girl kept saying, that she's from an alternate universe and that we're living in a book or a film or some crap."

Baba remains composed. "Well, that is quite simply preposterous, wouldn't you say?"

Nate snorts. "Says the five-hundred-year-old woman with no face."

Thorn raises his hand to deliver another blow, but Baba intervenes. "That's quite enough, Thorn. Show our guests a little respect. I like them."

"They're responsible for Rose's death." He continues to stare meaningfully at an invisible target on Nate's head.

"Yes," Baba says, like she's addressing a child, "and when one flower dies, another blooms in its place."

His hand flops to his side, dejected. "I don't know what you mean."

"That's the thing about the viola flower. It's little, but it's rather special. It contains a scent that turns off the receptors in the nose, making it undetectable for moments of time."

"Don't talk in riddles, old woman," Thorn says.

She laughs and dismisses him with a flick of her hand. "Leave me with them, and go and figure out this old woman's riddle."

He fidgets with his eye patch, not used to receiving orders. "And why would I do that?"

"Don't be difficult," she says. "You forget that I already know you're going to leave. It's one of the benefits of being a precog."

He turns on his heel and marches from the room, his features fighting to hide his annoyance. The door slams behind him and the rush of air stirs the flames—shadows dance across the granite. Baba yawns, her toothless mouth like a baby's mid-cry. "His bark's worse than his bite."

"You sure about that?" Nate says. "He nearly slit my throat."

"OK, they're both pretty bad. He's been through a lot, but I guess you already know that." She gestures around the room. "Take a seat, Nate. Make yourself comfy. I need some time with your sister."

He plunks himself down, missing the cushion but not seeming to care. "You're going to mind blend, aren't you? This is so cool—do me next."

She ignores him. "Come now, Violet, let me rest my hands on your brow."

I kneel before her, just like Rose should have done, and once again, I feel that sense of loss. But something more toxic runs beneath—guilt. It should be her, not me, resting her knees on these stone slabs, her dark hair falling forward as she offers her brow. I close my eyes to prevent a giant tear splashing on the ground.

Baba lays her palms on my head like she's checking an infant's fever. The anticipated bolt of pain shoots through me, swelling my tissue, cracking my bones. It's so much worse than the description in the book. I want to scream but it's like there's no air in my lungs. I see a knife slicing a peach, the palest blue eyes I've ever seen, a minidress torn by grabbing hands, Saskia's hair fanning around her face as Matthew weeps, a stage set hurtling toward me, a girl in a mirror dressed in a tunic.

The pain migrates toward my frontal lobes, intensifying to a single spot between my eyes.

I see Mum . . . Dad . . .

Home.

The pain grows and grows until I teeter on the edge of consciousness. And just when I think I will surely die, when I start to long for the peace of death, it begins to fade. The colors, the feelings, the pain, all leak from my temples, drawn through my skin into the warmth of her palms.

I open my eyes and see only white. I blink several times and realize I'm standing in a snowstorm. I'm about to shout for help, to reach blindly for Baba, suddenly united by our lack of sight, when

the snow thins. Only it isn't snow. It's thistledown. Swirling, dancing, spiraling through the air like a flock of tiny white birds. The
air continues to clear and I see Baba standing beside me. Same
doughy skin, same toothless smile, but her back is straight, her
legs strong, and her eyes finally open to reveal two apple-green
irises. She inhales deeply through her brand-new nostrils. "That's
better," she whispers to the air.

I slowly spin, taking in my surroundings. We stand in the
Coliseum. High stone walls dotted with gun towers. To the front, a
wooden stage displays nine hungry ropes. I know that on one side
rests London, broken and gray, and on the other stretches the
Pastures, fresh and green. Just like in canon. Just like earlier today.
Yet it seems so different—empty and still, like a playing field at
night. And I feel strangely calm. The sky looks clear and the air
tastes delicious, fresh—lemony perhaps.

I find myself inhaling, too. "How did we get here?"

"We're in your mind, dear. I thought it apt to visit the Coliseum,
the place where it all started." She laughs and catches a piece of
thistledown. "Bet you feel like Dorothy right now?"

I nod.

She releases the thistledown back into the air as though freeing
a dragonfly. "There's no place like home . . . There's no place like
home."

The word *home* brings tears to my eyes, hot and fast.

She cups my face and dries my cheeks with her thumbs. "But
the thing is, your arrival rather knocked our story off-track. Rose
wasn't meant to die, she was meant to infiltrate the manor and fall
in love with Willow. A love so strong and pure it transcended the
Imp-Gem divide, and eventually reunited mankind as one. But
you know this, don't you?"

I try to nod but she holds my face stationary.

"And some stories simply need to unfold," she says. "They need to reach their beautiful climax, existing almost like a life cycle, an entity in their own right."

"I—I don't understand."

"Don't you feel it, Violet? Our story—the canon, you call it—pulling you back in, dragging you along. It's almost impossible to resist, is it not?"

I think of the two pieces of thread, running in parallel, twisting together, and I nod.

She drops her hands to my shoulders and spins me so I face the stage. I see each noose, waiting for another neck to choke.

Her voice heats my ear. "You must save the Imps, Violet. Through self-sacrifice and love, *you* must complete the story. Only then will our world release you."

I laugh—a nervous trill—and my breath disrupts the path of a lazy seed. "How am I supposed to do that?"

"You take Rose's place. An insert. You put right what you made wrong. Then you can go home."

Nausea rises in my stomach.

I turn to face her, the green of her eyes knocking me off balance. "This isn't *Quantum Leap*!" My voice sounds a little petulant, completely out of place in the grandness of the Coliseum.

She closes her eyes for a moment. "*Quantum Leap* . . . the fictional man who jumps between realities . . . your dad's favorite show."

"Putting right what once went wrong—how do you do that? And come to think of it, how do you know about *The Wizard of Oz*?"

"It's in your head. If it's in your head, it's in my head." She smiles. "And did Sam Beckett squash a main character when he entered those realities?"

I see something in my peripheral vision, a streak of black falling from the top of the wall and thumping into the ground. My hand sails to my mouth as I whisper the word *no*. I manage to focus and see the ruby butterfly wings opening across the slabs. Rose. My head reels and I stumble forward.

Baba catches me. "Well, I'm afraid that you rather squashed our main character." She glances at the broken girl behind her. "And you didn't squash the Wicked Witch of the West, you squashed the plucky heroine, the one person our reality simply can't do without."

I shake my head, heavy with guilt and disbelief.

"I'm not plucky, and I'm not a heroine." My voice crumbles at the edges as though proving my point.

She shrugs. "Then you and your friends can stay in our reality forever."

My parents' faces appear in my mind's eye, the grief etched into their skin, still waiting for me and Nate to return from Comic-Con. My legs go weak and I find myself slowly crumpling to the ground, only yards from Rose's body. And the loss just keeps on growing, expanding in all directions until it loses all boundaries and edges and fills my whole brain: hot showers and TV shows and Instagram and Ben & Jerry's and makeup and comfy beds and Google and camping and Kindles and Nando's and parties and university entrance exams and then going to university and getting a job . . . raising my future children in a world that values them and treats them justly . . .

I shove my hands into my scalp and feel this scream building inside.

Baba kneels before me and gently teases my fingers from my hair. "This may only be a story, Violet. It may be generated by your world, from a book or a film." She points to the crest of the wall, and I see another figure. A female—Sally King. The late author of *The Gallows Dance*. I recognize her from the book cover; her long, mousy hair pulled taut from her face, the heavy frame of her glasses swamping her childlike face. And I remember the news reports when she died. *Up-and-coming author of bestselling dystopian novel throws herself from high-rise after long struggle with mental illness.* She looks straight at me, smiles, and then steps forward as though she's stepping onto an escalator. Her body twists through the air and lands next to Rose.

Baba strokes my hair. "Our reality may be generated by a single author's vision or an audience's collective conscious . . . Who knows? But it is *our* reality. It matters to us just as your reality—your home—matters to you." She uses a finger to raise my chin so my gaze meets hers, but her green eyes only heighten my loss, reminding me of forests and meadows and Christmas wreaths, all things I will never see if I remain in this God-awful city. She blinks like she knows I need some kind of respite. Her words, however, offer none. "A story is like a life cycle, Violet. You will be released only when the story concludes. Birth to death."

Birth to death. A burst of adrenaline travels through me. Birth to death.

Again, she turns me to face the stage, her fingers curling through my tunic like talons. "The place where it started, and the place where it must end."

I look at the nine loops of rope and gain a sudden clarity. I fill my lungs with the lemony air.

"I'm going to hang in Rose's place," I whisper.

"Yes."

"Next week, at the Gallows Dance?"

"Yes. For your friends, your family, and, above all else, love."

The justice is almost poetic—we killed Rose, after all. I laugh, but it quickly morphs into a sob. "Exactly one week from today, I will hang." And upon speaking these words, I finally pass out.

CHAPTER 13

EXACTLY ONE WEEK from today, I will hang.

I will hang for my friends, my family, and, above all else,
love. A thought that offers surprisingly little comfort when I
think about the noose closing around my neck, my feet searching
for solid ground, my legs flailing . . . dancing in midair.

This morning I was clueless. This morning I was at Comic-
Con, inhaling the scent of hot dogs and sweat and perfume, taking
in the brightly colored costumes, the flash of the cameras, the bass
drums and the violins. And yesterday I was in school, stressing over
some stupid English presentation and wishing I were in another
world.

Be careful what you wish for, because sometimes the reality
truly blows.

"Violet?" I hear Nate's voice. "Violet, are you OK?"

I wake somewhere warm and soft—on my sofa back home or
snuggled in bed. The fragrance of burning wood mingles with
pollen, and candlelight pools on the walls. I hear low, pulsing voices
and wonder if Mum and Dad are talking in the kitchen. But I
quickly realize the voices belong to Baba and Thorn.

Nate leans over me. For a fleeting second, I recall my dream, but I see no chasm opening across his chest.

"What happened?" I whisper. It feels like I've been screaming, the lining of my throat cracked.

"Baba did her weird thought-sucking thing and then you passed out. Are you OK?"

I shake my head. The vast, empty space of the Coliseum, Rose's body hitting the floor, the empty noose . . . Memories fill my mind until my skull feels like a sieve, incapable of containing them all.

"Violet? What is it?" Nate asks.

I open my mouth to explain, but Thorn raises his voice at that same moment.

"I refuse to believe it," he says.

Baba—once again bent in her chair, her apple-green irises sealed firmly behind her lids—clasps his hand. "She's the one, Thorn." The same words Baba spoke to Thorn in canon, right after her mind blend with Rose.

Nate turns to me, his face full of wonder. "They're talking about you," he mouths.

"She will save the Imps," Baba says. "Through self-sacrifice and love."

Nate's eyes widen, his face all apexes and points in the firelight. "You're going to take Rose's place?"

I nod.

The concentration nips at his face as he bites his bottom lip. "But if you take her place . . ." His features twist in alarm as he follows the concept to its natural end point. It amazes me how clever he is sometimes.

"It's OK." I try to smile, though it feels more like a grimace.

"Soon as I hang we'll all get transported home. All of us. I won't feel a thing."

"But . . ."

"Baba promised, I won't even know it's happening." I'm not sure for whose sake I'm lying—mine or his.

"But, Violet . . ."

"Let's not dwell on it, OK, bro. It is what it is."

And I bury those terrifying, bleak words in some distant part of my brain—*Exactly one week from today, I will hang.*

Thorn crosses the floor in three long strides and pulls me to my feet like I weigh no more than a doll. "Come then, Little Flower, I'll brief you on your assignment."

I follow him from the chamber, my arm linked through Nate's for stability. I forget to say bye to Baba, too focused on the ache in my head and the weakness in my limbs. Only when I hear her voice following us up the corridor do I remember her. "You don't need to brief her," she shouts. "She already knows what to do."

Nate and I wait on a pew near the front of the church. All the other pews have been removed to make room for desks and chairs, so this one stands alone, making it seem more like a random park bench. It's the exact same pew Rose and Thorn sat on after their meeting with Baba. But current-Thorn stands, statuesque, glowering once again at the plaque beneath the bombed-out window. He hasn't bothered to rebind our hands, and I find myself just staring at Nate's fingers as they spread over his thighs. They look so delicate, the skin unblemished by time.

A muffled shriek pulls our attention to the back of the church. Matthew half drags, half carries a gagged Alice toward Thorn. She arches her back and digs her heels into the ground, but Matthew easily overpowers her. Saskia follows with Katie, who also puts up a fight, but her petite frame makes little impact against Saskia's viselike grip.

"Sit them all together," Thorn says, not even bothering to turn.

Alice and Katie slide along the pew so they sit beside us. My thigh presses into Katie's—I can feel her shaking.

I try and still her knee with my hand. "It's going to be OK," I whisper, mistaking her tremors for fear, but when she replies, the gag absorbing her words, she sounds pissed off, not afraid. *Thank goodness she's gagged*, I think. Katie has no idea just how violent, how brutal, Thorn can be. She'd probably call him a toasted knob-cheese sandwich or something.

Saskia and Matthew stand behind us, their shadows fragmenting across our laps as a draft stirs the candle flames.

"God knows how you're still alive," Saskia whispers into my ear.

Thorn circles the desks and stops when he reaches the pulpit at the front of the church. He has this look of self-importance, like he's going to climb the wooden steps and start preaching, but he settles on clearing his throat. "Turns out we may have a use for our visitors."

"Firewood?" Saskia mutters. "Bet they'd spit and sizzle like pork chops."

Thorn pulls the gags from Katie's and Alice's mouths, taking more time over Katie's, letting his fingers brush up against her freckles. She turns her face away and he inhales sharply, as though her gesture wounds him. But whatever Katie stirs inside him leaves as quickly as it arrived—his face hardens and he wipes his hand against his blazer. He addresses Saskia and Matthew, speaking over our heads. "Violet has agreed to take Rose's place in the Harper mission."

Saskia and Matthew begin to laugh.

"I'm serious," Thorn says.

The laughter stops abruptly.

"But—but—she can't possibly take Rose's place." Saskia raps on the pew with her knuckles, as though trying to drum all the frustration out of her.

"What choice do we have?" Thorn says. "Rose is dead. And we still need a pretty young Imp to infiltrate the manor house and befriend Willow Harper. Little Flower here is the best hope we have."

I hate the way he calls me Little Flower; he never called Rose that.

Saskia's knocking increases in volume. "But we don't know anything about this girl. How do we know if we can even trust her? She and her idiot friends killed Rose, for Christ's sake."

Thorn looks a little unsettled, but he papers over it with a stern expression. "They didn't kill Rose, the Gems did. The day we start blaming one another for the sins of the Gems is the day we fall apart. But I share some of your concerns, Saskia, which is why you and Matthew won't let them out of your sight. You will make sure they're onside and on-task every second of every day."

Dammit, I think. Saskia and Matthew worked at the Harper manor for almost a year before they pulled Rose from that street fight—that's how they identified Willow as a target. They helped Rose blend in at the estate, told her about Willow's routine, and just generally supported her. But they're coming with us to criticize and kick us if we fall.

And it seems Saskia isn't too happy about it, either. Her knocking crescendos and then cuts out. "Who the hell are these weirdos?" She hurls the words like weapons. "At least tell us that. They turn up in the Coliseum claiming to be spies, dressed up as . . . God knows what."

Katie turns to me and whispers, "Was she this much of a spunk rocket in the book?"

I risk a little shake of the head, wishing I could replace that gag.

Thorn arranges his features into a controlled expression. "I don't have to explain myself, Saskia. I want them on that Imp-bus tomorrow night. Got it? They aren't from this city and they've never worked in the Pastures, so make sure they pass for slaves. OK? If they get shot for trying to cross the border illegally, I will hold you personally responsible."

Silence.

"All of them?" Matthew finally asks.

"No, only Little Flower and the boy."

"Don't send the lad," Matthew says. "It could be really danger-ous, and he's only young."

"I'm fourteen," Nate says.

Thorn smiles. "And Violet's obviously very protective of him. His presence will serve as a constant reminder of what's at stake if she fails in her mission."

I think about that knife pushed into Nate's throat, and the words I'm about to say fade to a whisper in my mouth. "What about Alice and Katie?"

Thorn studies Katie. "So, the one in black, Katie is it?"

"That's right," she replies.

He lets his gaze linger on her a little too long. "Well, Katie, you're my insurance, my leverage. If Violet is successful in her mis-sion, if she gets those secrets, then you will live. But if Violet does a runner, or betrays me, or simply fails in her mission, then I'll kill you myself."

Katie's tremble becomes more pronounced, sending rhythmic waves up my forearm. "You can't be serious?" She gives him *that* look, narrowing her eyes and pressing her lips together like she's back in class dealing with Ryan Bell.

"Katie, don't." I squeeze her thigh.

"No," she says, her voice rising with indignation. "If this dicksplat thinks he can intimidate us, then—" She never gets to finish. Saskia whacks her around the back of the head, pretty hard judging by the sound of it. Her red hair whirls forward and she nearly falls from the pew.

"Katie, don't," I say to her again.

She must see the panic in my eyes, because she falls silent.

Thorn kneels before her and leans in close. "I admire your spirit, Katie, but you must never insult me like that again. Do you understand?"

Say yes, say yes. The words repeat over and over in my head, but the pause keeps on stretching until it becomes a full-on tumble-weed moment, and Katie just stares back at him, tight-lipped and hard-eyed like a cowboy waiting to draw.

"Do you understand?" he repeats. He stands, looming over her, his single eye flitting up and down her form. He adjusts his eye patch and I'm reminded of the wolf in *Little Red Riding Hood*, hiding his fangs beneath a poor disguise.

"Katie, please," I whisper.

Very slowly, she nods her head.

He runs his tongue across his bottom lip, a flash of pink against the darkness of his skin. "Then we'll get along just fine, Katie."

"And what about this one?" Saskia says, jabbing a finger into Alice's back.

"Ah, the Gem look-alike?" Thorn shifts his gaze to Alice. "Gem on the outside, Imp on the inside. At least her blood is decent," he says.

"We could cut her open and see," Saskia says.

Thorn laughs. "Steady now, Saskia. I need to keep her Gem casing intact . . . at least for now. I've got a very special job for her."

"What do you mean?" Alice asks.

The shadow of something more youthful, mischievous, crosses his face. "And then you would know everything, and where would the fun be in that?"

CHAPTER 14

WE'RE BACK IN the ocher room again, the four of us curled into one another, our breath misting in the cold. I spend a few minutes telling Katie and Alice about the recent encounter with Baba. They listen intently; the red marks left by the gags reach toward their ears like some bizarre tribal makeup. Matthew pulled the cords from their wrists when Saskia wasn't looking. He also smuggled in some bread, which we devoured in seconds.

"So *our* universe created *this* universe?" Nate asks.

I nod. "That's what Baba said: that this universe, the *Gallows Dance* universe, was created by Sally King . . . or the readers. She was kind of vague."

Alice laughs. "Kind of vague. Whopping understatement."

We pause, torn between denial, confusion, and shock.

Finally, Katie speaks. "Since when was Thorn such a sleaze-bag?" She rubs each finger in turn, stimulating the blood flow.

"He's like a super-mean version of himself," I say. "Saskia, too. I suppose we did screw up the thistle-bomb mission."

"And as a result, the Harper mission," Nate adds.

Katie looks a little awkward. "Has anyone else noticed the way he looks at me?" The paleness of her skin fails to hide her blush.

Alice nods. "Yep. He clearly fancies you."

"Gross," Katie says, but a shy smile reshapes her mouth—like me, she's unused to male attention, having lived in Alice's stream-lined shadow for the past year or so.

Alice makes a noise that sounds a bit like *humph*. "He only fancies you 'cause you're so clearly an Imp."

Katie does her eye-narrowing trick, her pink lips whitening as she pinches them together. For a split second, I fear a full-on cat-fight will break out, but Nate speaks before the fur starts to fly.

"It's because you remind him of Ruth," he says simply.

We look at him. He shrugs like it's completely normal for one fourteen-year-old boy to have more romantic awareness than three seventeen-year-old girls. "It's a no-brainer," he says. "Remember? Thorn's flashback in the film? Ruth had red hair and green eyes."

I laugh, amazed I hadn't thought of this before. "He's right."

"Great," Katie says, examining a lock of her copycat hair. "The most gorgeous man ever to fancy me is a raving psycho who'll probably murder me on our first date."

"In a nutshell," Nate says.

"It could work to your advantage, Ringo," Alice says. "There's no harm in flirting a little."

Katie raises an eyebrow. "Surely, that's your domain." She hates it when Alice calls her Ringo. It's normally followed by a cry of, "I play the cello, not the drums"—I never know if Katie's missed the Beatles/Liverpool connection, or if she's just acting dumb.

"For real," Alice says. "It could keep you alive. He's a scary man, and it would really help if you could keep him on your side."

Katie pulls her hair from her face like she can somehow become less Ruth-like. "There's no way I'll ever flirt with that spermpiper. He's evil personified."

"You felt sorry for him when we told you about Ruth," Alice says.

"Yeah, well, that was before he bashed Vi over the head and treated us like cockroaches and threatened to kill me and locked us in a cell." She stares at the floorboards, tears darkening her eyelashes as though she suddenly appreciates the reality of the situation.

I touch her hand. "Are you OK?"

She looks up and squeezes out a smile. "Yeah, 'course. So, what happens when you reach the Harper estate?" Her voice clicks into a more practical gear, like she's trying to deny the tears moistening her eyes.

Alice stretches out her long body, her feet poking out from the bottom of a threadbare blanket. She still has this air of serenity, like she's lounging on a beach somewhere. "So Violet gets to the Harper estate, she meets Willow, acts all mysterious and sexy, and ta-da . . . he's got a raging Gem horn."

"Alice," I hiss, "Nate's here."

But Nate just grins. "Should be easy enough, Violet, you look a bit like Rose and you know all the right things to say."

"No pressure, then," I grumble.

Alice continues. "Then Willow declares his undying love to Violet, but Violet has a major attack of conscience and realizes she can't betray the man she loves. So she purposefully botches up the Harper mission by telling Willow that she loves him, but she belongs in the city. It's a mercy dump."

"Is that even a thing?" Nate asks.

"It is now," Alice says.

Nate grins. "Sounds like she ate a curry and took too many laxatives. Get it? A mercy dump."

"That's not what I meant and you know it," she says.

"Can you tell the story with Rose in it, not me?" I ask, fidgeting with my hands. "I just don't think I'm quite ready to, you know, think of myself as *her*."

"Well, you're going to have to be ready pretty soon," Alice says.

Katie smiles at me. "That's fine, Vi. Isn't it, Alice?"

Alice nods, determined not to let Katie be the better friend. "Yeah, 'course. Anyway, where was I? Oh yeah, the mercy dump. It was tragic. Heartbreaking. *Rose* crossed the border that night and returned to Rebel Headquarters to tell Thorn that she'd failed in her mission, that Willow didn't fancy her. She did it so the rebels would leave him alone forever."

"That's the turning point in the plot," I say. "The midway twist Miss Thompson was talking about."

"It was kind of noble of her," Katie says.

"Rose is—sorry, *was*—noble," I reply sadly.

Alice ignores me. "But Willow didn't give up. He dressed as an Imp and followed Rose across the border, into the city, all the way to Rebel Headquarters. It was so brave and heroic. But the rebels caught him peering through the keyhole of the church."

Katie scoffs. "He sounds more stupid than brave."

"You leave him alone," Alice says.

Nate looks thoughtful for a moment. "We can influence stuff directly, I get that, but how do we get other people to do what we want? I mean, how do we make sure the rebels still catch Willow?"

After a long pause, I say, "Baba told me that the story wants to unfold, that the canon will drag us along or something."

Katie frowns. "Yeah, and you've talked about the canon haunting us before. But it makes no sense. The four of us should be some kind of massive butterfly. Flapping our wings and cocking everything up."

"What are you talking about?" Alice snaps.

"Jesus, Alice, the butterfly effect," Nate says. "You know, a butterfly flaps its wings and causes a hurricane halfway around the world."

Alice looks a little confused. "It's a film, yeah? My mum likes it. It's got Ashton Kutcher in it."

I nod and smile so as to offer encouragement. It's hard when a fourteen-year-old knows more than you.

"Well, we're the butterfly," Nate says. "Flapping our wings, changing everything just by breathing."

"Only we're not," I say. "That's what I'm trying to tell you. The canon keeps dragging us back. It *wants* the story to be completed as it should."

"All the same," Nate says, "we should stick to canon as much as we can. Avoid taking any risks."

Nate and I nod. Even Alice nods.

But Katie looks unconvinced. "I don't know, guys. Do you really think it will be that easy? You stick to the script and everything will just fall into place?"

"Yes," Alice and Nate say in unison.

"What other choice do we have?" Nate says.

Stick to the script. This comes as a huge relief—I like plans, I like schedules, I like predictability. And in this crazy, dirty, mental universe, having a script in my head, a perfect plot structure, makes me feel safe again.

"So remind me again what it is we're sticking to . . ." Katie says.

Nate slaps his hands to his head. "Jesus, Katie, you really need to watch the film."

"Well, I don't see a freaking DVD player anywhere, do you?" she replies.

I pick up the story where Alice left off. It's the only thing keeping me sane right now. "So after Willow was captured by the rebels, the rebels raided an Imp brothel—"

"A brothel?" Katie wails. "I thought this was a kids' book."

"Young Adult, actually," Alice says.

"The rebels raided an Imp brothel," I say, "and the lovebirds used this as a distraction so they could escape."

"So Willow just forgave Rose for not telling him about the whole being-a-rebel thing?" Katie asks.

I nod. "Yeah, because he knew she'd tried to protect him in the end."

"So, then what happened?" Katie says, leaning forward, unable to hide her interest, and for a lovely second, it feels like I'm back in Miss Thompson's class doing that presentation again. Life as normal. Home.

I smile. "Rose and Willow dropped into the disused sewers, got kind of lost, but eventually emerged to find an old Humvee. They drove to the river and tried to cross to No-man's-land in a boat."

"No-man's-land?" Katie says.

"Yeah, these abandoned stretches of city and countryside where there aren't any Imps or Gems. But they never made it. The Gem authorities tracked them down and lifted them from their little boat."

"You see," Katie says, "it's like I said at Comic-Con. The government's always the baddie in dystopian fiction. It's so predictable."

"Katie, focus," Nate says.

I rush to the end, avoiding the dreaded hanging word. "Then Willow declares his love for Rose at the Gallows Dance. The crowd turns, they pull down the gallows, a revolution is sparked."

"How long until the next Gallows Dance?" Katie asks.

"One week from now," Nate answers.

"One week?" Katie says incredulously. "This all happens in one week?"

We nod. Katie's got a point. It sounds so ridiculous, and I suddenly feel completely inadequate. How can I possibly make all this happen? How can I possibly be like Rose?

Katie shakes her head in disbelief. "People fall in love quickly in dystopian chick lit."

"It's a dystopian *love story*," Alice says.

Nate nods vigorously in agreement.

Alice sighs. "It's so romantic. Like when Rose leaves an actual rose on Willow's windowsill instead of telling him her name."

"And when she waitresses at his coming-of-age ball," Nate says. "And they wait till all the guests have gone and they . . ."

"Dance to no music," they chorus together.

"For God's sake," I say. "You're both still acting like it's just a book or a film. But it's not anymore. This shit just got real."

We fall silent, my words seeming to echo around the ocher room.

"So after all this, can we go home?" Katie finally asks, her voice filled with a yearning quality that breaks my heart.

I nod. "So long as I complete the story, just like King wrote it, so the gallows get ripped to the ground and a revolution is sparked."

Nate scrunches up his face. "And you're sure the universe will release us when you hang? Otherwise, you're just going to hang, you know that?"

"Will everyone please stop using the word *hang*?" I realize I've started gripping my neck. "From now on it's banned. Got it?"

They nod in turn.

"So, you fix the canon," Alice says. "You always did want to be Rose." She chews on her bottom lip, which, totally devoid of lip gloss, looks thinner than normal.

"I can't be Rose," I whisper. "She's so . . . awesome."

Katie rests a hand on my knee. "What's in a name?"

"Eh?" Alice says.

Katie blinks in disbelief. "A *Rose* by any other name . . ."

"You're seriously quoting Shakespeare at a time like this?" Alice says.

"Sorry, One Direction just didn't cut it. Maybe I should quote some Bieber, instead."

"Both of you—stop," I say.

Alice rubs my arm. "Sorry, Vi. Come on, think positively. You get to be Rose . . . You get to . . ." She wiggles her eyebrows.

My muscles tense. "I thought I said not to mention the *h*-word."

She just laughs. "No, you miserable cow, you get to kiss Willow."

I exhale suddenly and get a slightly giddy feeling, like the first time I rode the carousel—wind on my face, hair streaming, knuckles white as they gripped the metal pole. I remember begging Mum to make it stop but, in the same breath, wishing the wooden horse would go faster and faster. That's how I feel now, terrified and yet exhilarated—I can't stop this massive grin spreading across my face. I'd been so focused on the dying part, I'd completely forgotten the kissing part.

Alice smiles. "And think how much fitter Ash is in this universe. Just imagine how hot Willow is going to be—he's going to burn out your eyes. I kind of hate you right now." She laughs, but I can't work out if it's the bare walls or a lack of humor that makes it sound so hollow.

The next morning, Matthew leads Nate and me into a small vestry house. The air inside smells stale and damp, like it hasn't been disturbed in a long time. I know what's about to happen—we're going to get slave tattoos, just like Rose did. Our story threads are twisting together again, becoming one, which can only be a good thing—the more this happens, the more likely we are to go home.

Saskia perches on a tattered chaise longue, needle in one hand, pot of ink in the other. "I need to get to your neck." She doesn't even raise her eyes, as though we're not worth looking at. *Spunk rocket*, I think to myself, and smile.

I yank my tunic over my head, determined to appear brave. I stand in my leggings and vest top, the damp air chilling my arms, just waiting for the needle to pierce my skin. It looked pretty unhygienic and painful in the film, but I'm surprisingly calm about it all; it kind of pales in comparison to the whole noose thing.

Saskia cackles. "So, which design would Madam like? The dragon or the flaming eagle?" She dips the needle into the ink.

Matthew gently pulls my hair over my shoulder. "Now keep still. If it looks fake, the guards'll shoot you."

Saskia repeatedly pricks the skin on the back of my neck, returning to dip the needle in the ink every so often. My eyes water and I can't help but whimper as the needle passes over a nodule in my spine.

"Dammit, Violet," she spits. "You're making the five wobbly."

She finishes and lays a damp piece of gauze over the wound. "This stops infection and speeds up healing. We swiped 'em from the Pastures."

It also numbs the pain, for which I feel hugely grateful.

Nate is next. He remains completely still; only his fingers betray him as they dig into his thighs.

Saskia admires her handiwork. "You *should* fool the guards."

I glance at Nate as a knot forms in my stomach. "*Should* fool the guards?"

She shrugs and gathers up her kit. Rose crossed the border with only a minor run-in with a guard. But she was lucky, and she didn't have a wonky five. I try not to think about it, focusing on the Pastures . . . on Willow.

We pull on some regulation overalls. The material itches and rubs whenever I move, as if it's objecting to the fact it covers me and not Rose. I watch Nate scratching his arms through his sleeves, and I feel enormous responsibility pressing into my windpipe. But I also feel like I'm back on that carousel, the wind on my face and the rattle of a metal pole beneath my hands. I'm going to meet Willow. Not Russell Jones, but *the* Willow.

We leave headquarters with no ceremony. They don't even let us say good-bye to Alice and Katie, which may be a good thing, because I'd probably cry. If I get this wrong, if I fail, Katie dies. And then there's Alice, my best friend. I turn Thorn's words over and over in my head—*I've got a very special job for her*—but I'm just left feeling frustrated and none the wiser.

The journey through the city takes most of the day. We take the longer, more meandering route to avoid the controllers who tried to lynch me yesterday. Alley after alley, wall after wall, till it feels like we're lost in a gray, stinking maze. My feet smart, my stomach growls, and my skull continues to ache from the mounting head blows, but still, I feel a sense of loss for the London I know and love. Sunken buildings, faded street signs. I say each street name in my head again and again, thinking of how the sounds have slept for centuries, the city filled with illiterate Imps.

We continue to walk until the city wall looms ahead, snaking into the distance and merging into the gray sky so that it seems endless. A large, windowless building sits to the right of the gates; a cube with metal doors. The city wall appears to cut straight through it like a train through a tunnel. I recall this building from canon. The decontamination block, where the Imps are sprayed with a cocktail of chemicals and their tattoos are checked for fakes before entering the Pastures. It looks even more soulless than on the silver screen. Even more soulless than I'd imagined after reading the book, and that's saying something.

I remember Rose feeling anxious at this point in the story, sneaking across the border, her counterfeit tattoo fresh and stinging just like ours. But words on a page, a scene in a film, can't do this awful feeling justice. It's like my body has solidified, but my thoughts have turned to popping corn, firing again and again inside my skull. *What if we get caught? Will they kill us? Can we really die in a story? Is it just a story? It seems so real.* Like my brain is this screaming, writhing, red-hot mess, and yet my body is heavy with fear and powerless to act.

I glance at Nate and notice the tendons on his neck standing proud.

"You remember what happened to Rose in the decontamination block?" I whisper to him.

He nods. "Yeah, 'course. The guard with eyes the color of cornflowers."

"The unicorn," I reply, hoping to lend him some strength.

He nods, but his neck remains stiff. Saskia demands my silence with a firm glare.

I want to remind him that not all Gems are bad. Within the block exists at least one Symp—a Gem who's secretly an Imp sympathizer. A guard with the most amazing, bright-blue eyes searched Rose and noticed her tattoo looked fresh, but instead of arresting her for trying to enter the Pastures illegally, he simply warned her to avoid the guard with the mustache and the steel-gray eyes. Rose thanked him, and told him that she always thought Symps were a thing of magic and myth—like unicorns.

It's always been one of my favorite lines, and I'm secretly hoping I may get to say it.

I watch the Imps traipse toward the building like they're part of a funeral procession. There's just so many of them. I remember this from canon. Imps carry out most of their manual labor under the cover of darkness so as not to offend the Gems with their normal, imperfect, human bodies. This means there exist far more Night-Imps than Day-Imps. And even though the Night-Imps miss the warmth and the colors of the day, they enjoy more freedom, able to roam the Pastures in peace. And I'm starting to understand that freedom is its own form of sunshine.

We join the back of the line. I practice slouching and lowering my head, trying desperately to blend in, but my tattoo burns, a constant reminder of the wet ink and that wobbly five. We approach the iron doors and I focus on the dirt underfoot, avoiding the glint of the guards' pistols. Finally, we enter the block, plunging into the dense, congealed air, stiff with the odor of bleach.

We shuffle in a line down a windowless corridor, strip lights flickering overhead, throwing into relief the stippled gray of the cinder-block walls. I watch the nape of Nate's neck oscillate between white and black, his tattoo just hidden by the collar of his overalls. I feel this crushing pain in my chest, this feeling of helplessness.

A whirring noise builds and builds, and soon I can just make out a cloud of steam swelling, then diffusing, every thirty seconds or so. As we shuffle nearer, I begin to pick out a contraption—it looks like a car wash, only smaller, Imp-sized. I remember it from the film, only now it looks dangerous—hungry. As the line passes through, a burst of steam engulfs each Imp before they move on, sterile and Pasture-ready. Nate glances nervously over his shoulder, and I wish I could go first, but swapping places now would only draw attention from the guards. The steam engulfs Matthew, then Saskia. Next, it's Nate.

He steps into the contraption and I watch him vanish in the haze. Up close, it looks slightly green and stinks of bleach and something acrid I can't quite place. I hear a strangled cough and my heart leaps in my chest, but I don't dare move, a guard's pistol gleaming in my peripheral vision. The fog thins and Nate's silhouette reappears. He steps away, grinning over his shoulder like he's enjoying himself.

I take a deep breath and follow suit. Inside the metal cylinder there are nozzles and pipes and other strange mechanical equipment. I hear the steady fizz as the green gas squirts around me, and I get an overwhelming urge to flee. The gas assaults my nostrils and seeps beneath my overalls, stinging my skin and igniting my tattoo so I feel like I've been branded. I try desperately not to gasp or gag or both. The fizzing stops, the air clears, and I walk forward, trying to swallow down the sourness.

We pick up the pace and march down a long corridor. A large sterile room awaits, with thirty or so Imps lined up inside. We join the end of the row and the door slams shut. I lower my head, linking my hands together, afraid their shaking may betray me.

Several guards begin running their hands up and down the Imps, feeling for lumps that don't belong, any weapons that may be smuggled into the Pastures. They move farther down the line toward me and Nate—every inch of my body freezes as though blinking or breathing might somehow attract attention. I stare at my boots until my eyes itch, listening as the steady *clunk* of their step intensifies.

The footsteps pause.

"You," a guard says. "Come with me."

I lift my head and see his finger pointing straight at me. He has steel-gray eyes and a mustache.

CHAPTER 15

EVERYTHING GOES MUFFLED and my tongue sticks to the roof of my mouth. The guard from canon stands before me, the one the Symp warned Rose about. He leads me to a separate chamber—an inspection booth with unpainted walls and an acrylic screen—and pushes me forward so my palms push into the plaster. Then, he grasps my ankles from behind and winds his hands quickly up my calves. I fight the instinct to kick out and run. His hands move to my front and he pushes his palms over my thighs, around the back and up the insides. I've never been touched so intimately by a man. And it doesn't feel loving or tender. It feels brutal and quick. I think I might cry, so I bite down on my lip, so hard I can taste blood beneath the caustic tang of the chemical spray. Briskly, he stands and slips his hands up the sides of my chest and over my breasts. A scream catches in my throat.

"Arms up," he says.

I raise my arms and begin to shake. At any moment he could notice my tattoo, still raw and fresh and irritated by the spray. But he spins me around so I face him, snaking his palms across my back.

Only now do I meet his eyes. The hatred there makes me gasp.

He grips my shoulders and pins me against the wall. "We've got ten minutes." His breath tastes of stale coffee.

I feel like a moth in a display case, pinned beneath a sheet of glass, totally exposed and unable to move. "I—I don't know what you mean."

"Don't act all innocent, Imp." He pushes my hair from my face. "There's some Gem coin in it for you. Extra if you smile."

Every one of his muscles pushes against me. I feel sick.

"Come on, this can't be the first time, a pretty Imp like you. Now step out of the overalls."

"But—but, you've already searched me." Tears well in my eyes.

In one sudden movement, he throws me into the acrylic panel—the breath rushing from my lungs. Beyond my ghostly reflection lies a vast dimness strewn with movement, shapeless figures forming a line. I squint into the gloom and realize the shapes are people, a line of naked bodies, clutching at each other's hands so they look like one of those paper doll chains we used to make when we were kids.

"Do as I say or I'll put you in there," he whispers in my ear. "With the rebels and the wannabe slaves with fake tattoos."

I hear the disjointed beat of gunfire, the sound of muffled groans. The chain crumples and bodies slump to the ground. I think I say *Oh God*, my breath clouding the pane.

"OK," I whisper—the word stings my lips.

I begin to unzip my overalls with numb, trembling fingers. It feels like I'm removing my skin.

The door opens and a foot soldier with eyes the color of cornflowers appears. The Symp. I could cry with joy.

He examines me for a moment and scowls. "We're about to load them onto the bus."

Coffee-breath freezes. "Go ahead."

"We need *all* the Imps."

They glare at each other for a moment.

"Now," the Symp says.

Coffee-breath responds by taking a step back and lowering his head.

I follow the Symp down the corridor, my fingers scrabbling with my zip, tears leaking down my face.

"Are you OK?" he asks, his voice quiet and soft.

"Yeah," I manage to say. I want to tell him he's magical and mythical and brave and wonderful. I want to throw my arms around his neck and tell him thank you over and over. But all I manage is a weedy, "Thanks."

By the time I reenter the waiting room, I'm all zipped up and I've wiped my cheeks dry. Nate risks glancing at me, a terrified look hanging on his face. I offer a little nod—*I'm OK*, it says.

The guards march us outside onto an expanse of concrete, segmented by yellow markings and encircled with stone barricades crowned with loops of barbed wire. The sky may look drab, but it's vast and limitless and the same as back home. The fresh air of the Pastures fills my lungs, carrying scents of roses and bark and pulling me back to vacations in the Lake District. I suddenly feel this huge sense of relief.

A line of parked Imp-buses vanishes into the distance, their uneven windows shimmering in the ever-decreasing sunlight. We follow Saskia to a bay marked 753 and approach a rusting bus. The scent of bleach sends my heart into overdrive.

"This bus will take us straight to the manor," she whispers as we climb the steps.

The driver is clearly an Imp, but two Gem guards sit on the

front seat, pistols docked in their holsters. Panic takes hold again; each of my muscles tightly coils like a snake before it strikes. But the guards simply ignore me. I move down the bus and slump into an empty seat next to Nate. The seat feels hard and the stink brings tears to my eyes, but just knowing we're about to leave the decontamination block and the guard with the steel-gray eyes makes my bottom lip quiver like a toddler's.

Nate examines my face. "Jesus, sis. What did they do to you?"

"Nothing," I reply, my breath tart in my mouth. "That guard, you know, the one with cornflower eyes, he kind of saved me."

Nate gasps. "It's like Baba said—the story's dragging us along."

"It's so much more than just a story now, though, isn't it?" I whisper. "The poor Imps, I know we've read about it, watched it on the telly, but now that it's real"—I get this mass in my throat that makes talking hurt—"I think it may be worse."

We wait for about half an hour until the bus is full with Imps. The engine starts and we roll through huge metal gates into the Pastures. The world of the Gems.

It's like entering Disneyland—that sudden injection of color. I swear the sun shines brighter and the birds sing louder on the Gem side of the wall. The green stretches around us in all directions—trees, grass, hedgerows dotted with yarrow and clover and the deep purple of brambles. I was raised in the suburbs and I'm used to green—I've missed it, even after two days.

The Imp-bus trundles along the roads, far noisier than any vehicle I've ever traveled in. The Imps nap, including Nate, his head resting on my shoulder. I study his face. Normally, he looks like Dad, so animated and full of life, his face all pointed and excited, his sandy hair sticking up like he's stuffed his finger in a power socket. But now he's completely relaxed, he looks more like

Mum—the same softness around his mouth. My stomach twists and that mass in my throat grows. I miss my parents, really miss them. The safety, the belonging, the way they always make everything OK.

The rhythm of the bus and the warmth of the sleeping bodies lull me into sleep. I know this because I dream—the seat has been replaced by something soft, a mattress perhaps, and my eyelids flicker, the walls of a darkened room throbbing in and out of focus. I see the outline of a man, feel the warmth of a hand wrap around mine. I smell this tinny hospital smell that reminds me of the dentist and, weaving beneath, coffee and stale tobacco—the smell Dad gets when he's stressed. He squeezes my hand. *Wake up, Violet. Please, darling. Just open your eyes and wake up.* But the silhouette loses form, blurring around the edges and growing dimmer by the second.

And suddenly, I see Rose, standing on the wooden stage, rope around her neck. A voice soars above the crowd. *I love you.* Her hair falls from her face, and I see that it isn't Rose anymore. It's me. The hangman pulls the lever and I hear the crack of the trapdoor flying open, see the sudden jerk of my body as it pulls against the rope, watch my feet pirouette as they frantically search for solid ground. I hear Baba's voice: *A story is like a life cycle, Violet. You will be released only when the story concludes. Birth to death.*

But it doesn't release me. I feel the air choking from my lungs, the lines of the Coliseum dissolving, the sounds of the crowd fading. And yet still, it doesn't release me.

"Violet! Wake up," Nate says.

I wake gasping for air, like someone is squatting on my chest, crushing my lungs to the size of pockets. My skin feels raw—so raw I can't place the sensation. I could be on fire, or trapped beneath a frozen lake, or covered in hundreds of tiny contusions. I know that I'm crying because I can hear my sobs, feel the tears dampening my cheeks.

"It's OK," Nate says. "Look, we've reached the Harper estate."

"What's going on back there?" a guard shouts.

I fall silent, biting my tongue with the effort of keeping quiet.

We enter the Harper estate the back way. We see no sweeping vistas of the manor, proud and watchful, nestled in acres of meadows. There's just a load of privet hedges and the outline of an orchard against the evening sky. I can't help feeling a little disappointed. The bus pulls to a halt and we file off.

Saskia leads us down a path. "We're heading to the Imp-hut."

Nate's whisper is barely audible over the crunch of gravel. "Don't worry, we're only here for a few days."

"That's what I'm worried about."

"What? Returning to the city?"

I sigh, insecurities eating away at my insides. "No—getting Willow to fall for me in a few days."

"Rose managed."

"Katie's right, nobody falls in love that fast."

Nate stops in his tracks. My gaze follows his and we stare at the Imp-hut.

"Grim," he whispers.

I remember it so fondly from canon. A haven where Rose, Saskia, and Matthew sat in their bunks, playing cards and plotting. It looked a little like a gingerbread house, nestled in greenery and sheltered by oaks. But the reality is a wonky shack, built from corrugated iron and rotting beams. And things only deteriorate inside. It smells of wet dog and human excrement, and the fine layer of hay dusting the floor barely hides the mud beneath. The quirky furniture and bohemian curtains from the film have been replaced by a few upturned crates and a rotting pine table.

"Where's the bathroom?" I ask in a small voice.

Saskia laughs. "There's a couple of lean-tos out back with toilets and a communal shower."

"The shower's bloody freezing," Matthew says. "It's better just to smell."

"Grab a bunk," Saskia says.

The bunks look more like shelves covered in straw. They line the back of the hut, divided by plain, threadbare sheets hung like curtains, offering little in the way of privacy. I take Nate's hand and we wander toward the bunks, slightly shell-shocked.

The other slaves mill around us, making cups of tea, gathering up tools, and heading out into the evening. They seem to take it in turns to scowl at us, and I figure there'll be no card games. I find myself searching for Ash, for the palest blue eyes in existence. But he's nowhere to be seen. He must be arriving on the next bus. I can't help but feel a little disappointed.

Saskia plunks herself on one of the shelf-bunks. "We'll sleep here instead of returning to the city in the day. It's safer to stay put for a while, avoid the searches at the border."

Nate yawns. "I'm so ready for a sleep."

"You'll be lucky," Saskia says. "You're Night-Imps now. You don't get to sleep until morning." She turns to me, a malicious smile crossing her face. "And you'll be taking that freezing-cold shower tonight, girlie—I don't want you stinking of the decontamination block."

"Why not?" I ask, my brain still numb from it all.

She gawks at me like I'm an idiot. "Because when that sun sets, you'll be meeting Willow Harper for the first time."

CHAPTER 16

THE SHOWER IS beyond cold. I feel it in my bones, the skin on my chest mottled and blue. But at least it momentarily distracts me from my nerves. I'm about to meet Willow for the first time. I wait for that lovely feeling of anticipation, but instead I just feel like I'm competing with Rose's ghost—and coming up short.

Rose and Willow. An epic love story. Their first meeting was just fizzing with electricity. They had this instant attraction, a connection. She waited for him in the orchard beneath a plum tree, knowing he would take this path on his midnight walk. She then attracted his attention by cutting her own hand and yelping—and I don't mean high-pitched dog yelp, I mean stunning-damsel-in-distress yelp. Willow ran to see what was wrong, took one look into those big, brown eyes, and everything he knew about the world began to unravel. He had fallen for an Imp.

He'll take one look at me and run screaming in the opposite direction.

Saskia teases my hair into curls and pinches my cheeks, murmuring something about Rose having more of a natural glow. I couldn't feel more deficient if I tried. Once she's finished prodding my face and my ego, she leads Nate and me toward the orchard, navigating the estate in the dark like a bat.

The Harper estate is large, even by Gem standards. Hundreds of acres of woodland and meadows and landscaped gardens. I imagine I could easily get lost, so I stay close to Saskia, even though her constant frown unsettles me.

We cross a paddock, climb over a fence, skirt around the edge of a lake—this route actually seems familiar, echoing the set of the movie, but I feel so far from being a film star. With every step, my nerves seem to build, and now they fill my entire body, making even my fingers tremble. I begin to long for that beyond-cold shower again.

You see, I've always been terrible with the opposite sex. I've been on one date, which ended with me choking on an olive, and I've only been kissed twice. Once I was so drunk I barely remember it, the other time it was like having a wet gherkin shoved into my mouth. It's hard scoring boys when you're constantly overshadowed by Alice, the human mannequin.

Violet the Virgin. Ryan Bell called me that for a whole semester, until Katie kneed him in the balls and called him a scumbag.

Just thinking about Katie and Alice makes my heart feel like it's going to explode. I *have* to get Willow to fall for me or we're all stuck here. The image of my feet pirouetting through the air bursts into my consciousness—*in six days, I will hang*—but I push it down into that shadowy part of my brain along with the olive and the gherkin and all my other insecurities.

Saskia pauses by a leafy archway laced with trailing wisteria. "That's your best bet, the orchard." She gestures beyond the archway. "His evening stroll should take him right near here. Attract his attention somehow, do your thing. Thorn trusts you, God knows why." She looks me up and down. "If you let us down, I'll kill you."

I suppose a "Good luck" is out of the question then, I think to myself.

She grabs Nate by the arm. "Come on, young 'un, best not cramp the lovebirds."

"No." My voice comes out a little desperate.

Saskia glares at me.

"Can he stay? Please, I don't know if I can do this on my own."

Nate interrupts. "She needs me to prepare, we're a team, you see."

Saskia curls her lip at the word *team*. "Whatever." She walks away, and I get this awful feeling she wants us to fail so she can follow through on her threat.

Nate runs through my lines with me, quoting the scene from the film. He takes Willow's lines, using this deep, manly voice, which makes him sound like the girl who played the prince in last year's pantomime. And I say Rose's lines, wincing at how stale my voice sounds:

WILLOW
Are you OK? Are you hurt?

ROSE
No, thank you, I'm fine, it's just a little graze. You must be Willow.
You look like a Willow.

WILLOW
And what does a Willow look like?

ROSE
Tall and lanky.

WILLOW
(laughs)
And you are?

ROSE
Just another Night-Imp.

WILLOW
Really, I hadn't noticed.

Fortunately, the dialogue from the film remained pretty true to the book, so we at least don't feel torn about which lines to choose. I have a different problem: The words have lost all meaning and swirl around in my head like a series of disjointed sounds. And I can't believe I never noticed how cheesy they sound. Saying them out loud makes me cringe.

I raise a hand to show I've had enough. "It's not helping, sorry."

"It's OK, you know it backwards, anyway."

I stand next to the plum tree, my hands sweaty, my breathing shallow. I try leaning against the trunk like Rose, but my hair sticks to the wood and I worry I'll get a bark pattern imprinted on my forehead.

"I don't think I can do this." My voice seems to disappear upward, between the leaves and branches.

"Of course you can," Nate replies.

"But Rose and Willow . . . they're like Edward and Bella, Lancelot and Guinevere, Tristan and Isolde . . ."

"Kermit and Miss Piggy."

This makes me laugh, but only for a second. "What if he doesn't like me?" I wish I hadn't said this, because even in the dark, Nate's face acts like a mirror, reflecting my anxiety.

He catches himself and smiles. "'Course he will, just stick to the script. Say the lines and try to look, you know, half-decent . . . Don't dribble or fart or pick your nose."

"But what about that *connection*," I say.

Nate recites a line from the book. *"And after only the briefest of encounters, Willow knew that he could wander the earth for the rest of his life and never find another soul who made him feel so complete. It's like they were born to fit together."*

"Seriously, Nate. I don't need to hear that crap right now."

The clock tower strikes midnight. I imagine a stage curtain lifting.

"You ready?" he says, handing me a knife.

The knife. In all my anxiety, I totally forgot about cutting myself. Thank goodness Nate remembered. He must have lifted the blade from Saskia on the way here.

I hold it above my outstretched palm. *I am Rose. I am strong and fearless.* I squeeze my eyes shut and will myself to stab my own hand. But my arm just wavers midair, puppetlike and uncertain.

"Violet," Nate hisses.

Panic forces my eyes open. "I can't."

"You have to, it's canon."

"But I don't do pain."

The clock finishes chiming, the curtain has lifted, and yet here I stand, unbloodied and wobbling like a giant marionette.

Nate grabs at my overalls and whispers in an urgent tone, "Come on, you've got balls of steel. Think Rose, think Tris, think Katniss."

I flatten out my palm, now dappled with sweat. "Balls of steel, balls of steel." I say it like a mantra, letting the adrenaline build inside. And just as I'm about to thrust the knife blindly downward, hoping I somehow hit my palm, I hear the *crack* of twigs.

"It's him." Nate dives behind a nearby trunk, his slim frame easily swallowed up by the orchard.

Necessity pulls the blade down in a graceful arc, but I lose my nerve at the last moment and whip my palm away. The tip of the blade just catches my thumb, sending a sharp pain up my wrist like I've been stung. "Ow! Bastard knife!" I drop it—handle first—on my foot. Mid-hop, I remember Rose leaned seductively against the tree, and I kind of headbutt the trunk in my eagerness.

Willow skids into view. I clasp my foot with one hand and my head with the other, my heart tries to escape my rib cage, and I think I may be mumbling a stream of swear words. But when my eyes fall upon his face, everything stops. My head empties. I forget it all—the mission, my insecurities, my pirouetting feet. I see only him.

He looks a bit like Russell Jones—same high cheekbones, same full lips—but his eyes seem kinder, like two puddles of molten copper. And his bone structure looks more delicate, his Adam's apple less pronounced, lending him a more feminine quality. The film didn't do him justice. Even my own imagination didn't do him justice. The man before me is an *Adonis*. I suddenly become aware of the fullness of the moon, the scent of apples and wood smoke, the bite of the cold on my throat.

"Are you OK? Are you hurt?" His voice sounds like the chiming clock, resonant and lyrical and yet somehow distant. He ambles toward me with long, sinuous steps. I notice the top two buttons of his white linen shirt have come undone, revealing a triangle of honey-colored skin. I freeze, unable to blink, unable to breathe.

He stops an arm's length from me. Even in the dimness, I can see the warmth of his colors—copper eyes, honey skin, caramel hair—like a sliver of sunshine in the night. I inhale quickly and the tang of his aftershave finds me. Citrus and coriander.

I know it's my line, but my thoughts mush together. I open my mouth and my breath uncurls in a single wisp.

He studies my face for a moment—in the book he's supposed to be reminded of tree sprites or nymphs or something. I suddenly feel very awkward in my overalls, more goblin than sprite.

I hear a faint cough from a nearby tree. I feel so dissociated from reality it barely seems strange a tree should cough. The actual, real-life Willow stands before me, all concerned and perfect and warm—of course the greenery's coughing. No, not the greenery. Nate. *It's my line.*

My synapses begin to spark and, finally, my throat opens. "No, thank you, I'm fine. It's just a little graze." I look at my palm and realize with a rush of shame that I failed to draw any blood, but I push on with my lines regardless. "You must be Willow, you look like a Willow."

He smiles his faultless smile, two long dimples framing his mouth. "And what does a Willow look like?"

"Tall and lanky."

He laughs, the heat of his breath closing the gap between us. "And you are?"

"Just another Night-Imp."

"Really, I hadn't noticed." He moves toward me so his chest almost touches my chin. The words don't seem cheesy at all now, they seem romantic . . . perfect. And this close, I realize just how tall he is—all the moisture leaves my mouth. He lifts my hand and examines the scratch on my thumb.

I order my voice to stay true, to stay on-script. "The trouble I would get in if anyone saw you touching me. I shouldn't even be talking to you."

He continues to hold my hand and lifts his gaze to meet mine. "I'm sure the trees won't tell."

"No, but the stars might."

He laughs like he's meant to. "It's a risk I'm willing to take."

I let the scent of apple and smoke and aftershave fill my lungs. It's going really well. Not an olive in sight. "Why are you being so nice? I thought all Gems were cruel."

"And I thought all Imps were stupid."

"Looks like we were both wrong." I smile. I mean, *really* smile, not just because that's what Rose did, but because pretending to be confident and sexy makes me feel confident and sexy.

He releases my hand. "You really aren't going to tell me your name, are you?"

"We don't have names . . . only numbers." I spin around and lift my hair so he can see my tattoo. The cold hits my neck and a thin veil of sweat evaporates.

He sucks air over his teeth. "That must have hurt."

I nod and suppress a little smile. *Willow is gazing at my neck.*

"You seriously want me to call you Imp 753811?" he says.

I let my hair fall back across my tattoo and turn back to face him. "You really want to know my name? Why don't you guess?" I would never say anything so brazen, especially not to a boy; it feels liberating.

"Rumpelstiltskin."

I laugh. It's meant to sound like a bell, but it comes out a bit snorty. "Almost."

He touches the fabric of my overalls like he wants to touch me, but can't quite muster the courage.

Right on cue, we hear a car door slamming. He runs his fingers through his hair, ruffling it up so it's all gloss and color in the moonlight. "I'd better go." He smiles as if to say, *Another time*, and turns toward the manor.

This is the point in canon when he glances over his shoulder and says the words, *Can I see you again?* But he doesn't, he just keeps on walking. I watch him saunter away, the leaves and bark closing around him as though he sinks into a bog. Swallowed up forever. *Look over your shoulder*, I scream in my head. *Look over your shoulder and say your line . . . please.* Fear shoots through my veins—I've failed the mission. Thorn will kill Katie and we'll be stuck in this world forever. But another emotion simmers beneath the fear: disappointment. He didn't like me.

I'm about to admit defeat, hot tears gathering in the corners of my eyes, when he stops. And he doesn't just glance over his shoulder, he turns his whole body. His face hovers in the dark like a bronze heart. "Can I see you again?"

It feels like someone has yanked a plastic bag off my head. I want to gasp and heave and suck in great mouthfuls of air, feel my rib cage stretch and my head fill with blood. But instead, I offer a demure shrug, just like Rose. "Perhaps."

He laughs. I watch the triangle of his back disappear and stand completely still for a moment, listening to the rush of blood in my ears.

Nate dashes out from behind a tree and embraces me while jumping on the spot. "Oh my God, Violet, that was *awesome*."

I start jumping, too. "I know, I know."

"You were word perfect."

"Did you see him touch my hand?" I feel like my body can't contain this much joy, like my skin's going to rip from the pressure.

Nate opens his mouth to reply when we hear another voice—familiar and yet faintly bitter. "Why didn't you just tell him your name? It's so pretty . . ." It comes from the sky, and for a brief second, I think God himself is talking. "The color and the flower." A rustle of foliage followed by a shower of dust and leaves and splinters.

Ash lowers himself so he hangs from a nearby branch, overalls pulled taut across his chest, fingers white and claw-like. He lands a few yards away, absorbing the fall with his knees like he really is part cat. "I never took you for a Gem lover." A wry smile unfurls across his face, but his voice sounds a little wounded.

After staring at Willow, Ash doesn't seem nearly so cute. His nose seems a little on the large side, his smile a little lopsided, but something about him looks so *real*. And those eyes . . . My mouth hangs open for a moment.

"Ash!" I finally say. I knew I would run into Ash eventually, but Rose didn't meet him until later tonight, in the Imp-hut. He certainly wasn't watching her from a tree in canon. I don't know what those two threads are playing at right now, but after being entwined for so long, they've decided to diverge. "I wasn't expecting to see you so soon," I say.

"Ash?" Nate still clings to me, though he's at least stopped jumping. "As in, Ash from canon? Rose's *puppy*?"

Ash ignores him. "I figured."

"How does he even know you?" Nate asks me.

But I ignore him, too.

We stare at each other—Ash and me—this awkward silence hanging between us, lips parted like we want to speak but don't know how. The paleness of his eyes alarms me and I feel a sudden urge to apologize. I move like I might take his hand, but instead make this strange fluttering motion in front of my face. I suddenly remember how useless I am with boys, how much I need that script.

I see Nate in my peripheral vision, studying my face and mumbling, "Oh no." He pushes his hands into his hair and grimaces. "This is *not* canon."

I just keep gawking at Ash. This muddle of emotions pushes up my throat—sheer pleasure just because he's here, awkwardness, like my limbs don't quite fit on my body, and this guilty feeling like I've been caught cheating.

Nate looks from me to Ash and back. "Oh no, oh no, oh no." He leans against a trunk like it's all too much. "Why didn't I notice before? He's even got the stupid dystopian-love-interest name— Ash—like Gale or Four or something." He slithers to the floor, all the joy leaking out of him. "This is going to screw up everything."

CHAPTER 17

I SEE ASH IN the Imp-hut later that night—this was the point when he first met Rose in canon, completely unaware of her true identity as a rebel, completely unaware of her relationship with Willow. He offered to show her the ropes and took her apple picking. He looked so affable, so naive. But this Ash, *my* Ash, looks positively suspicious, pissed off even. I guess it isn't just Gems who disapprove of Imp-Gem relationships.

I pretend I don't notice him, and instead focus on Saskia's instructions. She sits opposite me and Nate at the pine table. We warm our hands on mugs of hot tea, and she inadvertently blows steam at us while she speaks. "So if you want to blend in, you need to get on with chores for the rest of the night. Some of the Night-Imps choose to travel back to the city come morning, the ones with families and responsibilities, but we're better off sleeping here, minimize your contact with the guards as much as possible."

The mention of the guards sends a shiver down my spine.

Saskia pretends not to see. "Nate, you can help mow the lawns, Violet—"

Ash cuts over her. "I could always do with a hand picking apples."

This surprises me. Judging from his expression, I'm the last person he wants to spend time with. Maybe I'm due an ear bashing.

Saskia shrugs. "Yeah, whatever, just don't work her too hard, Squirrel."

I step from the dank air of the Imp-hut. The moon casts the estate in a milky glow and the stars stretch into forever. I follow Ash across the paddock and around the lake, which sits like a giant opal in the night. The air feels at its coldest, and the scent of smoke finally dwindles, overpowered by wet leaves and soil. I resist the urge to rub my eyes, the lack of sleep and the stress gradually pulling at my seams.

At this point in canon, Ash bombarded Rose with questions, hanging on her every reply, studying her face with large, puppy-dog eyes. *So, what's your name? What part of the city do you come from?* But right now, I'm met with an awkward silence. I begin to wish we could follow the movie script, but with our history, it would make no sense.

"So why did Saskia call you Squirrel?" I finally ask. I know the answer of course, but I can't bear the tension anymore.

He continues to plunk one foot in front of the other. His reflection in the water shoots away from him like a spike. "It's just a nickname."

"Yeah, I guessed that, but why?"

Finally, he meets my eye, causing a tiny ripple of excitement in my belly. He then runs at a nearby oak tree, planting the ball of his foot on the trunk and jumping from the other foot. One arm wraps around the trunk, the other grabs a low-hanging branch, and he lugs himself up so his pelvis rests on the bough. He swings his legs up so he sits, back bolt upright, arms folded like an elf. He looks down at me and laughs. He's hardly broken a sweat.

I laugh, too. "OK, OK, I get it . . . it's because you've got buck teeth, right?"

"At least you didn't crack a joke about me liking nuts." He grips the branch with his legs and lets his body fall back so he hangs upside down like a bat. This makes him look really strange, his hair falling away from his face and his cheeks sagging toward his eyes. I can't help thinking of the upside-down kiss in the old Spider-Man movie. Maybe following the script isn't all it's cracked up to be.

"Now you're just showing off," I say.

"Maybe." He places his hands on the branch and lets his body unfold, landing on his feet with a gentle *thud*.

We pass beneath the trailing wisteria and enter the orchard. I glance nervously at the spot where I spoke with Willow. That guilty feeling worms around in my gut again. Ash squats down and whacks a black cube with the side of his fist. A bulb flickers into action like an old movie projector starting up—a portable floodlight coating the orchard in a sticky white light. He grabs a wicker basket, his arm sending a giant shadowy butterfly wavering across the trunks.

We start picking apples from a nearby tree—they make a soft *thump* as they hit the bottom of the basket, chucking up dust and releasing their sweet, earthy aroma. This scene mirrors canon very closely—Ash and Rose picking fruit together—but the conversation differs dramatically.

"It's all very strange, Violet." His words interlace with the beat of falling apples. "I save you from getting hanged, then you turn up in my orchard. Are you stalking me or something?"

"No, 'course not."

He smiles his lopsided smile. "I was joking. You were practically drooling over that Gem . . . Willow." He sticks out his hip and bats his lashes. *"You look like a Willow—tall and lanky."* He mimics my voice and bites into the skin of an apple with relish. This Ash is so much more vibrant than canon-Ash.

I throw an apple at him. It explodes against the bark and releases a fine spray of juice that catches in the floodlight like beads of glass. "You can't blame me, he looks like an angel . . . a demigod."

He places another apple in the basket. "He's about as far from God as any creature could be—all tweaked and fake."

"I didn't say he *was* a demigod, I said he *looked* like a demigod."

"Well, aren't we the superficial one?" The trunk forms a divider, shielding his expression, but his voice sounds small and a little hostile.

I push my hands between the leaves in search of fruit. My fingers find only twigs. "I can't help who I'm attracted to. You said it yourself, we're all just animals."

"Yeah, well, they'll hang your animal ass if they find out you've been canoodling with a demigod."

"We were just talking."

"He was undressing you with his eyes."

My hand finally locates an apple—I snap it free almost triumphantly. "Are you jealous?"

"Of course I bloody am." He laughs, but I see a fleeting glimpse of that vulnerable puppy dog. I was wrong, he doesn't disapprove of Imp-Gem relationships; he disapproves of me with somebody—*anybody*—else.

I resist a little smile. "Look, Ash . . ." But I don't know what to say. I study his slightly asymmetrical features for a moment.

"What were you and the kid doing?" he asks suddenly.

"What, you mean my brother, Nate?"

"Yeah, the kid. You were reciting lines or something, right before the demigod turned up."

"We were just messing around. Sibling stuff."

He passes an apple between his hands. Back and forth like it's too hot to hold. "It was like you were rehearsing for something, and then the demigod actually said some of the things the kid said." He raises his eyebrows expectantly.

I can't tell him the truth, so instead I change the subject. "I never thanked you properly for saving me and my friends, back in the city, I mean."

He picks up the basket and moves to another tree. "That's OK. Couldn't very well let 'em hang you, could I?"

I follow him, partly because he has the basket, and partly because I feel lonely, just me and the shadows. I stand beside him and notice the hairs on his forearms, dark against his skin and raised in the cold.

"Well, you saved our lives. Thank you," I say.

He screens his eyes with his heavy lashes, which seem even longer than usual, extended across the pink of his cheeks by their own spidery shadows. He suddenly looks very sad. "I just can't believe you want a Gem, after how they treat us, what they do to us."

I recall my face pressed into the acrylic screen, the crumpling paper chain, and I feel like I might cry. I shake my head, trying to dislodge the images from my brain. "But it isn't Willow who does those things. You can't blame him for the sins of his people."

He raises his gaze. His irises, so pale they look like glass in the floodlight, his pupils, two intense dots. "Who, then? Who do you blame? Nobody else is going to rise up and stop the barbarity against the Imps if it isn't the Gem people."

I wish I could tell him everything, but it's too risky. Besides, he would probably think I'm mad. So, I steady my voice. "Maybe he will, one day, if he falls for an Imp. Maybe he will make a stand."

"What do you mean?"

I realize I've already said too much and return to picking apples, pretending those frosted blue eyes don't pierce my skin as they study my profile. At this point in canon, Rose was making up some crap about having worked in the Pastures before. Just small talk, really. Polite answers, eager nodding, puppy-dog eyes. I wish we were back on-script again—this is way too hard.

"Nothing," I say. "I'm just thinking out loud."

"Just don't get killed, OK?" He scoots up the tree so he can reach the fruit on the higher boughs.

I strain my neck to look up at him, and he drops a couple of apples into my outstretched hands. "I'll do my best," I lie.

"Because I didn't save you from one noose just to see you wind up hanging from another." He drops an apple straight into the basket. "Bull's-eye," he shouts.

Ash returns home on the Imp-bus that morning. I watch him shuffling up the line and climbing the steps, adopting his subservient Imp pose, so at odds with the squirrel I witnessed earlier in the night.

I slump into the bunk above Nate.

He pokes his head up so it's level with mine. "So, how did it go with Ash?"

"Rubbish. I think he may hate me."

"Well, it doesn't matter whether Ash likes you or not. He's just a side character; it matters whether Willow does."

I know Nate's right, but it kind of matters to *me* that Ash likes me. "I guess," I reply.

Nate pats my arm. "Get some sleep, heroine extraordinaire, gotta look your best."

It makes me smile when Nate goes all nurturing on me, like he's the older sibling. "Thanks," I say.

He bobs back down, and I soon hear the rhythmic pattern of his breath as he falls to sleep.

The Day-Imps begin to arrive, and their movement, combined with the light seeping through the cloth dividers, keeps me awake. Plus, my mind is just a whirl of conflicting thoughts and emotions: I think of Katie, back in the bell tower, at the mercy of a patch-wearing sociopath with a bit of a crush; I think of Alice, wherever she may be; I think of Ash and those winter eyes; I think of the way Dad always touches Mum's hand as she pours milk on his cereal; and finally, I think of my feet, dancing midair, searching desperately for solid ground, never to find those ruby slippers and return home.

In five days, I will hang.

I roll into the fetal position and imagine all these thoughts pooling in the side of my head, seeping into the pillow below. Finally, I fall into an uneasy sleep, punctuated with twisting shadows and screams and a feeling like I want to move but can't, like rope binds my limbs. The dream changes, and suddenly I can move again. I feel surprisingly free, like all of the weight has been lifted from my chest. It's summertime—the smell of lupins and freshly cut grass, the sound of children playing mixed in with birdsong.

I'm seven years old, standing in my parents' garden with Alice and Nate. Alice looks so young—her feet not yet crammed into heels, her hair free to kink around her face. And Nate, he's only four years old. His legs still have that lovely, chubby fold at the ankle and the knee, and his shorts drown his petite frame. I'm blowing bubbles, watching them sprout from the wand and float into the air, perfect spheres shining in the sun. Alice and Nate run this way and that, trying to catch them, squealing as they pop in their cupped hands. *More*, Nate cries, *more bubbles, Violet, more bubbles, please.*

I aim the wand upward and spin in a circle. The bubbles fly high into the sky, hovering just out of reach, carried by the breeze and catching on the tops of the buddleias. *Too high*, Alice cries. *Too high, Violet.* But I keep on spinning, keep on blowing, spurred on by their laughter and the sense of freedom. Suddenly, Nate screams, *Look, Violet, look!* Alice and I freeze and track the invisible line traveling from his finger. A single bubble survives the buddleias, climbing higher and higher, bobbing over the garden fence, beneath the telephone cables, up, up, and over the tops of the sycamores.

We watch that bubble until it is no more than a tiny dot, floating into the horizon. Nate turns to me. He grins so wide I can see all of his baby teeth, all pearly and wet. *Will it land in the stars?* Alice and I laugh. *Yes, Nate, it will land in the stars.* And that's when I hear it, the rhythmic *pip* of a hospital machine, like the ones you hear on *Holby City*. *Pip. Pip. Pip.* The scent of antibacterial soap and detergent replaces the perfume of summer.

Alice turns to me. *What's that noise?* We look across the lawn, under the flowers, behind the wooden bench. But we can't find the machine. *Pip. Pip. Pip.* Nate nuzzles his head into my stomach. *I don't like it, Violet, make it stop.* I climb on the stones, peer into the neighbors' gardens, check the windows into our house. But still no machine. That sense of freedom makes way for a growing sense of dread. *Pip. Pip. Pip.*

The *pip*s begin to mutate, changing into the hollow tap of knuckles against wood. I wake to Saskia's stern face, her fist rapping against the edge of my bunk. "Come on, Violet. You need to use your charms on that useless hunk of a Gem."

I'm covered in sweat, my pulse banging repetitively in my ears. "Willow," I say, my voice muffled with sleep.

She frowns. "Yeah, I know his name."

I blink the grit from eyes and tell myself those *pip*s were just the sound of Saskia's impatient knocking, or my own blood gushing through my body. There's no other explanation.

CHAPTER 18

I shove some tasteless gruel down my throat and grab another shower, almost enjoying the way the cold hammers into me—freezing the anxiety, transforming it into a shimmering block I can step away from and leave behind.

I walk to the manor with Saskia and Nate. I can feel the worry taking over—the next part of the story requires more than just reciting lines and avoiding farting. This is when I really fall short of Rose's ghost, because the next part of the story requires physical activity. And there's a reason I'm always the last one to get picked for the basketball team.

"So how are you going to get lover boy to notice you this time?" Saskia asks me.

"Last night, he asked me my name. Tonight, I'm going to show him."

She raises an eyebrow so it meets the dark stain on her head. "What d'ya mean, show him?"

"I'm going to leave a rose on his windowsill," I reply.

Nate pulls a rose from his overalls and hands it to me. The plumpest, reddest one he could find in the rose garden earlier that evening. I take it from him and rotate it in my fingers. We both look at Saskia, awaiting her excited response, the one she gave Rose in canon: *That's a brilliant idea, lure him out of that bastard manor house.* But instead, she scrunches up her face like she's just smelled something really bad. Maybe I did fart.

"That's effing ridiculous," she says. "Leaving a rose on his windowsill! Where do you two come up with this shit?"

Nate and I exchange a little smile.

"It'll work," Nate says. "Just you see."

Saskia snorts. "Well, it's wrong if you ask me, calling yourself Rose. It's disrespectful of the dead."

"Thorn said I should keep her name," I reply. "To remind me of her bravery and to keep me on course." Thorn didn't say this, but I hoped if I took on her name, I would somehow take on some of her beauty and daring. Besides, a mess of viola flowers sprawled across a windowsill wouldn't look nearly so romantic, as Nate so keenly pointed out earlier in the day.

"Thorn ain't always right, you know," Saskia grumbles, brushing her fingers against the scar on her collarbone.

The manor falls into view. It looks similar to the building used in the movie; stately and grand, with two parallel towers puffed out like the breasts of a peacock, and so far removed from the Imp city it may as well be a painted backdrop. It always struck me as strange how the Gems, with all their technological advancement, should choose to live in such classical-looking environments. I know the exterior of the manor is merely an illusion and inside there exists every futuristic gadget imaginable: artificial intelligence; matter-transporting drains; simulation pods; I could go on. But I could never work out why the Gems chose to modernize original Imp buildings, why they didn't just build from scratch. Now, living as an Imp, gazing at this beautiful Georgian hall, I finally get it. They did it to piss us off. To remind us that they won—they're the superior race. They live upstairs, we live downstairs. They *stole* our beautiful Georgian halls.

Bastards.

I try and cleanse my brain of such thoughts. Anger toward the Gems won't help me lure Willow. Instead, I focus on the grass yielding underfoot as we creep across the lawns, the grip of Nate's fingers around mine, the taste of smoke and cold on my tongue. We circle toward the back gardens, nearer and nearer to Willow's window. I notice the light in Willow's room remains off—third floor, fourth from the left.

We huddle beneath a large oak, the one Rose shimmied effortlessly up, bloom poking from her cleavage. I swear this tree is bigger . . . meaner.

"So, *you're* going to climb that huge tree?" Saskia says.

I begin to tuck the rose down the front of my overalls, imagining how awesome I'm about to look. But instead, my lack of cleavage lets the stem wilt to one side and the thorns stick into my chest like the little bastards that they are. I am so *not* Hollywood. But I force a little smile, pride getting the better of me. "How hard can it be?" And if I say it, I might believe it.

She shakes her head and links her hands together to form a stirrup. I place my foot in it and grip the lowest branch. The bark scrapes my fingers and the bough flexes beneath my weight, yet somehow I manage to haul my body into a sitting position. I'm no higher than the top of Saskia's head, but I still don't dare to look down; it freaks me out that I could just lean back and topple to the ground.

I honestly don't know what I thought would happen. I knew I wouldn't magically transform into Rose and scoot up a giant oak with ease, I knew the spirit of Katniss wouldn't suddenly possess me, allowing me to scuttle into the treetops while shooting a bow and arrow. But I didn't think I would be *quite* so devoid of upper-body strength. I take a few deep breaths and let my head fill with images of Katie and Alice and Nate. I *have* to do this. I *have* to complete the story so we can go home.

I stand carefully, hugging the trunk like a koala, my feet splayed across the bough. Another branch lies within reach on the other side of the trunk. I flail through the air and end up straddled between two branches, acutely aware of the fact only air and wood separate my body from the ground.

"This is going to take all bloody night," Saskia says. I can hear the pleasure leaching into her words.

My fingers slip, scraping across the bark, and when I finally risk looking down, I get this giddy feeling. But when I look up, I see only branches and leaves and twigs—the window seems unreachable. So I finally utter the words I'd been secretly avoiding. "Can someone get Ash?"

"Ash?" Saskia says. "He's not part of this, you know? He'll start askin' questions and if word gets out we're, you know"—she lowers her voice—"rebels, it won't be safe. Not all Imps are trust-worthy, that's what I'm saying."

"Well, it's Ash or a broken arm," I say, hysteria rising in my voice.

I hear Nate pleading below. "Yeah, come on, Saskia, Ash isn't going to tell anyone. He fancies Violet way too much."

I hear a reluctant sigh from Saskia, and I look down just long enough to see Nate dashing from view.

By the time Ash arrives, I've returned to the first branch and I'm back to hugging the trunk. I'm just so relieved he's back from the city—if he'd taken the later bus I'd be screwed. I glance down and see his massive grin. In the dusk, it's pretty much all I can see.

"You enjoying yourself up there?" He's unable to mask the laughter in his voice.

"Yeah, it's great up here . . . the views are stunning . . . lots of bark."

I feel the tree shudder as he hauls himself onto the branch opposite. I can't see him, but I feel the warmth of his hands as they cover mine. I suddenly feel very safe. He sticks his head around the trunk and smiles. The compassion in his face pushes away any doubts I had about requesting his help.

"You OK?" he asks.

I shake my head.

He smiles. "When you're a beginner, you should only ever have one limb free from the tree at a time. Got it?"

I nod.

"And always test a hold before you put your weight on it. Because if you commit to a weak branch, you're only going one way."

"That's really helpful, but I was kind of hoping . . ."

"I'd climb it for you?" he asks.

"Yeah."

"So why exactly am I climbing this tree?"

I risk freeing a hand, and I pull the rose from my overalls. It looks more like a wilted strip of seaweed.

He takes it from me and frowns. "You want me to put a rose . . . where exactly?" He looks up and must figure it out because he makes this "ah" noise.

"Third floor, fourth from the left."

"And why should I help you with this . . . whatever it is . . . daft idea?"

I don't know what to say. I just stare into his face—the night robbing his eyes of any blue—and mouth the word *please*.

"OK, OK, don't use those big brown eyes on me," he says.

The next thing I know, his feet disappear up into the leaves like he's being vacuumed toward the sky. Leaves and bark rain down on me, and I have to lower my head to stop my mouth and eyes from filling with debris.

Several minutes later, he's a bloom lighter and helping me back down to the ground.

Nate slaps him on the back like they're best buddies. "Thanks, mate."

Saskia just looks grumpy. "Well, let's just hope it works after all that." She stomps across the grass away from the manor, dragging Nate with her.

I turn to follow, but Ash grabs my arms and whispers into my ear, his breath like hot water. "You know Saskia's got a bad reputation here? There are rumors that she and Matthew are . . . rebels."

"Would that be so bad?"

"Not really, it's just, if you're caught up in some rebel plot, it will probably end with you dancing on the gallows. What is it with you and hanging? It's like you *want* to hang."

I don't dare tell him he's right on. I don't dare speak the words—they're just too scary. Instead, I take his hand. It sits like a hot stone in my palm—all heavy and dusted with leaf fragments. "Thanks for helping me, Ash. You're a real friend."

"I'm a bloody idiot." He looks kind of sad, his lashes hiding those night-bleached eyes, but he doesn't move his hand. We stand for a moment beneath the oak canopy, all these words forming on our tongues but never leaving our lips.

A light flicks on in Willow's room. It filters through the leaves and causes shadows to dapple our skin, pointing out how far we are from safety, a sharpening of reality. Our hands part. We sprint away from the manor, into the trees and the privets and dark. And I know that somewhere behind me, Willow has just figured out my pseudonym.

CHAPTER 19

I WAIT FOR WILLOW in the orchard again, same spot by the plum tree. There's this light drizzle, barely visible in the dark, but I feel it dampening my nose and eyelids, the leaves offering little protection. Nate and I decided I should meet Willow alone this time—in this scene there's just too much movement for Nate to remain hidden. But he paced the route through with me only moments ago, reminding me of my lines and when I should say them. I can't help smiling, thinking of him as he turned his slight body toward the stables and ran his hands up and down his back so it looked like he was kissing someone. "Ooh, Willow . . ." he said in this silly girly voice, which I prayed sounded nothing like me.

I lean against the plum tree and try to make my body look lean and sexy, but the nerves flicker in my stomach and I struggle to keep my limbs from fidgeting. Tonight is the first-kiss scene; hopelessly romantic and beautiful. I should feel excited, but I just feel terrified. What if he doesn't kiss me? Or worse, what if he does and it makes him puke? And I just can't get that damned gherkin-tongue out of my head. All my insecurities hover in my peripheral vision like fat droning insects. Quickly, I recap my lines in my head, the lines that led up to that first, perfect kiss.

WILLOW
I've never met anyone like you before.

ROSE
An Imp, you mean?

WILLOW
No, anyone so free.

ROSE
I'm not free. I'm a slave. Your father's slave, to be exact.

WILLOW
*I know, I'm sorry, I didn't mean it like that . . . It's just, I
don't know, it probably sounds stupid me saying this, but I
wish I could be more like you.*

ROSE
(cups his face in her hands)
You can be.

And then he kissed her.

Passionate. Heart-wrenching. Perfect.

But the reality is I've been sharing a moldy toothbrush with
Nate for three days, and my mouth tastes of feet.

I hear Willow's step before I see him, fast but not urgent. My
pulse quickens and the taste of feet grows stronger. He steps through
the arch looking even more beautiful than usual, the moon illuminating the fineness of his features. He sees me and chuckles, strok-
ing the underbelly of his chin with the petals of the rose. And

then, just like he should, he delivers his opening line: "Rose . . . You look like a Rose."

My fingers tremble, but I force my voice to remain strong, my words to remain true to the script. "And what does a Rose look like?"

He laughs. "Prickly." He crosses the remainder of the orchard and we sit side by side beneath the plum tree. I sit on my hands so they don't fiddle, and I study his profile—so perfect he almost looks like a CGI prince from a kids' film. I bite my lower lip and suddenly I'm very aware of the skin on my chest growing hot under my overalls.

His eyelashes beat slightly as he contemplates the stars. "I love the estate at night."

"I only really see it at night."

He turns to face me, his skin already dewy in the rain. "So you sleep in the day, right?"

"Mostly."

A puzzled look crosses his uniform features. "Do you sleep at the estate, or do you catch that big old car thing back to the city?"

I laugh, playfully tapping his shoulder just like in canon. It feels kind of flirty and a bit alien, but I say my line all the same. "Big old car thing? You mean the bus?"

"Is that what it's called?"

"You're so privileged."

"I think the word you're looking for is *ignorant*."

We stare at each other. The strength of his gaze almost robs me of my next line. "I tend to sleep here at the manor. I don't have a family to return to, and I avoid crossing the border if I can—the guards can be a bit rough."

He touches my arm. "Have they ever hurt you?"

I recall the acrylic screen and the steel-gray eyes. I know I should stay on-script, just reply, *Not yet*, like Rose did, but I feel this anger welling inside me like something dark and evil, and I can't seem to stop it pushing up my gullet and forcing out my own words. "If you try to sneak into the Pastures, the guards shoot you on sight, did you know that? They just line you up and gun you down like you're nothing." I can't believe I just said this, that I would risk deviating from canon when there's so much at stake.

He looks a little taken aback. "But they need to stop rogue Imps crossing the border."

Willow knows about the decontamination block? He knows and yet he does nothing? *Just stick to canon, Violet*, I think. But the anger reaches a new level, transforming to rage, and I simply can't stop the words—hot and pleading—pouring from my mouth. "You know about this? You know about this and you haven't tried to stop it?" I know I should just get back on-script, I know I should just focus on the end result of returning home, but I just can't get that paper doll chain out of my head—the way it crumpled to the floor like used-up newspaper. I shake his hand from my arm.

Now it's his turn to look angry. "Look, Rose, until I met you . . . I never really thought about it . . . it's just the way it's always been."

"Not always," I snap.

He suddenly looks very deflated. His beautiful features sag and he places the rose on his lap. "I'm sorry, you're right, of course."

I look at his soft eyes, his look of earnestness, and the anger fades. I need to get the scene back on track. So I take a deep breath and, true to canon, leap to my feet. "Come on, I'm sick of this bloody orchard."

I begin to run through the trees, batting the branches with my hands as I run. In the film, Rose looked so free-spirited, but I think I just look clumsy. One of the boughs smacks me across the face. Thankfully, Willow finds this hilarious, his laughter spurring me on.

The orchard comes to an end and we burst onto a meadow, silver beneath the moon. Already, he streaks ahead, aiming for the gate at the far side. I focus on closing the gap, head down, arms and legs pumping, chest heaving. It feels so exhilarating. The ground yields, and for a brief moment I think I might slip, but I steady myself and continue to climb. I glance up to see the gap closing. I can make out the feathered point at the nape of his neck. I reach out, so close I swear I can feel the heat of his body beneath my fingertips. But he must sense me and zips forward. My hands fall empty through the air.

We slam—laughing and panting—into the gate. The wood groans beneath our weight and tries to push us back like a springboard. He has this amazing smile.

"You're fast." I lean on my knees to catch my breath.

"All Gems are fast."

I feel the cool night air against my neck as my hair falls forward and my overalls slip back, revealing the upper nodules of my spine. Just like in the book.

His breath gradually slows as he traces each tattooed digit with a finger. A wave of tremors spreads beneath my skin—concentric circles in a lake.

"What does it mean?" he finally asks.

I recite my line with ease. "The first number is the city. So the seven means I live in London. The next two numbers show which estate I work at—all of the Imps working here start with 753."

"And the 811?"

"That's my number. The eight hundred and eleventh Imp to work at the manor." I smile. "They know how to make a girl feel special."

He presses his palm into my neck, blocking out the numbers. I absorb the clammy warmth of his skin. *Willow is touching my neck.* I feel a bolt of excitement.

"It's just ink," he says. "A collection of shapes—it only means what we say it means."

We smile at each other. Then, following the script, I give him a gentle nudge. "Enough stalling, Gem."

I recall Rose vaulting over the gate in one smooth action, but I suspect I would fall flat on my face, so instead I just climb over it. I try my best to seem feisty and brave, but my boots squelch in the mud and I feel like a bit of a fraud. I begin to run again, hoping I'll get enough of a head start to make sure we end up at the stables.

"Not fair," he calls after me. "I don't know the estate like you do."

"You're the superhuman," I call over my shoulder.

I see the stables and feel an enormous sense of relief, followed quickly by the realization that this is it—he's about to kiss me. I order myself to stay focused; I'm so close to pulling this off. I slip down the side of the stables, hogweed and brambles catching at my ankles, causing me to trip and bump into the wood. He stumbles behind me, and we both begin to giggle, waking up the horses.

I reach the back of the structure and lean into the planks, grateful for the rest, my chest rising and falling from all the exertion. The scent of pony kibble and horsehair mingles with our sweat. He leans beside me, still giggling, a piece of hogweed clinging to his ankle. I can feel the cords of his arm muscles as they push against my overalls. I'm only moments away from the first kiss. My mouth suddenly feels like it's stuffed with cardboard—shoe boxes, judging from the taste. God, I would kill for a breath mint.

He turns to me and pushes my hair from my face. It kind of catches in my mouth and pulls my lip to the side. "Agh," I mumble.

But he just laughs. "I've never met anyone like you before."

I take a moment to study his features. A collection of shapes. This close, I can see the trellis of pores and the fine covering of tiny hairs on his skin.

I untangle my hair from my mouth. "An Imp, you mean?"

"No, anyone so free."

He toys with the back of my ear and I can't help turning into his hand, it feels so large, so solid, against my cheek. *Willow is touching my ear.* I focus on the perfect bow of his upper lip. "I'm not free. I'm a slave. Your father's slave, to be exact."

His hand drops to his side, weighed down with shame. "I know, I'm sorry, I didn't mean it like that . . . It's just, I don't know, it probably sounds stupid me saying this, but I wish I could be more like you."

This is it. He's about to kiss me. I cup his flawless face in my palms and force his eyes to meet mine. I think my heart may have stopped beating, just turned to grit in my chest. But I deliver my line with confidence. "You can be."

He stares at me for a moment. I anticipate his sudden movement, the taste of his lips against mine. I get this unexpected shudder in my windpipe, this feeling like I've just come inside from a snowstorm, my skin hot and cold at the same time. I let my eyelids close. *This is it.*

But he remains still, the kiss never arrives.

Instead, he says, "It's my coming-of-age ball tomorrow."

He's moved straight on with the lines, he's left out the kissing bit. My heart jump-starts and my brain fills with all those insecurities: *Is it because my breath smells? Is my hair too messy? Is it because I went off-script and talked about the decontamination process? Maybe I'm just not good enough.*

But I stick to my lines. "Yeah?"

Maybe I should kiss him? But what if he doesn't want me to? He's so tall, I might miss and just kiss his chin. The four-letter word fills my head, all angular and spiked.

But he just smiles, completely oblivious to my inner turmoil. "Are you waitressing at it?"

"Yeah."

"I'll probably have to dance with every Gem socialite in the region . . . but I'll save the last dance for you."

"I'd like that," I reply, my outer voice on autopilot, my inner voice still screaming profanities.

"I better head back," he says.

I realize I'm still clutching his face. I try to let go casually so he barely notices, but my palms kind of stick to his chin. "OK, then."

"I'll see you tomorrow? Yeah?" He flashes his beautiful smile.

"I'll wear my dancing shoes."

He kisses me on the cheek. *On the cheek.* And then he leaves.

CHAPTER 20

RETURN TO THE Imp-hut, completely dejected, my worst fear confirmed—I'm hopeless with men. Even with a script, even without my gorgeous BFF cramping my style, I'm hopeless with men.

Nate takes one look at my face. "He didn't kiss you, did he?"

I shake my head.

"Why not?" he says. "You didn't dribble and fart and pick your nose, did you? Because I warned you against that look."

I don't dare tell him I went off-script and risked so much, just because I lost my cool. I'm just too embarrassed, too ashamed. Instead, I slump onto my bunk. "I guess he just doesn't find me as attractive as Rose."

Nate slaps his palm to his forehead. "Violet, it's Monday night. Willow is meant to declare his undying love for you on Thursday night and follow you into the city. You've got three more days. If you don't get him to fall for you, we're stuck here . . . as Imps, in a world where Imps are lower than pondweed. You know that, yeah?"

"I know," I snap. If I don't get Willow to fall for me, we're stuck here. If I do get Willow to fall for me, I end up pirouetting on a rope. I think I'm about to start crying. "Don't pile on any more pressure, OK? I feel like I'm about to crack as it is." I suddenly long for Katie's grounded presence, to hear her gentle Liverpudlian voice telling me everything's going to be OK.

Nate sits beside me. "But Willow said the thing about the last dance?"

"Yeah. And I said that cheeseball line about dancing shoes."

"OK, so that's when we get it back on track." Nate smiles, like he's the older sibling again. "Don't worry, sis. It was a crappy first-kiss scene, anyway. Behind a stable? Come on now, Sally, sort it out."

Ash enters the Imp-hut. He looks tired, the blue of his eyes somehow dimmed, his skin almost gray. But when he sees me, the tiredness lifts and his oversize smile explodes across his face. "You ready for another night of hard labor?" he asks.

I swing my legs from my bunk, sending a shower of straw onto the floor. "Always."

"I'll come, too," Nate says.

The smile never drops from Ash's face, but I can tell from the firmness in his voice he isn't about to argue. "Sorry, buddy. It's a two-man job."

"Yeah, I bet it is," Nate says.

I accidentally-on-purpose clip Nate with my boot heel as I dismount from the bunk.

Stepping out into the night with Ash feels good. In canon, Rose and Ash spent several nights together, working on the estate. But most of these scenes were alluded to in the book and never made it into the film, so there's no script even if I wanted one. Surprisingly, this thought leaves me feeling relieved—I don't have to say the right thing or stand in the right way.

We cut around the back of the hut and into the meadows. Without the heady scent of pollen, the air seems a little lighter, cleaner.

"Why don't you sleep on the estate?" I ask. "In the hut with the rest of us? Why do you go back to the city every day?" I remember Willow calling the Imp-bus the big old car thing, and I wince.

"It's my home." He kicks a stray fir cone from his path and it bounces off a squat stone wall.

"But it's so dirty and unclean."

"Yeah, well, it's what I know. It's where my family lives."

There's no place like home. I get this aching in my gut. "Have you ever had any trouble crossing the border?"

He shrugs. "Yeah. Once I tried to smuggle out some supplies for Ma. This guard found them."

I study his profile, almost silver beneath the moon. "What happened?"

"They took the supplies and beat me unconscious."

My knees seem to jam up. I turn to face him. "Were you OK?"

He rubs my upper arm like I'm the one who needs comfort. "Yeah. It was lucky I passed out. They didn't bother shooting me and, when I woke up, I somehow managed to crawl back home."

"That's awful." I feel anger pushing through me in waves.

"That's the Gems."

I think of Willow again, his perfect mouth forming those hateful words: *It's just the way it's always been.* I begin to feel very guilty for trying to kiss him behind the stable.

"What about you?" Ash asks.

"Yeah. Nearly, but this Symp stepped in." I feel my cheeks fill with blood, and I fold my arms across my chest.

"I'm sorry," he says.

"Thanks. What were the supplies for?"

"Just basic things—antiseptic, bandages. Stuff for Ma."

"Do you ever help her?" I ask.

"Deliver babies, you mean?"

I nod. *Deliver babies.* He makes it sound so simple, so clean, like the postman just turns up and hands over a baby with a stamp on its head. But there will be no medication, no antiseptic or equipment. I bet it's horrific.

"Yeah, sometimes I help. I mostly just hand her a wet cloth and clean up the mess. General gofer."

"You must see some pretty scary things."

He smiles. "Did I ever tell you how I got my name?"

I shake my head. More backstory King didn't write, but it doesn't feel like a backstory anymore, it feels like something real and human. Something I desperately want to know.

He stares at the moon as though trying to remember. "So Ma labored for hours before she had me. The midwife, this old lady from the other street, kept Ma calm by singing old nursery rhymes. Do you know the thistle-counting song?"

"No."

"Seriously? You didn't used to skip to it as a kid?"

"Never."

He launches into the rhyme:

"Count the thistles, one, two, three,
Soon the Imps will all be free.
Count the thistles, four, five, six,
Take up your guns, your stones and sticks.
The ash trees turn from green to red,
Spring has gone, the summer's dead."

He looks a little embarrassed. "Anyway, I came out with the cord wrapped around my neck, not breathing. Ma thought I was dead, but the midwife untangled the cord and smacked me on the back. She kept on singing the whole time. Ma swears I gasped my first little breath just as she heard the word *ash*. That's why she decided to become a midwife—to replace the old lady when she died."

This tale makes me a little teary, thinking of how close Ash came to never breathing, thinking of the old lady and Ma, dedicating their lives to help Imp women and babies for no reason other than kindness.

Ash grins, his teeth bright in the dark. "Good job I didn't breathe on a different word, hey? Or I could have ended up with a really stupid name, like Four or something."

I wish Nate was here—he would have busted a gut laughing.

We swing around the end of the wall and approach a large vegetable patch. A series of raised beds and a huge fruit cage, bigger than my living room back home.

"So you're a slave by night and a midwife by day. When do you sleep?" I ask.

He laughs. "I'm a slave by night and a gofer by day, and never. I never sleep. Come on, you're on black currant duty." He gestures to some wooden baskets stacked against the metal frame of the cage. "I'll see to the peas."

I can't help feeling a little disappointed we won't be working together.

After a few hours of fruit picking, my thighs ache from crouching, my fingers feel crampy, my eyes have started to sting, and I really, really miss the sun. And seeing the berries in the dark proves really tough, even with the flashlight Ash gave me. The only good thing about this job is the tang of the black currants when they explode in my mouth. I'm sick of apples and stale bread.

Ash helps move the baskets into a wheelbarrow and grins. "Come on, fess up, how many did you eat?"

I laugh. "Probably more than I picked." I offer him a stem with stained fingers. "Try them, they're good."

"Nah. Horrible little things. Why do you think I chose pea duty?"

He parks the wheelbarrow behind the cage and beckons for me to follow him. We climb over a fence and I notice for the first time a wooden shack, about the size of a garden shed but with no windows and a small square door like a giant cat flap.

"What's in there?" I ask.

"Let's go and find out." He drops down onto all fours and approaches the cat flap.

I follow suit, giggling at how daft we must look. "Ash? What are we doing?"

"You want some proper food?"

"Always."

"So it's an early breakfast."

He pushes his way through the flap until his feet disappear. I hear the soft buzz of a match striking and the gaps around the door glow ever so slightly. He holds the flap open for me, his face soft and amber in the lamplight. I squeeze my chest through the gap and headbutt his armpit. I start to laugh.

"Shhhh." Ash points to a row of sleeping chickens. They look so peaceful perched up high, feathers puffed out and gleaming.

I continue to push my way into the coop, crushing dung with my hands and knees. The smell of creosote and warm feathery bodies makes me feel safe for some reason. I try and pull my legs under my body, but my arms kind of give way and I face-plant into the straw. Ash helps me up, shaking uncontrollably with laughter, his cheeks all pink and lovely with the effort of keeping it in.

"Piss off," I whisper, blowing straw from my mouth.

He pulls a strand from my hair. "Your breakfast awaits."

"Won't we get caught?"

"Not likely. The Gems never venture this far from the manor."

Quickly, I gather up some eggs, all smooth and warm in my hands like paperweights. I pass them to Ash and he places them outside the coop. He turns to me and nods when he's got enough. He's about to climb out when my stomach rumbles.

He places a finger over his lips and stands so he faces me. "It's very important you don't wake them," he whispers.

"Why?" I mouth back.

"Because if you wake them, this happens." With no warning, he arches his back, turns his arms into wings, and sticks out his chin. He crows so loudly I worry he'll wake up the whole estate. Hens shriek, wings whoosh, and breasts bump into each other. I scream and laugh and shield my face with my hands.

But he clamps my arms to my sides and shouts, "Don't miss it, Violet."

We freeze, surrounded by wings and feathers. And in this chaotic, messy moment, I think to myself, *Now*, this *would make a good first-kiss scene.*

CHAPTER 21

WE EAT ALL of the eggs—scrambled over a campfire—
and fall asleep on a bed of grass beneath a silver birch.
I dream of feathers and thistledown, broken leaves
and pieces of exploding apple. The air fills with glittering specks
that stick to my lips and make it difficult to breathe. The flecks
turn to bubbles, sea foam, and I suddenly realize I'm underwater. I
glance down and see a fish tail sprouting from my torso like it
belongs. I open my mouth to scream, but I have no tongue. I have
no voice. Katie bobs opposite me, still wearing her black catsuit,
her red hair circling her face like a lion's mane.

She smiles. "You must win the prince's heart, Violet, or we will
turn to sea foam."

I open my mouth to tell her I don't know what to do, but a load
of froth emerges, spewing down my chest like vomit.

I wake with a start. I think I'm going to cry out, but the dream
retreats and I remember only the bones of it—something about
Katie and water and an overwhelming sense of threat. I glance to
Ash. He looks so peaceful, his long eyelashes flickering slightly,
and the dream slips from me completely.

I touch his cheek with the back of my fingers. He feels warm and soft and real. We fell asleep barely touching. But now we coil together, swaddled in our own body heat, our chests rising and falling in complete synchrony. I notice how well our bodies fit together, and for the first time in forever, I feel completely at peace.

The sun begins to fade, and I realize we've slept most of the day. Which means I will hang in four days . . . which means the ball starts soon. This thought shatters my peace. I sit up, knocking Ash with my shoulder, opening my mouth in panic. For some reason, I'm surprised by how free my tongue feels as I shout the words, "Shit! The ball."

We run all the way back to the Imp-hut, sleep blurring our eyes.

"Where have you been?" Nate says as we push through the door.

Saskia's gaze swings between me and Ash, her face locked in this suspicious frown. "Come here, bedhead. We need you to look waitress-ready."

She washes my face with a scratchy cloth and pulls the remaining strands of straw from my hair. I'm hoping she assumes they're from the bunks, but judging from the amount of huffing and puffing, I'm fooling no one.

She rubs rouge into my cheeks and arranges my hair in a tousled updo. Ash watches me with a shy smile on his face. "You look beautiful, Violet."

An echo from canon: the exact words Ash said to Rose just before she headed off to the ball. But real Ash—*my* Ash—sounds more assertive, less needy.

Saskia and Nate both glare at him.

"Yeah, well, she's off-limits. Got it?" Saskia says.

Ash shrugs. "Doesn't stop her looking beautiful."

I try and bury the little smile that tugs at the corners of my mouth.

I arrive at the ballroom an hour before the party begins. I remember that Willow called it his coming-of-age ball, probably to save my feelings, but its real name is a Gallows Ball, thrown for a Gem debutante just before they attend their first Gallows Dance. Yet another way of mocking the Imps. My jaw clenches.

I banish the thought from my brain and focus on successfully completing the next part of the story; on making sure those two pieces of thread stay closely intertwined. All I need to do is serve at the ball, gaze longingly at Willow all night, and then hang back when the guests leave. Then, I get to star in one of my favorite scenes. Willow and Rose dancing to no music in the deserted ballroom, the bloom that Rose gave him pinned to his lapel. It was so beautiful. Loads better than that crappy stable. Hopefully, it will set the scene for our first kiss.

I take a second to absorb my surroundings—my favorite set. Double doors lead to a sweeping staircase that takes you onto the marble floor—a giant, polished ice rink. It looks more like something from a fairy tale than a dystopian novel, and so removed from the Imp city that it possesses a dreamlike quality. Lilac walls reach toward a white, domed ceiling. A cluster of chandeliers form the shape of a flower, several smaller petals blooming from a larger centerpiece. And something the film simply couldn't capture is the way the light bounces off everything—the crystals, the marble floor, the silverware. I think I would've stood and gaped forever if the Imp in charge, a stout, middle-aged woman with a mustache, didn't bark up the stairs, "Move it, new girl, you're on drinks."

The Imps busy themselves, setting out hors d'oeuvres and floral arrangements. They watch the food hungrily, and I feel a sympathetic grumble in my stomach. We look smarter than usual, dressed in the regulation gray suits reserved for special Gem occasions such as this. I should feel masculine, but four words beat over and over in my head: *You look beautiful, Violet.* I try and hide these words away, aware that I shouldn't be thinking of Ash when I need to get the canon back on track, but they just keep popping back into my head.

I set out the champagne flutes on trays, my white regulation gloves preventing contamination from my dirty Imp hands.

"Attention," Mustache calls.

We stand in a neat little line. Heads bowed and gloved hands clasped before us. The string quartet begins to play, and I try not to stare at their impossibly elegant Gem fingers dancing up and down the strings. I think of Katie, the way her hair falls across her face as she strikes her bow against the strings of her cello. There's something far more alive, far more beautiful, about her imperfect face scowling with concentration when compared to these airbrushed, uniform Gems.

The guests arrive. The women look like a parade of Disney princesses, the men all handsome in tailored suits. I try to remain invisible and avoid eye contact while offering drinks, a difficult task that requires all my effort.

"Oh my, Howard! Look," one Gem cries. She looks Asian, and has amazing long black hair and full red lips. I remember this scene from canon. Two horribly patronizing Gems talking really loudly about Rose as though she couldn't hear. Howard Stoneback, the nephew of the Gem president, and his wife. At least it means the canon is dragging us along, even if I do want to smack them in the face. "This Imp is *almost* pretty." She points a manicured nail right in my face.

Howard laughs, his blond curls bounce around his face. "Oh, yes. Stranger things, darling, stranger things."

"Get a photo." She stands next to me and smiles, her sticky perfume invading my nostrils.

"Darling, don't stand so close to the Imps. They've scrubbed up tonight, but they're still . . . you know . . . dirty." His voice strengthens, in search of an admiring ear. "And as the president's *only* nephew, I demand that standards be upheld."

Standards, indeed! I know from canon that Howard regularly frequents brothels. *Imp* brothels, at that. I look at my boots so they don't see my smirk.

Mrs. Stoneback steps away. "Quite right, darling, the champagne's making me giddy." This doesn't stop her grabbing another glass, her scarlet nails tapping on the stem. They hurry away, laughing. I force my features into a neutral expression and imagine spitting in their drinks—this cheers me up.

Before long, the room swells with music and laughter and the air is thick with perfume and the fizz of champagne. I continue to navigate the thirsty masses by their reflections in the marble floor, clutching a tray of glasses and ordering my arms not to tremble.

A deep, sonorous voice cuts through the chatter and the violins. It must be Jeremy Harper. I risk a quick look, aware that all other eyes will be trained on him. He looks like Willow, but with none of the warmth, none of the softness. He doesn't look much older than thirty, but the skin around his eyes looks a little too tight, a little too shiny, and I suspect a surgical knife has slowed down the aging process. Even genetic enhancement can't prevent aging completely. "Thank you for joining us for our son's Gallows Ball. For eighteen wonderful years, we have watched him mature into the man he is today. And next week he will attend his first

Gallows Dance, and now . . ." He leaves a dramatic pause, just like he did in canon, and a drumroll builds, reminiscent of the count-down to death at the Gallows Dance. I shudder in spite of the heating. ". . . the time has come for him to dance his very own Gallows Dance. So let's get this party in full swing." He mimes pulling a rope around his neck, sticking out his tongue and cross-ing his eyes. The crowd laughs. This pissed me off when I read the book and watched the film, but now I feel this hot fury, this sense of injustice filling my chest like a noxious gas. I notice the flutes on my tray quivering slightly. I glance at the other Imps, but they con-ceal the dark, twisting shapes that must fill their heads as their misery is openly mocked. Years of practice, I guess.

The music builds and Willow appears at the top of the stair-case. He looks stunning—hair swept to one side, skin even warmer beneath the bright light of the chandeliers—and he wears a navy suit that really contrasts with the copper of his eyes. I try to let some of the anger go, anticipating his gaze meeting mine, that shy, boy-ish smile. But something is very wrong. My heart jams in my chest. Not only is he missing my rose stem from his lapel, but an equally stunning Gem girl stands beside him. *Oh God, in canon he attended the ball alone.* I feel the tray tip and some champagne spills from the flutes. I try to steady it, try to focus through the fog of my own panic.

Who is this mystery Gem girl?

She wears a flowing dress, the color of trees after too much rain, and a simple tiara, matching the gold of her hair. Her honey-glazed skin is exactly the same shade as Willow's, making it diffi-cult to tell where his hand finishes and hers begins. For a brief moment, I almost laugh, just the thought that he might want *me.* Of course he wants this beautiful, honey-colored doll—every Ken needs a Barbie. They walk down the staircase in perfect sync, and she smiles like a bride approaching the altar.

Their feet touch the floor at precisely the same moment and he sweeps her into the center of the room beneath the grand chandelier. The crowd breathes a collective sigh as the couple begins to waltz. I can feel sweat beading between my inferior breasts, the air growing clotted and dense. *How am I meant to compete with her?*

The Gems begin to waltz in their pairs, closing around Willow and his mystery partner, obscuring my view. I stand completely still, just trying not to drop my tray. The not-staring rule completely evades me now, but nobody seems to notice. Through glimpses of fabric and flawless skin, I see Willow laughing.

The waltz finishes and Barbie walks in my general direction. I stare at her reflection in the marble and shamelessly wish I were her. She moves closer, and I continue to avert my eyes, not yet daring to steal a proper look. I decide to wait until she passes—that way she's less likely to notice the slave studying her face. But she seems to walk straight toward me. I lift my tray slightly, my heart trembling beneath my shirt. Her hand connects with a champagne flute, her nails smooth and long and perfectly formed, and I snatch a quick glance at her face. To my surprise, she smiles at me.

Only when she speaks do I finally recognize her. "You've got to try some of this, Vi. It's so much nicer than the cheap pear stuff." She takes a massive slurp and coughs a little.

"Alice!" I feel this huge surge of relief, just knowing she's OK. "Alice, what are you doing here?"

"Shhh, I can't be seen talking to the riffraff." She winks a long, fluttery lash, and as she glances toward the exit, I notice how the curls piled on her head look slightly paler, slightly waxier, than her natural hair. "Meet me outside in half an hour and I'll explain."

The minute hand on the grandfather clock seems to crawl forward, the air seems to grow even thicker and more resistant, my tray heavier in spite of the diminishing load. In canon, Willow watched Rose all night, his eyes darting feverishly to her mouth as he recalled the texture of her lips. But he doesn't even look my way. He's transfixed by Alice. I get this feeling in the pit of my stomach like I'm back at Comic-Con, watching Anime Alice with Russell Boozer-Jones. *Well, you really are in Wonderland now.* I know I should feel angry, scared even, about Alice messing up canon like this, but I just feel jealous. And I can't quite unpick my matted thoughts. How did Alice infiltrate the ball? Was this the special job Thorn mentioned back at headquarters?

Finally, Alice kisses his cheek and dashes out the door. I almost expect her to lose a glass slipper on the way. I tell Mustache I need to pee and slip out of the room, using the staff door at the back.

The cool evening air catches in my nostrils, and the stretch of lawn—the stillness of twilight—calms me for a moment. I close my eyes and listen to the lilting melody floating on the air. Something beautiful I can't quite reach.

I tread lightly, moving across the gravel, heading toward the side of the manor where I expect her to be.

"Violet!" Her golden head bobs around the side of the building. She beckons me.

I reach her and she pushes me back so a privet hedge shields us from view.

"It's so good to see you," she says.

We embrace and the jealousy grows blunt at the edges, the familiar scent of cherry blossom and lemongrass filling my head. The whaleboning of her dress digs into my ribs, but I continue to hold her, allowing myself to acknowledge just how much I've missed her.

She holds me out at arm's length and looks me up and down. "You make a good Rose."

"Thanks, you make a good Gem."

"Aw, thanks."

I fail to return her smile. "Alice, what's going on?"

She smooths down the fabric of her dress, avoiding eye contact. "So Thorn asked me to pose as a Gem."

"Yeah, I kind of guessed . . . But why?"

"He wants me as a backup plan, in case you fail. There's more than one way to skin a cat and get those Gem secrets. He doesn't believe the alternate universe thing, can't blame him, really—he thinks Baba may have lost the plot, excuse the pun."

Just at that moment, the band bursts into a lively jig. She turns her head as though she can see the music floating on the breeze.

My body grows rigid, paralyzed, and frustration builds deep inside, pushing upward and outward until I think I might burst. "But that's not why we're here. In case you've forgotten, we're here to make sure Willow still falls for Rose. To make sure the story runs its course so we can go home. Remember? The psychic lady with no face . . . 'You must save the Imps, Violet.'"

"Yeah, but Thorn's priority is still getting Willow to blab about Daddykins."

"And your priority is . . . ?"

"To help you, obviously."

"By hitting on Prince Charming." I tap my foot—she hates it when I do that.

She wrinkles up her nose, her makeup cracking like a china glaze. "Look, Violet, things have deviated from canon already.

You're not Rose for a start—you may know her lines, but you're still not her. You need all the help you can get."

This tugs at some deep-rooted insecurity. "What's that supposed to mean?"

"Do you know how eligible Willow is? Seriously, every unmarried Gem girl wants a piece of him, he's gorgeous and kind and rich—"

"Says the unmarried Gem girl."

"Violet, don't be an idiot. If I'm seen with Willow, then I'm putting off the Gem competition and you stand a better chance."

"A likely story," I snap.

"I'm just trying to help."

The insecurity grows and grows until all I can hear are the words *Violet the Virgin*. "What, you think I can't do this on my own? You think I can't make a guy fall for me?"

"Not just any guy—Willow Harper. You know, the most perfect man in the universe . . . this universe and ours." She makes a circular motion with her finger.

"Oh, so if he was an ugly loser, then I'd stand a chance."

"That's not what I'm saying."

"Then what exactly are you saying?" My tone rises, and I realize this is the first argument we've had since she stole my red dress and wore it to a party back in Year Ten. I remember feeling so angry, not because she didn't ask me, or even because she slopped garlic dip all down the front, but because she looked better in it than me.

She exhales quickly. "I'm saying, we just need to get Willow to fall for you and follow you to the city. How it happens doesn't matter."

"Jesus, Alice, this isn't some little fanfic exercise—you can't just rewrite the plot and hope for the best. We're the butterfly, remember, flapping our massive wings. Just the slightest change and the consequences could be drastic."

"Yes, but you also said the story *wants* to unfold. Anyway, I'm not rewriting the plot, I'm ensuring it hits its key climax moments."

A bitter laugh erupts from my lips. "Yeah, I can see climaxing is your main concern."

"Now you just sound jealous."

"Well, maybe I am. You get to be with Willow, the most perfect man in existence, and I have to slum it in the Imp-hut, worrying about me and Ash, Saskia breathing down my neck, and you get to live like—like . . ."—I gesture around me, to the manor, the estate, the stars—"a Gem."

Her brow knots. "You're worried about you and Ash?"

I stutter on my words. "Well, not worried . . ."

"Seriously, the hero with the big dong and the massive crush? He's just background noise in canon, you know that, yeah?"

I study the ground, dodging her accusatory stare, banning thoughts of feathers and potential first-kiss scenes from my mind. I notice how intricate her diamanté sandals look in comparison with my boots. "Of course I know that."

"You're a hypocrite, Violet."

The band stops and the world seems strangely empty. Flat. Like a reflection of itself. I open my mouth to respond, but only a strange hissing noise escapes.

We stare at each other for a moment, and then she does this familiar thing—she rubs the little split heart between her thumb and forefinger. A sign she's anxious. I hadn't realized she was wearing it till now.

I feel myself soften. "Where are you staying?"

"With a Gem family who live nearby. Thorn has a lot of connections—there are Symps in all sorts of places."

"So they know you're—"

"An Imp?" She laughs. "Yeah, they know. I don't think they believe it, though."

"Try not to sound too pleased."

She glares at me. "Look, I need to get back to Willow."

"Wait." I catch her arm. "How did you end up as his date?"

"I need to get back to Willow," she repeats. "If he comes looking for me and sees us together he's bound to get suspicious."

I know she's right, but I can't bring myself to agree. "Yeah, and I need to get back to waiting on you and your Gem friends, slave that I am."

"For God's sake, Violet, I'm an Imp, too."

But I think of those honey hands wrapped around her waist and the jealousy combines with anger, a lethal combination. "You're also supposed to be my best friend—turns out you don't know how to act like either." I turn on my heel and slam my feet into the gravel, my head full and hot and ready to burst.

CHAPTER 22

THE REST OF the night passes in a blur of perfect teeth and multicolored dresses. I complete my duties robotically, just trying not to drop that blasted tray. Gradually, the music ends and the guests disperse. I watch Alice and Willow walk up the stairs together, his hand resting on the small of her back, and I feel the pressure of a thousand tears building behind my eyelids. He will never kiss me now, and I may never go home.

I know it's pathetic, desperate even, but I hang back just like in canon, sweeping the floor. The rhythmic action soothes my mind, the swish of the broom drowning out the words in my head: *Violet the Virgin.*

I sweep and sweep until the first signs of dawn push through the windows. I've let everyone down—Nate, Katie, even Alice, though I think she may deserve it. Finally, I let the tears flow. They drop from my chin and splat on the floor, transforming to smears beneath the bristles of my broom. The treachery burns deep in my chest—how could Alice sabotage our only hope of going home? I know she's always had this bunny boiler, fangirl crush on Willow, and I know she loves being a Gem, but this is different, this is our lives. Now I have to return to the Imp-hut and look Nate in the

eyes as I tell him what's happened. And then an even more terrifying thought rams its way into the forefront of my brain . . . *Thorn
will kill Katie.*

Katie. I wish she was here instead of Alice. She would never
sleaze all over Willow. She would never put the Gems on a
pedestal—she would call them a bunch of fuckturnips and follow
it up with a quote from Shakespeare. I really miss her.

I pull my sleeve across my face and step into the cool of the
dawn. The faint outlines of last night's stars still blink in the sky,
speaking of what could have been. Slowly, I drag my boots over the
lawn, hoping that if I walk really slowly, I may never reach the hut.

"Rose." The voice moves through the air like a song.

I turn and see Willow striding up the hill toward me. He's lost
the bow tie, and sweat glistens on that triangle of honey-colored
skin. He looks tired, but he smiles and lifts his hands. "I promised
you that last dance."

It feels like my feet have sprouted claws and I'm unable to
move, except for the huge smile reaching across my face. "You took
your time." Beneath the excitement, I feel this surge of panic—
we're totally off-script. I have no lines to recite. And this isn't Ash,
this isn't some background noise, this is Willow—this *matters*.

But Willow just smiles. "I prefer fashionably late." He places
one hand at the base of my spine and gently takes my hand in the
other. The heat of his body travels through my clothes. The skin on
my throat suddenly feels very exposed. He hums a soft melody
under his breath and we begin to turn.

I decide to just take a risk. "Who was that girl?"

The humming stops, but we continue to revolve.

"Who? Alice?" he says.

I nod. And I can't help feeling a little peeved that his mouth has formed her real name and not mine.

"I met her yesterday at some social—a friend of a friend. She just seemed to . . . really know me. It felt like she could read my mind. And Mother had been nagging at me to get a date."

I tuck my face into his chest so he can't see my scowl. She used her knowledge of his character to her advantage. It feels like she's cheated.

"Well, you looked good together." I try to keep my voice light. This close, I can smell his aftershave and the scent of champagne on his breath.

He laughs, his chest vibrating beneath my ear. "No, we didn't, we looked awful, like a copy of a copy. We all look the same, us Gems, I get so bored of looking at us."

"You should mix with us Imps a bit more, you know, slum it."

"Is that an invite?"

"Yeah, anytime you fancy hanging out at the Imp-hut, just let me know."

We stop revolving and he holds me away from his body so I can really take in the beauty of his face—so perfect, it's almost bland.

"Alice was quite charming," he says. "But she said a few things that really made me . . ." I get this twinge in my stomach, anticipating the stab of further betrayal. But he chuckles softly to himself and says, ". . . miss you."

The betrayal thins in my veins. "Like what?"

"Oh, you know, she said something about intrigue being at the core of attraction, and of course I thought of you. I know I said I loved the way you were so free, but I also love the way you can be so, so . . . awkward, and real. You're such a strange combination, you really fascinate me." He pauses. "You remind me of what it is to be *human*."

This really makes me smile. Not just because he uses the word *human*, an old-fashioned term never used in the world of *The Gallows Dance*, as it implies the Imps and Gems belong to one species, but also because he likes *me*. Violet. The branches slapping my face, the hair in my mouth, he finds it fascinating.

He takes both my hands in his. "And then Alice said something really beautiful. She said that you could spend your whole life wandering the earth and never find that one person who makes you feel complete. So if you ever meet that person, you should cling to them with both hands and never let them go." He pulls my hands into his chest and smiles.

The quote from the book. Alice was helping me all along. I feel like a maple seed, spinning and floating through the sky. The betrayal disperses completely, replaced by pure love for my best friend.

"Rose?" he says.

I shake my head. "Sorry, yes. Never let them go." I take a deep breath. It's time to seal the deal—to get the canon back on track and go home. I smile into his beautiful face and say, "It's like we were born to . . ."—and as if to prove the point, he joins in, and we utter the same words—". . . fit together."

My mind reels back to earlier this evening. How Ash and I fitted so perfectly together beneath the silver birch, curled up in the grass. But I order my brain to stay on track, to stay in the moment. I stare into Willow's eyes and notice how bright they look against the watery morning sky. He studies my face, tracing a line from the corner of my mouth to my cheekbone with his index finger.

Then, finally, he kisses me.

We kiss for a long time, neither of us pulling away. I love the scent of his skin, the pressure of his lips, the gentle flick of his tongue against mine. It's a perfect kiss, not a gherkin in sight. But I don't feel moved. I no longer spin like a maple seed. It just isn't how I'd imagined it all those times I sat on the sofa, dreaming it was me in his arms. Maybe my expectation was just too high—he is, after all, only human. Genetically tweaked, but still just a man.

Eventually, the kiss comes to a natural end. He stands tall and smiles down at me. I ignore that nagging, disappointed feeling and tell myself I'm only doing this to go home. I'm about to kiss him good-bye when a slight movement draws my attention. In the elm trees on the horizon, peering at us through the leaves.

The palest blue eyes I've ever seen.

CHAPTER 23

I spend the rest of the morning looking for Ash. I scour the estate while the sun lights up the sky all orange and pink, this burning sensation growing in my chest. I finally give up and return to the Imp-hut, the contents of my head turned to pulp.

I push through the door, amazed by how heavy it feels. Nate sits at the table, drinking tea next to Matthew. I notice with a pang of jealousy that they're playing cards.

"Well?" Nate says, his face a real mixture of excitement and fear, like he's just sneaked a horror film past Mum.

"Nailed it." I try to look happy, but I think of Ash's face peering from the leaves and I just feel like crying.

I roll onto my bunk, let the cotton divider separate me from the world, and I pray for the numbness of sleep. But Nate ducks under the makeshift curtain, his sandy head bobbing into view. He speaks quietly so Matthew won't hear, but an unfamiliar sharpness hardens his voice. "You've just scored Willow . . . why do you look like someone's died?"

I exhale heavily. "It's just, I don't know . . . Ash saw."

"Saw what?"

"Me—scoring Willow."

"So?"

I cover my eyes with my hands, secretly wishing Katie were here, even Alice. You can't really talk girl-stuff with your little brother. But right now, he's my only option. "So . . . it felt weird."

"Violet, Ash is just some little dweeb who follows you around looking lost and in love. Remember that."

"No, you're thinking of Ash from canon. My Ash is completely different."

"Since when was he *your* Ash?"

"You know what I mean, *this* Ash, *real* Ash." I roll onto my front so I can see Nate better. It feels like we're in a tent, the light sifting through the dirty white divider, contained and safe in our own little pod. "He's so different from canon-Ash, he's funny and edgy and not in the least bit lost . . . He delivers babies in his spare time." Nate opens his mouth to object, but I keep on talking. "But you know, part of me wonders if he's different because *I'm* so different from Rose, maybe he can be himself with me, maybe I bring out a different side to him, a *better* side to him. Maybe we've just got that thing, you know, that connection."

"Oh God," Nate says. "You've fallen for the wrong guy. I *knew* this was going to happen. The stupid way you gawk at him."

"No . . . no . . . it's just . . ." I process the end of his sentence. "I gawk at him?"

"Look, sis, you're Cinderella, and Willow's Prince Charming and Ash is . . ."

"Buttons," I say. This analogy keeps popping into my brain, especially with the ball so fresh in my memory.

"Yes. Bloody Buttons."

"Nate, don't swear."

He shakes his head, irritated. "Cinderella does not end up with

Buttons. She marries the prince and lives in a palace and—and—
she hangs at the Gallows Dance so we can all go home."

"OK, OK." I roll onto my back again, indicating the end of
the conversation.

"Just forget about Ash," Nate says. "Focus on what really
matters, and quit flapping those wings of yours."

I know he's right. I just need to stick to the script—play it safe.
And what kind of a lame fairy tale has the princess falling for the
butler, anyway? But *Cinderella* always was my favorite fairy tale,
and I've always had a soft spot for the underdog.

" 'Night, Vi," Nate whispers, even though it's late morning.

"Yeah, 'night. Sweet dreams."

"You, too."

But when I finally fall asleep, my dreams are anything but
sweet. I'm kneeling—bent double—over these flagstones, scrubbing at a hearth that is covered in red paint. I dip my scrub brush in
a pail, slop water on the paint, and I scrub and scrub and scrub. But
the red won't budge. And then I hear a voice narrating my favorite
fairy tale. It sounds like Dad. *Poor Cinderella desperately wanted to
go to the ball, but her evil stepmother would not allow it.* I wipe a giant
tear from my cheek, leaving a crimson smudge across my skin. The
narrator changes his tone, like he talks to someone offstage. *I feel
kind of silly, are you sure she can hear me?* I hear a woman's voice. *Yes.
I'm sure. Carry on.*

I can smell medicine and detergent and aftershave and coffee.
*Poor Cinderella cried all night, dreaming of waltzing and shimmering
ball gowns.* I look up from my scrubbing. "Dad?" I shout. "Dad?
Where are you?" I stand, knocking over the pail, its contents spilling onto the floor. But it isn't water—it's just more of that damned
red paint. A noise draws my attention, a smothered groan mixed

with squelching like oozing liquid. I look up, and that's when I notice them for the first time—strewn across the beams like in some disgusting slasher movie. A paper chain of dead Imps, dripping blood onto my floor.

I look at my hands. They're covered in blood and they hold a noose.

I wake, choking on a scream.

In three days, I will hang.

I lower myself from my bunk, careful not to wake Nate, and cross to the sink. It's dusk, and I console myself with the thought that I at least slept for most of the day. Tentatively, I rinse my face with the cold, brown-flecked water. These dreams . . . they seem so real. Sometimes I wonder if *this* is the dream and real-Violet lies asleep in bed. But the water stinging my skin feels too cold, and the pain in my back from sleeping on a block of wood feels too intense, and the early evening chatter of the Day-Imps as they leave and the Night-Imps as they arrive sounds far too cowed and subdued to be generated by my unconscious. It's just too lifelike, too coherent, too detailed. *Shame*, I think to myself.

Saskia's voice cuts through me. "We got word from headquarters."

I turn around, my face still dripping with icy water. She looks at a tattered envelope in her hand as though debating whether to give it to me or not. She sighs, her conscience finally winning the battle, and slaps it against my chest. "It's from your little redheaded mate."

"Katie?"

"Don't pretend you got more mates than you have—of course Katie."

"Is she OK?"

"Read the bloody letter."

I dash to my bunk and pull the divider back into position again, cocooned in my own little world. *Please let her be OK, please let her be OK.* I can't open the envelope fast enough, yet my fingers seem to be on a go-slow, trembling and stumbling over the seal. I slip the letter out, trying not to tear it in my desperation.

A page of Katie's handwriting. I love it—it's an extension of her, neat and small with a bit of an edge. I'm used to seeing it scribbled across a notebook in English lessons, sentences like, *Will this bloody lesson ever end? I'm starving! What I wouldn't give for a Nando's right now!* It's so peculiar, seeing that same writing stare at me from a sheet of crinkled, ancient parchment while I hide behind a dirty sheet. I steady my hands and start to read.

> *Vi,*
>
> *Thorn said I should write to you. He thinks it will help keep you focused on your mission. At the very least, it's something for me to do. Christ, I am soooo bored. I'm still in that horrible little room, although Thorn gave me a beat-up old sofa and helped me clean the window so I can watch the sunset, so it isn't AS bad.*
>
> *I wish I could somehow help. I feel so bloody useless stuck here day and night. And I've started eating the rat stew—you're right, it tastes OK. Who knew? Anyway, I was trying to think if there was anything I could do to help, other than Alice's suggestion, and I decided the only thing I can offer is some words of infinite wisdom. Sadly, they're not my own.*
>
> *All the world's a stage,*
> *And all the men and women merely players,*
> *They have their exits and their entrances,*

And one man in his time plays many parts.

(As You Like It, Shakespeare)

What I'm trying to say is, you can do this, Vi. I know
you can.

And did you know that Shakespeare first coined the
phrase spunk rocket? (Alice believed this for a whole
week, daft cow!)

Anyway, good luck, my lovely Viola. I know you can
do it. Stick out your tits and smile like a hooker.

Lots of love, K xxxx

P.S. If you're reading this, Thorn, see . . . I told you I
was literate!

Viola. She's never called me that before. I think she's refer-
ring to a character from *Twelfth Night*, one of her favorite plays. I
don't know it well, only from what she's told me, but I think
Viola is the one who pretends to be a boy. I can see why she made
the parallel, me pretending to be someone I'm not. What I can't
remember is how the play ended. I just hope Viola didn't die a
hideous death.

I fold the letter and carefully slip it into my overalls, her words
warming my chest like I've just tucked a hot-water bottle down my
front. She's safe, at least for now. And she's taken Alice's suggestion
on board, which I think is code for flirting with Thorn. I hope
she knows what she's doing. Current-Thorn is so unstable, even
more so than canon-Thorn. If she overdoes the flirting, he may get
a little too friendly, but this thought makes me feel sick, so I push it
from my mind.

Nate's sandy head appears, his eyes sticky with sleep. "So what scene is it tonight, sis?"

"It's the one where Willow teaches Rose to read." I smile at the irony—receiving Katie's letter the same night I have to pretend to be illiterate.

"Oh yeah, well, that should be easy enough."

I nod. "Katie's doing OK." I think about showing him the letter, but I feel an odd sense of possession and I don't want to share it. "We just got word from HQ. Apparently, she's bored out of her tree but she's doing fine."

Nate grins. "Has she got down and dirty with Thorn yet?"

I whack the top of his head. "God, you're nearly as bad as Alice."

Later that evening, I perch on a grassy edge of the road, waiting for Ash at the bus stop, the sharp evening air drilling beneath my overalls. I'm desperate to talk with him about the kiss, but completely unsure of what to say. Eventually, he arrives, the bus fumes causing him to cough.

He sees me and smiles. "Hey."

"Hey," I reply. Well, that wasn't so bad.

We fall into step, side by side, making our way toward the Imp-hut. He drags his hand along the privet hedge, rustling the leaves as he goes. He seems fine. I begin to relax a little.

"To what do I owe the honor?" he asks.

I raise a quizzical eyebrow.

He laughs. "My welcoming party of one."

"Oh yeah, right. I just, you know, wanted to check you were . . ." I fumble with my words. "That you were . . . you know . . . OK." *Smooth, Violet.*

"Yeah. Why wouldn't I be?"

"No reason."

Denial. This actually works well for me. We just won't acknowledge my thing with the Gem—the enemy. The blood on my hands. Ash never knew in canon, after all, so why should we talk about it now? I'm just ensuring those two pieces of thread continue to wrap around each other. I know this should make me feel better, but it doesn't. I realize I was hoping he would be upset—jealous. What's wrong with me?

"So, you enjoyed yourself at the ball last night?" he says in an overly casual voice, like he's trying a little too hard not to care.

"Yeah. It was OK."

"You certainly looked like you were enjoying yourself."

"I guess."

He stops walking and takes my arms in his hands. I can feel the heat of his skin sinking into mine. "Look, Violet—or Lily or Daisy or whatever floral name you're going by today—sorry about last night. I wasn't spying or anything, I was just worried about you 'cause the rest of the Imps serving at the ball had all come back. I just thought, you know, you might have gotten hurt, or lost, or something."

I think I may implode from guilt. *He* is apologizing to *me*. "Don't be daft. I didn't think you were spying," I say.

"You just looked pretty shocked when you saw me."

"I was."

He looks at the path and fidgets with the fabric of his overalls. "So you—you really like this Gem guy?"

I shrug. "I dunno."

"It's just . . ." He takes both of my hands in his. "It's just, I think you should know what you're getting involved in, for your own sake."

"I'll hang if I get caught, I know that." The word *hang* still causes my stomach to lurch.

He meets my gaze—causing my stomach to lurch once again, but for a very different reason—and shakes his head. "That's not what I meant. I meant the *type* of people you're getting involved with."

"Willow's OK. I know he's a Gem, but really, he's a nice guy."

He explores my face with his eyes like he's searching for a hidden answer. I can still pick out the blue of his irises, even in the half-light—the color of a blackbird's egg. "There's something I've got to show you," he says. "But we need the cover of complete darkness."

I try not to look too interested, my curiosity roused. "But I'm meeting—"

He laughs. "You're meeting Willow."

"Yeah."

"OK, then after you've met Willow. I'll wait next to the chicken coop. Promise you'll come. But don't tell anyone, OK? It's really important it stays between us."

I think of that bastard butterfly, inadvertently spreading her natural disasters. I think of the canon and of home, and Katie's letter feels like it's burning a hole in my skin. A few unscripted conversations, the odd innocent stroll, well, I can justify those, surely. But a secret nighttime unveiling? I may as well give the butterfly a baseball bat and let the havoc commence.

But when Ash trickles his fingers down the backs of my arms, he leaves two parallel trails of light, and before I can stop myself, I've already said the words: "I promise."

Later that night, I meet Willow. It's the scene in canon where Willow taught Rose to read. A sweet, tender scene that showed their fledgling relationship really starting to fly. Willow smuggled this ancient book out of the manor. He'd stolen it from a museum when he was just a boy and kept it hidden under his bed. A book of Imp poems, one of the few to survive the Gem burning of the Imp books all those years ago.

The lovebirds huddled in the loft of the old hay barn, crouched over a paraffin lamp, running their fingers over the letters. I follow the script, cuddled into Willow's chest, but I struggle to concentrate. Not just because I know how to read, but because I can't stop thinking about what Ash said.

"So the curly letter there, that's a *C*," Willow whispers into my ear. It really tickles.

I nod, but my mind won't stop turning. What does Ash think is so important? There's nothing in canon to give me any clue. I should probably just leave it, stick to canon and focus on my end goal—returning home.

"Rose?" Willow says.

"Sorry, yes, *C*, like *cup* and *card*."

"That's right." He turns the page, eyebrows raised, unable to hide his surprise at what a fast learner I am.

My mind wanders again. Why would this mysterious revelation make me think so badly of Willow? Surely, that can only be a bad thing. I mean, I don't need to like Willow to complete the story, but it kind of helps. No, I definitely shouldn't go to the chicken coop tonight.

"Rose, are you even interested?" Willow says.

Dammit. We're off-script. I kiss him on the cheek to distract him. "Sorry, go ahead, what's that letter there? The one shaped like a zero?" Imps can read numbers because of their slave tattoos.

"That's an *O*. As in *orange*."

We launch back into our lines, but my brain is elsewhere. I barely notice when Willow starts to kiss me. I'd forgotten about the making-out scene. It seemed so romantic—Rose and Willow nestled in the straw, basking in the flickering glow of a paraffin lamp. But in reality, the straw pricks my face and the lamp is a massive fire hazard, and I just feel guilty for kissing Willow when I'm thinking about Ash. I suddenly wish we *were* in a movie or a book, then I could just hit the fast-forward button or flick through the pages at record speed.

"So, I'll see you tomorrow?" Willow asks.

"I'd like that."

Willow helps me down the wooden ladder, book tucked beneath his arm. I feel a swell of relief—the scene finally drawing to a close. I can't believe I didn't enjoy that. What's my problem? It's *Willow*, for Christ's sake. My fangirl crush since I was fifteen.

This place must be getting to me.

We share a final kiss, which is a little on the sloppy side, and I watch him meander back to the manor, his silhouette fading into the dark. I think I said my lines right; he certainly seemed happy enough. More than happy—I think he has genuine feelings for me. I guess this isn't a script for him. It's real.

And I think I've just figured out what my problem is. Love can't be prescribed or thrust upon you. Love doesn't follow a script. Falling in love is about falling into unpredictability—it's about taking a risk.

And on that note, I run toward the chicken coop.

CHAPTER 24

I SEE THE FLICKER of Ash's flashlight—like the beam of a dying lighthouse—before I see him. I move toward it until I can hear his breath. He leans against the coop, and I notice how monochrome he looks in the dark, the white of his skin against the black of his hair. I catch his scent on the breeze, weaving beneath the smell of creosote, and I inhale a little deeper.

"I wasn't sure you'd come." He whispers, even though there's nobody else around.

"You said it was important."

"It is." He shines the flashlight in my face. "But you have to promise not to tell a soul."

"Yeah, 'course."

He moves the beam across my face, as though trying to see beneath my skin and into the contents of my head. "Because it could end up getting us both killed . . . I mean it."

"Shit, Ash. Just show me." I hate change, I hate surprises. I should be hiding in the Imp-hut, practicing my lines with Nate. Yet, being here with Ash, I find I actually want to take a risk— perhaps this universe is forcing me to let go a little, desensitizing me to all things new. Or maybe being with him just makes me feel safe enough to shut my eyes and jump. Maybe he brings out a different side of me . . . a *better* side.

He takes my hand—I think through practicality rather than intimacy, but it thaws my insides all the same—and leads me away from the coop, even deeper into the estate. We walk in silence for a mile or so, Ash constantly glancing behind his shoulder like we may be followed. This makes me a little uneasy, but the curiosity chips away at the fear, and that safe, steady hand gripping mine stops me from flipping out. We walk through meadows, climb a stone wall, cross a wobbly bridge, and, finally, enter a wood.

The temperature falls and a rich scent of pine and damp grass fills my head. The leaves block out any ambient light and the beam of his flashlight only just alerts us to the trunks before we bash into them. I can't remember ever being in the woods at night, only in the day back at home, picnicking among harebells—more Mary Poppins than Blair Witch. But everything seems scarier in the black—especially the noises. Cawing, hooting, caterwauling. I focus on the sound of Ash and me, crunching through the undergrowth, drawing in mouthfuls of stiff night air. It's slow going; zigzagging between trunks, stumbling on tree roots and bundles of weeds.

"We're nearly there," he whispers.

Something bursts from the undergrowth. A whirl of feathers, a loud clacking noise, something warm and soft brushing up against my face. I fall to the ground, too scared to scream.

"It's just a pheasant," he says.

He follows the brown body into the tops of the trees with his beam. I try and catch my breath, my heart punching into my rib cage.

"Come on." He helps me stand. I can just make out the glint of his teeth, no doubt he's grinning that massive grin.

"Don't you dare laugh, you massive dolt," I whisper, before laughing myself.

He places a finger over his lips and hushes me, and it feels like we're back at the chicken coop the first time round, like he's going to arch his back and start clucking like a hen.

"There's nobody here," I say.

He places the flashlight beneath his chin so it lights up his face. He looks like an evil hobgoblin. "We'll see about that."

A few more trunks, a few more roots, and suddenly I realize I can see without Ash's flashlight. A clearing. The moon high above, its light thinned by a smudge of clouds.

"Ta-da," he says, his voice still low.

"There's nothing here."

It's just a clearing. A stretch of dirt, surrounded by a dense forest and a lattice of weeds. A pocket of stillness.

He runs his flashlight beam over a few of the nearby trunks, then slips his hand into a tree nook. "In here, there's a little switch."

"That's what all the fuss is about, a little switch?"

"This place is so far from the estate, nobody ever comes. But you know me, I like to explore." He fiddles with something inside the nook. The switch, I'm guessing. He looks at me, his eyes wide. "Don't you think there's something weird about this place?"

I look at the clearing. Just a load of trees. "In what way?"

He gestures with his head. "That side of the clearing looks exactly the same as this side. A mirror image. All the knots and branches and hollows . . . everything."

I peer across the stretch of dirt. I can just make out the nook of the tree, and next to it, two pale blobs—not blobs—faces. I'm about to freak out again, but something about those faces looks so familiar. "Is that *us*?"

He laughs. "It took me a while to find, but it's a cloaking device, a clever mirroring gadget. It filters out human forms in the day, but at night, I don't know, it just seems to miss us."

I hear a sharp click. He pulls his hand free.

The air in the clearing seems to shimmer for a moment. Instinctively, I grab Ash's hand. A large gray cube materializes. A bunker. I suppose it was always here, but it's as though it's fallen from the sky. A basic structure built from concrete, shorter than the trees but more than tall enough for someone to stand inside.

"What is it?" I ask.

He squeezes my hand. "It's what's inside that's more important."

Together, we circle it. It's no bigger than my bedroom back home. No windows, no door.

"There's no way in," I say.

"There is for a squirrel." He loops his hands together and boosts me up so I can reach the top of the bunker. My fingers close around the ledge of the flat roof, wet with moss and slime. I think I'm supposed to haul myself up, but it's like that bloody tree all over again, and I just kind of dangle. I hate the way I'm so helpless sometimes. Ash jumps up beside me, catching the roof with his hands and using his feet to climb the wall. Within seconds, he's peering down at me, his hair flopping over his forehead.

"Show-off," I mutter.

He pulls me up, my wrists cracking from my own weight. This high, the woods look alien, the leaves thicker, the trunks narrowing into the black of the sky. We crawl toward the center of the roof, approaching what looks like a manhole cover.

"The only way in," Ash says. He pulls a pin from his overalls and begins to tinker with the lock. I hear a reassuring *clunk*. He looks at me and grins, his eyes glass-pale in the starlight.

"Are you some sort of secret criminal mastermind?" I ask.

He shakes his head. "Just an enterprising street rat."

I help him slide the cover to one side. A faint circle of light falls on a concrete floor below, but other than this, I see only darkness.

He rests his hand on my arm and his voice suddenly changes, heavy with concern. "I know I said you needed to see this, but now we're here . . ."

"It's OK. I want to."

"Are you sure? Because once you see this, you'll never think about the Gems in the same way again."

He means Willow. I know I should probably just climb off this roof and run back to the Imp-hut. I know I should just stick to canon—safety, predictability, home. But when I stare into Ash's open face, all soft and muted in the night, I realize it's not just about taking a risk, it's about truth. And I'm sick of all these secrets, all these lies, this bloody disguise. Katie's letter feels like it's on fire again, but I don't care. I want to tell him who I really am. It's like there's an invisible wall between us, built from white lies and omissions and every type of deception known to man. I look at the weak shaft of light below and I decide one less secret can only be a good thing.

"Let's do this," I say.

Ash nods, and ever so gently, he lowers me into the bunker.

CHAPTER 25

ASH DROPS DOWN next to me. He swings the flashlight around the room. I see the odd shape, the glimpse of a reflective surface, and I get the sense of things surrounding me. "It's OK, you're safe," Ash says. He can probably hear I've stopped breathing.

I force my lungs to work again. The air tastes surprisingly clean—medicinal almost. I know that smell. Then there's the earthy scent of coffee, the freshness of star anise. And I swear I can hear Dad's voice. *Goldilocks came upon a little house in the woods. She knocked on the door, and as nobody replied, she went inside.*

I spin around, staring into the darkness. "Did you hear that?" I ask.

"What?"

Silence. Just the strange sound of bubbles and the soft whir of machinery.

"It's nothing." I must be losing my mind, all the stress, the change in sleep patterns.

"You're sure?"

"Yeah, yeah. I'm just tired."

He drapes a protective arm around my shoulders. "You ready?"

"I guess."

He raises his voice. "Lights on."

The lights overhead hum into action. The bluish glare stings my eyes, especially after stumbling through darkness for so long. I blink several times, a combination of excitement and fear chewing on my guts, and slowly, I survey the room.

A series of large cylindrical tubes line the walls, reaching from the floor to the ceiling. Each cylinder is filled with transparent fluid. Judging by the lazy motion of the bubbles, it's more viscous than water. It looks almost like a giant lava lamp, the way the fluorescent light catches the shifting globules of air. My brain struggles to make sense of the shapes suspended inside the fluid—limbs, hair, faces.

Each cylinder contains a person.

Lifeless. Naked. Eyes that stare blankly ahead.

I can feel my stomach shrinking, my soft palate arching, my tongue pulling back in my mouth. I think I'm going to puke.

"Violet, are you OK?" Ash holds me up and rubs my back.

"Are they . . . ?"

"Dead?"

I manage to nod.

"No, no, they're not dead," he says.

I swallow down something foul-tasting and approach one of the tubes, my entire body trembling. I look at the floating person. It's Willow. His tanned body completely limp. He has a tube going into his mouth and his nose, and his caramel hair wafts around his face, long and unkempt, disturbed by the bubbles that slowly drift by.

"Ash?" is about all I can manage to say.

"It isn't Willow."

For some reason, this comes as a huge relief. My pseudo-boyfriend isn't some weird alien hooked up to machines. But if he isn't Willow, who the hell is he? As if in response, the floating boy blinks.

I step back, a cry catching in my throat.

"It's OK," Ash says. "They do that sometimes."

Drawn to that face—that slack, unfeeling face—I take a step closer, the tip of my nose connecting with the glass. Ash is right, it isn't Willow. It just looks like him. But this floating boy's nose is a little crooked, his lips not quite so full. My eyes flick down his form. His body's less muscled and his legs look shorter.

I can't help but stare at his genitals. I've never seen a naked man before. Not unless you count that porn magazine Ryan left in my locker with the word *virgin* scrawled across it, or the time Mitchel Smith streaked across the football field. But up close, in real life, I've never seen a naked man. It looks kind of shriveled.

"Are you staring at his dick?" Ash asks. My gaze moves to Ash's reflection. He's smiling, his eyes full of laughter. My cheeks start to burn.

A plaque marks the base of the cylinder. DUPLICATE #1.

"Who is he?" I ask.

"Willow's brother."

"Willow doesn't have a brother."

Gently, Ash takes my shoulders and turns me so I look at the next cylinder along. "No. He has three. They're Duplicates."

Three floating boys. All so similar to Willow, just not quite so perfect.

My stomach starts convulsing again, that foul stuff fills my mouth . . . Duplicate #3 has no legs.

"His, his legs are missing." I can't tear my eyes away from the point at which his legs should join his torso. They've been removed at the pelvis, leaving his genitals intact. A perfect, surgical slice.

No blood, no scraps of tissue, just sealed-up stumps. I can hear someone breathing heavily, a panting in my ear. I realize it's me. I begin to feel dizzy, the scent of medicine returning. Coffee and star anise. *One was too hot, one was too cold, but one was just right.*

I spin in a tight circle. "There it is again."

"What?"

"That voice."

"Violet, there's no voice."

Oh God. It's in my head. The shock's making me hear things. That's just what I need, mental health problems.

"Don't worry." Ash strokes my arm. "This place plays tricks on you, it's creepy as hell." The gentle motion of his skin against mine lifts me from the panic. He's right, it's just this creepy place.

Slowly, I look at the other cylinders. Two versions of Willow's dad, three versions of Willow's mum. And lodged between Duplicate #5 and Duplicate #6, a control box—a dusty monitor and an array of switches and buttons.

"What is this place?" I finally say.

"Storage," Ash replies. "The Gems decide what they want their baby to be like—looks, talents, those kind of things. They preorder and grow them in artificial sacs."

I nod. I know this from canon. I cross the room to look at an almost identical Mrs. Harper. She has a fine red scar across her chest, and pink sores on her inner thighs. I look closer. It's as if pieces of skin have been peeled away from her legs.

Ash follows. He stands so close, I can feel his breath on my neck. "Genetic enhancement isn't as precise as you may think," he says. "It takes several attempts to make the perfect baby, so they grow several fetuses at the same time. The obviously flawed ones are flushed before birth."

"One was too hot, one was too cold, and one was just right," I whisper to myself.

"What's that?"

I shake my head. "Nothing, just a story my dad used to tell me."

Ash rests his hand against the glass, just above almost–Mrs. Harper's face. A tender gesture. He sighs. "I'm guessing that these babies were too good to flush."

I trace her features with my gaze. She looks nothing like Willow. Blonde hair, pale skin, slender shoulders. But those lifeless, staring eyes are the exact same shade of copper.

"They keep them for spare parts?" I finally say.

"It's the only explanation."

I look back to that fine scar, and I notice she's hooked up to a small pump by a loop of bloodred tubing. Mrs. Harper must have had a heart problem. I guess the Gems didn't eradicate all diseases like Sally King wrote, I guess they just found other ways of defying death and illness. And judging from those missing patches of skin, I'd say Mrs. Harper's wrinkle-free face has had some help. I know from canon that she's in her sixties, even though she only looks about thirty.

I can't help thinking of Frankenstein's monster, assembled from different body parts, held together with coarse stitching. I've heard that comparison before. Nate called Alice a filthy, Frankenstein Gem on the way to Comic-Con. Such a strange coincidence, like Nate somehow predicted this. Unless it wasn't a coincidence. Unless Nate somehow made this happen by saying it. Or maybe the phrase lodged somewhere in my unconscious and I made it happen. This reminds me of that sash, the one I wore to Comic-Con . . . Did I somehow create Rose's belt of blood?

I immediately dismiss the idea, partly because it's ridiculous, and partly because I don't have the headspace to process it.

"Are you coping OK?" Ash asks.

I shake my head. The shock, the disgust, makes way for a cleaner emotion—anger. How could they do this? How could they mutilate their own siblings? I look toward Willow's truncated brother. I remember the backstory from canon now. Willow was in a terrible riding accident when he was twelve and spent several months in the hospital undergoing regenerative surgery. But King never mentioned anything about dismembering an unconscious sibling.

I think about Nate—his pixie grin and his spiky hair and the way he always knows random facts about everything—and the anger intensifies.

"They'd do that to their own flesh and blood? To their siblings, to their children?" I say.

Ash's fingers entwine with mine. "The dangers of playing God, I suppose."

I turn to face him. He looks pale, even for Ash. "So the Imps don't know about this?"

He shakes his head. "There's rumors of big storage warehouses filled with Duplicates in secret locations in the Pastures. I've never heard of relatives keeping them on-site before. And as far as I know, nobody's ever seen one, or at least admitted to seeing one."

My throat clamps shut, but I manage to force out one single word. "Willow?"

"He may know."

"I could ask him?"

"No." Ash suddenly looks afraid. "Why do you think I haven't told anyone? It will put you in grave danger. The government obviously doesn't want this getting out. And according to the rumors, most of the Gems don't even know. It's probably just the wealthy, powerful Gems who can afford backups."

"They're not backups, they're *people*." I wipe my face, the anger returning. "You should have told someone about this, someone who could help."

"Violet, sometimes it really is like you're from a different universe. If I speak up about this, you can guarantee I'll wind up dead in some alley, or dancing on those gallows. And then who would help Ma? Who would bring back the Gem coins for food? I've got to put my family first."

"So why did you show me this?"

He looks sad for a moment. Remorseful. "I—I wanted you to know what the Gems are truly like. The lengths they'll go to in their quest for perfection." Unexpectedly, he wraps his arms around my neck and pulls me in really close so my face rests on his shoulder. The scent of sweat and soap stills my pulse, and for a moment, I feel OK again. When he speaks, I feel his breath in my ear. It doesn't tickle like Willow's did, it just feels amazing. "And I just had to tell someone—it felt like a weight inside me, the secret, that is. You're the first person I've ever really trusted."

I begin to cry again. And not just because of those dead-eyed, floating Duplicates, or because of the empty space where almost-Willow's legs should be, or the missing heart beneath that fine red scar. But because Ash will only ever know almost-Violet, the Duplicate, the player.

He will never know the real me.

CHAPTER 26

I ROLL ONTO MY bunk. The sun is rising and I need to sleep. I only hope my dreams allow me to escape the glassy, dead eyes of the Duplicates.

Tonight is a big night. The turning point, the midway twist. Willow must declare his love to me, and I must tell him that I love him but I'm returning to the city—the mercy dump, as Alice put it. I'm just about to let my eyes close when Matthew and Saskia duck under the mangy cotton divider, leaning on the end of my bunk and destroying any hope of privacy or rest.

"Come on, sleepyhead, we've got a job for you," Matthew says.

I sit up, blinking heavily. "What?" This wasn't in canon. Rose slept today, I'm sure of it. I think I may cry, I'm so tired.

Saskia smiles at my discomfort. "While you were out canoodling with Gem boy, I've had me ear to the ground. Word is, he's got another date with that pretty bit of fluff from the ball."

I don't tell her the pretty bit of fluff is Alice. They obviously haven't communicated with Thorn since we left headquarters, and I'm just too ashamed to admit my best friend might still sabotage the mission, intentionally or otherwise.

"He's taking her into town for a bit of shopping," Matthew says.

This definitely wasn't in canon. The anger from my argument with Alice returns. She's risking everything just so she can live out her fanfic fantasies, taking us further and further from the story. Further from home. I get this sick feeling in my stomach because, deep down, I know I'm partly to blame—I should never have gone to the bunker with Ash, I should never have let that butterfly flap its bastard wings.

Saskia looks a little smug. "If you want to convince that Gem brat to give up Daddy's secrets, you better be the only girl he wants to . . ." She makes an obscene gesture with her hands. Matthew bursts out laughing.

"So what do you want me to do?" I ask.

"You can work at the market today," Saskia replies. "You and Nate."

Matthew nods. "The Gems love to visit the market, makes 'em feel all superior, watching us Imps toil. Just make sure you remind him who he really wants."

We travel on an Imp-bus through the market town. This set wasn't in canon, so I see the sleek lines of the Gem town—forged from glass and steel—for the first time. They look like an artist's impression of the future, all airbrushed and clean. Already, scents of garlic and caramel weave toward us as the restaurants prepare for lunch. I see Gems through the smeared panes of the bus, strolling by, making small talk, or stopping to absorb the window displays, tilting their chins and revealing their CGI-perfect profiles.

Without permission, my eyes dart up and down the boulevard, seeking a glimpse of Alice, her hand wrapped in Willow's. But I can only see the signs that adorn every shop window, every restaurant door. A picture of an ape trapped behind a diagonal red line. No Imps allowed. My tongue sticks to my teeth as a stream of anger passes through me. They're the animals, not us. They're the ones that chop up their siblings, their children, all in the name of perfection.

We follow the curve of the boulevard, which eventually leads into a market square. This must be the old part of town, where the glass and steel is yet to reach. The stone facades of the modernized Imp buildings surround us, and fixed to a nearby wall is a large sign boasting a picture of an ape. I'm guessing it's a warning that we've entered a mixed zone. My muscles tighten and I feel a bit like a jack-in-the-box.

Nate sighs. "It's no fun being the ape, is it?"

I consider telling him about the Duplicates from last night, but I promised Ash I wouldn't tell a soul, and I don't want to burden Nate with it. So instead, I just say, "No fun at all."

We file off the bus and join the throng. Imps move gracelessly between the stone pillars that demarcate the individual stalls, buying and selling goods for their Gem masters. There's this wonderful smell of cooked meats and spices, and bright splashes of color as spools of yarn turn in the breeze. The Gems stand out immediately. Tall, lean, and self-important. Mostly soldiers, their rifles on display, but the occasional Gem civilian glides past, chin raised like a bad smell fills their nostrils, like we're nothing more than animals. I twist my fingers together as though I can wring the anger from my body.

"You can help me on the bread store," Saskia says, gathering her streaked hair into a loose plait.

We approach a wooden stall boasting an array of loaves. That warm, yeasty aroma reminds me of a family holiday in Brittany. Dad was always dragging us into the *boulangeries*, and Nate would laugh every time he tried to say it, pronouncing it with a hard *g*. I get this searing pain just thinking of Dad, baguette crumbs lodged in his stubble.

Saskia hands us some pristine white gloves. I inch my fingers into them and begin straightening the loaves, so fresh their crusts fracture beneath my touch. Nate picks up a baguette and grins, and I suspect he remembers the hard *g*, too.

I'm wrapping a loaf in a sheet of waxed paper when I spot Ash on a nearby apple cart. He sees me and raises a dark eyebrow. He walks over, his limbs fluid and natural, and presents me with an apple, scarlet against the white of his gloves.

"Push off, Squirrel," Saskia says.

"I just wanted to talk to Violet. I'll keep it brief, promise."

A guard loiters nearby and Saskia obviously doesn't want a scene, so she returns to counting out the coins and mutters, "Five minutes."

He helps me wrap another loaf, but remains silent.

"I thought you'd be back with your ma," I finally say.

"I wanted to check you were OK after . . . you know." He lowers his voice so Nate and Saskia can't hear. "I think I made a mistake showing you those *things*."

"I wanted to know the truth," I whisper back.

Our fingers connect momentarily as we reach for the same loaf, the material of our gloves bunching together. He glances up and smiles.

A voice cuts through the air. "Where are your gloves, Imp?"

The guard looks straight at us. My heart leaps into my mouth. I glance down and see the white cotton of our hands. Which means he's either talking to Saskia . . . or Nate.

I spin around, my worst fear confirmed, the peach of Nate's uncovered hands peering through a light dusting of flour.

I watch the terror cross his face as he realizes the guard is addressing him.

"I—I—" His words knot together. "My hands were . . . hot."

The guard narrows his emerald eyes. "Your hands were . . . hot?"

Nate's body seems to shut down—chest stops rising, eyes stop blinking, fingers dig into the edge of the counter. I feel an overwhelming urge to rush to him, to scoop him up and protect him. But Ash whispers, *"Don't,"* and the fear of making things worse stills me.

The guard tightens his grip on his rifle. "Have you been putting your grubby Imp hands all over our Gem food?"

Nate tries to shake his head, but instead just moves his eyes from side to side.

The guard scowls, his face pinched, like he's just yanked a drawstring that connects all his features together. "Cat got your tongue *and* your gloves?"

Saskia steps forward, eyes lowered, palms up like she's surrendering. "I'm so sorry, officer. I will see that he's suitably punished. I will cane him myself when we return to our estate."

I've never heard her sound so obliging. I guess she's trying to save him from a worse fate than caning. Sweat pricks the back of my neck and I can feel my thighs beginning to shake.

The guard dismisses her with a wave of the hand. "Shut it, slave. Unless you want to lose your hands, too."

"NO!" It bursts from my mouth without permission.

The guard swivels. "Who said that?"

I open my mouth to reply, but the world looks kind of fuzzy and I forget where I am for a second.

"I did," Ash says.

The guard laughs. "That's a remarkably feminine voice you've got there, Imp." He glares at him. "Seems like we could do with a good amputation, just to keep you all in line."

He hauls Nate from behind the stall.

The reality of the situation smashes into me and it feels like my body plunges into a vat of lava. Hot and brimming with outrage. "NO!" I scream again. I lunge forward, but Ash and Saskia hold me back. I kick and punch, trying to break free, but they're too strong and I bounce between them like a pinball. Several guards arrive, pointing and laughing at my outburst.

"They're going to chop off his hands," I scream, trying to fish the sense from the words. The image of that Duplicate appears in my consciousness—half-formed, half-dead. Not Nate, not Nate. They can't do that to Nate.

Ash smothers my mouth. "Violet, they'll kill him if you carry on like this."

But I can't stop thrashing, just hoping that if I can somehow get to Nate, they'll let me take his place.

They drag Nate over to a corner in the square, their giant bodies swamping him. Quite a crowd gathers, but even from this distance, peering through the spectators, I imagine I can see the smooth, adolescent skin of each finger stretching toward his nail beds. The white of his palms. The map of veins hovering just beneath the surface of his narrow wrists. Vomit rises in my throat and I begin to cough.

They shove him to his knees and twist a plastic tourniquet around his forearms. *This can't be happening.* I suddenly feel strangely disconnected from my body; I don't even know if it still fights, or just flops like a doll. I watch his sandy head bent low, tears plopping on the ground before him. I remember us high-fiving when he wasn't even a year old, and then, when he was two, banging our fists together and shouting, "Yo!" I remember his first piano lesson, his little fingers barely able to span a fifth. I feel something wet and hot leaking down my cheeks and onto my tongue. It tastes like brine.

The crowd falls silent and the guard raises a great curved knife above his head. It hovers in the air, a glowing crescent in the mid-day sun.

"GUARDS!" A female Gem pushes through the crowd, beau-tiful yet clearly riled, followed closely by an equally beautiful male Gem. I recognize them even through a gauze of tears and horror: Alice and Willow.

"WAIT." Alice throws herself over Nate so that the guard would have to first slice through her. But Willow hangs back, uncertainty flickering across his face.

"I demand that this stop immediately," Alice shouts, her crim-son dress fluttering in the breeze.

Saskia gasps. "Isn't that : . . ?"

The guard shifts his weight, the knife still poised. "What is the meaning of this?"

Alice turns her head but doesn't budge. "I know this Imp, he works for my father. If he loses his hands, Papa will be furious."

Another guard steps forward. "Miss, with all due respect, there are so many Imps out there. Just find another one."

Alice smiles. "Oh no, this one's irreplaceable."

"This is quite unorthodox, Miss . . ." The guard with the knife searches for a surname, his suspicions clearly roused.

Willow finally steps forward. "Alice, her name's Alice. And if you hadn't noticed, she's with me."

The guards see him for the first time, their faces stripped of any pride. "Master Harper, I am so sorry." They tip their cloth caps.

The blood starts moving around my body again, the world falls back into place. I feel Ash loosen his grip.

Willow clears his throat, clearly a little embarrassed. "If Miss Alice says this Imp should be spared, then I back her unquestionably."

The guards do this groveling little bow, followed by a chorus of, "Yes, of course, Master Harper."

Alice stands and the guards dash to release the tourniquet. Something goes off in my head like a starting pistol and I streak across the market square, Ash's feet pounding behind me, slightly out of sync with my own. I gather Nate up in my arms and bury my head in that soft curve between his shoulder and his neck. He just kind of slumps into me, all limp and heavy. I choke back the tears and smooth his hair from his face. "Jonathan, Jonathan," I whisper, guiding him back to the stall. I use his given name, the name Mum and Dad use. I'm the closest thing to a parent he's got right now. His body trembles and his hands are this strange blue color.

"Are you OK?" Ash says, wrapping a protective arm around us both.

Nate sobs. "They were going to do it. They were going to cut off my hands just because I took off my gloves."

"They're monsters." Ash shoots me a meaningful look.

The crowd disperses and the guards move back to their posts. If it weren't for my pulse drumming in my head and the ashen look on Nate's face, you would think nothing had just happened, like it's completely normal for the Gems to hack off a fourteen-year-old boy's hands.

Willow eventually notices me—huddled around Nate and crying. A look of shock and guilt disturbs his perfect face. I stare back at him, shamelessly, refusing to look away. We both know he wouldn't have spoken out, wouldn't have stopped the amputation had Alice not been there. I remember his words from the orchard just the other night: *It's just the way it's always been.* I think of the nine loops of rope, that crumpled paper chain, the no-ape signs, the truncated, floating boy, and I feel anger inflate my entire body, making me twenty, thirty, forty feet tall. I don't want to tell him I love him, I want to throttle him. And judging from his face, he can tell.

Alice gently tugs his arm. Just before they walk away, she looks over her shoulder.

"Thank you," I mouth at her.

She smiles her beautiful smile and winks.

CHAPTER 27

MY DAD ONCE told me something really cool about frogs: "If you drop a frog in a pan of boiling water, it hops out immediately, clutching his burned froggy arse with his flippers. But you stick that same frog in a pan of cold water and slowly turn up the heat, the daft bugger just sits there. He sweats off his little froggy balls until, eventually, the water boils and he croaks. Literally." (He's funny, my dad. And he knows a lot of random crap. I guess that's where Nate gets it from.)

Well, I feel like that first frog. Like I've been shoved into a pan of boiling water and my arse is on fire. But the other Imps, they're like the second frog. They've sat in that pan so long, they've grown used to the heat. A boy nearly gets his hands chopped off and it's business as normal. You get called an ape, carry on as always. You get sexually assaulted, maybe even shot by a guard—just another day in *The Gallows Dance*.

But unlike the first frog, I've got nowhere to jump to. I'm stuck in that bastard pan, just counting down the days until I hang.

As soon as we return to the manor, Nate crawls into his bunk. Even Saskia seems concerned, making sure he eats an extra hunk

of bread and tucking the covers up around his chin. Dusk falls and
I know I must head to the orchard to wait for Willow one last time,
but before I go I kiss Nate on the head, inhaling his scent. He stirs
in his sleep and I kiss him again, just for good measure.

As I leave, Saskia catches me by the arm. "Remember. You're
just pretending to fancy him."

"It's OK, Saskia. You saw what happened at the market." *And
he keeps his truncated brother floating in a tank*, I think to myself.

She smiles like she knows everything and I know nothing.
"Imp or Gem, men are all a bunch of scumbags."

I manage a weak laugh and shuffle to the orchard, still numbed
by shock and immune to the chill, trying to rehearse my lines in my
head. I know this is the most important scene yet—the midway
twist, the scene that ultimately results in Willow following Rose to
the city. But the lines stick together and I can't quite separate them,
because I don't want to tell Willow I love him, I want to tell him
he's a massive turd.

As I walk beside the lake, I notice the moon, a perfect sphere
in the water. I smile in spite of myself—funny how the reflection,
the echo, can look as real as the thing it reflects. I reach down and
fumble with a stone. Then I lob it so it smashes the sphere into a
thousand silver pieces.

"Violet."

I turn and see Ash approaching. He tilts his head to the side
and something reaches inside my gut and starts to pull.

"What's going on with you?" he asks.

"What do you mean?"

"I recognized that Gem, the girl from the market."

I must look confused because he sighs, a little irritated. "Let
me give you a clue: massive man feet."

I don't know how to explain it, and I don't really have time. I have to meet Willow in a few minutes. "Look, it's really complicated."

"You told me she's not a Gem." He sounds a little hurt, betrayed even.

"She isn't."

"So she really is a spy?"

My hand connects with his. "One day I'll explain, I promise."

"You're keeping secrets from me, after I showed you . . ." He tails off. We both know what he means, and I'm not surprised he's pissed.

"I'll tell you, I promise . . . just not now. I have to meet someone."

He examines me with big, searching eyes. "You're not seriously going to meet *him*?"

"Yeah."

"You can't really like him, not after you saw those Dupes, not after he was going to let those guards cut off Nate's hands."

"I know."

"And you know he's never going to be with you, not properly, the law forbids it. You'll end up dancing on those gallows."

"Ash, I know."

"So why are you doing this?"

I want to tell him everything, starting at Comic-Con and ending right here at the lake, I want to tear down that wall of secrets and lies and I want him to see me for who I really am, but most of all, I want to throw my arms around him and lay my head on his shoulder, knowing that we will fit together perfectly. But I know I can do none of those things. There's just too much at stake. My body feels like a selection of interlocking parts. I've lost all sense of wholeness, of completeness, as though I'm some strange, corrugated puppet held together by pegs.

He sighs—his breath hangs between us like mist. "Do you have real feelings for him?"

"I—I don't know."

"Because you shouldn't want someone just because"—his mouth twists a little—"because they have a perfect chest-to-waist ratio, or the perfect cheekbones, or the glossiest hair. You should want someone because they're . . . I don't know . . . real, true."

I can't help but glance at the water, tiny fragments of moon still dancing across its surface. I look back at Ash, his slightly proud nose, his unthinkably pale-blue eyes, and the mouth that I know has the ability to completely overshadow the rest of his features when it cracks a smile. Then I think of Nate and Alice and Katie and home. I *have* to carry on with the canon. I *have* to make those two pieces of thread weave together again. I used to cling to the script, to predictability, but now it feels like someone's ripping me down the middle. "I know, I know."

"I mean, he doesn't even know your real name, and it's such a pretty name, so much better—"

But he never gets to finish his sentence because I've already leaned forward and started to kiss him. He returns my kiss, his lips warm and soft, his breath filling my nostrils, and I'm spinning and floating like a maple seed, filled with joy and launching into the sky. He weaves his fingers along my spine, an elaborate pattern, and I get this feeling like I can't inhale any deeper, like my lungs will burst. I pull him closer so his body presses against mine—we really do fit together perfectly.

But my head fills with Alice and Katie and Nate, and that awful ripping feeling returns.

The damned canon.

That bastard butterfly.

I pull away. "I'm sorry."

He studies my face. "You—you just want him?"

The lie sticks in my throat like something barbed and sharp. And for some reason, I think of the quote from Katie's letter. *All the world's a stage.* I swallow hard and push the words out one by one. "Yes. I just want Willow."

And without saying anything, he turns and walks away.

CHAPTER 28

I REACH THE ORCHARD, firmly blinking the tears from my eyes and wiping the kiss from my mouth. I'm such a mess, kissing the wrong character, falling for the wrong guy. Maybe Sally King was right, maybe you can fall in love in just a few days, if the person's right, if you and they just fit together. *For God's sake, Violet*, I tell myself, *he's from another reality, another universe, and you're going home.* The image of my body falling heavily against a rope flashes into my mind—*in two days, I will hang.* I push it away, blinking hard.

I turn these thoughts in my head again and again, briefly recalling the times when my worst fears were failing an exam or choking on another olive. I almost don't notice how cold I've grown, how dark it's become. Eventually, the clock chimes midnight.

The bottom of my stomach falls away.

Willow isn't coming.

The most important scene yet, and Willow's stood me up. It feels like my skin is missing. I've failed. For whatever reason, he doesn't want me. Nate was right. I should have stuck to the script. I run through it all in my mind, the Gallows Ball, the kiss, the market.

Something clicks. The market. He's embarrassed, of course. He failed to stand up for an Imp, an Imp clearly important to me.

He let me down, and he knows it. I feel my heart rate slow. I just need to go to him, show him that it's OK and get the canon back on track.

I push aside thoughts of Ash, thoughts of the noose tightening around my throat, thoughts of that truncated, floating body, and I feel a renewed sense of purpose. I take a huge mouthful of apple-scented air.

I run to the manor, loop around the back, and stare up the oak. Light spills from Willow's window. He's awake. I try chucking a few stones up, but the branches get in the way and I fail to draw his attention. There's only one thing to do: I have to climb that stupid tree.

I recall Ash's advice and slowly, steadily inch up the branches, never freeing more than one limb at a time, testing the boughs before I put my weight on them. I get numerous twigs in my face, leaves in my hair, and I graze my hand a couple of times on hidden shards of bark, but I make pretty good progress.

I near the top, never looking down, always looking up, anticipating the break in the leaves and the view of the stars, enjoying the wind in my face as the branches thin. And as I near Willow's window, ready to reach out a trembling fist to rap on the pane, I actually have a massive grin plastered across my face. Me—Violet—climbing a monstrous tree, making a Gem fall in love with her. I feel invincible. I shimmy across a bough, fortunately strong enough to take my weight, and a little giggle escapes my mouth. The light from his window illuminates my hands as they splay before me. And finally, I pull my body upward so I look straight into his room.

He lies in bed. I can see the satin bedding crumpled around his perfect, muscular body. The shape of his hips, the line of his torso, the faint scars encircling his upper thighs. He sleeps, his chest rising and falling rhythmically.

And he isn't the only person naked in that bed—my own personal midway twist.

She lies beside him, her golden hair strewn across the pillow, her long, bronzed legs entwined with his.

And all the men and women merely players.

Alice.

CHAPTER 29

ALICE'S EYES SNAP open. She looks straight at me. At first, she must see only what I see, reflected back at her from the panes, a world of soft light and bronzed shapes. But I see her focus change, her expression move from contentedness to shock as she looks through her own image and meets my gaze. Slowly, her expression shifts to acceptance, like she always knew I would find her here.

I have only one instinct: to flee. I shuffle back down the branch, tears landing on the wood before me, and begin the mad scramble down the tree. I forget all of Ash's advice—tumbling, scrabbling, bouncing through the boughs, a haze of twigs and leaves biting at my hands and my scalp. I lose my footing on the final branch and the ground seems to rise up from nowhere, smacking my back and knocking the wind from my lungs. I just lie there, glaring up at that bastard tree, gulping down empty, air-free mouthfuls, feeling like I'm going to suffocate, trying to get that hateful image from my brain.

I hear her before I see her. The crunch of her feet on the gravel, the soft yet frantic cry of my name. "Violet. Violet."

She skids into a kneeling position beside me. "Did you fall badly?"

"Yes," I manage to squeak.

"Did you hit your head?"

My hand travels to my brow. "No."

She helps me into a sitting position. The zingy sweetness of her perfume calms me, but then I just feel angry with myself. I study her for a moment. She wears no makeup, her hair extensions curl freely around her shoulders, and she's wrapped a white satin sheet around her body, probably to hide her nakedness rather than protect her from the cold. She looks so natural, and for a moment, she's just Alice again.

"What's going on?" The vulnerability in my voice surprises me as much as her.

"I'm . . . I'm sorry. I don't know what else to say."

"Don't you want to go home?"

"I thought I did. But then this happened."

"What? Willow?"

"I guess . . . and more." She sweeps her hand in a dramatic circle. "Wonderland."

"Shit, Alice. You're not doing this for love. You just want to be one of *them*." I bumble to my feet. My lungs still ache, my body's still oxygen-starved, but the anger gains strength and I'm able to pull myself upright.

"Why not?" She stands, too, the sheet folding around her like a carefully sculptured piece of royal icing. "The Gems are kind to me. The Imps treated me like a leper, they cut off my hair, tried to hang me, locked me in a tower."

"Yeah, they tried to hang me, too, remember?"

"So you get it, then?"

"No, as a matter of fact, I don't. If you'd seen what I've seen, the way the Gems *really* treat the Imps, you'd soon change your tune."

"And maybe, if you were in my shoes, you'd change yours."

My fists clench in frustration. "For God's sake, Alice. The Gems only treat you like that because they think you're one of them."

"So?"

"So . . . what happens when you catch a cold, or you start to age like a normal person, or you, I don't know, you go to a pub quiz and can't answer all the questions 'cause your IQ isn't stupidly high?"

I clearly hit a nerve. She takes a step back. "Are you saying I'm stupid?"

"Well, you must be if you want to stay here." I sidestep her and walk toward the trees, my boots slapping the grass, my body rigid and prickling with rage.

But she runs after me, catching me by the arm. "Violet, please try and understand, I've never fit in, not anywhere. This is the first place I haven't felt different."

"Poor Alice. It must be hard being so beautiful." I wrench my arm from her grasp.

"That's not what I mean." She circles in front of me, blocking my path. "I'm happy here."

"Oh, and it's all about you, isn't it? Have you even thought about Katie? About what Thorn will do to her when he realizes you're only here to get naked with Willow?"

Something crosses her face, an expression I can't quite read. Guilt? Regret? And that's when I notice for the first time that she no longer wears her split-heart necklace.

The treachery deepens in my gut. "You're not just sabotaging our chances of getting home. You're risking our lives."

"Thorn won't hurt Katie, he fancies her too much . . . It was clearly just a threat."

"You tell yourself that. And you tell Nate, next time some guard tries to hack off his hands, you tell him it was clearly just a threat."

This unnerves her—her brow knots together. "Look, Violet. I know the guards were out of order, but Willow and his family, they're actually really *nice*. They would never do anything like that."

The anger fills every part of me. I think of that boy floating in a tank, hacked in two, and that promise I made Ash seems so very far away. "Is that right? So why don't you ask Willow what he keeps in that bunker at the bottom of the estate?"

She doesn't look confused, as I anticipated. Her eyebrows don't pull together, her inky gaze doesn't falter—she looks sheepish, ashamed.

"But you already know, don't you?" I say.

She looks away, adjusts her sheet. "I saw the scars on Willow's legs, and when I asked him what happened, he told me."

"About his dismembered relatives?" My voice rises.

"The Duplicates? Yeah."

I glower at her, daring her to meet my gaze. "Calling them Duplicates doesn't stop them from being people." I pause, momentarily thrown. "Wait. Willow told you? So Willow knows, too?"

"Yeah, 'course he does. They're his legs."

I could punch her right now. I clasp my hands together—a desperate prayer. "No. That's the point, Alice. They're not his legs." I spit out every word to try and make her understand. "He. Stole. Them. From. His. Brother."

"You're being melodramatic."

"Oh really?" I'm shrieking now, but I feel so full of rage, so incensed, I've lost all volume control. "Well, maybe you shouldn't have stopped them from amputating Nate's hands after all. You and your new mates could have had a spare-parts fundraiser."

She steps toward me, her voice calm, like I'm the unreasonable one. "Look, Violet. It's not as bad as it sounds. All of the Dupes are in comas, it's not like they're in pain, or even aware they exist."

"Oh well, that's OK, then, so long as they can't look you in the eye when you carve out their vital organs."

She ignores me, continuing in her balanced tone. "And the Harpers built their Dupes a special hiding place to keep them safe."

"Yeah, I know. I found it. And believe me, they're anything but safe."

"Calm down, Vi." Only Alice could look so collected, so poised, wearing a sheet from *my* pseudo-boyfriend's bed, while discussing organ theft. "After they heard those rumors about the guards at the warehouses . . . you know . . . fiddling with the Dupes, they built them a special hiding place to keep them safe."

"Fiddling . . . as in . . . ?" I slip over my words.

"God, you're naive. As in sexual stuff."

I shove my hands over my ears, unable to process this extra information, trying to hold my brain together. "Holy crap, Alice. This just gets worse and worse." My voice sounds funny, like it's inside my head. "I don't want to hear anything else you have to say. I don't *know* you anymore." I drop my voice to a low snarl. "You disgust me." I've never spoken to Alice like this, not even when she stuffed my favorite T-shirt down the toilet 'cause Alfie Peach asked me to the disco when we were twelve. Not even when she stole my algebra homework and pretended it was hers and I got detention. I expect her to crumple, to burst into tears.

But she just laughs. She actually laughs. "You're just jealous."

"Of what, exactly?"

"Of me. Of the Gems . . . we're perfect."

"Well, if being perfect means losing your humanity, you can bloody well keep it." The silver heart rests in my fingers and I suddenly notice how sharp and cold it feels. I tighten my grip around the chain and yank it with all my might. Either the buckle warps and breaks, or the weakest link gives way, but it falls from my neck with disappointing ease. I hold it out for her to see.

Her fingers brush her naked throat. "Violet . . ." Her voice tails off and we stare at each other for a moment.

"I'm sorry," she finally says.

"Don't bother." I jab an angry finger toward the manor house. "Better take the toga party back to lover boy." I sound so bitter I hardly recognize myself.

She winces at my tone. "I'm doing this for both of us."

"Bullshit."

"I don't want to watch you . . ." The word sticks in her throat.

"Say it." My head feels swollen and about to pop. "Say it."

"Hang," she shouts. "I don't want to watch you hang."

"Bullshit! You just don't want to go home."

I turn and run toward the trees, the chain hanging limply from my palm, and this time, she doesn't follow.

CHAPTER 30

THE DASH BACK to the Imp-hut feels strange and unprocessed, like a clip of a movie that's been stretched in places and cut in others, dreamlike and fragmented. The wind numbs my cheeks and fills my ears, but it can't drown out that one line: *My best friend has betrayed me.*

I throw open the door of the Imp-hut, my expression acting like a siren, drawing looks from every slave inside.

Saskia dashes toward me, her spiky facade momentarily dropped. "Violet? What is it?"

"Alice," I say, almost to myself.

Matthew guides me to a chair.

"Alice," I repeat, like saying it again can somehow make it hurt less.

Nate scoots across the room, pushing through the gathering crowd. "What about her?" he asks, his face a mixture of concern and pain.

Saskia snarls at the bystanders. "The next Imp to stare at stuff that don't concern 'em will have to deal with me. Got it?"

They go about their business, pretending we don't exist.

"Well?" Nate says.

I take a great, shaky breath, for once barely noticing the stink of damp. "I saw them, together. Willow and Alice. In bed, they were, you know . . . or at least they had been . . ."

"Bitch," Nate says.

"Nate, mind your language," I mumble out of habit.

Saskia leans into the table and exhales slowly. "OK, OK, this isn't so bad. Alice is on our side, right? She's working for Thorn? I'm guessing she's his fallback in case you fail to seduce Willow."

"It's not just about seducing Willow." I place my hand on hers, wishing I could somehow make her understand. She snatches it away, but I carry on regardless. "There are more important things than getting Jeremy Harper's secrets."

"Like what?" Saskia spits.

Like completing the canon and going home. The words remain heavy on my tongue, causing my mouth to hang open.

Saskia turns so I can't see her expression, but she holds herself stiff and balls up her fists. "OK, well, if Alice is doing her job, we're best off removing you from the equation. Let's head back to head-quarters and see what Thorn wants to do."

I can't bear the thought of letting Alice win. I can't bear the thought of leaving Ash. And I just can't bear the thought of never going home. I can feel the panic rising inside. "No. I want to stay." My voice sounds stronger than I feel. "I want to win him back and put this right."

"I ain't asking you, I'm telling you." Saskia turns to face me, a tic developing just below her right eye. "You think I'm happy about this? Months in the bloody making this plan was, and all me and Matthew's own work, and then doll-face-bloody-long-legs comes swanning in and steals the show." She turns and says to herself, "This would never have happened if Rose were here."

If I thought I couldn't feel any more inadequate, I was wrong. Her words wither my insides. And it just seems so unfair—I was so close. If only Alice hadn't interfered. Nate rests his hand on my shoulder, which helps stem the tears for at least a moment.

Matthew finally speaks. "Come on now, Saskia. We don't know that."

She puts her hands on her hips and looks me up and down. This bitter laugh erupts from her mouth.

The panic hardens, turns to anger, my insides still raw from my run-in with Alice. "You think I wanted this? To come to this awful place and get strung up by that controller, and nearly assaulted by a foot soldier, and watch Nate almost get his hands cut off, and get called an ape and treated like I'm barely human and get no sleep and be permanently hungry and watch my best friend betray me." I tug at my clothes. "And these God-awful overalls, how can you even bear them, it's like having nits or something."

The skin around her eyes tightens. "Steady now, princess. The way you're talking, anyone would think you're not really an Imp."

"Of course I'm an Imp. I'm five foot bloody four!"

"We leave on the next bus. Now gather your things." She storms from the hut, slamming the door so hard it groans on its hinges and dislodges the dust and muck from the beams.

"What things?" Nate gestures to our empty bunks, his voice sarcastic, full of bravado, but he leaves his hand on my shoulder like I'm some sort of crutch.

Matthew disappears behind a cloth divider. I hear him roll onto a bunk. "The next bus isn't till dawn, better get some sleep. We've got some walking ahead."

Even though I've hardly slept, I don't feel tired. I can still feel the remnants of the adrenaline, and my body's forgotten whether it's night or day. Eventually, I move to the kitchenette. Nate follows, and we begin stuffing bread in our pockets, filling bottles with cloudy water.

"How could she do this?" I whisper over the rumble of the taps.

"What? Alice? Do something completely selfish? Screw the man of her dreams? It's a mystery."

"Nate, language."

He laughs. "*Screw* doesn't count." He twists the lid onto one of the bottles, his knuckles blanching, and when he looks up, he looks serious. "She clearly wants to stay."

"That's what she said."

"You talked to her?"

"More like yelled."

He nods in approval. "Did you remind her about Katie?"

"Yeah. She's hell-bent on ruining the canon so she can stay." I think about the paper chain, the glinting scythe, the Dupes suspended in fluid. "How could she want to be one of them?"

Nate sighs. "It's like those Zimbardo experiments Dad told us about."

I shake my head, slightly irritated by the tangent.

"You know, they took a bunch of students and made half of them prisoners and half of them guards. Within days, they were acting like it was real."

I smile. "How do you remember this crap? You're only fourteen."

"Because I clear my brain of all other clutter, like where I live and what my name is."

For a moment, it feels normal again—just me and Nate carrying on. But it quickly fades. I sigh. "What are we going to do?"

"Baba will know."

"She didn't know this."

He doesn't reply.

We leave the estate on the first bus that morning, the four of us shivering in the dew-soaked air. I stare at the battered headrest in front of me, letting the fibers pixelate before my tired eyes, and I don't risk glancing out the window until the Harper estate lies far behind—a world spun from sugar. Beautiful, sweet, and yet painfully brittle.

I'd tried to find Ash, but he'd done his vanishing act again. I never got the chance to tell him good-bye, or even part of the truth. Now he will always think I wanted Willow. I swallow back the tears.

The hypnotic rhythm of the bus eventually rocks me into a world of dreams. Alice, Katie, and I stand on the school stage—the one in the gym that never gets used because it's too small and filthy. Alice wears this amazing Elizabethan gown, all silvers and greens, like she's the queen of Slytherin. She really does look like an hourglass—the fullness of the skirt narrowing into her tiny waist, only to flare out into an elaborate, white-lace collar. Katie and I look more like wenches, dressed in dour black smocks and aprons, our dirty hair tucked into equally dirty mop hats.

"Come now, servants," Alice says, addressing us in a regal tone. "Do not keep the audience waiting."

I notice for the first time that spectators fill the hall, each one of them gawking at us. It's my line. I know it's my line, but I can't for the life of me remember what I'm supposed to say.

"Vi," Katie hisses. "Vi, come on, I'm depending on you."

The crowd begins to whisper, but they're quickly drowned out by the pounding of my heart. I prize open my jaw, force down some air, beg the words to form in my brain and migrate to my tongue. But it's like my mind has been stripped down, left bare.

The crowd begins to laugh. That's when I spot Mum, standing in the midst of the audience. She shakes her head like she's disappointed, that same shake she did when I came home drunk and puked on the sofa. Then, her lips begin to move. And even though she's thirty-odd feet away, it's as if she whispers straight into my ear. *Come on, sweetheart. Say something. For me. Please just say something and wake up.*

I wake with a start, Nate beside me.

"You OK?" he asks.

"Yeah." My hand settles on my overalls, just above the place where Katie's letter should nestle. I left it at the Imp-hut, stuffed down the back of a crumbling sideboard. I was worried the guards would find it when we crossed the border. It would rouse suspicion and put us in the firing line, a supposedly illiterate Imp carrying a letter. But it seems those words sunk through my skin and into my veins, like my blood would flow ink-black if you cut me open. I feel like crying. All the world's a stage, and I am the worst actor ever.

Leaving the Pastures proves a lot easier than entering. There's no decontamination process, because you can't contaminate a city already filled with disease and raw sewage. Just a quick pat-down from some apathetic soldiers, who throw my bread in the trash and laugh when my stomach snarls.

We trail through the city gates with the rest of the slaves, and I brace myself for that rotting-bird smell. But this time, rather than overwhelm me, it seems strangely reassuring. At least it knows it stinks. And being surrounded by the misshapen, badly proportioned physiques of the Imps, not a Gem in sight, I get this strange feeling like I've returned home from the zoo.

Regardless, the trudge through the city is soul-destroying. I spend half of the journey recalling how, at this point in canon, Willow was secretly following Rose across the city—dressed in a pair of gray overalls, hair mussed up and dirt rubbed into his face—and the other half preparing for my future conversation with Thorn. *I knew you wouldn't be able to replace Rose. It's a good job I sent Alice, too. Now you will all have to stay in this place for the rest of your lives.*

At least I'll see Katie again. I've missed her soft Liverpudlian accent, her grounded approach to life, the way she always makes me laugh. I want to tell her about Ash, about the Dupes, about what a bitch Alice has been. Katie will call her a spunkbucket, and I'll momentarily forget how crappy everything is.

Katie, I suddenly think. *Thorn will kill Katie.* I begin to unravel—my hands begin to shake, my joints seize up, my gut clenches. I've always known this was true, but only as we near headquarters does the reality sink in. Maybe, just maybe, Alice was right and he fancies Katie too much to hurt her.

"Violet? What is it?" Matthew asks.

"Katie," I say. "I failed the mission."

"We'll try and talk to him," Saskia says.

Matthew nods. "He listens to Saskia."

"He doesn't listen to anyone, arrogant jerk." Saskia glances at my tense face and tries to smile. "But he won't kill your mate, promise. He likes her, I reckon, as much as Thorn can like anyone."

I hold on to these words, and just hope Katie managed to befriend him, at least enough to stop him from killing her, but not so much that he tried to get it on. I shudder when I think of what a difficult position Katie's been in, the role she may have had to play. And I just can't lose Katie. These past few days, I've realized just how much she means to me. Not just because of Alice's betrayal, but because it's always Katie I've longed to tell when something's gone wrong. It's her voice, punctuated with hilarious swear words, that I've imagined telling me it will all turn out well. Alice has been my best friend since I was four, a history that can't be ignored, a history that practically elevates her to sister status. But if I were to walk into a room completely oblivious to the past thirteen years, my friendship slate wiped clean, it would be Katie I'd choose to slam tequila with, not Alice.

I let my eyes skim over the forgotten, ghostly street signs, the monotony of the gray and the *thwack* of my step eventually stilling my mind. The sun slowly moves across the sky, its rays barely penetrating my skin. That's when I first notice it, a flash of gray fabric in my peripheral vision. The tiny hairs on my arms stiffen and I have this overwhelming sense that somebody's watching me, following me. I get a soft flicker of hope in my chest. Maybe, just maybe . . . but I can't bring myself to even think it, because if I'm wrong, I will experience that crushing disappointment all over again.

Nate fishes some undiscovered bread from inside his overalls and hands it out. Saskia grabs a piece and gives half to Matthew. "We can eat as we walk," she says.

A few crumbs fall from Nate's mouth. He looks at me and grins. "Hansel and Gretel made it home, didn't they?"

"Yeah, but the birds ate the crumbs," I reply.

Saskia jabs me in the back. "Who said you could speak?" It sounds aggressive even for her—she's worried about seeing Thorn, too.

"So how did they get home?" Nate whispers, after a tokenistic pause.

"They killed the witch," I whisper back.

"Shhh." Saskia jabs me in the back again.

"Tempting," Nate says.

We both giggle.

By the time the church spire comes into view, hunger and tiredness have weakened my limbs, and I have to concentrate really hard not to cry. That flash of gray hasn't reappeared and I left the flicker of hope behind with Nate's bread crumbs.

We approach the church, the scent of fish thick in my nostrils. Just the sight of those porthole windows, the gothic spire, and I get this pain in my stomach, this tightness in my throat. Saskia and Matthew push through the wooden doors and I follow, Nate's hand wrapped in mine. Thorn leans against the altar, just like in canon. I'd forgotten how beautiful he looks, his dark skin gleaming in the evening light.

"I hear you've arrived empty-handed, Violet," he says.

He must have received word from Alice. All the fear and tiredness seem to lift, and that anger hardens in my rib cage again. He's the one who sent her. If it wasn't for him, the canon would be on track and the rebels would be about to discover Willow peering through the rusted keyhole in the church door. It was a heart-wrenching scene—Willow all roughed up and hauled into the church to face Thorn. The hurt expression on Willow's face when he saw Rose with the rebels and finally realized her true identity.

My brow sets in a determined line. Because of Thorn, Willow is currently feeling up my bestie. "I take it you mean those Gem secrets?" I say. "He chose Alice, by the way."

He laughs. "Ah, so the Gem look-alike won in the end. I thought she might."

I weave through the desks and stride up to him, pushing myself onto my tiptoes so I can meet the glare of that single, lavender eye. "Do you remember your conversation with Baba?" I whisper so the others can't hear. "This is bigger than just getting those Gem secrets. It had to be *me* that Willow fell for. You sabotaged me."

Thorn places two heavy hands on my shoulders, forcing me to take a step away. "I see your stay in the manor has made you bold."

I catch myself. He's a brutal psycho, after all. "Sorry . . . I—I just thought Baba explained it all."

"She spoke in riddles. She always does."

"But she knows things—"

"I am the rebel leader, not Baba, and when a Gem look-alike fell into my lap, I chose to cover my bases. *You* failed this mission, not me, and certainly not Alice."

It sometimes amazes me how quickly I can feel weak again—all the strength draining from my body, my arms dangling by my sides, my eyes itching with tears. I look at my boots and clutch my head, trying to think of what to say next. I need to see Baba. I swallow hard and open my mouth, but the sound of the door bursting open silences me.

A group of rebels haul someone into the building, muffling his shouts and steadying his blows. That soft flicker of hope returns ten, twenty, thirty times stronger, beating its wings like it's going to burst from my chest. I look at Nate and can't help but smile. In spite of Alice, in spite of everything, I did it. Willow chose me. The canon is back on track.

Thorn looks at me and begins to laugh. "I take it back, Violet. You aren't empty-handed at all."

The tussle ends and the rebels part. But it isn't Willow bowed on his knees, a ribbon of blood streaming from his mouth. It's Ash.

CHAPTER 31

A sh, Ash." I hear my voice shout his name. I lurch toward him, but Thorn pulls me back.

Ash looks up, his eyes vivid blue, staring from the pink of his beaten face. I gasp at the sight of his blood, and my hand touches my own cheek as though I can somehow feel his wounds.

"Do you know this Imp?" Thorn's breath catches against my ear.

I nod. "He's a friend."

"And why is your friend sneaking around my church?"

Ash raises his voice. "Violet? What is this?" He looks at me and then at the rebels. He wears the exact same look Willow wore in canon—hurt, betrayed.

A rebel whacks him in the temple with the butt of a gun. He splays on the floor.

"Stop it! Please!" I shout. I can't believe I dragged him into this mess.

Saskia steps forward. "He's just a kid from the Harper estate who's sweet on Violet, that's why he's here."

Thorn walks toward Ash with slow, purposeful steps, accentuating the rhythm of his speech. "And now he's just a kid who knows where Rebel Headquarters is, and what we all look like."

Ash manages to scrape himself off the floor, rocking back into a kneeling position. "Who am I going to tell?"

"Some Gems work for the Imps," Thorn says, "and some Imps work for the Gems. Not everyone is true to their own."

I follow Thorn, nausea rising in my stomach. "Please, Thorn. He's no threat to you."

"His nickname's Squirrel, for God's sake," Nate says.

Thorn squats down before Ash and seems to study his face for a moment. "Lesson number one, boy—never think with your dick."

Ash smiles his lopsided smile. "I was thinking with my heart."

"Lock him in a cell," Thorn says.

The exact same line Thorn said in canon. It's like the story wants to unfold—Baba was right.

I watch as the rebels pull Ash to his feet, stomach acid burning the lining of my throat. He glances over his shoulder at me—his long eyelashes shielding his expression—and a cocktail of guilt and longing swirls in my stomach.

"I'm sorry," I mouth at him.

But they cart him away before he can respond.

The church suddenly feels very cold. I squeeze my arms around my body, wishing I could disappear into myself, sucked into a vacuum of my own guilt. If it weren't for me, Ash would be stirring Ma's pot, or sitting on an Imp-bus, or lying on a bunk, or climbing a tree. I should never have deviated from the script and taken all those risks. My lips tingle as I recall last night's kiss, and his words loop in my head. *I was thinking with my heart.*

Matthew breaks the silence. "Honestly, Thorn. He's a good lad."

Thorn ignores him and steers me away from the others to the front of the church. I hear Nate mutter something about being left out again, followed by a sharp smack, probably Saskia clipping him around the ear. But it all seems a little unreal. My knees feel like they won't bend anymore, and my steps become jerky and small. Thorn leads me to the pulpit and gestures for me to sit beside him on the stone lip. The chill of the stone pushes through my overalls.

He sits beside me and stares at the ceiling. "Before you ask if you can see him, the answer's no."

"I was going to ask if I can see Baba."

"Why?"

I lean forward, letting my hair form a screen so he can't see my tears. "Because I don't know what to do."

"You don't do anything. You just hope Alice comes up with the goods—it isn't just Katherine I've got locked in a cell anymore."

"Katie," I say, almost to myself. The guilt multiplies as I realize she hasn't entered my head since I arrived back at headquarters. But something about the way he used her full name, the way he rolled it around his mouth like he was exploring its contours with his tongue, makes me fear less for her safety.

"You can't see her," he says.

"Is she OK?"

He nods. "For now."

I take a deep breath and push my hair behind my ears. I need to convince him to let me see Baba. I steady my voice. "What if Alice doesn't deliver the goods?"

"She's doing OK so far." His single eye flits between my own.

"Last time I saw her, she was enjoying being a Gem a little too much. It's a lot to give up."

"I managed it." He raises his eye patch to remind me of his origins. This close, I can see his pupil shrink to a dot, unaccustomed to the light.

"Yes, but the Gems haven't killed the man she loves."

"Speaking of love, it seems your mission may have been compromised by a certain Night-Imp."

My cheeks flush. "Ash is just a friend."

He laughs like he doesn't believe me and pulls a silver flask from his jacket. "Go on, then, what makes you think Alice loves the Gem brat?"

"Back in my world, Alice is a fanfic writer, a really good one. She gets thousands of hits every day."

He hands me the flask, his features controlled and still. "A fanfic writer?"

"Alice didn't write the original book, but she expanded on it, twisted it, wrote new bits." Tentatively, I take a sip. It tastes pungent, gouging a path of fire from my tongue to my belly.

"She makes shit up."

I laugh softly. "Yeah."

He plucks the flask from my hand. "I trusted Baba when she said you were the one. But she got it wrong. And I'm not about to believe her bizarre idea that you're from a different dimension and our world is just a . . ." He tails off and takes several hungry slurps. I notice his hand tremble slightly, a sheen of moisture on his brow.

I press on. "Alice's favorite thing was to write stories about girls who could win Willow's heart, made-up girls . . . and they were all tall and blonde, and called things like Abby and Ada and Amelia. She's imagined being with him since she was fifteen."

"What are you trying to say?"

"You still need me, because Alice isn't on our side. She's on Alice's side. She always is."

Thorn tucks the flask into his jacket and flips his patch back into position. "It seems you share a similar view to Katherine. Let me show you something, Little Flower."

He leads me to the dark crucifix screen at the front of the church. A golden bird spreads its wings, trapped beneath a circle of angels.

"The bird is a pelican," Thorn says. "In ancient Imp mythology, it fed its young with its own blood by plucking the feathers from its breast."

I don't know what he wants me to say, so I just mumble, "Gross."

"There is nothing gross about self-sacrifice, Violet."

He looks past the painted cherubs to the high vaulted ceiling for inspiration. "You get one minute with her."

"Who?"

"Baba."

I smile. "That's all I need."

Baba hunches in the corner of her cell, watching the fire and humming a tune. The scent of lilies and wood smoke transports me to my first meeting with her. I think of the gallows and the falling bodies and my mouth dries up.

She turns her head toward me, her eyes wavering beneath her sealed-up lids as though she's dreaming. Her lipless mouth puckers at the corners. "Violet. You seem . . . different."

"Hungrier and sleep deprived."

"Stronger." She offers her withered hands, and I cross the slabs to hold them. They feel surprisingly warm. "Where's Thorn?" she asks.

"He gave us one minute."

She laughs, causing her frame to rock slightly, the firelight moving across her skin. "He's so mean when he's stressed." She gestures to the ground before her. "Come, kneel, my child."

I kneel—letting the stone cool my shins—and bow my head. This time I want the pain. Something to numb the ache of guilt and failure. She cradles my temples and that bolt of pain shoots down my neck, glancing off my sternum and ricocheting around my body. Every part of me hurts. I inhale, but my lungs reject the air and my throat closes. I get the sense I'm drowning without any water. I see a paper chain of Imps crumpling to the ground, a floating, half-dead boy, a scythe-like blade raised high and glinting in the sun, a muddle of bronzed legs cushioned in satin sheets.

Then, just like before, the pain collects in that space between my eyes. I see Ash kneeling between the rebels, a ribbon of blood running down his chin. *I was thinking with my heart*, he says.

And as swiftly as it arrived, the pain vanishes.

I know where I stand before I even open my eyes. I breathe in the scent of freshly mown grass, hear the chatter of the birds and the soft *thud* of falling apples. The orchard. I've never been here in the midday sun before. It's so vibrant—bursting with color and perfume. The wind shakes the leaves, and my skin becomes a collection of strobe-like shadows. I smile to myself.

Baba stands before me, her back straight and her eyes open. She surveys her surroundings. "So, *this* is where the magic happened?"

"Yes. But Willow didn't fall for me. The magic didn't work— I'm Neville Longbottom, in the early books, before he gets good."

Baba laughs, and I notice she now owns a set of teeth. "I wasn't talking about Willow. I was talking about the other one—the one with the baby blues."

Just the mention of Ash and tears sting my eyes. "It's all gone wrong, Baba. What am I going to do?" I'm aware I sound like a small child, but I don't care.

She ignores me and reaches into the boughs of a nearby tree, every strand of her gray hair alive in the sun.

"How could I have been so stupid?" My voice comes out high-pitched and whiny. "I knew Alice loved Willow. Did I really think she was just going to step aside?"

She plucks an apple from the branch and inhales its scent, her newly found nostrils sucking together from the force. "Alice gave you a poisoned apple, but that doesn't make her a wicked hag. And just because you took it, doesn't make you Snow White."

"She betrayed me."

Baba shrugs. "You were willing to betray Willow, to seduce him for your own gain. The end justified the means. Alice just has a different end in mind." She sinks her teeth into the skin of the apple, juice dribbling down her chin. "Ash. That's his name." The pulp moves across her tongue. "I like him."

"What am I going to do?" I repeat, slightly annoyed by her lack of direction.

She swallows. "You still have those ruby slippers, maybe you walk a different path."

"I don't understand."

"You find your own way, Violet. Stop trying to be Rose."

"But, I thought sticking to the script was the right thing to do. I thought the story needed to complete so we could go home."

I must look really perplexed, because she offers me a sympathetic look and says, "But you took the odd risk, didn't you, Violet. And what happened?"

I reply without thinking. "I fell in love with the wrong character."

"Or is that *why* you took those risks? Chicken and egg. Everything's just a loop in the end."

"Baba, please, you're making no sense."

"Look at it another way—if you were stuck here, here in our world, how would you live your life? What kind of an Imp would you become?"

I can feel the irritation building inside. "I can't stay here, Baba. I *have* to go home—me, Nate, and Katie, we don't belong here."

"Belonging is just a state of mind, ask Alice."

She sounds like one of those wall stickers in my auntie's living room. *Learn to dance in the rain.* "Please, Baba. Stop talking in riddles, just tell me what to do."

"Now, where would the fun be in that?" The apple reappears in her hands, a bright, shiny orb. She hurls it into the air like she's releasing a dove—it punches through the branches and sails into the infinite sky. Her laughter dissolves into birdsong. The colors of the orchard run together like paint, and the scent of apples gradually fades.

CHAPTER 32

We're back in the chamber, her hands still resting on my head. I look at her, almost surprised to see those waxy lids in place of the green.

She smiles, her teeth long gone. "Thorn's here."

Moments later, I hear the *thud* of his boots approaching.

He strides through the door. "Your minute's up."

It felt so much longer than a minute, and I suspect time passes more slowly during a mind blend.

"Let her see the boy," Baba says.

"No way."

Baba pulls her hood over her head. "Will you ever learn to trust me?"

We enter the corridor, but instead of leading me back to the main body of the church, Thorn leads me deeper underground until we reach a blue rusted door. I recognize it from the film—Thorn took Rose to see Willow in this very cell. I'm tracing Rose's footsteps again, and it feels like the canon has started to mock me, constantly reminding me of what I should have been doing had I not screwed it all up at the manor.

Looking at that blue door, the skin on my scalp begins to crawl. That scene from canon scared the life out of me—Thorn nearly killed Willow, shoving him against the cell wall and wielding a knife right next to his cheek, Rose screaming in the background. Alice and I bawled at the telly, "No, no, don't you dare damage his perfect face." I think Nate even threw Doritos. But Willow saved himself by telling Thorn top-secret Gem information about an underground, Gem-run brothel: the Meat House. Information Thorn used to raid the Meat House that very night. Alice and I high-fived at the point when Thorn lowered his blade. I thought it was romantic, the way Willow gave up Gem intel so he could be with Rose. Now I just think it was a bit pathetic, spilling the Gems' secrets like that. Typical Willow.

But it isn't Willow slumped behind that blue door, it's Ash—my lovely, brave, honorable Ash. I think about Thorn's knife, probably at this very moment stashed in his belt, and my heart begins to race.

Thorn opens the door. "One minute. That's all."

I step into the cell. The door clicks back into place and darkness surrounds me—darkness and the smell of wet moss. I hear the faint rhythm of someone's breath syncopated with the drip of water.

"Ash?"

"Over here," he replies. I recognize the timbre of his voice, but not the tone—it sounds so flat. I follow the direction of his words and my eyes grow accustomed to the dimness. I begin to pick out his silhouette, hunched in the corner, knees pulled to his chest. I scoop his hands into mine. "Jesus, Ash. Are you OK?" Even in the gloom, I can see how badly his face has started to swell.

"You're a rebel?" he says. "You didn't think to mention it?"

"I'm sorry, I'm sorry. That night, when you helped me put the rose on Willow's windowsill . . . I thought you knew."

"You think I would have shown you the Dupes if I knew you were a rebel?"

"I guess not." I couldn't feel more guilty if I tried. "I'm so sorry, really I am. I didn't want to put you in danger by telling you the truth." The truth. That unattainable thing we can never share. I brush the hair from his forehead and inspect a deep cut. In the dark—against the pallor of his skin—it looks like a black gorge. He sucks the air over his teeth as I gently pinch the skin back together.

"You need stitches," I say.

"Oh, well, drop me at the nearest Imp hospital."

We lock eyes for a moment and begin to laugh.

"Why did you follow me?" I leave my palm pressed against his head. I no longer need to pretend I have feelings for Willow. I feel slightly giddy at this thought, like I'm back on that carousel. And I suddenly grow very aware of my own exposed skin, how my face, throat, wrists all seem to absorb Ash's body heat.

He lets his eyelids close and turns his head into my palm. "I thought you were in trouble. You see, I didn't go back to the city after you kissed me—"

"You kissed me back," I say, and then blush for being so petty while he's lying beaten in a cell.

"I didn't get much of a choice. You were all over me." He tries to wink, but his eye looks too swollen. He settles on a half smile. "I went to the orchard and when I came back to talk to you, you'd gone. All the slaves were talking about how Saskia had been really angry and you'd all left in a hurry. So, I caught the next bus back to the city and tracked you down. It wasn't hard, I remembered where you were headed the first time I met you. And you've got this really noisy way of breathing, kind of like a pig." He makes this snorting noise and I laugh.

A pause hangs between us. I notice the scraping of a rodent's claws, the drip of water keeping time. My voice cracks. "After I told you I wanted Willow, I thought—"

"I'd just give up?"

"Yeah."

"You know what I told you about climbing? How you always keep one limb on a branch so you don't fall."

I nod, realizing my fingers have begun to twine through his hair.

"Well, I broke my own rule." He catches my fingers with his own. "And now I've fallen way too hard."

My insides feel warm and I can't help grinning, in spite of our current situation. "Are you comparing me to a tree?"

"A big, old gnarly one." A sudden look of panic dislodges his smile. "What are they going to do to me?"

"If you have no use, Thorn may kill you. It depends if Saskia can talk him round." I try to sound calm.

His head thumps against the wall. "I'm a dead man."

"We just need to make you useful to them—indispensable."

Light floods into the cell. Thorn stands in the doorway. I hurriedly untangle my fingers from Ash's hair, angry at myself for dropping my guard, desperately trying to think of a way to make him seem invaluable.

"OK, Little Flower, time's up." Thorn draws a knife from his belt, the same knife he held against Willow's face in canon. Ash's breath quickens against my cheek.

Thorn looks at the blade and then at Ash. "Now I just need to take out the rubbish."

"Wait." I stand, forming a barrier between Ash and the knife. Beneath my overalls, my legs feel like paper.

"Violet, don't . . ." Ash says.

Thorn sneers at me. "Are you going to tell me another story about Ruth? It won't work this time."

My brain aches as I try desperately to think. Not Ruth, not Ruth, another part of the canon. I stare at him, speechless and floundering, my eyes drawn to that rusted, bloodstained knife. I'm reminded again of the canon, and suddenly, I know what to say. "It turns out Alice doesn't know everything. Willow *did* tell me some of the Gems' dirty secrets, before she got her claws into him. But I'll only tell you if you agree to spare Ash and Katie."

Thorn knocks me out of the way and hauls Ash to his feet, ramming him against the wall and sticking the blade into the masonry right next to his cheek. "Tell me," he shouts.

This sudden burst of aggression shocks me. Even though I half expected it, feeling the rush of air and the spray of mortar dust against my face, inhaling the tang of anxious sweat, and seeing every tendon protrude from Thorn's wrists—it's so much scarier than anything on the telly.

I talk fast, my gaze never leaving the blade as it bends and scrapes against the stone. "I know where all the rich and important Gems will be tonight. Ambassadors, generals, even President Stoneback's nephew—Howard." My brain can hardly keep up with my mouth, pulling Willow's lines directly from canon. "There's a brothel known as the Meat House. It's run by some twisted foot soldiers, offering the Gems whatever Imp meat the customer desires—male, female, some disabled, some children. As long as the customer can pay the price, the concubine will be provided." I hear Ash grab a shaky breath. The point of the blade rotates against the wall, releasing dust and sand. The desperation climbs in my voice. "And I know where it is. I can take you there."

Thorn looks at me, the knife still hovering millimeters from Ash's face. "These brothels are disturbing, but they are not new."

"But the customers are not your average Gems," I say. "You storm the brothel, free the Imp concubines . . . you ruffle some very important feathers."

"OK, but to launch an attack on the other side of the border would be suicide. We would be behind enemy lines."

"That's the thing. This brothel has got an extra thrill factor. It isn't in the Pastures, it's in the city."

Thorn begins to laugh, the brilliance of his smile practically illuminating the cell. "Well, well, not so shrinking anymore, are we, Violet?"

"You get treated like an ape, you get pissed."

"Pissed at whom?" Thorn asks.

I recall the decontamination block, those prying hands on my body, the crumpling paper chain, the dead eyes of the Dupes, Nate's arms stretched before him in the marketplace. This anger flares in my stomach and I begin to shake. And when I finally speak, I speak not as Violet, avid fan of *The Gallows Dance*, but as Violet the Imp. "Those bastard Gems deserve everything they get. They deserve to dance on the gallows and know how it feels."

I watch Thorn's blade lower, just as it did in canon. He's going to let Ash live. The relief washes over me.

Thorn turns, a dark expression clouding his face. "But I'm afraid only Katherine wins the reprieve." He spins back to Ash, blade drawn back and ready to strike. In that awful sliver of a second, I realize Ash is going to die.

"Wait!" I cry. The blade hovers. "I know more, I know more . . ." The canon can't save Ash now. I need to take a risk, I need to stop relying on the script, like Baba said. The last time I took that leap,

I was holding Ash's hand. It was when he took me to see . . . "The Duplicates!" My words trip over each other. "Ash, tell him about the Duplicates."

Ash looks at me, his face a muddle of swellings and abrasions, all pinks and blues against the white. But his eyes look sharp, alert, his gaze intense. I nod softly to him and the understanding spreads between us like something concrete and real.

He begins to talk, his voice surprisingly clear. "I found a cloaking device in the Harper estate, deep in the woods where nobody goes, not even the other Imps. I disabled it, and this strange bunker appeared. Inside, there were eight Duplicates. Three Willows, two Mr. Harpers, and three Mrs. Harpers. One of the Duplicates has no legs, and I think one has no heart."

Thorn blinks long and slow. "You found Duplicates?"

"Yeah, suspended in tanks of fluid."

"Duplicates are *real*?" Thorn gasps.

Ash nods. "I've seen them with my own eyes."

"Me, too," I add.

Thorn releases Ash, his disbelief morphing into excitement. "This is . . . *huge*. I thought Dupes were just some sick rumor the Imps made up to turn the average Gem against the government." He pushes his hands through his hair, the knife sandwiched between his thumb and forefinger. "This is beyond huge." He turns to me. "How many Gems know about this?"

"I don't know," I reply. "Just the really wealthy ones, I think. Alice said most of the Dupes are stored in secret warehouses. The Harpers moved theirs because some of the guards were . . . you know . . . doing disgusting things."

"To the Dupes?" Thorn says.

I nod.

Thorn exhales. "So, it's widespread among the Gem rich and elite, but a very well-kept secret. The average Gem obviously hasn't got a clue, otherwise I would already know about it. If this gets out, well, it would really shake things up. Turn the average Gem against the government." A smile spreads across his face and he turns to Ash. "And you said you found this bunker?"

"Yeah."

"With no help?"

Ash shakes his head. "No help at all."

"When?"

"A few months ago, I guess."

Thorn laughs. "And you figured out there was a cloaking device, and then you didn't tell a soul until you met young Violet here?"

Ash nods. "I kind of like being alive."

Thorn tucks his knife into his belt. "Enterprising and secretive. Maybe you aren't rubbish after all." He turns to face me. "The Meat House, Duplicates. You've excelled yourself." He pauses in the doorway, the smile still stuck to his face. "I'll send Darren to get you in five minutes. Consider it part of your reward, Little Flower."

Ash and I slump against the wall, our arms and hips pressed together.

"He is one scary guy," Ash says.

I rest my hand on his. "Seeing him with that knife—"

Ash silences me with a kiss and I feel the anxiety gradually begin to lift.

He pulls away, a thoughtful look on his face. "Little Flower."

"Thorn always calls me that. I hate it."

"It's just strange, you know. Ash and Little Flower. I never thought about it until now."

I shake my head, confused.

"I guess I never told you the last bit of that skipping rhyme," he says.

"No."

He begins to speak, just out of time with the constant drip of water.

"*Count the thistles, one, two, three,*
Soon the Imps will all be free.
Count the thistles, four, five, six,
Take up your guns, your stones and sticks.
The ash trees turn from green to red,
Spring has gone, the summer's dead.
Count the minutes, not the hours,
'Cause hope starts as a little flower."

CHAPTER 33

HOPE STARTS AS *a little flower.*

This line really gets under my skin. I follow Darren through the stone corridors and up some stairs, but I still can't shake that line from my mind.

Hope starts as a little flower.

It seems to be about . . . *me.* Could I be the little flower? The little flower who left spring back home, missed summer, and arrived here in autumn. The little flower who's supposed to bring hope? It can't be about Rose. After all, roses are large if anything. And I remember Baba's words when I first met her: *That's the thing about the viola flower. It's little, but it's rather special.*

This rhyme wasn't in canon, which makes sense if it's about me—*I* wasn't in canon. But it sounds more like a prophecy than a children's rhyme, like I was always destined to save the Imps, which makes no sense. I understand how my clumsy butterfly wings can affect the present, the future, but this rhyme existed long before Ash's birth. Surely, I can't change the past and create a prophecy? And more important, if it is a prophecy, it's an unbelievably crap one. I've screwed up big time—there's no way I'll be inciting a revolution anytime soon.

It's just a rhyme, I tell myself. *A dumb kids' rhyme. At the moment, my very own personal prophecy is more likely to be Humpty-bloody-Dumpty.*

I've been so buried in my thoughts, I barely notice that we've climbed the stairs and reached the wooden door that leads to the ocher room—to Katie. A sense of calm spreads through me, just thinking about her soft Liverpudlian accent.

Darren unlocks the door. "The boss said you get one last reward."

I push through into that musty, dank smell. The door slams behind me.

Katie lounges on a tattered gray sofa pushed up against the back wall. Her delicate features spring into a smile. "Violet!" She throws her arms around me.

I hug her back.

"I can't believe it's you," she says. "It's just a massive pile of scum here."

It can't be much fun for her, still stuck in this poky room, but at least there's some daylight now, the window cleared of grime just like she said in her letter. I visualize Katie and Thorn, working side by side, and can't help feeling a little curious about their conversations.

She no longer wears her catsuit, but a blue linen dress and a brown woolen cardigan. And judging from her slightly floral smell, Thorn's been allowing her to bathe frequently. She looks even more Jane Austen than Sally King right now—her cheeks all rosy like she's just come in from a stroll across the hills.

I hold her at arm's length. "I've been so worried about you."

"*You've* been worried. I'm not the one who's been gallivanting around this horrible place for days. I'm just so glad you're back."

"Not for long."

Her face falls.

I give her a sympathetic smile. "I'm still trying to sort it all out."

She slumps onto the sofa, clouds of dust billowing around her. "So, how's it all going?"

I sit by her side, unable to look her in the eye. "I messed up, Katie, big time. Alice ended up sleeping with Willow, so he never followed me into the city like he was supposed to. The canon's way off-track and I don't know what to do."

Her body stiffens. "Alice did what?"

"Don't make me say it again."

She slams her fists into the cushions, sending more dust eddying into the air. "That filthy little scumbag. I thought she looked a little too happy waltzing off to Gem-land, you know, considering you're going to hang . . . Sorry, I know you hate the *h*-word."

"That's the thing. I hate it, but I hate the thought of staying here more."

I can't quite pinpoint the emotion that crosses her face. Sorrow, anger, denial. "It's not over yet, Vi," she says. "There's still one day left."

"One day . . . and Willow loves Alice, not me. It doesn't look good for Team Violet right now."

"Love?" She narrows her eyes and tightens her mouth. "More like lust. You know what Alice is like, dirty spunkweasel—she probably jumped the poor lad and flashed her tits. He'll soon realize what a shallow knob gobbler she is and want you."

"By tomorrow?"

She sighs. "So, what happens if you don't hang? Do we really just stay here?"

"I guess."

Her hand finds mine. We stare into space, just watching the dust move back and forth, following the tide-like pattern of our breath.

"Thanks for the letter," I finally say.

She grins. "Yeah, I had to be careful what I said because I knew Thorn would read it, but I knew you'd understand."

"So, how's it been?" We're both talking about the whole flirting with Thorn thing.

She smiles. "OK. He's been kind of nice. We've spent a lot of time talking about Ruth. He's still in love with her, even though it's nearly twenty years since she hanged."

"Twenty years? I didn't know it happened that long ago." The canon never specified, but it doesn't surprise me; this universe has a habit of embellishing the backstory.

"Yeah, he looks good for his age, doesn't he? He must be pushing forty. I guess that's the Gems for you."

"You haven't forgotten he's an evil spermpiper, have you, Katie?"

She laughs. "God, no. I could never forget how mean he was when we first got here. But I've been bored, you know, and lonely. It's been nice having someone to talk to. And I do feel kind of sorry for him . . . The way he looks at me sometimes."

I study her face. "It's creepy, you know that, yeah? He's nearly forty and he's sleazing on a seventeen-year-old."

"I guess. It never feels sleazy, though, it feels, I don't know, protective. And he's never *done* anything, he's been the perfect gentleman."

"Just be careful, though." I sling my arm around her neck and pull her copper head onto my shoulder. "You're playing with fire."

"Is Nate OK?" she suddenly asks, changing the subject.

"Yeah, he's just Nate, you know."

Her face relaxes and I notice how pretty she looks compared to the Gems. The slight irregularity of her eyebrows, the smattering

of freckles across her nose, the interesting way her lips pull slightly
to the left when she smiles.

"So, what happens next?" she asks.

"I really don't know. If everything had gone according to plan,
Willow would be here with me now. We'd be planning our escape
from the rebels, tonight. Remember? They were meant to raid that
brothel."

She nods. "And if he *was* here, if you *did* escape, you'd get
caught by the Gem authorities, yeah?"

I nod. "Yeah. Willow and Rose made it as far as the river.
They were trying to reach the safety of No-man's-land, but that's
hardly going to happen now. Willow's probably banging Alice as
we speak."

Katie looks deep in thought. I notice her fingers tapping the
fabric of the couch like she's practicing a cello piece. "What if *you*
got caught? Without Willow, I mean. What if you still end up hanging at the Gallows Dance tomorrow?"

"It wouldn't work. Not without Willow announcing his love
for me. That's what captured the Gems' sympathies and caused the
revolution." *Take up your guns, your stones and sticks*, I think. But I
force my attention back to Katie. "Without Willow, the story can't
complete. And I'll . . ."

". . . just die on the gallows." She finishes the sentence so I don't
have to. We hold each other's gaze, and I wonder if she's wishing
she never met me, never came to Comic-Con. But instead she says,
"Well, we can't have that. If I'm going to live in this shit-tip for the
rest of my life, I at least need my favorite person here."

I smile. "Thanks, Katie."

"Just try and stay alive. You and Nate, yeah."

"Yeah. You, too."

Thorn enters the room. He looks at Katie and smiles, an unfamiliar softness to his face, but when he looks at me, the hardness returns. "Time to go, Little Flower."

I wish he'd stop calling me that. It just reminds me of that rhyme and how far away hope seems right now. "Just another minute?" My voice sounds fragile. I want to tell Katie about Ash, about the Dupes, about the skipping rhyme, about Nate nearly getting his hands chopped off. I want to lighten some of my load. But Thorn shakes his head.

"Can I come, too?" Katie asks.

"No. I'm sorry, Katherine, but I need you here. You're my insurance policy."

And I can't help wondering if Thorn keeps Katie locked away in this tower Rapunzel-style not for insurance, but because he wants her all for himself.

CHAPTER 34

WE WALK DOWN the stairs toward the main body of
the church. Thorn tells me he's prioritizing the Meat
House over the Duplicates. "It's a matter of timing,"
he says. "The Dupes aren't going anywhere."

The rebels did just this in canon—raided the Meat House on
the Friday night, the night before Rose hanged. Willow and Rose
accompanied them to the raid, pretending they wanted to help.
They hid in the alley with the rest of the rebels, waiting until
Saskia had conned her way past the Gem guards. But instead of
helping, the lovebirds used the distraction to escape the rebels—
dropping down a manhole cover into the disused sewage system,
slinking away like rats, trying to reach the river and the safety of
No-man's-land.

When I think about it now, this was a really sucky thing for
Rose to do; abandoning her fellow Imps so she could shack up with
her dream man. I always thought she was romantic and impulsive.
But now, knowing what I know, she just seems selfish.

I tell Thorn everything I remember about the Meat House—
location, timings, risks. We enter the church and Thorn whispers
something to Saskia. Within an hour, dozens of rebels fill the

church—assembling weapons, studying plans, exchanging muted, excited words, same as in canon. And I think about those threads again, how they keep winding together in spite of everything.

I find Nate sleeping on the front pew. Someone's laid a green blanket over him, and only the top of his sandy head pops out. I sit beside him. I can't bear the thought of him growing up in this bloody awful place. Toiling all night at the manor, and breathing in the stinking city air in the day. But I can't see how to fix it. I mull over Baba's words. *If you were stuck here, here in our world, how would you live your life? What kind of an Imp would you become?* Maybe this is all I have left—being true to myself. And right now, that means keeping Nate, Katie, and Ash alive, and sticking it to those bastard Gems.

Night falls and I wake Nate. We leave the protective walls of the church, lurching from the archway into the cold night air. Clouds obscure the sky and I can barely pick out the skeletons of the surrounding buildings. The rebels start loading weapons onto a collection of beat-up vehicles—Humvees, hovercycles, trucks—all originally Gem vehicles, stolen or salvaged.

Thorn guides us to a faded-yellow pickup truck; the jagged, dark shapes of weaponry fill the cargo area. It's the same truck Willow and Rose traveled to the raid in, and it feels like the canon is mocking me again.

Nate and I wriggle into the back of the truck, the dirty floor scraping our palms, and pick our way over the collection of boxes and rifles. We perch on a small wooden plinth, our backs pressed against the hard metal of the cab, just like Rose and Willow.

"Mum would have a fit," Nate says. He's right. She's always been such a stickler for road safety—seat belts on, no loose groceries in case some rogue can of beans flew at our heads in the event of an accident. *Death by beans*, Dad called it, and Mum playfully kicked him under the table. I push the image from my mind; seeing their happy faces just makes my chest ache.

I watch Matthew lead Ash into a Humvee. Ash's movements look fluid, and I feel huge relief he hasn't sustained any major injuries. He watches me from the back of the vehicle, his face distorted by the smeared pane—a mosaic of washed-out colors beneath a black smudge of hair. The hovercycles whir into action, and he vanishes behind a layer of hot, sandy air.

Saskia jumps in beside Thorn and the truck begins to vibrate. It may look like a regular truck, but it doesn't run on gas, so emits no noise.

"Hydrogen," Nate says. "I want this truck."

"I'd settle for a seat belt," I reply.

We accelerate. The g-force hurls us forward and I nearly head-butt a crate of ammo. But the speed soon evens out and we steady ourselves against the cab, our arms linked for stability and comfort. The shelters lining the streets blur together, gray shot through with plastic, rainbowlike beneath the headlights. I can just make out the other vehicles following us, their headlights dipped and muted like a collection of glowworms. The cab offers some form of slipstream, but the wind still makes my eyes water and my ears ring, and I can't stop thinking about the danger ahead. I try to concentrate on breathing—in, out, in, out.

Nate turns to me. "Is this a good idea? The raid, I mean."

I can't bring myself to look at his face, which I know will be all innocent and pixie-like. "It's our only option."

"Rose and Willow only went so they could escape from the rebels. They used it as a distraction, they didn't even enter the Meat House."

I watch the buildings flash by, the windows and bricks merging into one long brushstroke. "I had to tell Thorn about it, there wasn't a choice." The wind steals all the confidence from my words.

"Why?"

"Look, it's tricky to explain, just let me be big sister for once."

He exhales quickly, snatching his arm from mine. "Stop treating me like a kid."

"You are a kid."

"I'm nearly fifteen."

I look at him. The wind has flattened all the spikes from his hair, and in the starlight the top of his head looks like a bullion bar. The weight of responsibility feels like it's going to crush me. The truck swerves at a corner and I fall against the metal side panel. "I had to tell Thorn something or he would have killed Ash."

"Oh, so this is still a love story, I see."

"Thorn had a knife. I was thinking really fast."

"So, you chose one Gem with one knife over many Gems with many guns."

"Well, I don't hear the Imp concubines complaining." It comes out a little snappy, which I immediately regret.

"Soon as the rebels enter the Meat House, we should do exactly what we're meant to—find a manhole cover and drop into the sewers so we don't get shot."

"What about Katie?"

"I don't know." Guilt hangs in his words.

"If we run, they'll kill her. And—and—"

"And what?"

"And what about the Imps? The way those bastard Gems treat us."

"So, now you're a rebel?"

"I didn't say that." I chew my lip. "But if we can't complete the story, if we can't go home, we need to think about what sort of a life we want to live here." Another line of that rhyme gets stuck in my head—*take up your guns, your stones and sticks*. Maybe I can bring hope to the Imps even if I don't hang at the Gallows Dance. Maybe I can help incite a revolution a different way.

The panic in Nate's voice drags me back to reality. "Don't say that, Violet. Of course we'll go home."

How? I want to scream at him. *Exactly how are we going to go home now? Willow loves Alice. He doesn't love me. How am I supposed to fix that in one day?* But I think he's about to cry. So instead, I don't say anything. I just gaze at the stars, which remain remarkably still in spite of the wind in our hair and the relentless movement of the buildings.

"I miss Mum and Dad," he finally says.

"Yeah. Me, too."

"And food."

"And sleep."

He watches me for a moment. "Violet?"

"Yeah."

"Do you ever have . . . any really weird dreams?"

I shift my weight against the cab. "All the time."

"No, I mean, *insanely* weird dreams, where you hear . . . voices. You know, like they're real."

"Mum and Dad?"

He looks excited. "Yeah, saying things like, *Wake up, Jonathan, you can do it.*"

I nod. "And sometimes I can smell the inside of a hospital."

Nate bites the skin around his fingers, nudging his lip as the truck hits a bump. "Do you think *this* is the dream?"

I wish he hadn't said this. The thought has plagued me since we arrived in this world, but it messes with my head, so I've dampened it down, shoved it to one side, just trying to maintain my sanity. I study the stars for a minute. Is earth—*our* earth—really up there somewhere? Eventually, I speak. "Like a coma-induced dream, or something?"

"Maybe."

I consider telling him about the *pip*s of the hospital machine and about the fairy tales. About my sash and Rose's belt of blood. About his Frankenstein insult and how it may have created the Dupes. But my head hurts from thinking, from the relentless wind pushing through my pores and under my skin, and I can feel the idea gradually undoing me at the seams. No, this can't be a dream, it's too bloody scary.

The braking of the truck pulls me from my thoughts. It slows and turns down an alley, the glowworm-headlights expanding into white, sparkling plates. We grind to a halt, hemmed in by two crumbling brick walls. A line, heavy with laundry, blocks out the stars.

Nate sighs. "I love this truck."

"I'll get you one for your birthday."

"Nah. DeLorean all the way." He pats the side of the cargo area. "No offense."

I feel the air—hot against my cheeks—as the hovercycles approach, disturbing the water in a nearby drain, chucking up mud particles and slime. The rebels dismount, checking their weapons and talking in hushed tones. I look for Ash, but I see no signs of the Humvee.

Thorn slams the truck door and hauls me from my perch, the sharp edge of the truck's side scraping against my shin. "You can play canary," he says.

"What?" I try to straighten myself, but I feel like I've stepped off a fairground ride.

"You know, in the old days, before the Gems, when people were just people, they'd send canaries into the mines first to see if the poisonous gases would kill them."

I must still look blank, because he rolls his eyes and says, "You're going in first, Violet. This was your idea, you pay the price if you're wrong. You pretend you're one of the girls, then you slip this into the Gems' drinks." He pushes a vial of orange liquid into my hand. "You've got ten minutes, then we bust through the doors and the windows. Just keep yourself out of trouble until then."

I silently curse. In canon, Saskia went in first—conned her way past the guards, drugged the Gems, and summoned the troops, all in less than ten minutes. I'll never manage that.

Thorn fluffs Nate's hair. "You do a runner, Violet, you turn us in, and I've got my own little canary right here."

Saskia dashes toward us. "Let me go first, she'll only screw it up like everything else."

Thorn shakes his head and grabs a shotgun from the back of the truck. "I want to see what our Little Flower here's made of."

"She's only seventeen." She grabs Thorn's arm, her eyes wide. "Please."

Her concern surprises me. I feel a sudden rush of tears. It's like I'm eight again, falling off my bike and walking two miles home with a busted-up knee, only to start crying when I see Mum.

But Thorn seems unmoved. "The Gems will think her a tastier piece of meat."

Saskia doesn't argue, but her disapproval stiffens the muscles around her jaw. She begins fussing around me, pinching my cheeks and detangling my hair with her fingers. "You sending Ash in, too?" Her voice sounds clipped. "'Cause he's only eighteen, you know. They're both just kids."

"He can come along with the rest of us," Thorn says. "But don't take your eyes off him, I'm not having the lovebirds running off together in the commotion."

I catch Nate's eye. Current-Thorn is smarter than canon-Thorn. But then I remember the main difference: He trusted Rose, he doesn't trust me.

Saskia lowers the zip on my overalls and frowns at my lack of cleavage. "Pretend you belong, that's the secret," she whispers to me.

I try not to laugh—that's what I've been trying to do since I arrived in this world.

"And if you get into trouble," she says, "knock the main light off, OK? We'll come for you."

Ash jumps out of the Humvee. "What's going on?" He dashes toward me.

"I'm the canary," I reply.

"The canary?"

"You know, they're going to send me in first to see how safe it is."

"No way. I'll go," Ash says.

"Well, well, quite the little hero, aren't we?" Thorn waves a hand and several rebels surround Ash, preventing him from reaching me. Thorn turns to me and shrugs, a tight smile gripping his mouth. "Turn left at the end of the alley. Thirteen rows, remember?"

I hold Ash's gaze. "I'll be fine."

Nate squeezes my hand, his eyes moist. "Balls of steel," he whispers.

"Like Katniss, like Tris, like Rose," I whisper back.

And before his tears start to fall, before Ash receives another beating, I slip the vial of sleeping draught up my sleeve and begin to walk down the alley into the unknown.

CHAPTER 35

EMERGE FROM THE alley and get my bearings. To my right lies an arterial road, a straight stretch toward the Coliseum, and to my left lie rows upon rows of terraced houses. I recognize the pink glow that falls from a distant window, and I know that distant *thump* of drums. It's the same as the Meat House from canon—several nondescript terraced houses linked together on the inside, filled with cerise light and futuristic music.

Carefully, silently, I tiptoe down the pavement, the drums gathering strength. I try to swallow, but my body has diverted all its moisture to my sweat glands. The door appears before me. My finger connects with the frayed plastic of the bell, my brain frantically sifting through information, searching for a plan. I have no idea what Saskia said to the guards. The canon showed this scene from Rose's point of view, peering around the corner of the alley, waiting for an opportunity to flee.

I hear the creak of metal sliding across metal, the groan of the wood as the door parts from its frame. My gut knots. A guard stands in the doorway, his broad shoulders silhouetted against the light.

He cocks his rifle. "What do you want?"

I try to speak, but the sight of his weapon dries my mouth even further.

"Well?" he shouts.

"I—I were told I could make a few Gem coins—extra if I smile." I put on my best Imp accent and force my eyes to his face. All angles and symmetry—typical Gem.

"And who told you that?"

The click of the safety hits my ears. Adrenaline hones my thoughts, an idea takes shape. "I work at the Harper estate. I served at Master Harper's Gallows Ball. There were a gentleman who asked me to attend tonight."

He narrows his eyes. "OK, then, slave. What did this gentleman look like?"

"Tall, with all this curly blond hair. He said he were related to someone very important." I try to look demure rather than terrified. "Howard something."

He nods, a little too hurriedly. "Howard Stoneback. OK, then. But any trouble and you get a bullet between those tits of yours." He shoves the nose of the gun into my sternum.

"No trouble, I promise," I say.

He gestures for me to enter. I slip past him, my chest still aching with the imprint of his gun. The scent of incense and stale sweat fills my nose, and I find myself hankering for the stink of rotting bird. He locks the door and leads me down a corridor. The pulse of the drums grows more insistent and the bulbs cast the walls in a fuchsia glow.

He looks me up and down. "So, Howard Stoneback took a shine to you? I bet you think you're really lucky. Well, the last slave he was left alone with didn't look too pretty after he'd finished."

My face must fill with fear.

He laughs. "Too late now."

I begin to wish I was just following blindly in Rose's footsteps. Right now, I'd be running for freedom, not waiting to be molested by a genetically enhanced pervert.

The guard opens a door into a small waiting area—no windows, crimson walls, another cerise bulb that flickers out of time with the drums. Four Imps wait in line in front of a plain white door. I join the back of the queue. They turn and study me for a moment. Three girls and one boy. But something strikes me as unusual about each of them. An angry scar extends from either side of the boy's lips; a Chelsea smile, I think Dad called it once. A large burn covers the back of one of the girls, her dark hair tied up and her smock cut to show the shiny, tight skin. The other girl has one eye that is gummed up like a slit on a tree trunk—she reminds me of Baba and I can't help but stare. She notices me and opens her mouth in a giant yawn, revealing a tangle of scars where her tongue should be. I look away.

It's as though the Gems have grown tired of the blandness of perfection, and this awful place is some sort of warped tonic. Or perhaps it's even more basic than that, perhaps humanity needs imperfection—*craves* it—because without flaws, humanity ceases to be. But still, the sick bastards could just embrace a unibrow.

I glance at the girl directly in front of me. She's the only one here—except for me—who lacks any kind of scar. She looks younger, maybe only fifteen, and wears a beige smock, handstitched from burlap, darted to fit her body. Her red hair falls over one shoulder, a sheet of fire beneath the raspberry light. She reminds me of Katie, and I feel sick just thinking about what the Gems will do to her.

She catches my eye and smiles. "First time?" she whispers.

I nod. "What's happening?"

The door opens. A surge of music. The boy with the Chelsea smile disappears into the room. The door slams shut and the line shuffles forward.

"So, we're waiting to go into the display room. That's where the Gems bid for us. The highest bidder gets to take you upstairs." She glances at my overalls. "Try and look, you know, desirable . . . you want them to want you. No bids is very, very bad."

"What happens?"

Her amber eyes grow wide. "A bullet . . . if you're lucky."

"They kill us?"

"They can do whatever they want, so long as they pay."

The door opens. The girl with the burns disappears.

"Can't you tell someone?" I ask, but even as the words leave my mouth I realize how naive I sound. I can almost hear Ash's voice. *You really are from another universe, aren't you?*

"And risk getting killed? Anyway, nobody could do anything. We're just Imps." Her eyes lower, shame disturbing the lines of her face. "And some of them are good tippers. I can't exactly work in the Pastures anymore." She holds up her hands—but there are no hands, only skin, unevenly stretched over the nubs of her wrists. "And they pay extra for a freak."

The image of Nate kneeling in the market bursts into my mind, followed by the floating, legless Dupe. I want to reassure her, to tell her help is on the way. But the fewer people who know, the better. I feel the vial pushed against my wrist and inhale. "I'm sorry."

I notice that the girl with no tongue has disappeared.

The girl with red hair stares at the door. "I'm next."

"It'll be OK." I reach for her hand, finding only the puckered skin of her stumps.

She shrugs. "Yeah. So long as I don't get that blond creep again . . . Howard something."

An almighty shudder spreads up my body. Howard Stoneback. Of course he's here. I feel so stupid for not thinking through my earlier lie. The fear and anxiety must have clouded my brain. The guard who let me in will expect Howard to bid for me, maybe even address me directly. My only hope is that the rebels arrive before my lie is revealed. And I still have no idea how I'm going to drug the Gems.

The door swings open and she pulls away from me, her red hair replaced by the blank white door. I stand alone in the crimson room, surprised that it should be loneliness rather than fear that threatens to immobilize my trembling, bowing legs. Tentatively, I rest my ear against the door in search of voices. They call out numbers in distant tones. *5,000, 7,000, 8,000.* I don't notice the young Imp boy enter the waiting area, but I hear him clear his throat. I spin around like I've been caught out.

"Sorry . . ." I begin.

He smiles and moves toward the door. And that's when I notice he's clutching a bottle of champagne. He's a serving boy, not a prostitute. My first response is relief because he just looks so young. But my second reaction is to come up with a plan as the vial pushes into my skin—cold and insistent.

I block his path. "Hang on, you've got a smudge"—I point to his cheek—"right here." I maneuver the vial so I can unscrew the lid.

He scrunches up his button nose and mumbles something indistinguishable under his breath.

"Here." I take the bottle from him.

"Thanks." He spits on his tunic and frantically rubs it against his face. He doesn't see me tipping the contents of the vial into the smoking neck of the bottle.

"Is that better?" His cheek looks red and sore.

"Much."

The door opens. I fix my mouth into a shy smile and order my legs to carry me forward, my skin dappled with sweat. I enter a large living room—several smaller rooms knocked into one. The walls look typically Imp—cracked and sagging and waiting to collapse—but the furniture looks Gem, a series of armchairs and stylish leather sofas lining the walls. Several customers remain, sipping champagne and smoking cigars, and several guards stand at the doors. They all hold a drink.

My eyes settle on Howard Stoneback. I recognize him from the Gallows Ball. Same floppy blond curls, but he wears a pin-stripe suit and a perverted leer. I try to swallow, but my earlier lie blocks my throat like a lump of half-chewed gristle. At least the guard from the front door isn't here to rat me out.

A male Gem leans forward. "Come on, ape. Let's see if you're covered in hair under those clothes."

I stumble into the middle of the room to the sound of laughter. Their eyes move up and down my overalls, skimming my features, the shape of my breasts. My stomach turns. But above the drums, I hear the fizz of fresh champagne hitting glass.

A female Gem throws a cigar at me. It bounces off my collar-bone, a shower of sparks landing at my feet. She turns to a guard. "If I wanted a bog-standard slave, I would have stayed at home."

The Imp boy fills the final glass and silently leaves the room. I just need to buy a little more time. I reach toward my chest and clutch my zip with sweaty, trembling fingers. Even though I'm fully clothed, I've never felt so naked. I feel like I'm back in the decontamination block, a moth pinned behind glass.

"Come on, show us the goods," a guard shouts.

"Stick a bullet in her," another woman shouts, her beautiful mouth drawn into this ugly snarl.

A guard aims his rifle at me and the room seems to shift a foot to the right. "Wait," Howard says. "I know this ape. She's from the Harper estate. This is marvelous—I love playing with Jeremy's toys." He sucks the champagne over his teeth, waving his hand for me to continue.

Slowly, purposefully, I lower the zip, inching my shoulders out of the material. My skin looks almost blue against the pink of the walls, and I become painfully aware of every bruise and graze collected since my arrival in this world, my vest speckled with filth and sweat stains so that I resemble a piebald pony. My cheeks feel hot with the expectation of tears.

"This is embarrassing," Ugly Snarl says.

Howard laughs. "It's hilarious, darling. Let's see if we can't make her cry."

I slowly turn, angry with my tears for betraying me, angry with myself for taking so much longer than Saskia, and, above everything, angry at the bastards who humiliate me. But the champagne is nearly gone, so I just grit my teeth and continue to rotate.

A man with muscular hands leans toward me. "Are you hiding a wooden leg under there?" He reaches for my thigh.

A gasp escapes my mouth and I shake him off.

Howard chuckles. "No handling the meat without a bid. You know the rules." He moves to set his empty glass down, but his hand slips and he ends up smashing it into the table.

Muscular Hands slouches back in his chair. "There are no rules, that's the bloody point . . ." His voice trails away and his eyes roll back in their sockets.

"Albert? Are you OK?" Howard asks, but his voice wavers. He grabs the back of a chair, grinding it across the floor.

One of the guards attempts to raise his weapon. It barely reaches his thigh before he sags into the wall. I survey the room—every single one of my tormentors has wilted, their tongues slopping from their mouths.

I ram my zip up. "Bunch of perverts."

The door opens. I expect to see Thorn's face, but instead I see the guard from the front door. Of course he didn't drink any of the poisoned champagne. I could kick myself for making what could literally be a fatal error.

"What the hell?" He aims his gun at me for the second time that night.

"Please, I don't know . . ." I flatten my body against the wall, wishing I could somehow sink into the bricks, become the plaster.

Never dropping his aim, he picks up a nearby glass and sniffs it. He looks at me, his jutting cheekbones highlighted by the overhead lamp. "You sneaky little brat."

I want to slam my hand against the light switch, signaling to Saskia, but I freeze. He smiles in slow motion and aims straight at my chest. I hear the sound of cracking bone. He crumples to the floor, his finger depressing the trigger. Plasterboard sprays my face as the bullet lodges an inch or so from my head.

Thorn steps through the doorway, bat raised for another swipe. "You OK?"

I nod.

He surveys the room and smiles. "That's my girl."

I feel an unexpected surge of pride, but it quickly fades at the staccato beat of gunfire and the sound of wood shattering. The rebels arrive, carrying weapons and rope, shouting instructions.

Thorn races across the room to the door that leads upstairs, the rebels close behind.

"The ones upstairs aren't drugged," I shout after him.

He laughs. "I love a moving target."

They disappear as quickly as they arrived. This is my chance to turn around. To just run and run into the night, never looking back. The need to feel safe pulls against the need to help the Imps. I feel like a Russian doll. Layers of different Violets reducing in size, each one constructed from a different set of memories and emotions. Violet the girl, blowing bubbles in the family garden. Violet the teenager, mooning over Russell Jones. Violet as Rose, desperate to go home. Violet the Imp, repressed, assaulted, and full of rage. I'm not sure who I am anymore.

As if to remind me, someone shouts my name. "Violet!"

I turn to see Ash. He holds a small pistol a little awkwardly, but the smile lodged on his face is as big as ever. He rushes toward me and we embrace. The warmth of his neck against my cheek, the smell of his hair—wood smoke and hay—makes my earlier humiliation evaporate.

"Nate?" I ask.

"He's fine, Saskia and Matthew are watching him. Come on, let's get you out of here."

But something deep-rooted propels me forward. That angry Russian doll, which still feels the pressure of those Gem eyes all over her. "Wait. There's this girl I have to help."

"You can't be serious. We can wait outside where it's safe."

Baba's question echoes in my head again: *If you were stuck here, here in our world, how would you live your life? What kind of an Imp would you become?*

I take Ash's hands in my own and gaze into his beautiful eyes. "I have to do this," I say.

CHAPTER 36

H<small>E LOOKS AT</small> me, the blue of his eyes blissfully cool after what feels like a lifetime of blinking into magenta lights, then he sighs and lifts the pistol. "I've never shot one before."

"Hopefully, you won't have to."

We cross the display room and steal up the stairs—backs pressed into the wall. Upstairs is a warren of corridors. We pass several entrances, each revealing its own tale; rebels rounding up Gems, foot soldiers bound and gagged, young Imps looking disheveled. Door after door, tale after tale . . . no girl with red hair.

We creep up a second, smaller flight of stairs. Sweat dribbles down my neck and beads between my breasts, and the beat of the drums exactly mirrors my pulse, making me feel invaded, like the house has somehow wormed its way into my arteries. A long corridor sweeps away from us, cast in the light of a dying apricot bulb. We must be in the attic, the ceilings sloped and low. I suddenly feel thankful for the continual *thump* of the drums, sure our steps fall heavily against the boards as our desperation climbs.

I notice that these doors remain closed and undisturbed.

"There's nobody here," Ash whispers.

We're turning to leave when a squeal catches my attention. My eyes pivot to a nearby door. I press my ear against the wood and hear a young girl sobbing. I glance at Ash. He cocks his pistol, and with no further thought, we barge into the room.

We enter a darkened chamber. A purple net hangs from the ceiling, surrounding a four-poster bed. Candles glimmer on the walls, the air laced with oil and sweat. The girl with red hair sits on the bed. The neck of her dress has been slashed, revealing the sphere of her shoulder, and I can't help but notice the tremor of her bottom lip. The nose of a shotgun presses into the side of her head. At the end of the shotgun sits a Gem—shirt unbuttoned.

His gaze locks onto Ash. "Something's going on, I can hear the gunfire. Let me go, or I shoot the Imp."

Ash raises his gun. "Where are you going to go? The house is teeming with rebels, and they're seriously pissed."

I step closer to the Gem. "Give us the girl or he'll put a bullet between your eyes." My voice remains strong. He doesn't see that beneath my clothes, my skin is coarse with goose bumps.

Ash glances at the girl. His eyes momentarily dip to the space where her hands should be, and his aim wavers. The Gem seizes his opportunity, turning his gun so it points at my chest. But this time, I don't freeze. This time, I'm filled with rage. My body responds before my brain. I knock the gun from the Gem's hand. The sudden movement must startle Ash, because he fires, the noise fracturing the air. The Gem yelps and clutches his shoulder.

I clasp the girl's arm, no thicker than a bird's leg. "Follow me."

We dash downstairs, scanning the empty rooms—furniture tipped over, carpets glittering with glass fragments, bedsheets stained with blood. No signs of life—Imp or Gem. We stumble into the display room. Again, only ghosts remain.

"Go home," I say to the girl.

She nods, tears gathering in her eyes. "Thank you." She scuttles from the room.

Ash and I stand alone, listening to the music and the sound of our own breath. His hands tremble and the gun knocks rhythmically against his thigh.

"Where have they gone?" I finally ask. In canon, the rebels freed the concubines and left the Gems behind—battered and humiliated and unlikely to open another Imp brothel for a very long time.

"The Coliseum," Ash says. "Thorn told us to take the Gems to the Coliseum."

I don't bother asking why, I already know the answer—I'm the clumsy fool of a butterfly who put the idea in Thorn's head after all. A convulsion grows at the base of my spine threatening to empty my stomach as I remember my earlier words: *They deserve to dance on the gallows and know how it feels.*

CHAPTER 37

THE COLISEUM. I have to go back to the Coliseum. It's like the canon's beckoning, keeping me on track. I just can't seem to escape those gallows.

The city gates come into view. I see two soldiers drooping in their podiums, bowing to the gallows with blood in their hair. We approach with caution. The closer we get, the more the floodlights sting my eyes.

"They must have looped the security feed," Ash says.

"Quickly," I say, grabbing his hand. "We have to stop Thorn from hanging the Gems."

"Sorry, what? Why would we do that?"

"Do you remember what you said to me in the orchard?"

He looks at me blankly. "Don't screw the demigod, screw me?"

I smile. "No, you said that only the Gem people can rise up and stop the barbarity against the Imps."

"I said that? Sounds clever."

"Well, the whole point of this mission was to show the Gems that *they* are the ruthless animals, not the Imps. If we simply kill them, they'll never think of us as humans. They'll never rise up."

He studies my face. "You never did fancy the demigod, did you?"

"Hell, yeah! Did you see those abs?"

Ash laughs and kisses me on the lips.

We slip into the Coliseum, using the same wooden door I stumbled from a week or so ago, still dressed in my cosplay outfit, confused and scared. It all looks so different beneath the stark beacons, all peaks and dips, angles and shadows, more like the vision from my mind blend with Baba. And I feel so different, so full of purpose. When I think of the canon, of Rose and Willow running through the sewers, just skulking away to the river, I feel a sense of pride that I chose to help the Imps. *Hope starts as a little flower*, I think to myself.

In the distance, I see rebels guarding the various entrances. Backs stooped, guns tipped skyward, alert and ready to shoot. At the other end of the Coliseum looms the rickety stage, topped with a broad beam and dangling ropes. The tiny hairs on my body awaken, a ripple of nervousness passing beneath my skin. A line forms before the gallows. I can tell they're Gems from the breadth of their chests, the length of their legs. The rebels wave their guns, forcing the line to climb awkwardly onto the stage. Imps crawl across the top of the beam like insects.

I'm about to move when a familiar voice pulls me back.

"Wait up." Nate stands at the door, looking smaller than ever.

I run to him. "You're supposed to wait with Saskia and Matthew."

He grins, his face all teeth and dimples. "I gave them the slip—ooh, they'll be pissed."

"Jesus, Nate, this is too dangerous."

"This affects me, too." He puffs out his chest, trying to seem older.

Ash takes him gently by the shoulders. "You're a kid. You need to leave."

Nate shakes his head. "And you haven't got a clue, Squirrel." He ducks to one side and breaks into a run, streaming across the Coliseum toward the gallows. We follow, stopping only when we reach the stage. This close, I can make out Darren perching on the beam, checking the lashings one by one. Thorn stands beneath, his forearms tensing as he fastens a series of slipknots.

I shove past the terrified Gems and vault onto the stage. "Thorn, wait."

He sees me. "You want to help?"

"You can't hang them," I say.

"Why the hell not? They hang us every Saturday."

"And it's wrong. You know it's wrong."

He grabs a nearby Gem and positions him above a trapdoor. The blond hair twinkles in the stark lights. Howard Stoneback— his eyes still glassy from the draught. A gag muffles his words, but I can tell from the whimpering that he's attempting to plead with me.

Thorn plows his fist into Howard's ear. "Shut it." He turns to me. "The condemned Imps are innocent. These Gems are rapists, sadists, some are pedophiles. If you don't like it, then look away."

The violence still shocks me. I can't help but look at Nate— hovering at the base of the stage, face drawn in horror. I should have forced him to leave, carried him kicking and screaming back to Saskia.

"This is murder," I say.

"It's the price of freedom." Thorn shoves a rope over Howard's crown, pushing the knot into the base of his neck. "Half of these Gems are politicians. Do you realize the publicity we'll get, the stand we'll make, when their bodies are found hanging from the gallows?" He crushes Howard's cheeks so that his lips stick out around his gag. "This bastard here is Howard Stoneback. Howard bloody Stoneback."

The rebels begin to follow suit, pushing the Gems onto trapdoors, fumbling with lengths of cord. Only Ash stands motionless, his hand resting on my shoulder.

I grip Thorn's hand, the one that encircles a length of rope. "If we behave like animals, they will never think us human."

"They deserve to dance on the gallows and know how it feels," Thorn says. "Your own words, Little Flower. If you were a true rebel, you would make them dance."

A few Gems begin to weep. A puddle of urine stretches across the floor, nudging up against my boots.

Ash steps forward. "What if we could still get the publicity— still make a stand?"

"Go on," Thorn says.

"We sit them on the stage, nooses around their necks, and then we write across their chests, telling the world of their crimes. Then we alert the Gem media. Even the government couldn't spin a story like that."

"That's brilliant," I say. "We take the moral high ground."

Thorn glances from my face to the trapdoors, gouges both hands into his eyes, and makes a strange noise like a balloon deflating. "But they deserve to die. They have to be punished."

"Look at them," I say. "Gagged, crying, standing in their own piss. They'll be humiliated and shunned. It's worse than death."

Thorn seems to stroke the noose for a moment. His eyes fill with tears, his beautiful lips press together. I know he's thinking of Ruth. My heart swells with pity, and the sobs of the Gems sound so very far away. Maybe I would want to hear the snap of the ropes, see the flailing of Gem boots, if she'd been taken from me. I suddenly know how Katie must feel, pitying Thorn.

Very slowly, I unpeel his fingers. "You have to trust me."

He grips my hand for a moment, searching my face for some unspoken truth. "OK," he finally whispers.

A siren cuts through the air. So loud I feel it pass through the soles of my feet. I turn to Ash, just in time to see his lips forming the word *ambush*.

The floodlights cut out, plunging the world into black.

CHAPTER 38

SILENCE. NOTHING BUT darkness and silence. Even the Gems on the gallows seem to hold their breath. From far away, I hear the ocean, a distant roar as it rises and falls, smashing into rocks. The ocean grows louder, angrier. Helicopters.

"FALL BACK!" Thorn roars.

The rebels begin to shout, feet slap the tarmac, gun barrels click into position.

I hear Ash. "We need to get out of here."

But I stand completely still, my legs jammed in position. There was no ambush in canon. The rebels never even went to the Coliseum. How do the Gems know we're here?

Helicopters swarm above, pouring shafts of white light into the black, like giant streamers probing the ground. I see fragments of movement as if captured by a strobe. Cables arcing over the Coliseum walls. Rebels retreating, their weapons raised. Figures crawling over the wall like spiders. A helicopter passes directly overhead. The pulse of the blades travels through my skin. All the tiny hairs on my face—even my eyelashes—stretch toward the ground, caught in the downward draft. My nose fills with dust, my ears feel ready to burst, and in the blinding white light, I see the blanched-out faces of the Gems beside me, ropes twisted beneath their chins.

My hand still grips Thorn's. He pulls me near as if I'm a doll. His normally lavender eyes are almost colorless, his pupils two black pits. "Did you do this?"

I open my mouth to respond, but he leaps from the stage, pulling his gun from his holster in one swift motion. And then he's gone. The helicopter passes and the world swings back to darkness.

Ash tugs my overalls. "Violet, come on."

Gunfire erupts and I see a spray of embers in the distance. Beneath the searchlights, more spiders drop into the Coliseum, their helmets glistening like beetle shells. A light moves over us. Ash pulls my arm and we spring from the stage. The earth hurtles toward me, and I see my boots colliding with the black puddle of my shadow. The searchlight flits away.

"Nate!" I reach blindly for him.

"I'm here." His voice, shrill with terror, finds me above the gunfire. Another flash. His face dives toward me. I pull him from the searchlight into the blanket of darkness. Ash encases my head, pushing me low to avoid the bullets that zip above. Bent double, we begin to run.

We reach the outer wall of the Coliseum and edge toward the wooden door near the Imp-pen. A noise splinters the air, silencing the gunshots and the cries. A noise like no firework I've ever heard, screeching through the sky like a comet. I turn, just in time to see a helicopter crashing into the center of the arena. Its searchlight pours across the ground like a ghostly blood pool. The blades still attempt to turn, causing the body to twitch like it still clings to life. Smoke balloons into the sky and a dreadful snapping sound resonates between the Coliseum walls.

Two figures, molded from flames, stagger from the heap. Foot soldiers rush to the wreck, but an explosion pushes them back, tossing them high in the air as though flicked by a giant hand. The blast ripples through me. I turn into the stone wall, shielding my face as best I can.

I glance back to see the remnants of the helicopter illuminating the Coliseum like a bonfire. The air fills with the scent of gas and smoke, and this faint greasy smell I can't quite place. It smells a bit like pork. Bodies surround the metal shell, forming a perfect circle, some dazed, but some black and red and smoldering. Flesh. I can smell roasting human flesh. Nate grabs at my overalls and a muffled gasp escapes my lips.

"Keep moving," Ash shouts.

We near the door and the gunfire seems to diminish. One by one, the floodlights sputter back into action. My heart lurches. I can see the devastation clearly now. Scraps of fire mingling with black smudges, which I think may be bodies, lines of smoke reaching toward the sky, the helicopter still smoldering like a giant centerpiece. The Gems we captured have long since vanished, and most of the rebels are now being marched from the Coliseum. The Gems could have killed all the rebels if they'd wanted. A blanket of explosives, a few canisters of gas. They must want them for questioning, or a fresh supply of meat for the Gallows Dance. I start to shake uncontrollably, my stomach contracting and expanding in quick succession.

"Hurry," Ash says.

I can see that wooden door, we're so close.

I hear the soldiers approaching. But I don't look. I can almost taste the air beyond the doors, free from the scent of burning flesh. The *thwack* of boots on concrete grows louder. "Drop your

weapons! Raise your hands!" I grab the handle, but a row of fin-
gers pincer-grip my upper arm and a gun pushes into my back.
Any hope of escaping disappears. I look across the Coliseum to see
Howard running toward us.

"Her . . . yes, her!" he shouts. Blood still trickles from his
ear where Thorn belted him, and the gag—dampened by spit—
encircles his neck. "That's the dirty little slut who's behind it all.
She drugged us so her barbaric friends could kidnap us." He pushes
his face into mine, I can smell the blood and champagne on his
breath. "I will see you dance on the gallows tomorrow, ape."

It's the canon, dragging me back, forcing those threads to
intertwine. But my death will be pointless unless Willow runs forward and announces his undying love. And there's no chance of
that now he's got Alice. A fresh wave of panic rushes through me.

The soldiers march us toward the giant electric gates at the far
side of the Coliseum—the exit that leads to the Pastures. We pass
the remains of the helicopter and the side of my face burns hot and
sore. I hear Nate whimper behind me. I want to turn, to tell him
everything will be OK—even though I know it won't—but I can
sense the foot soldiers watching me, their weapons trained on the
back of my head.

Beyond the exit, I see an army of Gems awaiting us. The outlines of the rebels' faces stare from helicopters, hovercrafts, and
trucks alike. I can't believe I ever thought of them as extras from
my favorite film, just background noise to an epic love story. Their
fight for freedom, their quest for justice, now seems so much bigger
than the needs of two love-struck teenagers.

We walk farther away from the Coliseum and I get a strange,
unsettled feeling in my gut just knowing I'm back in the Pastures.
Back in the cotton candy world of the Gems.

A sergeant approaches. Unceremoniously, he snatches my arm. "These three are coming with me."

The soldiers salute him. He guides us between a cluster of vehicles. I see groups of soldiers, some peeling away their armor, others sipping at cups of hot liquid, steam unfurling into the cold. We approach a grounded hovercraft, slightly removed from the rest of the squadron. It crouches on the pavement, a giant pewter disk. A hatch opens, offering a series of metal steps.

"Wait here," the sergeant barks at Ash and Nate.

Strangely, I feel relieved. If word has gotten out that I'm the ringleader, maybe they'll go easy on the others. The guard nudges me up the steps, the pressure of his gun at the bottom of my spine. I enter the craft, stooping slightly, and see a line of soldiers, their perfect Gem faces staring at me.

And in the pilot's chair, leaning casually against a control panel like a cockerel in a henhouse, is Willow.

CHAPTER 39

WILLOW?" THE NAME feels alien in my mouth.

He speaks to the guards, his gaze never leaving my face. "You can go now."

The sergeant leads the foot soldiers from the craft. They move rhythmically—a line of identical clockwork toys. Willow and I stand alone. My ears still buzz from the bullets and I realize I haven't slept or eaten properly in days. I try to focus on his beautiful face, but it swims in and out of focus, the sharp, metal lines of the hovercraft smudging around him.

"Rose? Are you OK?" His voice reaches me above the fuzz, and for a moment, I forget my other name, my canon name. I open my mouth to reply but only a mess of vowel sounds emerges.

"Here." He guides me to a metal stool and passes me a cup of something hot. "It's just tea, it will help with the shock."

I stare into those copper eyes. I can't decide whether I want to hug him or smack him. All my emotions kind of muddle together, forming this ugly, amorphous ball in my gut. I'm so glad he isn't with Alice, and there's something about his perfectly organized face—the symmetry and order—that makes me feel safe. But I also feel angry. Furious. Not only because he slept with my so-called best friend, but because he knows about the Dupes and yet he does nothing, and he would have let those guards amputate Nate's hands if Alice the slutbag hadn't stepped in—how could he be so weak?

"What are you doing here?" I ask.

"I kind of hoped I could be your knight in shining armor. I came to save you."

Save me . . . why does he want to save me? That flicker of hope is back and I begin to think maybe he still has feelings for me. But I order myself to remain composed—he's disappointed me before.

"How did you even know I was here?" I say.

"Rose, I know you're a rebel, and it's OK, I'm not angry. I was at first, but when Father told me about the Gems' plans to ambush the rebels tonight, all I cared about was your safety."

I can't help but frown. "How do you know I'm a rebel?"

"Alice. The girl from the ball, the one from the market."

"Oh . . . *her.*"

He ignores my tone, but can't hide the shame in his eyes. "Why did you take off like that? We kissed and then I couldn't find you again."

Because you screwed my best mate, manwhore. I force a little smile. "Really? You don't know?"

He lowers his head so I see his crown for the first time—each caramel strand spirals outward from a single center point. It reminds me of a pinwheel. He sighs. "I made a terrible mistake. It was just the once, but I guess that's all it took."

"Yeah, I saw you with her the night I left. It broke my heart." This is true. Knowing my best friend could betray me like that, but I let Willow believe he did all the breaking—his guilt could work in my favor.

"Rose, I'm so sorry." He takes my hands and pulls me forward so I can smell the citrus of his soap and the peppermint on his breath. "You see, she told me she worked for the government as some sort of agent, rooting out Imp spies. When she said that you were only getting close to me to spy for the rebels, I was so upset and . . . It was stupid. I regretted it immediately."

Alice told Willow I was spying for the rebels? If Willow had blabbed to the Gem authorities, she could have got me killed. I know that's unlikely, seeing as Willow forgave Rose for being a rebel, but it was one hell of a risk to take. The shock and anger move through me in waves, unsettling the contents of my stomach and robbing me of breath. Could she really be so willing to gamble with my life?

And she never told me that she'd tricked Willow, unsettled him, she'd just let me believe she was better than me. Maybe Alice doesn't possess some weird voodoo power over men, maybe she just schemes and plots and flashes her tits like Katie said. Well, I can compete with that—though maybe not with her double Ds. I begin to feel stronger, empowered. I fill my lungs with air and touch my neck where my necklace used to sit. "She was sort of telling the truth. I am an Imp rebel. I was supposed to win your trust and uncover the Gems' secrets, but as soon as I met you, all that changed."

"I know, I know."

Arrogant manwhore, I think, but I keep on smiling, desperate to get the canon back on track. "I knew I could never betray you, even after I saw you with Alice. It's one of the reasons I left the manor, so I could tell the rebels I'd tried and failed. Then they would leave you alone for good." I know I'm being manipulative, but so much depends on winning him back, I just don't care.

And it looks like he's buying it. He smiles and gazes into my face. "Even after you saw me with another girl? You're amazing, Rose, and I don't care that you're a rebel, I don't even care that you're an Imp." He grabs the cup from me and scoops me into his arms. "It's why I came—to take you back to the manor. The sergeant's a family friend and he said he'd help me smuggle you and your brother out of here."

For a moment, I'm tempted. The stink of the smoke and the burning flesh have yet to penetrate this far. I smell only the Pastures— crisp and pure and laden with pollen. But I know it's all a lie.

He pushes my hair from my face. "Plenty of Gems have Imp lovers. But you would be more than that, of course. I mean, eventually I would have to marry a Gem girl, but it would be for show."

A plan starts to form in my head. I squint slightly with the effort of thinking. I wish I had a pen and paper to write it all down so I don't get snarled up in all the layers. If I get captured by the Gems tonight, Willow could still declare his love for me at the Gallows Dance tomorrow. I just need to get away from him without rousing his suspicion. Then I need to get Nate, Ash, and Katie to safety before surrendering to the Gems.

This could actually work. The excitement builds on my earlier panic so that I feel like I'm about to overflow with adrenaline. I could still incite a revolution. Still go home. Still save the Imps. *Hope starts as a little flower.*

I snake my arms around Willow's waist, hoping to add weight to my words. "There's nothing I want more than to be with you. But I need to get my friends to safety first. Will you help?"

"Of course."

"Just fly us clear of the guards, and when I know they're in the clear, safe inside the city walls, I'll return to the estate."

"I'll come with you."

I shake my head, remembering that lynch mob with a shudder. "The Imps will kill you if they figure out you're a Gem." *And then you can't complete the canon*, I think to myself, followed by a spike of guilt.

He sighs, giving up a little too easily perhaps. "Please be careful." He kisses me on the mouth. Only it doesn't feel like kissing anymore—it just feels like two people bumping lips.

I gently pull away. "I will, I promise."

"Quickly, then." He crosses to the hatch.

"Willow?"

He pauses and turns, his hand drifting above a shiny green button.

"How did your father know about the raid on the Meat House?"

He shrugs. "He didn't say. Why?"

This has niggled at me since I heard the roar of the Gem helicopters. How could the Gems have known we were going to raid the Meat House? In canon, Willow made the raid happen. But in the current, I made it happen. Not a single Gem could have known, unless there's a mole in our midst.

"I was just curious," I say, waving a blasé hand.

He hits the button and the door pops open. He strides across to the entrance. "Send in the two boys, please."

Ash and Nate emerge from the darkness. I hear the hatch swoosh as it seals behind us. After staring into Willow's clean, perfect face, Nate and Ash look like a couple of dirty, half-dead rats, covered in grime and blood and bruises. I feel an overwhelming urge to hug them both.

"What's *he* doing here?" Ash asks.

I shake my head, urging him to fall silent.

Willow loops an arm around my shoulder and plants a kiss on my cheek. "I'll fly us away from the soldiers, then."

I've never seen Ash scowl quite so deeply.

I can't help but grin—I've just had an idea. I wink at Nate. "We just need to find a manhole cover."

"Manhole cover?" Willow says.

"Oh my God!" Nate squeals in delight. "We're going into the sewers."

CHAPTER 40

THE IRON RUNGS of the ladder feel gritty and damp beneath my fingers, like I'm grasping at wet sand, and the cylindrical walls close around us—the rhythmic peristalsis of a giant throat. I feel grateful to the circle of light hanging above, delivering a blast of fresh air, a sense of escape. But Ash begins to slide the lid back into place, and I feel anxiety taking hold. The grind of metal on concrete, the shrinking crescent that eventually clunks to black; it's like watching a terrifying lunar eclipse. And it reminds me briefly of the Dupes, stuck in that windowless room with only a circle of ceiling removed.

I hear several splashes as Nate jumps from the ladder. The flashlight Willow gave him clicks on, highlighting the texture of the bricks, the jagged rungs stained red and orange by time. I follow him into the water, which soaks into my boots, thick and cold.

I survey my surroundings. A tunnel, similar to the ones in canon, arched above and flat beneath my feet, stretching endlessly in both directions. Smaller tunnels branch from it—a row of black, staring eyes. I can stand in the passage with ease, but I still feel confined, thinking about the tons of earth pushing down on us, held back only by a network of ancient, damp-mottled bricks.

Nate sloshes up to the wall and runs his finger over a yellow marking. It looks like an angle, two lines connected at a point. "The lovebirds never figured these out, remember? They ended up hideously lost."

I nod. The markings were made by the rebels years ago, signaling the various exit ladders. But they were coded, a precautionary measure in case the Gems ever made their way down here. And Rose had never been told how to interpret them. Eventually, she found a rebel safe house—an old garage with a Humvee stashed inside—but it took her several hours. They ended up crossing the rest of the city in it so they could reach the river. *We need that Humvee*, I think to myself.

I look at those yellow markings and can't help but smile. It's like the canon never gave up on us, like it knew we would catch up eventually. Just like Baba said—a story needs to unfold.

Ash pauses to examine the markings while Nate sloshes in my direction, seizing the opportunity to grill me. "So, what was Willy doing in that hovercraft?"

"He's still into me," I whisper. "The canon's back on track. If I get myself captured by the Gems, Howard Stoneback will see that I make it onto the gallows, then all that needs to happen is Willow saying his lines and . . . voilà!"

"You're serious?"

"Nate, we can go home tomorrow."

His face unfolds into a massive smile, the same one he used to wear when I pushed him full force on the swings. "Oh my God, Violet, this is immense. OK, OK, so how do we get you captured?"

"Well, the canon seems to come true whatever we do."

"So, we go to the river? Where Rose and Willow were finally caught?"

"That's what I'm thinking. We get the Humvee from the safe house, we bust Katie out of headquarters, we head to the river, then you and the others cross to No-man's-land. I'll wait for the soldiers and surrender."

"My God, sis, check out your balls, they're positively gleaming."

I grin. "Katniss and Tris—they're just a couple of Girl Scouts."

Nate looks thoughtful. "Is there time? Maybe Katie and I should find another hiding place?"

"No-man's-land is the safest place. If we hurry, you can easily cross the river before the soldiers arrive—we just need to navigate the sewers better than Rose, buy back some time. Can you remember where she went wrong?"

"Maybe, these tunnels all look the same," he says.

Ash joins us. The movement of his legs causes a gentle wave to lap against my calves. "So, what's the plan?" he asks.

"We're just discussing our next move," I say.

Ash looks at the bricks above, purposefully avoiding eye contact. "I thought that was what you and Willow were doing."

"Oh, get over it, Squirrel," Nate snaps. "She wasn't about to dick off the only person who could set us free."

Ash exhales sharply. I can tell he isn't convinced.

"We find a vehicle," I say. "Get Katie, then we all cross the river to hide in No-man's-land." *Except for me*, I think. *I'll be surrendering to those Gem soldiers.*

"There's just one problem," Ash says. Even in the gloom, I can tell he's blushing. "I can't swim."

None of the Imps can swim. I know this from canon. The only water available is filled with sewage and debris.

"Don't worry, there's a boat," I say.

Nate swings the flashlight beam over the first marking. "If we could figure these markings out, life would be a lot easier."

Ash glances at the markings again. "Two lines, one slightly shorter than the other. Are all the markings like this?"

"Yeah," Nate says. "Just a load of different angles."

"They look like the hands of a clock," Ash says.

He's right. A minute hand and an hour hand. I can't believe I never noticed this before—a result of living in a digital age, I suppose. *Count the minutes, not the hours.* Where have I heard that recently?

"The skipping rhyme," I say to Ash.

"Count the minutes," he replies. "Do you think the rebels hid the answer in an old nursery rhyme? One that only the Imps would know?"

I nod. "The minute hand must point to the correct tunnel. Clever."

Nate grins. "OK, then, let's buy back some time. Follow the human sat nav." He runs down the corridor, kicking up his boots so the water sprays around him, arcing from his feet and catching in the flashlight.

"Keep up, slowpokes," he yells over his shoulder.

Ash and I follow. The air grows increasingly humid the farther we get from the manhole, and running requires more and more effort, like pushing through molasses. Nate pauses at another pair of clock hands before jogging down a different corridor.

"So, what did the demigod want?" Ash says, the damp and the moss of the walls absorbing his voice.

"Look, Ash, what you saw in the hovercraft—"

He cuts over me. "It doesn't matter."

"I had to keep up the act so he'd let us go. It wasn't real."

"It looked pretty real to me."

We round a bend, pass another clock face. The passage tightens.

"Bear right," Nate shouts.

The ground below us suddenly curves. This tunnel is entirely tubular, and my feet take a moment to adjust. Ash catches me as I lurch toward the murky water. I collect myself, only to see a rat weaving past my boots—slippery and black, half-running, half-swimming. I grip Ash's hand, the warmth branching up my fore-arm, and push on through the warren. Something about that skipping rhyme bugs me. Where did it come from? The clock mark-ings were in canon, so perhaps the coded skipping rhyme was, too. But could a rhyme exist in canon if Sally King didn't write about it? Perhaps not. Rose never figured out the yellow markings, after all. And she would have known the rhyme had it existed; Ash made it sound like it was well known by all the Imps. Maybe the rhyme really is a prophecy about me.

Hope starts as a little flower.

Nate stares up a ladder. "You have reached your final destina-tion." He gestures to a single yellow brushstroke on the wall. "It's the mark from canon. It means the safe house is overhead." The beam of his flashlight explores the manhole cover resting above.

"What's he talking about?" Ash says. "And what's this canon you keep mentioning?"

"You wouldn't believe us if we told you," I say.

"More secrets?" Ash twists his hand from mine and begins to climb the ladder.

I feel a stab of loneliness. Right now, that wall of secrets feels more like an impenetrable forest of thorns and brambles. A voice interrupts my thoughts. Deep and familiar, and so very out of reach. *And the princess slept for a hundred years. Though she never did have the face of the dead, her cheeks remained pretty and pink like the day she was born.* It's Dad's voice again.

I look upward. "Dad?"

A mixture of excitement and concern crosses Nate's face. "You heard Dad again?"

I pause, listening intently to the drip of water, the scuffle of rats, the clang of Ash's boots on the rungs. I shake my head. "No, no, I'm just hearing things. Ignore me." I don't have space in my head for anything else right now.

I place a hand on the ladder, ready to haul myself upward, but Nate shines the flashlight in my face and whispers, "Violet, I've been thinking . . . How did the Gems know about the raid at the Meat House?"

"I don't know, and Willow couldn't tell me in the hovercraft."

He wrinkles up his nose. "I can't figure it out. In canon, the only Gem who knew about the raid was Willow, because he made it happen. But in the current, Willow wasn't even captured by the rebels, so how could he have possibly known about the raid . . ." He shoves his hands in his hair. "Agh, it's messing with my head."

Ash interrupts from above. "Are you guys coming or what?"

I look up at him, the soles of his boots so badly cracked I swear I can see the blisters on his feet. "Yeah, just a sec." I turn back to Nate. "Willow said his father told him about the raid."

He frowns. "What really gets me is the Gems knew we would be at the Coliseum—that didn't even happen in canon."

"I know. But the Meat House is only a few streets from the Coliseum. If the Gems knew about the raid, likelihood is they flew over the Coliseum and saw us. There must be a mole, maybe one of the Imp rebels. Someone we don't know, or maybe even Saskia or Matthew."

"Maybe. Or someone else who knows the canon."

We stare at each other. The realization scrapes out my insides. I reach for the split heart and end up pinching my bare throat instead.

"Why would Alice do that?" I ask. Everything seems to slow. The dripping water, the scuffling rats, even my own heart.

Because I already know the answer.

I can't complete the canon if I'm dead.

CHAPTER 41

LOVE. PEOPLE TALK about it like it's a mental illness.

Crazy in love, addicted, lovesick, obsessed . . .

And maybe they're right. Alice has loved Willow for two years. And I don't just mean the actor, Russell Jones, I mean the fictitious character, Willow. That's verging on insanity, surely? And if anyone should know, it's me, having suffered from the same affliction.

OK, so Alice has dated the odd footballer, the odd boy band (yes—the whole band). But she always returns to her keyboard, tapping out her fanfic, the only place she could enact her Willow-related fantasies . . . until now, that is. But would she really have her best friend killed in the name of love? Perhaps, if she's lost her mind. I risked the canon because of Ash, after all. But kill someone?

"I've known her since primary school," I say.

"I've known her since I was born," Nate says.

"She's . . . *good.*" The image of those four bronzed legs wrapped in satin appears in my mind's eye. "Well, she's not a monster, at least."

Nate nods. "You're right. This place is making me paranoid."

"Come on, you two," Ash shouts. He's already shoved the manhole cover to one side and a downward breeze caresses my face.

My heart starts pumping again. We clamber from the hole, leaving a patchwork of soggy marks on the surrounding concrete—hands, feet, knees. Even though the night is cold and dark, just the movement of the air, the sense of space, makes it feel like we've burst from a grave into a summer's day. Of course Alice didn't tell the Gems about the raid. I feel guilty for even considering it.

I glance around. The safe house from canon—just another stinking alley with an orange garage door. We flatten our bodies against the wall. Ash circles his weapon through the air as though searching for trouble, but the alley remains still, just like it should. We creep toward the familiar door, coated in blotches of flaking paint. I pull the latch and it swings open.

"Bingo," Nate says.

I can see little in the dark, but the stagnant air tells me the door hasn't been opened for a while. Nate runs the beam of his flashlight over the contents of the room. Shapes rise up from the ground, concealed beneath oilcloths and sheets. A forgotten museum. More like I imagined it when I read the book. In the film, the room was bigger, better lit, less claustrophobic. Quickly, we pull the cloth from the Humvee, flipping up dust and matted cobwebs. I stifle a cough. Ash finds a water bottle in a cabinet and hands it to me.

I hadn't realized how dry my mouth feels—the inside of my throat caked in a fine layer of grime—until the cool liquid hits my tongue. I only think to stop swallowing when Nate coughs.

"Sorry." I wipe my mouth with my sleeve and pass him the bottle.

Ash climbs into the Humvee and runs his fingers over the controls. "I've no idea how to drive."

"You didn't know how to shoot a gun, but you managed that pretty well," I say.

Ash grins. "I missed. I was aiming for his balls." He flicks a switch and the headlights strike the alley wall, reminiscent of the helicopter searchlights.

We made it out of the sewers in record time thanks to the skipping rhyme; there should be plenty of time to get Katie and make sure they all reach No-man's-land safely. So long as the canon keeps true to form, haunting us, pushing us down the right path.

Nate inspects the front of the car, his smile wide. "Still not the DeLorean, but it will do." He steps back into the alley to survey the vehicle as a whole. And the way the headlights fall on him—illuminating his skin, turning his hair to gold—lends him the appearance of some heavenly spirit. Something draws his attention, something in the alley hidden from my sight. Fright darkens the taupe of his eyes. The water bottle slips to the ground.

I hear his words, ridged with panic. "They're here."

I see the shadows first, three beasts reaching up the alley wall, a collection of frenzied spikes beneath the yellow glare of the headlights. I dash to Nate, thrusting his body behind mine. Only now do I see the eyes of the foot soldiers, shadowy beneath their helmets. Guns aimed at our heads. There were no soldiers at the safe house in canon. How did they know where to find us? It can't be a coincidence.

They drag Ash from the Humvee, twisting his arms behind his back, wrenching the pistol from his grasp. It skids across the ground, landing in a nearby gutter. I can hear the throb of a helicopter landing at the far end of the alley, stirring up the dust and the hairs on my neck.

Ash bashes into me, whirling from the force of a guard's hands. I quickly do the math. Three soldiers—heavily armored, covered in weaponry, tall, broad, and trained. Three Imps—all unarmed.

Fear prevents me from crying, but I can still feel the tears forming in my lower lids.

"On the floor or we shoot," a soldier shouts.

We kneel, our movements disjointed, the lights of the Humvee burning our eyes.

A man runs from the chopper, initially no more than an outline, but he gains color and form as he nears. He looks different from the soldiers. Something about the way he moves is more upright, more formal, and beneath his body armor he wears a pinstripe suit. He approaches me and a familiar leer twists his handsome face. Blond curls corkscrew from beneath his helmet. Howard Stoneback. It definitely isn't a coincidence; Howard's been gunning for me since the raid at the Meat House, and it looks like someone's told him where to find me.

He stands over me. "There she is, the little brat who drugged us."

"What shall we do with them, Mr. Stoneback?" a soldier asks.

Howard takes his time, looking us up and down, prolonging the torture. Then, he leans in and strokes my cheek with a cold, dry finger. I feel like I'm standing back in that display room, zip clutched between my trembling fingers.

He straightens up. "I want to see this pretty thing spinning on a rope on prime time. I've just spoken with the president, and he's reserved a special place for her at tomorrow's Gallows Dance."

This could work to my advantage. I'd hoped to see Nate, Ash, and Katie safely to No-man's-land before my capture, but I'm learning fast that things don't always go as planned.

He pulls a pistol from a holster. I can see every line, every hair, on his hands, cast in the glare of the headlights, but his features become no more than a hodgepodge of shadows. His gun glints as his fingers lace around the trigger. "But I only need the whore." He looks at me. "Next time you piss someone off, make sure they aren't related to the president."

The cold water nips at the base of my gullet, threatening to climb higher. I push it down and find my voice. "Arrest me. But please, let the others go."

He laughs. "An Imp issuing orders—interesting." He leans in close again. I can feel his breath against my cheek, hot and peppered with spit. "Do these Imps matter to you?"

I nod.

"How sweet." He smirks and lifts the nose of his gun. "An important lesson in life: Imps don't matter."

I watch his finger compress the trigger. The noise rips through my head and bounces off the alley walls as though God himself is screaming. For a moment, I think I've been shot. I brace myself for the pain, glance downward, awaiting the stain of crimson spreading across my stomach.

But I feel no pain, see no crimson.

I see only Nate—rasping, spluttering, clamping his hands to his abdomen.

A red patch spreads across his overalls.

I reach for him, but my fingers swipe only air as he topples to the side. The soldiers shove me into the ground and I watch as Nate's blood colors the concrete, moving toward me like black, syrupy water.

My hearing goes woozy. I can just pick out Ash's cries, traveling through a film of shock. "You bastards. I'll kill you, you bastards." I see his face, mid-scream, splattered with Nate's blood. The soldiers knock him to the pavement with steel batons. I watch the steel shafts curving through the air, almost gold in the yellow lights of the Humvee. My gaze shifts to Nate's body, slumped and bleeding. And something solidifies inside me. A singular Russian doll forged from anger and righteousness, a doll that belongs solely to the Imps. Its lacquered shell grows hard and strong, encasing me with a sense of purpose.

I see my opportunity. My muscles swell with rage, tight and curled and ready to explode. I leap toward Howard Stoneback, barreling into his shoulder and catching him off guard. He falls to the ground, firing several futile shots into the sky. I hurl my fists at his chest, his face, anywhere I can reach, the rage pulsing through me, pushing out screams and sobs. But Gems are strong, and Howard quickly flips me away. I skid across the pavement, my fists still whirring before me like they don't know how to stop.

I can still hear Ash's voice, gurgling and weak. "Violet, no."

Howard points his gun at me, disbelief unsettling his faultless brow. I know I will die now. My eyes flicker shut, and I wait for the bullets to pierce my belly, arms, neck.

Four shots in quick succession. Four thuds.

I open my eyes to see Howard and the soldiers littering the ground like scraps of paper. Those blond corkscrews dipped in red, and that perverse leer finally gone. Strong hands grasp my arms, hauling me to my feet and clutching me to a muscular chest. Matthew.

"Are you injured?" he asks.

I don't reply. I can barely breathe, let alone speak.

Matthew hoists Nate over one shoulder and carries him to the Humvee.

Saskia dashes over to me. "Violet, I'm so sorry, Nate got away from us back at the Meat House."

Again, I don't reply.

"We need to get out of here." She helps Ash up. "We only came back for the Humvee seeing as the Gems trashed our rides. Lucky for you we did."

Matthew lays Nate in my arms. The weight of his body wakes me from my stupor. I support his fair head in the nook of my elbow, cradling him as though he's newly born, and climb into the back of the car. I notice the slight movement of his chest, the blood fizzing from the corner of his lips as he tries to breathe.

Saskia and Matthew climb in the front of the Humvee.

Saskia turns to Matthew. "There's obviously a mole in our midst. We torch the church before the Gems find it." She pops her face around the back of the headrest. For a second, I think a splash of Nate's blood has reached her forehead, then I remember it's just her birthmark. "Thorn's gone. Dead or captured, so it's up to us now," she says.

The thought that this news would sadden Nate crosses my mind, but I feel very little when I think of Thorn being dead. At least he can't harm Katie now. I feel the movement of the Humvee as Ash manages to hoist his body beside mine. He helps me apply pressure to Nate's side. The blood feels warm, oozing between my fingers.

"I need something to stem the flow." My voice comes out a string of breathy words.

"It's a stomach wound," Saskia says. She doesn't tell me Nate is dying, but I hear it, heavy in every word.

I look into Nate's face, so pale it almost disappears beneath the starlight. His golden eyelashes quiver, his breath catches in his throat. And that's when I first notice them, faint and distant, the rhythmic *pips* from my dream.

We burst from the garage, tires screeching. Matthew cuts the lights, so I'm not sure how he can tell which way to drive, but he powers down the alley regardless. *Pip . . . pip . . . pip.* I trace Nate's features with a finger. The pain ages him by at least twenty years, carving great trenches into his skin. I wonder if his face offers a porthole into the future he will never have. Nate as a man—perhaps with children of his own, my nieces and nephews. Tears fall down my cheeks and splash against his forehead.

This is all my fault. Alice must have told the Gems about the safe house. How could I have been so stupid? My inability to doubt her led the soldiers straight to us—straight to my little brother. The guilt feels like a black hole, sucking everything from me. Hope, joy, love; dragged into a pit of nothingness.

Pip . . . pip . . . pip.

"Violet," Nate whispers. Blood dribbles from the corner of his mouth, scarlet against the white of his cheek. "Tell Mum and Dad I love them."

"Tell them yourself."

His eyelids flicker as he loses focus, and I notice the *pip*s begin to slow, like a clock losing time.

"Are you afraid?" he asks.

"Of what?"

"Of hanging."

I let out a loud sob, tears pouring into his face. "No," I lie. "Of course not. It's just a story. We can't really die in a story—Baba told me. When you wake up, you'll be home with Mum and Dad."

"And real food, and football, and a nice soft pillow."

"Yeah." A moan grows in my stomach, threatening to rip me apart.

Pip . . . . . pip . . . . . pip.

I begin to feel strangely removed. I step outside my body and watch his features slowly settle. I grow increasingly aware of the space above me. An infinite sky—black and heavy and loaded with stars. And below, I see myself. Face warped, back curved, fingers plaited through strands of golden hair. I can almost see my love, a shimmering force field encircling our bodies, binding us together in a giant bubble. I could reach out and touch it if I wanted, but I'm afraid it may disappear.

Pip . . . . . *pip* . . . . I wait for the final *pip*. I know what they are, what they mean, of course I do. Tinny and hollow and terrifying—echoing around a hospital room. I wipe my eyes and watch as our bodies move as one, swaying as the Humvee corners the endless side streets. Nate's face now looks completely relaxed . . . . . *pip* . . . . And finally, his chest is still.

The monotonous tone of the flatline hits my ears.

And I know that he has gone.

CHAPTER 42

SINCE ARRIVING IN this world, I've experienced more physical pain than I thought possible. I've been kicked, shoved, pulled, strung up, not to mention the indescribable ache of Baba's palms resting on my temples. But it feels so insignificant when compared to the pain of losing Nate.

Whereas physical pain brought my body into focus—filled me up, made me swell, turned me into something bigger—loss does the exact opposite. It scrunches me into a ball, folds me in half, scoops me out until I'm not sure I exist—the world around me becomes a carbon copy. Or maybe I'm the copy. I can't tell anymore.

I don't know how long I sit in the back of the Humvee, lurching from side to side. Eyes parched, brain numb, just clutching at Nate's lifeless body. The flatline still rings in my head, and I pray and pray and pray that this is just a dream, just a horrible, twisted dream. That when I wake up, Nate will be smiling and laughing and telling me some random crap in his Sheldon Cooper voice.

I barely notice when we draw to a halt outside the church.

Matthew holds my eye. "Dead?"

Such a small word, yet so hard, so final.

I nod.

"I'm sorry." He pauses. "The sky's empty."

I know he means of Gem helicopters, but I can't help thinking of the stars.

"There's no time to lick our wounds," Saskia says. "We need to torch the church and then escape over the river."

No-man's-land. They've had the same idea as us—hardly surprising.

Matthew jumps from the Humvee. "Wait here."

"But I need to get Katie," I say.

He looks at Nate and his eyes well with tears. "Quickly, though." He lifts Nate from my lap. "We can leave him in the church. He'll get a true hero's funeral."

I nod, too numb to argue. I need to focus on the living, on Katie and Ash. I'm not sure I even care about completing the canon anymore. Home isn't home without Nate. I slide from the Humvee, my legs only just carrying my weight, soaked in blood and weakened from fatigue.

I follow Matthew to the church, Ash's arm wrapped firmly around my waist. I can't help but watch Nate's feet undulating to the rhythm of Matthew's stride. Up, down, up, down. I remember him much younger, soaring back and forth on a swing, kicking up the spray at the seaside, dancing in my bedroom to Abba. That black hole returns, sucking me empty.

The church looks as if a swarm of locusts has passed through it. Everything, bar a series of boxes, has gone. Nearly all of the rebels were arrested at the Coliseum, and the night-lights have long since been extinguished; only a few remaining candles offer pouches of light. I see Thorn, leaning against the altar, his head battered and covered in blood, his hands holding a small black box.

Saskia sees him and stops. "Thorn, you're alive."

He looks up, his eye patch gone, the full force of his beauty uncovered. His gaze falls on me, red capillaries spider-webbing across the whites of his eyes. "You did this, Little Flower."

His words barely touch me.

Matthew lays Nate down on the pew at the front of the church. The one where he slept only hours ago. I bend over his lifeless body, brushing the hair from his face, kissing his cheek. It still feels a little warm. I pull the green blanket over his legs, telling myself he'll wake up soon.

"How did the Gems know about the raid?" Thorn says.

"Leave it, Thorn," Saskia says softly. She hands me a piece of moist cloth, and I begin to wipe the dirt and blood from Nate's face. He looks so young again, his face no longer capable of holding any pain. A sob lodges in my throat. Ash rests a tender hand on my shoulder, and without thinking, I plant a kiss on his knuckles.

"The raid, Little Flower. How did they know about the raid?" Thorn persists.

But it's like he's talking behind glass. I don't care if he thinks I'm a traitor. What could he possibly do to hurt me more than this? Tenderly, I arrange Nate's arms so they cross his heart. I lean in close. "I'm sorry," I whisper. "I'm so sorry, Jonathan." I hear myself begin to cry, and I bury my head in his narrow chest, willing him to comfort me.

I sense Thorn standing behind me. "You betrayed us, and now your brother is dead. It is a fitting punishment, I think."

I turn my head and glare at him. "You never did deserve to be his hero. You can go to hell."

"First, you've got to kill me."

All the fury, all the injustice, bursts inside me. I look at his perfect Gem face and I suddenly get this overwhelming desire to hurt him, to kill him. I run at him, kicking and spitting. "I hate you," I scream, "I hate you." I scream it to all the Gems, to the universe that holds us captive and stole my little brother.

Thorn lifts me from the ground and carries me from the church. I thrash and twist, but it's no use. Ash tries to help, but Thorn bats him away like a fly. Saskia and Matthew follow, concern gripping their features.

"No," I cry. "Let me say good-bye. Please. I just want to say good-bye."

Thorn laughs. "Well, now you can say good-bye to your little friend, Katherine."

"No, not Katie, too. You wouldn't kill Katie."

He carries me toward the Humvee. "You can watch her burn. Along with all the rebel intel, years of work. It's all got to burn."

And I realize Thorn's hate—for me, for the Gems—now overpowers his love for Ruth. What started as something beautiful has grown and morphed into something ugly. A black, jagged mess of revenge and hate. We were so naive, so foolish, to think that his feelings for Ruth would offer some sort of protection to Katie. I get this ringing in my ears as I realize I'm about to lose Katie, too.

Thorn throws me to the floor and stamps a foot into my stomach, pinning me to the ground. Ash jumps on his back, but Thorn seems to just shrug him off. I wriggle and flip like a fish on a bank, but he possesses Gem strength and the boot won't budge. He jabs the button on that little black box. Two small explosions punch through the drone and shards of glass rain down on the pavement. The church windows begin to glow orange, the eyes of a Halloween pumpkin.

"No!" I scream. "Not Katie." Nate's dead. Alice has abandoned me. Even worse, betrayed me. The thought of being the only one left from the four of us fills me with such an intense loneliness, I think I may implode. "I can't lose Katie, too." The tarmac slaps against the backs of my thighs, my shoulder blades, as I continue to struggle against his boot.

"Do something," Ash shouts to Matthew.

"This ain't right, Thorn," Matthew says.

Saskia runs toward us. "You ain't seriously gonna let her friend fry?"

Thorn pushes his boot down so hard I hear something crack in my chest. "They set us up," he says.

Of course. He thinks Katie betrayed him, too. That's why he wants her dead.

"It was Alice." My voice starts to fade, robbed of breath and hope. "It was Alice who betrayed you . . . *us*. I swear it wasn't Katie."

"Nice try. But Alice didn't know about the raid."

"She did. Ask Baba, please, just ask Baba," I manage to say.

Thorn laughs. His boot bears down and I hear another *crack*, feel another round of pain. "What, the precog?" he says. "She can see the future, do you really think she'd stick around for our fireworks display?"

I feel the air flooding my lungs, the release of pressure from my ribs as Thorn lifts his foot, but the relief is short-lived. He pulls me onto my knees, squeezing my cheeks, forcing me to stare at the church. Flames push through the windows, reds and golds lapping skyward, writhing and shifting into ever-changing patterns of shadow and light.

He whispers into my ear. "Can you smell it yet, Little Flower? Stick a match to us and we're all just the same. Gems, Imps, brothers, friends. We all stink like roasted pig and we all turn to dust."

I feel sick thinking of Nate and Katie, their skin blistering in the heat. The flames climb higher, swallowing the church in reds and golds and smoke. *You can't lose Katie, too. Think, Violet, think.* I recall that golden pelican plucking at its sacrificial breast, and the ink from Katie's letter stirs inside me, those words appearing in my mind's eye: *All the world's a stage, and all the men and women merely players.* And suddenly, I know what role I must play to save her.

"You're right." My voice gathers its strength from somewhere deep inside. "I did betray you. I told the Gems about the raid. I set the ambush in motion."

"No," Ash shouts. "Violet, what are you doing? He'll kill you."

I know Ash is right, but I push on regardless. "Katie didn't know anything about it. I never told her because I was worried her allegiances had switched. I was worried she would tell you of my betrayal."

Thorn begins to laugh, tightening his grip on my face so I can barely breathe, forcing my eyes toward those reds and golds. "I knew it was you, Little Flower." He yanks at my cheeks so they feel stretched and clawed and hurls me forward. I headbutt the tarmac. He looks at me for a moment, really looks at me. "You thought Katherine had switched allegiances?"

I manage a nod, spitting up something salty and hot. "She's rebel to the core."

He gazes into the flames for a moment, his face cast in amber, and then whispers something I don't hear. And suddenly, his legs begin to move with the urgency of a man about to lose everything, pelting his body toward the church. I glance at Ash. *I can't lose Katie, too.* He must see this in my face, because without a word, he grabs my hand and we follow.

We burst through the wooden doors only moments after Thorn. The smoke hits me first—thick and dense, stinging my eyes and burning the inside of my nose—followed by a strange, pungent odor, like the Imp-bus when it backfires, or Dad's whiskey, stagnant in a crystal glass. Thorn is already just a silhouette, his broad shoulders giving him the appearance of a tombstone rising from the mist.

I tighten my grip on Ash's hand and we wade through the smoke into the main body of the church. I see the desks and crucifix screen ripped apart by flames. The golden pelican and the circle of angels brought to their knees. But our path remains miraculously free from flames.

Momentarily, I freeze.

Nate.

The thought of the flames devouring his tiny body threatens to immobilize me completely. But I focus on Katie—her soft Liverpudlian accent, her pea-green eyes—and I hold my breath and force my legs to move, following that tombstone and pulling Ash toward the tower.

I look up the stairs toward Katie's prison. Thorn already stands at the top, desperately trying to open the door. He sees me and shouts a single, bleak word: "Locked." He clearly hasn't got the key.

Tears spring from my eyes, coaxed by hopelessness and particles of smoke. I consider just sinking to the ground and weeping, when a loud noise draws my attention. The door reverberates, bowing toward us, rattling in its frame. I imagine Katie, terrified and trapped, flinging her weight into the wooden panels. Thorn does the same, and for a short while, they're caught in a strange call and answer song. But the door is sturdy and, without much of a run-up, Thorn's unable to use his weight to his advantage.

Ash pulls me up the stairs, two at a time. "Your knife," he screams at Thorn. "Give me your knife!"

The panic in Thorn's face is replaced by suspicion. But Katie still hammers on the door, a sound that reminds him just what's at stake. He pulls his dagger from his belt and passes it to Ash, handle first.

Quickly, Ash works on the hinges on the door, using the tip of the knife as a screwdriver and removing the bolts.

"Hurry," Thorn shouts.

Ash's fingers remain nimble and precise, like he's back at the estate picking apples or shelling peas. In less than a minute, he's removed all six screws. Together, the three of us maneuver the heavy slab of wood, lifting it from its hinges and prizing it from its frame. I dash through the opening, nearly bowling Katie over with my embrace, and I take a second to hold her to my body, inhaling the smoke-free air of the sealed ocher room.

"Violet! Thorn!" Her tears dampen my neck. "You came for me."

"We have to go," I say.

"Now," Thorn says.

Katie looks at Ash. "Who's this?"

"There's no time, Katherine," Thorn shouts.

I guess she sees the urgency in his face, because for once she doesn't argue. We bolt down the stairs, sinking into the choking fog. I didn't think it possible, but the flames have intensified, transforming the building into a bell jar of smoke. Searing, blistering, and unyielding. We fly toward the door, mouths shielded with sleeves, skin aglow and tender with heat. My tongue and throat feel as though the blaze has singed them. I try to hold my breath, but this makes me cough, and the more I cough, the worse it burns and the harder my lungs seem to suck.

We reach the exit and I take one last glance over my shoulder. Behind the wall of flames lies my little brother.

"Good-bye," I whisper into the fire.

Good-bye, the fire replies.

CHAPTER 43

A MIGHTY CRASH shakes the building. I shelter my face as a shock wave of heat and dirt hammers into me. Of course. The rebels planted more explosives. The church is predominantly stone, so there would be little to feed the flames once they'd devoured the wooden furnishings. We stumble from the door, clinging to each other, hacking and spitting.

And suddenly Saskia and Matthew are beside us, wrapping us in their arms and guiding us from the smoke. And when we're far enough away that the air feels cool against our skin, we all slump for a moment, transfixed by the flames, as if watching a procession of cobras dancing to Eastern music, the orange reflected in our eyes. Rebel Headquarters, gone forever. Strange to think, after centuries upon centuries of worship and humanity and war and technology, something as primeval as fire should tear it to the ground. And it's impossible to look away, like watching a lion take down a gazelle—in spite of the horror and the overriding sadness, you can't help admiring the sheer strength of the beast.

Finally, Ash leans into me. "We need to run."

But he's too late. *I'm* too late. Thorn hasn't forgotten my earlier confession, and as I try to stand, he's already pounced on me, dragging me back to my knees. And I'm reminded again of the lion. But I feel no admiration now that I'm the gazelle; only pain and indignity and pure terror.

"No!" Saskia screams. "She was just saying it to save her friend."

"Thorn, please," Katie yells.

Ash rams into him, but he makes little impact against Thorn's heavy frame.

Thorn turns to Matthew. "Keep a tight hold of her boyfriend. I want him to see this."

Matthew twists Ash's arms behind his back, murmuring something directly into his ear. I don't know what Matthew said, but it's enough to drain away all of Ash's fight.

"Are you ready, Little Flower?" Thorn asks.

Cold metal pushes into my temple. I can't breathe. White spots gather in my vision. My lips go numb.

Katie moves in front of us. Her body blocks out the church so it looks like she's on fire, like she's some terrifying demon. She shows us the white of her palms and fixes Thorn with *that* look. "You don't have to do this. Please, for me, let her go."

I hear his voice, filled with anger and hate. "She betrayed us, Katherine. She told the Gems about the raid on the Meat House, they ambushed us at the Coliseum. She led them right to us—she must have worn some sort of tracking device. They killed dozens of us, captured the rest."

Katie's voice remains measured yet firm, her hair merging into the red of the flames. "Violet would never betray the Imps."

"How do you know?"

"Because I know Violet." Her gaze clicks somewhere else for a moment, and I see the slightest of cracks in her calm demeanor.

"I had a lot of time to think about the things you told me when we were in the cell together," she says, changing tack.

He pushes the gun into my skin. "What things?"

"The things you told me about Ruth."

"You leave her out of this, Katherine."

But Katie continues in her gentle manner. "At first, I thought I reminded you of her."

"You do."

"Yes, but there's more to it than that, isn't there? The clue's in the timing—she hanged nearly twenty years ago."

He doesn't reply, but the tremor of the pistol makes me think he may be crying.

"You lost more than just Ruth that day, didn't you, Thorn?" Again, her focus slips to a point just behind him, like she's watching . . . waiting.

"Stop it," Thorn says. "Just stop it, Katherine, I warn you."

She takes a step forward. "You lost something—someone—just as important." She's dragging out her words, buying time.

The nose of the gun rocks against my skull. My breath grows increasingly shallow, my vision increasingly hazy, and I find looking at Katie too hard, the flames burning my eyes. I let my gaze slip to Ash—his wonderful, irregular face—and I just wait for the peace and calm of nothingness. But something behind those winter eyes doesn't meet my expectation. They don't look scared or sad or angry. They look full of hope. Excitement.

Katie takes another step toward us. "But the real clue was the way you looked at me," she says.

I force myself to look at her again. She looks so empowered, so in control, and I realize that the whole time I was at the manor, trying desperately to keep us safe, to send us home, she was back in that ocher room doing exactly the same thing. Buttering up the enemy, gathering information, looking for chinks in the armor. She takes another step forward so that she blocks out the flames entirely and I see only the smoke, gushing into the sky.

She smiles a soft, kind smile. "Because you don't look at me like a lover. You never did. You've always looked at me like a father." She takes one final step, closing the gap between us, and reaches a steady hand out toward Thorn. "Ruth was pregnant when she died, wasn't she?"

But he never gets to answer. I hear a strangled scream. Something hot and wet and metallic-tasting sprays into my mouth. The gun falls away from my temple. I turn to see it bouncing off the tarmac. Then, I see Thorn. Both hands clasped to his throat, blood spurting between his fingers and streaming down his forearms. He collapses to his knees and stares at me, blinking in slow motion. I imagine I can hear the moist *click* as his upper lids finally connect with his lower rims—a pair of camera lenses shutting. Finally, he falls onto his side, blood pooling around my knees.

He doesn't blink again.

Saskia stands in his place, bloodstained knife in her hands. And I finally understand that Katie was keeping him talking so Saskia could creep up on him. I inhale a huge lungful of air; a strange, shaky noise escaping into the night.

Saskia raises an eyebrow. "Sweet Jesus, he's a big bastard. I almost needed a ladder to reach that throat." But the frantic rise and fall of her chest belies her nonchalant tone.

Katie falls on me, squeezing my body against hers. "Are you OK, Vi? God, I thought he was going to kill you."

"Yeah," I manage to squeak.

Ash and Matthew help me up. Ash kisses my forehead and

wraps his arms around me, his eyes wet with tears of relief. "I was sure you were a goner."

I wipe my mouth and my hand comes away scarlet.

Saskia cleans her knife and sticks it back in her belt. "Gem blood, Imp blood—it all tastes the same."

I notice I can pick out every one of her features. The strong line of her nose, the sapphire of her eyes, the texture of her port wine stain, slightly rippled like crepe paper. Which means only one thing—the searchlights of the Gem helicopters are approaching. Thorn's cost us precious time. We need to hurry.

We look to the sky to see an army of helicopters arriving. Small, dark smudges fall toward us—a sheet of explosives that penetrate the blaze of the church and lift more stone and debris our way. A blast to my left sends chunks of pavement battering into my ribs. Another blast and the Humvee bursts into flames. We slide to a halt and watch as our escape route disappears beneath a blanket of fire.

I can hear only the crackle and pop of the blaze, the whir of the helicopters—no explosions, no flying tarmac. At first, I think my eardrums must have ruptured, but when I look to the sky, I see the bombs have stopped falling.

A series of cables spiral toward the ground.

"Move, move!" Matthew shouts.

We don't wait to see the spiders falling down, nor do we wait for the shower of bullets to nip at our heels. We just turn and sprint—as fast as our damaged bodies will allow—into the winding side streets of the metropolis.

CHAPTER 44

WE RUN THROUGH the city, bending through alleys, squeezing our bodies through narrow passageways. The footsteps of the Gems and the thrash of the helicopter blades grow dull and tired, unable to navigate the city like the Imps. Perhaps we will make it to the river in time for my friends—all four of them—to reach safety.

"Thanks for saving me." I struggle to breathe and talk.

"I was hardly going to let him shoot you," Katie says.

"How did you know Saskia would slit his throat?" I ask her.

"She flashed her knife at me and I just knew. Thorn stabbed her once, he told me, and I'm guessing Saskia isn't the forgiving type."

I smile, because it's more than that—Thorn isn't the only one with parental urges. And Saskia and Matthew's loyalty plants a warm glow in my chest.

We wriggle under a makeshift roof, a piece of corrugated iron slung low between two pillars of rock. The mud oozes between my fingers and slips beneath my knees.

"So, what's happening now?" Katie asks, emerging into the open air and scanning the skies for helicopters. "Is it the river bit?"

"Yeah." The others are far enough ahead not to hear, so I brief her as we run. "Willow and Rose tried to escape across the river in a rowboat, and that's what you're going to do, you and the others. You can hide in No-man's-land until I hang tomorrow. It should be safe there."

"Didn't Willow and Rose get captured on the river?" She stumbles on a mound of broken concrete.

"Yeah, but I think you've got time to make it across before the soldiers arrive."

She steadies herself and sucks in a huge mouthful of air. "What about you?"

"I'll wait to meet the soldiers on my own."

"Sounds risky."

She's got a point, so I don't waste my breath arguing—I need it too much right now. My legs have started to ache and my throat feels hot and sore.

"Where's Alice? Still banging Willow?" she asks.

I feel my mouth pull tight—it's a question I don't want to answer. "No. She screwed the lot of us, instead."

"What do you mean?"

"She told the Gems about our movements—she's trying to get me killed so I can't complete the canon and take her away from Wonderland."

Katie loses her step again, mutters, "Pork sword" into the night, and grabs my hand in solidarity. "Are you sure? Alice can be a bit of an airhead, but surely that's taking it a bit far."

"It's the only explanation."

"Really? I just find that a little hard to believe. Something else must be going on."

I shake my head, a stubborn gesture.

"And where's Nate?" she asks.

Now, this is the question I've really been dreading. "Dead." The word expands to fill my head, knocking me off balance.

"No!" It sounds more like a scream than a word, so loud the others turn to check we're OK. "What—what happened?" Katie asks.

"The Gems happened." My voice sounds so angry, so full of hate, I'm reminded of Thorn. I run to the rhythm of her sobs, unable to offer any comfort as I have only bitterness and regret in my heart. I look at the moon—fat and plump just a few days earlier, but now fading, soon to become no more than a sliver in the sky—and I vow to keep my friends safe, to get them to No-man's-land before surrendering.

I won't let them die, too.

Little ambient light spills from the sky, but Saskia and Matthew navigate the streets with ease. For the second time tonight, I feel hugely grateful for their help—I don't think I'd have found my way to the boats on foot.

The Gem bombs haven't reached this far, and buildings sprout from nowhere, blocking our path, throwing us off course. We move around them, keeping the stench of fish close, and the occasional glint of the water even closer.

"This way," Saskia shouts.

We exchange no words, but simultaneously begin to drop toward the water's edge. It's the same bay as in canon, an outcrop of stone concealing an area of silt. We find the tiny fleet of rowboats nestled in the mud beneath sheets of tarpaulin. The smell makes me think of camping trips with my parents and Nate. His face all ruddy and pink in the light of the campfire, a drizzle of hot marshmallow stuck to his chin. That black hole threatens to reappear, so I blink back my tears and focus on the task at hand—helping Saskia set flashlights in the empty rowboats.

"Decoys," Saskia says.

We launch the boats into the river.

"Thank you," I manage to say, my breath heavy. "For what you did back at the church."

Saskia rubs her collarbone, the place where Thorn sliced her all those years ago. "He's had it coming for a while. Nothing to do with helping you and your dopey mates, you know that, yeah?"

"I didn't set us up," I say, watching the flashlights bob into the distance, like will-o'-the-wisps or jack-o'-lanterns.

"Of course you didn't. You're useless." Only one boat remains. "You guys ready?"

"Yeah," Ash says.

I don't tell them I'm staying on the shore, I don't have time to explain or argue. And I just can't stand the thought of saying good-bye to Ash. I've already had to say good-bye to Nate, and that's quite enough for my lacerated heart. We splash through the shallow water. Saskia and Katie scramble into the boat, the wood creaking and slipping beneath their boots. Katie perches in the stern and manages to smile at me, even though the green of her eyes looks dull and tired.

I scrabble with the rope while Ash and Matthew lean into the stern. The ground whips away and the vessel bobs free. Ash and Matthew clamber in, spraying cold water onto my hands and face. Ash leans forward and offers me his hand. I hear the dull, oceanic roar of the Gem helicopters. They're early. No, not early—any time gained navigating the sewers was lost when Thorn tried to kill me and the Humvee exploded.

I ignore Ash's hand and keep on pushing the boat. The water reaches mid-thigh.

"Come on, Violet," Ash says.

The helicopters grow louder, the water reaches my waist, and I just keep on pushing.

"That's deep enough," Saskia says.

The current decentralizes my balance. But I don't stop pushing.

"Good luck, Vi," Katie says, her voice shaky and small beneath the night sky.

"Just stay alive, OK?" I reply.

She nods.

Ash reaches for me, almost toppling the boat with his weight. I grasp his hands and gaze into his face, taking one last look into the palest blue eyes I'll ever see. "That secret I've been keeping?"

Confusion touches his features. "Yes?"

I smile. "It's always been you." And with one final push, I watch them drift away.

CHAPTER 45

"VIOLET, VIOLET." I hear them call my name. The scratch of wood against metal as oars click into the oarlocks, the frantic splashing of water as they attempt to turn the boat and follow me. "Violet, wait." I ignore them and turn and wade toward the shore. The helicopters have nearly arrived, and I pick up my pace, pumping my arms like mad. The river glistens like a pool of tar—I can just make out the reflection of the stars, cragged and blurred by my motion. "Please, Violet, they'll kill you."

Large hoops of light appear around me. I raise my head to see shafts of white carving up the black. The helicopters. Until I saw them, I wasn't entirely sure they'd arrive. Perhaps Alice disclosed this location, too, or perhaps it's the canon again, haunting me, dragging me to the gallows.

I just need to get arrested, then hopefully the soldiers won't bother with the little wooden boat floating in the background—it's me they want, thanks to the fact Howard Stoneback's dead. I take some comfort in that the hovercrafts haven't yet arrived. I'll never forget them in the film. Black, glossy disks hanging in the sky like stones, generating this low whirring noise that traveled through the sofa and into the backs of my legs. They snatched Rose and Willow from their little boat with long, metal tentacles—scared the life out of me. But I shove them from my mind and repeat the words again and again, hugging them to my body like a life vest: *I won't let them die, too. I won't let them die, too. I won't let them die, too.*

I reach the shore. I think I've made it. But the joy of saving my friends is completely overshadowed by the fear of facing the Gem soldiers. I begin to run along the bank, waving my arms, trying to attract the Gems' attention. "Don't shoot," I shout. "I surrender." They want me alive, at least for now, but the sight of the guns still makes me want to puke.

I hear a shot. I don't know who fired first; the Gem soldiers or my friends in the boat. It doesn't matter. Once the bullets start flying, I lose control of the situation. I turn to see Matthew, caught by a bullet. He falls over the side like a bag of sand, tipping the boat. Every one of the passengers falls into the water, pulled beneath the surface. I forget about the soldiers—I only know I must reach Matthew. Shot and sinking. But then another thought finds me, even more terrifying, even more paralyzing. Imps can't swim. Which means Ash is likely drowning at this very moment.

I run toward the upturned boat, flinging my body into the water. I take a large breath and squeeze my eyes closed, just before a thousand nails drive into my skull. The river may look like tar, but it is undeniably water—ice-cold, endless. I kick my legs and force my hips to twist, propelling me upward. The surface breaks over my head and I take one enormous gasp of air. For a moment, I feel disoriented. I can't see *anything*—the stars, the flashlights, the soldiers. But I can hear. Muffled gunshots, the echo of my own breath, lapping water. My hands paddle and bash against something solid. I realize I've emerged beneath the upturned boat.

"Violet?" I hear Katie beside me, panting and treading water.

My eyes adjust, and I can just pick out Saskia, clinging to the upturned seat, holding the boat as though it's a giant shield. Her head bobs under the water until Katie pulls her up again, looping an arm beneath her chin.

"Imps can't swim." I spray river from my mouth. "Stay with Saskia."

I dive back into the cold and power through the black, not entirely sure which way is up or down, manically swimming in circles, my arms reaching for imaginary shapes. But there is no Ash. No Matthew. Only gray, watery phantoms. My lungs feel ready to burst, and I know I desperately need more air, but panic drives me on, reeling, spinning, groping through the dark.

An intense light pushes its way into every corner of the black, like angels have ripped a hole in the clouds, letting the heavens burst through. The underwater world can no longer hide. I see every piece of driftwood, every murky stone, every strip of seaweed carried in by the tide, my own hands, pale and hopeless before me.

My eyes find Matthew first. He lies motionless. His mahogany skin already part of the riverbed, his lifeless eyes like two freshwater pearls. A dark cloud billows from a hole in his chest. And although this is not what I wanted, the last thing I wanted, I feel thankful. Because I only have one pair of arms, and now I don't have to choose who to save.

Next, I see Ash, suspended and flailing, wrestling an invisible sea beast. Bubbles spiral from his hands, and his black hair fans around his pale, bruised face. I've never seen him look so scared, and for a shard of a moment, I feel completely flooded with love. Within seconds, I reach him, slip my hands beneath his armpits, and drive us toward the surface.

We break into the heavenly light, coughing and spluttering. I flip him over so he looks skyward, hook my elbow under his chin, and begin to swim toward the boat. I hear a strange noise, a low, whirring hiss combined with Ash's spluttering. As far as the eye can see, the surface of the river begins to wrinkle, the water almost vibrating, droplets sucked upward like it's raining in reverse.

"Violet," Ash manages to say.

I think he's trying to warn me, because he's already seen what I can't.

The light doesn't belong to angels.

It belongs to the four glossy stones hanging above us.

Next come the tentacles—scary when I read the book, even scarier on TV, *horrifying* in real life. A motorized arm snakes through the sky with strong, sinewy movements. There's no point even trying to escape, it moves with such speed. A large metal cuff girdles Ash's middle and rips him from the water, so quick and brutal I don't get the chance to look into his face one last time. He floats high above me now—a tiny version of himself—and disappears into the belly of a hovercraft.

I bob for a moment, completely alone, just water and panic and brilliant lights. It comes from nowhere, the second arm, winding through the river like a metal sea serpent. A shot of adrenaline, a burst of horror. It clamps around me, forcing the air from my lungs, and yanks me upward with such speed my neck cracks. The wind rushes through my wet clothes, and I watch the boat below shrink to the size of a child's toy. Saskia and Katie remain concealed from sight. At least they are safe for now.

The arm sucks me into the craft and dumps me on the floor. Before I can catch my breath, a team of soldiers descend, jerking my arms behind my back, cuffing my wrists and ankles. I don't bother fighting. I just search frantically for Ash—my eyes find him; a mound leaking river across the floor.

This is just like the scene from canon, only it isn't Rose and Willow coughing up silt onto the metal floor—it's me and Ash. I hear the buzz of a walkie-talkie. *"We got her, sir. Her and another gutter monkey to throw in the mix."*

I've done it. The canon is back on track. Tomorrow, I will hang. But I feel no relief, no sense of achievement. Because just before I feel the bite of a hypodermic needle sinking into my neck, just before I lose consciousness, I hear the walkie-talkie spew out its response. *"Good work. A double act for the Gallows Dance."*

It won't just be me dangling from a rope tomorrow.

Not Ash, I try to say. *Not Ash*. But my tongue just flops hopelessly around my mouth.

CHAPTER 46

I WAKE ALONE, THE taste of dirt in my mouth. The remnants of several nightmares swim in my head: blood reaching across concrete, two freshwater pearls staring from the riverbed, metal snakes moving through water. My eyelids flicker and the walls of a white, sterile room throb in and out of focus. A cell, similar to the one Rose woke in. I try to sit, but my arms bow under my weight. Not nightmares—memories. The images continue to hover in my line of sight, transparent and ethereal, like they're printed on the finest of silk sheets.

The door opens and a couple of foot soldiers enter. They set various things beside me—a towel, a hot drink, a white robe, a tray of food. They leave the room and the lock clicks into place. Soon, I will meet President Stoneback. The man who makes Thorn seem like Santa Claus. Whose nephew's death I witnessed back at the safe house. I close my eyes and take deep, steady breaths.

The food smells amazing, like Christmas dinner and birthday cake rolled into one—proper food. I realize I haven't eaten anything since yesterday's bread, and although I shouldn't be able to touch a crumb, the juices in my stomach begin to swirl. So I kneel before the tray and shovel the food into my mouth like I'm back in Ma's house.

I look around the cell, not used to the feeling of fullness in my stomach. A small bathroom sits in the corner. Clean and sparkling and floral-scented. I stumble toward it, and for a while I just sit on the floor, waiting for the food to reappear, finding some comfort in the hardness of the tiles. But after a while, the nausea recedes. I notice for the first time since I woke that my clothes cling to my skin like a thin layer of ice, and even though I can't stop trembling, even though my thoughts are muddled and my breathing jagged— the early stages of hypothermia setting in—I delay the inevitable moment when I undress. Because I know I'm hurtling toward the climax, the end of the canon. And maybe I will return home, maybe I will incite a revolution and become that little flower who brings hope to the Imps, but Ash is going to hang, too. He won't return home. He will just die. Tears pool in the corners of my eyes, but I know I need to think clearly if I want to ensure his survival. So I command myself to unpeel my clothes and place them in the drying pod.

I step into the shower. At first, the water scalds, like a hundred little irons branding my skin. But the pain subsides, and I feel the warmth penetrate my flesh, gradually reaching my bones. Slowly, my brain starts working again. I take some time trying to unravel the confusion. The ambush, the safe house . . . Alice's betrayal.

My thoughts turn to the noose and the flying trapdoor. I wonder how much it will hurt. Whether I'll be aware of Ash, his legs whirling beside mine as life escapes him. And I don't really know if Baba was right, if hanging will even work—one moment, the life choking out of me, and the next, lying in a heap of rubble back at

Comic-Con or maybe in a hospital bed. It all seems a little far-fetched now that I'm standing in the shower in a military bunker, preparing to hang.

The questions multiply along with the panic, spiraling out of control. Will Katie and Alice wake beside me? And what if Alice tries to turn Willow against me again? What if Willow doesn't profess his love and the canon doesn't complete? Will I just die for real, and will Katie and Alice live in this world forever? And what about Nate? My funny, clever, quirky little brother. Will he wake up, too? The questions build inside till my skin starts to feel tight and ready to split. I shut off the shower and towel myself until every bruise stings—a welcome distraction.

I know I should probably put that white, clean robe on, but I wrinkle up my nose and slip on my overalls. They stink of the city, itch to high heaven, and feel rigid with grime and dried blood—my own, Ash's, Thorn's, Nate's. But they make me feel safer. I don't know how long I sit on the edge of the bed, staring at the white ceiling, wishing it were a sky full of bubbles and Nate were beside me shouting, *More bubbles, Violet, more bubbles, please.*

I begin to wonder what the president will say to me. I remember his conversation with Rose. He was so condescending, I wanted to slap him. *Well, well. If it isn't Rose. The beautiful, fearless Imp rebel. The girl who stole Willow Harper's heart, only to lose hers in return. Please, come sit with me.* But I can forget about the script now. It would make no sense, seeing as I was pulled from the river with Ash and not Willow.

Eventually, the soldiers return. They escort me down a long, sterile corridor, perfumed with lilies and cleaning products. I see a large, wooden door, heavily guarded and boasting the colors of the Gem flag. I wipe my eyes out of habit, but I have no tears. Every last drop of moisture has been squeezed from me. I take small, shaky steps toward the door, half expecting my joints to creak, hoping my body will crumble on impact.

The guards open the door and I see him. The man from canon. Rose's nemesis. The Gem president. He lounges in a velvet tub chair, sipping from a porcelain teacup.

He smiles his plastic smile and says, "Well, well. If it isn't Rose. The beautiful, fearless Imp rebel. The girl who stole Willow Harper's heart, only to lose hers in return. Please, come sit with me."

My lips part, but I feel too confused to speak. These are the lines from canon. The exact lines he spoke to Rose when he met her. How does the president even know about Willow? I don't know what to do, what to say. So, blindly, I follow canon, forcing out my lines: "Willow. Where is he now?"

"Back at the manor. Licking his wounds. Don't worry. You will see him again. He will of course attend your hanging tomorrow."

Again, the president follows the script. Somehow, he must have found out that Willow helped me escape the ambush. I say my next line, unsure of what else to do. "Please, no."

The president smiles. "Come now, Violet, you can deliver your lines with more pizzazz than that."

At first, I think I must have misheard. The fatigue and the anxiety and the remnants of the sedative. "Pardon?"

"Oh, I'm sorry. Have I gone off-script?" He turns to the soldier. "Lieutenant, please pour our guest some tea. She has, after all, traveled a long way to be with us."

The world seems to shrink. Everything around me—the coffee table, the picture frames, the vases of lilies—reduced to a series of knickknacks. The lieutenant passes me some tea and I set the saucer on my lap. The dark liquid begins to tremble. "I don't know what you mean," I finally say.

"You don't need to play dumb with me, Violet. You're the new protagonist, isn't that right? The dashing heroine of your favorite tale." He looks me up and down. "And a pretty convincing one at that."

I stare at him, my mouth hanging open.

He smiles his strange, plastic smile. "*I* know the lady with no face, too."

"Baba." I say her name and it all clicks into place.

He nods. "Amazing precognitive abilities, she knows where you're going to be before you do, Violet. And what psychic powers— a mole who can visit me in my dreams. She may look a sight, but she is Gem through and through."

A black, ugly mess of emotions surges up my throat. Baba told the Gems about the raid, the safe house, the escape across the river. Baba betrayed us. Baba killed Nate. My teacup begins to clink in its saucer. "But, in canon . . ."

"She was on the side of the Imps?"

"Yes."

"Haven't you noticed? The 'canon,' as you call it, is just a framework, the bare bones over which we have draped our rich and detailed universe."

I screw my eyes up. Thinking really hurts now, like I'm peeling thoughts off the inside of my brain. "She told you about *our* universe, about the book?"

He nods. "I've known for a long, long time."

All my questions begin to expand. I can practically see the rips appearing across the backs of my hands, my wrists, my skin straining against the pressure. "But Baba only found out a week or so back, when she first met me at the church."

He chuckles to himself and sips his tea. "She played dumb. She's known for years. Since *The Gallows Dance* was first published."

"I—I don't understand."

"No. I imagine you don't. Your small ape brain will struggle to take it all on board." He stands and walks to a small window, veiled by an emerald curtain. He pulls a cord and the curtain is drawn back. It isn't a window, but a portrait. Sally King. "I painted her from memory. Baba introduced us in a dream. You know who it is, of course?"

I nod.

"I thought it fitting she should watch over me. She did, after all, create me." He stares at the painting, an unfamiliar softness in his voice. "I know that somehow her universe, your universe, created ours—the power of the collective conscious, Baba called it."

"The collective conscious?"

"Yes. When a group of people share the same beliefs, the same ideas—"

"You're talking about the Fandom?"

"You could call it that. In fact, let's call it that. The Fandom—it has a better ring to it. Well, the energy from the Fandom created something . . . something real." He circles his hand, a dramatic flourish. "This!"

He leans over the table and dips his finger in his tea. It still steams, but he doesn't flinch. He draws a circle on the coffee table with the moisture. "Baba told you about a story being a life cycle. Birth to death."

I try to nod.

He holds my gaze with his glassy eyes. "Well, that's what this is. A never-ending cycle. A perpetual loop . . . I know because I'm stuck in it." He dips his finger in his tea again and draws a series of lines around the circle so that it resembles a scant clock face.

This makes me think of the markings in the sewers and Nate's face, lit up with excitement as he traced the yellow paint. I get this throbbing in my chest that makes it difficult to breathe. But the president continues. He points to the top line—the twelve o'clock line. "The beginning of the loop. Here. I'm sitting in my office. I hear the news about a thistle-bomb at the Gallows Dance. *Some rebels freed the condemned Imps*, they said, *nothing to worry about, sir*, they said." He moves to the three o'clock line. "Here. They tell me that Willow Harper has gone missing. *The rebels are involved, nothing to worry about, sir.* We launch a search party." He moves his finger to the bottom of the circle. Six o'clock. "Here. They arrest some jumped-up little rebel ape called Rose." His finger hits nine o'clock. His voice rising with urgency. "I meet her in my office, she shows no remorse. I think how lovely she'll look dancing on a rope." He moves his finger close to the first line—the twelve o'clock line. "I watch the ape hang, the crowd turns and rips the gallows to the ground, then . . . *bam*." He jabs his finger to the top of the circle again. "I'm back in my office, hearing of the thistle-bomb like it's just happened."

He dips his finger in his tea again and refreshes the fading loop. "At first, I doubt my mental health. I'm the president, I'm under a lot of pressure. I take some pills and I go through the motions again." His finger continues to circle the table, gathering speed. "I meet the ape, I watch her hang, the gallows fall, and then, *bam*." He pushes so hard, I swear I see some blood mingling with the tea. "Office. Thistle-bomb. The ape hangs. The gallows fall. *Bam*." His finger gets faster and faster, until the circle is entirely red. "Office. Thistle-bomb. The ape hangs. The gallows fall. *Bam*."

He screams in frustration and knocks the table over. The sound of bouncing wood and shattering porcelain fills the room. I freeze. Only my chest moves—a series of shallow gasps. He turns to me, his features arranged into such a banal smile I struggle to imagine he was capable of such an outburst.

He then speaks in a soft, low voice. "Trapped in a loop, in a cycle, unable to break free. It's a nightmare, Violet."

The lieutenant silently replaces the table while the president straightens his jacket. And just before Stoneback pulls his sleeves into place, I notice the tiniest of marks on the inside of his wrist: a black mole with the middle missing, kind of like a small hoop.

"So each time the story completes, it resets?" I ask.

He nods. I feel the ghost of hope, heavy in my chest. It makes me feel a little brave. I lick my finger and darken the twelve o'clock mark, smudging his blood. "So when the story resets, what happens to the people who died?"

"They are reborn."

A shaky laugh escapes from my mouth. Ash will be reborn. Matthew will be reborn. The hope grows suddenly, bursting through me like something tangible and warm. "My brother?"

He places a finger on my own and slides it toward me. A mixture of his blood and my saliva forms a thin line. "Your universe is not cyclical. It is linear. If your brother died in this reality, *The Gallows Dance*, he will never be reborn, not in this universe or your own."

The clasp of grief tightens on my throat.

He lifts his finger and sits again, his posture straight and proper. "I suppose you're wondering how I remember this loop while everyone else in my world is blissfully ignorant?"

I'd been thinking only of Nate, his sparkling eyes and pixie grin, but I nod regardless.

"Some of us Gems are a little too enhanced. Just like the old precog you were so fond of. Whereas she ended up with psychic abilities, a few of us ended up with enhanced memories. The best scientists, the best engineers, the top politicians. We remember the echoes, the reflections, everything—every damned loop. And we're tired of it. Life is supposed to move, to progress." He stares sadly at the circle of blood. "And we can't change the story, we can't do a goddamned thing, because the consequences of the loop failing to complete may be dire. It's a risk we're not yet willing to take."

I shove my fingers into my head as if I can somehow reach into my brain and untangle all the information. "But if the Fandom created you, how do you have a childhood, a past? It makes no sense. Your existence could only have begun when the story started."

"There are many paradoxes involved in transdimensional quantum resonance, which I do not expect your monkey brain to understand. Perhaps an analogy will help. Another perpetual loop—the chicken and the egg."

"Which came first," I whisper. Baba used this same analogy; she was taunting me even then.

"Yes. Well done. I'll get you a banana. Did the Fandom create us, or did we create the Fandom? Did the book create us, or did we create the book? It matters not. It's a question that cannot be resolved. Both are true—our universes are symbiotic—the Gems have childhoods, we have a history, we even share a history with your universe. But time flows differently in our universe."

"I don't get it." I feel so stupid. I wish Nate were here; he would do his Sheldon Cooper thing and he would understand. I feel his loss intensely, a hollowing-out of where my heart should be.

"No, I don't suppose you do."

I swallow back the tears, try and slow my breathing. "So, why am I here?" I finally ask.

"That's the thing with a genetic super-race. We can solve most problems, given enough time. We devised a way to breach the layer between our universes. A way to reach her." He points to the portrait of Sally King.

"But . . . Sally King is dead."

"She is now. But she wasn't. You remember how she died?"

"She killed herself."

"Because of the voices in her head?" He taps his temple with a long, elegant finger. "Sometimes the mad aren't really mad."

"The voice was you?"

He nods. "I tried to convince Miss King to write a sequel and break the loop."

I look at Sally's face, the sadness behind those oversize glasses. "You killed her?" I feel such anger, such hatred, toward this man. For Sally, for Nate, for Matthew, for all the Imps he's killed. I lift my teacup to my lips to avoid speaking, afraid I might shout or scream or curse.

"Not intentionally. She was our only hope. The problem was, when she started *The Gallows Dance* sequel, we had artistic differences." He smiles to himself. "She wanted the Imps to prevail. I did not. I'm afraid I may have pushed her too far."

"She died protecting the future of the Imps?" I recall the pelican again—giving life with its own blood—and a brief smile touches my lips.

He ignores me. "But then a new hope emerged. A rising fanfic writer."

A clear image forms in my mind's eye. Bronzed legs wrapped

around bronzed legs, almost like two stems twisted together, opening out into two separate blooms. The sleeping lovers—the two blooms—almost form the shape of a heart. I reach for my necklace, then remember I broke it. My best friend, the fanfic writer, the beautiful Imp who loves a Gem. It almost hurts to say her name. "Alice."

The president nods. "Anime Alice. Thanks to her, a new Fandom grew, holding the promise of a new story, an existence beyond this eternal loop. We could feel their presence, this new Fandom. We began noticing tiny changes in canon, new characters appearing, little glitches here and there. Alas, nothing dramatic enough to change our future, to break the loop. But imagine if this Alice returned to your world and wrote a sequel, a published story that reached a whole new audience. We would have a Fandom powerful enough to break the loop. We would have a future."

"You would have another book—another loop."

He claps, long and slow. "You must be one of those clever monkeys that can sign and do tricks for peanuts. No. What we will have is an opportunity. Who knows what will occur once we are freed. Your A-plus-B-equals-C logic is rather antiquated."

I feel my brow knot together, hear the rattle of porcelain against porcelain as my legs continue to shake. "So why *am* I here?"

"We realized our mistake when Sally King died. Sally was pro-Imp, of course. She is an Imp, you all are in your universe. And telling her to be pro-Gem, it just didn't work. We needed Alice to live like a Gem, to *become* a Gem, to learn what animals the Imps truly are. So now, when she returns to your world and writes us our sequel, she won't remember her little adventure, but she will be Gem through and through. She will create a future in which we Gems would like to live."

I begin to feel sick. "It was you? You brought us here from Comic-Con?" The trill of the teacup crescendos and abruptly stops as the cup topples. Hot tea soaks into my thighs, but I barely register the pain.

The president just laughs. "Yes. Like I said, we have brilliant scientists. If you like I can bring one of them in. He will explain the quantum physics of transdimensional tunneling, but I fear your primate brain may explode, and I'm wearing my favorite suit."

I look at my cup, broken on the floor. Two perfect halves. "And does Alice know about this?"

"No. Alice knows nothing. As far as she's concerned, she's having a lovely time living with the Gems. She still thinks so long as you don't complete the canon, she gets to continue living here. If she knew the truth she would feel . . . manipulated."

"But why bring me? Katie?" I have to swallow before I can say his name. "Nate."

"We only meant to transport Alice. But things never go quite as planned. And when you all arrived, my word, did it get interesting. Baba's been keeping me posted."

"Rose wasn't meant to die?"

He scoops up my teacup and pushes the halves together so the cup becomes whole. "Not then, no. She was supposed to hang at the Gallows Dance tomorrow, inciting a revolution, completing the cycle, and sending Alice home." A glimmer of pride offsets his usual look of disdain. "I must admit, Violet, you surpassed my expectations as an understudy. Baba told me you would."

"So, I will hang in Rose's place."

He grins—his teeth remind me of that foam candy I used to love as a kid. "That is correct. It is the only way the four of you will awaken in your world."

"So we *are* unconscious?"

He smiles his patronizing smile. "In your world, yes. And if you and your friends ever want to wake up, you will dance on those gallows as I ask." He laughs.

"What a pickle you've found yourself in. To fear the thing you need the most—the hangman's noose. Don't worry, all good heroines find themselves in a double bind. It adds to the tension."

I recall the paper chain, the grabbing hands, the Dupes, the crescent scythe, the Imps at the Meat House. Nate's body dead on the concrete. I feel such fury. And then I think of Mum and Dad, Maltesers and Netflix and university entrance exams and sleepovers. The president was right; I am in a double bind, he just got the wrong one.

"I won't do it," I hiss.

"I beg your pardon?"

"I won't do it. I won't play along. When Willow shouts out he loves me at the Gallows Dance, I'll shout back that I hate him, that I used him. I won't complete the canon and then Alice won't be able to wake up to write her pro-Gem sequel. The Gems will never prevail."

"How interesting. Just as Alice has identified with the Gems, you've identified with the Imps."

"I *am* an Imp."

He sneers. "As I said earlier, failing to complete the loop has consequences that we can't determine. They may be dire. Not only will you fail to cross over, but this universe may just cease to be."

"Maybe that's a risk I'm willing to take."

"We're talking oblivion, Violet. Oblivion for you and that gutter-monkey boyfriend and all the Imps you love so much. You may gamble with your own life, but I seriously doubt you'll gamble with theirs."

He's got me. I know it and he knows it. Deflated, beaten, I shake my head.

"So when Willow Harper bursts forward at the Gallows Dance and shouts"—he leaps from his chair and clasps his heart in a melodramatic pose—"'I love you, Rose,' you will say?"

"I love you, too."

"The Gems tear down the gallows, a revolution begins, the story is completed, and you can go home." He glances down at me, a sneer fixed across his plastic face. "Good little monkey."

CHAPTER 47

LIE ON THE bed in my cell, staring at the door, knowing that the next time it opens, I will be taken to the Gallows Dance. My brain aches, struggling to process all the new information. The fairy tales, the pips, the flatline. Back in my world, the real world, I *am* unconscious. And yet I'm also here. Two universes. Two Violets. It just makes no sense. I think perhaps Stoneback was right—I have the brain of a monkey. Tears leak down my face, spilling over the bridge of my nose, leaching into the pillow. After everything I have done, all that I have lost, I simply can't win this one. The Gems win. Baba wins.

I reach into my pocket and find my split-heart necklace. I must have stuffed it there after our argument, too sentimental to chuck it in the dirt. It coils through my fingers like a delicate pewter thread, and when I open my hand, the split heart swings before my eyes.

My best friend. Sucked in by the Gems. At least the extent of her betrayal was limited to sleeping with Willow; at least she wasn't responsible for Nate's death. But she will destroy the Imps in the end, and I will inadvertently help her by completing the canon. I feel broken, like I'm made of eggshell and no amount of horses or king's men could ever make me whole. I stuff the chain back into my pocket.

"Self-sacrifice and love." I whisper the words to the walls. But they just sound stupid. And for some reason, an image of Miss Thompson pops into my head, leaning on her Formica desk, telling us about the black moment in literature, the moment when all hope seems lost. Only one side of my mouth smiles—right now, things couldn't look much blacker.

The door opens. I expect to see another khaki uniform, but instead I see Baba. She moves forward, suspended in air, her feet completely still. At first, I think she's a ghost, but then I notice the levers clutched in her shriveled hands, and realize she's using some bizarre hoverchair. I study her old, closed-up face, so relaxed and still, and the image of Nate bleeding out on my lap fills my mind. She told the Gems about the safe house. The anger stretches around my body, filling my veins, contracting my muscles until they feel like a series of jack-in-the-boxes ready to pop. I think I may kill her. Only her frailty stops me.

The chair pauses next to my bed. I don't dare look at her, but I can smell lilies, hear her voice, warm and measured. "I sense your rage," she says.

I jump to my feet, my fists clenched and shaking. "How could you betray us like that?"

Her eyes dart beneath her lids. "You're forgetting that I am a Gem."

"But the Imps kept you safe for hundreds of years!"

She pulls a little lever and the chair levitates so her face sits level with mine. I can see the soft hairs on her skin like silver down, a hint of green behind her lids, the tiny tooth buds straining against her gums when she speaks. "And that is why I would never betray them. Or you."

"But the president—"

"Is a scumbag. No wait, he's a wankstain, yes, that's my favorite." She pushes the lever back into position and the chair settles back on the floor. "Come, kneel with me, child."

I watch her suspiciously, unsure whether she speaks the truth, whether I should open my mind to her again.

She chuckles. "What have you got to lose?"

Slowly, I uncurl my fists. Curiosity, desperation, I don't know what, but something pulls me to the ground. She places her palms on my temples and I feel that pain blossoming in my stomach, pushing through my body, and focusing between my eyes. It chases away the image of Nate, loosens the clasp of grief on my throat. I almost feel sad when the pain lifts—it's all I have left of him. And when I open my eyes, I'm standing in my living room.

"There's no place like home," Baba says.

It looks so ordinary, so *beige*. I spin slowly, taking it all in. The tan leather sofa with the coffee smudge on the right arm; the photos of me and Nate slightly askew on the fawn walls; the battered coffee table Dad swiped from our previous, rented house. I feel the shag rug beneath my feet, smell the casserole in the oven, hear the familiar buzz of the TV behind me. My parents sit on the sofa, side by side, Mum balancing the remote control on her knee. I recognize the music from *The Gallows Dance*. This makes me smile—Dad always referred to it as "that dystopian drivel." I study their faces, every line and curve of their features, my heart inflating in my rib cage.

Baba sidles up to me, her hoverchair long gone. "They look happy."

I nod, but my heart suddenly deflates. "They mustn't know about Nate yet?"

"These people are not your real mum and dad, Violet. They are your projections." She lays a doughy hand on my shoulder. "And they are the reason you've been striving to complete the canon. The Holy Grail, the light at the end of the tunnel, are they not?"

"Yes." I look at their fingers, gently woven together, their slippers bumping up against each other.

"When you saved the girl with no hands, when you went to the Coliseum to stop Thorn from hanging those Gems, when you pushed the boat into the river and returned to shore, when you dived into that water to save your friends—did you do it so you could go home?"

"I—I don't understand." My focus never leaves Mum and Dad, terrified they could just vanish.

"After all that you have seen, all that you have become, are you really hanging at the Gallows Dance just so you can go home?"

I shake my head.

She spins me so I face the telly. The final scene of the film plays—Rose stands on the stage, noose around her neck. My hands automatically fly to my throat.

She moves her hand so it rests just above my heart. "Why, Violet? Why did you do those things?"

I speak with no hesitation. "To help the Imps."

"Yes!" she shouts. "You have become so much more than Rose. You care about a cause, about justice. That is why I betrayed you. That is why I told the president where you would be. You needed to see the atrocities, experience the barbarity of the Gems first-hand, in order to become a true Imp—an Imp who would stand up and fight for her people. Because only an act of true love and true sacrifice can complete the canon. This has always been a love story, Violet. But for you, it's about a greater love than the love between two people."

I tear my eyes from the screen and look at her. The apple of her irises is even greener against the beige of my living room. "Nate died so I could become a true Imp?"

A tear trickles down her face, funneled through a lattice of wrinkles. "I'm so sorry. My powers lack precision sometimes—some things, I fail to see."

A rush of unexpected sympathy passes through me. I know how it feels to fail, after all. I change the topic from Nate, for both our sakes. "But when I hang, Alice will return to our world and write a pro-Gem sequel. The Imps lose, no matter what."

"Perhaps."

"Can I stop her? Is there a way?"

"When Alice returns to your world, she won't remember the past week. None of you will. Perhaps the odd echo, a fragment here or there, more like a dream. But your experiences will stay with you. The sequel Alice writes will be shaped by her experiences."

"There's nothing I can do?"

"All is not lost, Violet. There's still time for you *both* to find your way. Perhaps you are not the only one capable of self-sacrifice and love."

"What does that even mean?"

She looks thoughtful for a moment. "Self-sacrifice. Love. They will mean something different to Alice, I'm sure. But they remain at the core of every great story, even hers."

I have so many questions, so many uncertainties buzzing in my head, but she closes her eyes and begins to sing.

"Count the thistles, one, two, three,
Soon the Imps will all be free."

The Imp skipping song. I open my mouth to ask her what relevance it has, but the colors of the living room begin to smudge together and the ground beneath my feet seems to fade.

"Count the thistles, four, five, six,

Take up your guns, your stones and sticks."

She takes my hands in hers. The sound of the television turns to static. The smell of casserole turns to antiseptic and detergent.

"The ash trees turn from green to red,

Spring has gone, the summer's dead."

"Wait," I cry, trying to snatch one last glance at my parents. But they have already gone. I can see only blackness, and I can hear nothing but those final lines.

"Count the minutes, not the hours,

'Cause hope starts as a little flower."

CHAPTER 48

ODAY I WILL hang.

I will hang for my friends, my family, and, above all else, love. But not for the love of one man. No, I will hang for more than that. I will hang for the love of my people. For the love of the Imps. For Ash, Saskia, and Matthew. For Katie and Nate . . . even Alice. For every imperfect fluke of nature who has the right to call themselves a human being.

A team of flamboyant, manicured stylists arrive in my cell just like they did in canon. They attack me with powders and blushers and various paints, stick bits to my eyelashes, paint my nails, buff my skin till it glows. They look me up and down with probing, critical eyes, and I fidget beneath my robe.

One of the stylists smiles, causing her red lipstick to crack. "Well, she certainly looks a little less ape."

I guess Stoneback doesn't trust Willow to declare his love if I look like a dirty street rat. They shove some underwear in my hands and watch me try and slip it on under my robe. I've only just secured it when they yank off my gown and wrap this metallic girdle around my waist. It seems to contract of its own accord, forcing my stomach into my chest. They squeeze my breasts into this magic bra that adds two cup sizes. This definitely didn't happen to Rose. In spite of my impending death, I still feel a little annoyed that my figure needs more help than hers. I pull on my overalls and look in the mirror. I barely recognize myself.

Two guards arrive. I remember them from canon. They clutch my shoulders with rough hands and propel me across a large concrete expanse toward the hovercraft. The sun has reached its highest point in the sky, glinting off the metal of the craft and the loops of barbed wire that crown the barricades. I frantically search for Ash, but he is nowhere to be seen.

They shove me up the ramp into the craft.

"Dead man walking," one of the guards says.

"Dead *ape* walking, more like," the other replies.

The craft looks just like the one from canon. The air feels cold, tainted with the tang of antiseptic and gunpowder. They lead me to the holding cell at the back of the craft and slide back the door. That's when I see him, the curve of his neck, the point where the black of his hair meets the white of his skin. Ash. His arms are raised high, his wrists pinned to a metal rail, and in that instant, he reminds me of a bird, wings outstretched.

The guards cuff me in the same manner, forcing me onto my tiptoes, the metal cuffs slicing through my skin. The door slides into position and we sway to the rhythm of the hovercraft, side by side.

The stylists seem to have bypassed him completely. His hair looks matted with dirt and blood, and his bruises are really starting to come out; a swirl of purples and yellows wrapping around his left eye like a bizarre monocle. I nuzzle deep into his neck; his skin and overalls retain the stench of the river and his skin feels clammy and hot against my forehead. But when I finally look up into his face, his eyes remain the coolest of powder blues. I feel a moment of peace, nestled into him. I think briefly of Rose, standing in this cell alone, traveling to her death with no company, and I feel sad for her.

He kisses my temple, so gently I barely feel it. "I'm so sorry, Violet. If I hadn't followed you, you would never have told Thorn about the Meat House . . . None of this would have happened."

"This isn't your fault."

He exhales suddenly, and I can tell from the acidity of his breath that he hasn't eaten or drunk anything since our arrest. I feel a pang of guilt, thinking about my shower and tray of hot food.

I push my wrists along the rail and manage to stroke my finger against the back of his hand. "Try not to worry. I promise everything's going to be OK."

He smiles his lopsided smile, the skin on his lips splitting in the center. "Who says I'm worried?" He tries to look brave, I think for my sake, but his voice sounds like a fragile version of itself and a tear hangs on his eyelashes. It looks like a drop of oil, refracting the colors of the bruising.

All I want to do is make him feel a little better, to try and ease the pain. I kiss his lips, the chapped skin rough against my own. "I wish I could somehow explain, but this isn't the end for either of us."

"I didn't realize you were the spiritual type."

"It'll be over so quickly, and then . . ."

"And then?"

I push my lips against his ear, all pale and curved like a seashell. "If I told you, you would think I'm completely mad, but nothing is as it seems."

He turns to me, his nose bumping into my cheek. "You've already told me you're a time-traveling assassin, what could possibly trump that?"

My mouth finds his again. And I feel every indentation of his lips, the one-off pattern of ridges. Like swirls in a fingertip. I think I might cry again, so I pull away.

He smiles. "Hope starts with a Little Flower."

The lines of the poem turn over and over in my head. I feel like I'm missing something, something really important, but every time I come close, it sinks from view.

He sees the confusion on my face and says, "What I mean is, the world came to life when I met you."

The clasp of grief tightens around my throat again—a reminder of further loss. I speak earnestly, a touch of desperation brightening my words. "Have you ever had any feelings of déjà vu? Any echoes or reflections, like you've already lived your life?"

His brow knots. "Are you getting all spiritual again?"

I try to mask the disappointment. But it feels like my chest has been punctured with something sharp and long and unforgiving. When I die, when the canon resets, he won't remember me.

"What is it?" he asks.

"It doesn't matter." I study every line on his face, every pore, every fleck in those winter eyes, trying to burn his image into my retinas, because an even more heartbreaking thought has arrived.

I won't remember him, either.

CHAPTER 49

THE HOVERCRAFT BEGINS to descend, and we hear an odd purring noise. It grows and grows until it becomes an angry buzz.

"It's the crowd," Ash says.

I'd forgotten about the crowd. Chanting, shouting, pushing—a seething mass of bloodthirsty Gems. Baying for the blood of the Imps. Me and Ash. The craft lands and it feels like the crowd surrounds us, hollering through the blacked-out windows, pounding on the metal panels with their fists.

A guard approaches us. He looks straight at Ash. "You're in luck, gutter monkey. The president wants a single hanging today—says it will have more impact, whatever the hell that means."

My body floods with relief. Of course the president only wants me on that stage. In canon, there was only Rose. Stoneback wants those two pieces of thread as closely bound as possible, ensuring the cycle is completed and Alice returns home. I know Ash wouldn't have died for real—he would have woken up at the beginning of the story, back in Ma's kitchen, stirring soup—but I'm still glad he doesn't have to go through all that pain. *All that pain*. I think I may puke.

"No, wait," Ash says. "You want a single hanging, then hang me."

The guards don't listen. They unclick his handcuffs.

"Wait, please," he cries. "Hang me, not Violet."

"Don't worry." The guard laughs. "You'll see your girlfriend from the Imp-pen."

"No, please, no." Ash strains against the guard, but he's no match for the burly Gem physique. He looks me in the eye. "I love you, Violet."

The emotional part of my brain dislodges like a jigsaw piece, and I find that I know things, yet no longer feel them. Ash is telling me he loves me. *My Ash*. Yet I feel empty . . . lost. In less than an hour, we won't know each other. We will be strangers divided by more than a few lies, more than a wall or a forest of brambles; we will be divided by an entire universe, a shift in time, complete memory loss. Our love story is to become a tragedy, just like Rose and Willow's. I appreciate this irony, even in my dissociated state.

Ash repeats the words over and over as he's dragged from the craft. "I love you, Violet. I love you." They fade into the roar of the crowd until I can't hear him anymore.

He's gone.

This thought snaps me from my inertia. That dislodged part of my brain falls right back into place and I no longer hover. The reality of the situation smashes into me: I will never see Ash again.

"I love you, too," I shout back.

But I'm too late.

CHAPTER 50

A GUARD UNFASTENS MY cuffs. My anxiety causes his features to blur together, but I see the glint of hate in his eye, sharp and clear. He drags me to the door and I prepare myself for the crowd, but when the doors slide back, I see only gray. The craft has landed in the city, beside the Coliseum. They want me to walk through the Imp gates, the gates of the condemned. Just like in canon.

I step from the craft and the stench of rotting bird hits me. For a brief moment, my heart soars. I take a moment to absorb my surroundings. I can see the walls of the Coliseum a hundred or so yards away. But I can't see Ash. He must already be in the Imp-pen. And I see no other Imps. I guess they've squeezed into their hovels, watching the proceedings on scavenged television sets. I search for the city gates, but a swarm of armed guards obscures my view—bumping up against me, sweeping me along so I become part of a single, khaki entity.

From the other side of the wall, a shiny fanfare erupts. *In ten minutes, I will hang.* My legs stop working and the guards have to pull me along, my feet dragging behind me like two simian hands, as if I really am an ape. I reach the gates and they push me into an upright position. One of the flamboyant stylists appears. He wipes cotton swabs beneath my eyes, rubs oil on my lips, combs out my hair.

I hear President Stoneback's reedy voice rising above the Coliseum walls. He says the exact words from canon. Only this time, he's talking about me.

"Welcome to the Gallows Dance, fellow Gems. We are about to witness the death of Imp number 753811. A Night-Imp who used her animalistic ways to trick an upstanding young Gem into thinking he might have feelings for her. A Night-Imp who seduced and lied her way into a young Gem's heart in order to access government secrets. A dirty little spy. Trying to bring down the Gems, trying to destroy our way of life."

The crowd roars.

They all step away from me—the stylist, the foot soldiers. I sway on the spot, shivering in my overalls, staring at the impenetrable metal gates. I start to shake uncontrollably, worse than when they pulled me from the river, and I think my heart may be about to burst.

The president's voice again: *"So let's meet this temptress, this spy."*

The gates begin to open. The crowd falls silent. I watch the slice of colorful Gem world expand and expand until it is all I can see. And despite the terror pulsing around my body, I still appreciate the irony that my very own black moment should be so filled with Gem color. Densely pigmented suits of emeralds and scarlets, glossy sheets of hair, every color of skin from porcelain to ebony. Yet every face looks the same. Symmetrical, perfect, and hungry for retribution.

The silence holds. I stand perfectly still, just breathing and blinking and staring right back at them. I realize how much I hate them. And it surprises me how intense the emotion feels—more consuming than love, a physical thing radiating from me in waves. And that lacquered Russian-doll shell is back, encasing me like armor plating, holding me upright, delivering strength to my legs, my arms, all of me.

They want a hanging? I will give them a hanging.

"And here she is, ladies and gentlemen. Guilty on two accounts. Relations with a Gem and high treason. It's a shame we can't hang her twice."

The crowd laughs. I begin to take strong, hate-driven strides toward the stage. I hear Nate's voice in my head and smile. *Balls of steel. Balls of steel.*

I don't look at the noose or at Ash in the Imp-pen. I can't risk cracking my armor or blurring my clarity of purpose. I try not to think of the helicopter, the giant bonfire lighting up the faces of the rebels only last night. Nate by my side, his excited face. I just keep staring at the mass of brilliant, symmetrical eyes.

In the crowd, standing near the front, I see Willow, his face clenched by an unknown emotion that hovers somewhere between fear and love. Next to him is Alice, her hands playing nervously around her neck. And I realize I hate her, too.

The hangman stands—a pillar of black—his hand cupped over the lever. I know that my armor won't let me down. I won't fall to pieces. Resolve hardens inside me and brings a welcome sense of calm. I climb the steps onto the wooden stage, stand on the trapdoor, and let the hangman place the noose around my neck. I don't know why, perhaps a last grasp at some sort of comfort to get me through the next five minutes, but my hand falls upon the chain in my pocket. I squeeze it as tightly as I can. There's no place like home.

The president speaks again. *"Imp. Your crimes are punishable by death."*

I look at Alice. Her eyes fill with tears, her upper lip covered with snot. She just can't bear to see the canon completed, can't bear to leave this godforsaken place. She has no idea that when she returns home, she will be used by the president to serve the Gems by writing a pro-Gem sequel for the Fandom. My jaw clenches, the empty feeling in my chest almost unbearable. I look away, and that's when I see them, standing in the Imp-pen. Not just Ash, but Saskia and Katie, too.

Katie looks beyond anxious, her knuckles white and threatening to slice through her skin as she runs her fingers through the red of her hair. We make eye contact and she manages a wink, like she's back in that classroom, listening to my presentation. Saskia looks devastated. Grief pulls her features together and tears drip from her chin. I fleetingly think how pretty she looks with all the anger bled from her face.

Next, I look at Ash. I wish I'd told him the truth, however crazy it would have sounded. I wish I'd told him about Comic-Con and the alternate universe and Willow and Alice . . . about everything. But most of all, I wish he'd heard me when I told him I love him. Even if we live the rest of our lives oblivious to each other's existence, at least for the tiniest of moments I could have looked into those gorgeous eyes and seen the truth reflected back at me.

The drumroll begins. Just like in canon. I turn to Willow. Any second now he will vault over the barrier and onto the stage, declaring his love for me. The drumroll gathers speed. Any second now . . . But he stands completely still, his hands trembling, his eyes closed.

My stomach falls away, my heart jackknifes. It never occurred to me that Willow would freeze. If he doesn't say his lines, if the canon isn't completed, who knows what will happen. I will probably die on this rope, and this universe and everyone in it—Ash, Saskia, Katie, even Alice—will just cease to be.

The drumroll builds, and yet Willow still doesn't move. His eyes remain firmly closed, his lips vibrating slightly like he's muttering a prayer. Perhaps it was the extra time he spent with Rose, fleeing across the Imp city, that solidified his feelings of love for her. Perhaps the fact he now stands beside Alice, a beautiful and fun replacement, weakens his resolve. Or perhaps current-Willow—*my* Willow—really is weaker than canon-Willow. Whatever the reason, I've failed. Hot tears stream down my face. I feel defeated, lost. All of this, everything, was for nothing.

Come on, I scream in my head. *Come on, Willow. You have to do this.*

The drumroll fills my brain, now louder than a firing squad. I look to Alice. I will her to intervene, to smack Willow around the head or something. But I know she thinks if the canon isn't completed, I will just die and she will stay in this world. If only she knew the truth, if only I could explain it all to her.

The drumroll reaches its climax. And yet, still, Willow remains completely motionless, eyes tight shut, not even daring to look at me. I look back to Alice. She blinks at me slowly, almost vacantly, just waiting for my body to drop.

She's chosen *them* over me.

The chain tumbles from my fingertips, just at the moment the drumroll stops. Silence. Except for the soft tinkle of the broken heart hitting the floor.

This is it.

I hold my breath and wait for the *crack* of the trapdoor as it flies open, the snap of the rope against my neck. But instead, I hear a voice. Loud and strong and filled with outrage.

"STOP!"

I look up to see her. Leaping over the railings, vaulting onto the stage, her pale hair flailing around her face. Alice. She stands on the stage, her hands trembling, her chest rising and falling as she snatches a series of quick, shallow breaths. She stares at me for a moment. She looks so different, her beautiful face pinched with fear, all of that honey color drained from her cheeks. And I notice it, in the dip where her collarbones never quite meet—the split-heart necklace, its jagged edge catching the sun. For a second, the guilt of doubting her engulfs me.

She nods at me slowly. We share a moment of understanding. Then, she turns to face the crowd.

"My name is Alice. And the Imp you're about to hang has a name. Violet. And she is the bravest and kindest person I have ever known. Imp or Gem, she is a human being." She quotes the canon almost word for word, sticking to the script for the first time ever. Her voice climbs above the walls of the Coliseum, daring anyone to disagree. "She isn't a temptress, or a criminal. She is my best friend. And I love her with all my heart." She holds me with her inky-blue gaze. "I love you, Violet."

I hear the gasp from the president on the screen behind me. He knows he has lost. Alice longed to live as a Gem, to stay in this world, but she is giving it all up for me. I suddenly understand what Baba meant. This is Alice's sacrifice, this is Alice's love. There's no way she will write a pro-Gem sequel now. I smile at her. The biggest smile I have.

I thought it would be difficult saying my final line, knowing what awaits—the tightening of the rope, the sudden jolt of pain—but it feels right, natural.

So without further ceremony, I fill the Coliseum not with thistledown, but with my voice.

"I love you, too."

And finally, the trapdoor opens.

CHAPTER 51

I'D IMAGINED HANGING as an all-encompassing pain—one that would fill every part of my being until it defined me, *became* me. But it actually feels quite precise. The noose tugging against my neck, the burning collar of fire, the downward pull of the weight of my body, my lungs desperately gasping for air, my feet cycling of their own accord, searching for solid ground. And I hear the screams of the crowd, changing from joy to outrage, washing over me in waves. The light dwindles and my vision is peppered with exploding stars.

I begin to feel like I did when Nate died; strangely removed. I step out of the pain, the collar, the stars, like they're no more than a bizarre costume. I hover above myself, watching the scene like it really is from a film.

I hear Alice's voice, strong and loud. "Will we continue to allow this government-sanctioned murder of innocent Imps?"

I hear another voice, a familiar voice. Mum. *That's it, Violet. That's it.*

Not yet, Mum, I try to say. I move farther away, up, up into the clouds, and far below me I see Alice and Katie, their faces craning upward like they can see my spirit escaping toward the sun. The scent of rotting bird and pollen fades in my nostrils, replaced by something cleaner, something man-made.

That's it, darling. That's it. You can do it.

I watch the crowd begin to turn. Moved by Alice's words, outraged by my death. The collective cry of indignation. The rising of fists in the air. Ash climbs onto the stage and carries my body into the crowd, his face soaked with tears.

"Who are the animals now?" Alice shouts at the top of her lungs. "Who are the animals now?"

And then I see the Imps swarming over the walls of the Coliseum, joining the Gems, united for the first time in centuries by my death.

That's it, Violet, you can do it. Open your eyes.

That sterile smell of medicine and antiseptic and freshly washed linen fills my nose. I hear a series of *pip*s, the clatter of metal on metal.

Not yet, Mum. I just need the cycle to be completed.

Pip. Pip. Pip. I watch as the crowd engulfs the gallows, ripping at the supporting beams, lifting up the planks. The stage buckles and the gallows topple like the masts of a sinking ship. Everyone stands motionless, Gems and Imps alike. Shards of wood and clouds of dust launch into the sky, twirling and dancing and catching in the sun.

The cycle is complete.

Pip. Pip. Pip.

At last, I open my eyes.

CHAPTER 52

ALICE HUGS HER faux-fur jacket around her body. "It's freaking freezing out here."

She's right. It's that kind of cold that seems to come from the ground, traveling through the soles of your boots, spreading across your feet, and crawling up your body until even your teeth feel raw and exposed. I pull my woolly hat down a little bit farther and try to make my body smaller, as though I can somehow dodge the chill.

"Stop with the whining, you southern softie," Katie says, "we're only five minutes away."

Alice frowns. "In five minutes my tits will have dropped off."

The stone face of the hospital seems to grow larger with every step, transforming from a solitary Duplo block into an imposing tower of bricks and windows, shimmering with glass and ice. I always wonder if I can see *our* window; the window of the room I woke up in about six months ago, clutching at my neck, gasping for air, flailing my legs, a haze of white sheets and nurses flapping around me. And I always wonder if my friends are thinking the exact same as me, silently hunting for clues, a familiar vase on a windowsill perhaps.

Alice and Katie woke from their comas within minutes of me. The Comic-Con Four, that's what the press dubbed us—a group of kids who lost consciousness at London Comic-Con and slipped into comas following a minor earthquake. Not a single detectable injury between us. Medical mysteries. And when three of us regained consciousness exactly one week later, we became minor celebrities for at least a day, until one of the Kardashian sisters got another butt implant.

We cross the road and the wind picks up, lifting snow dust from the pavement, the tops of the cars, the ridges in the brickwork of the shop faces, sending it twirling, spiraling, dancing through the air. This teases a familiar image from my brain. Thistledown. Hundreds of seeds encasing us in our very own snow globe. Or maybe feathers, white and brown, bursting around me and drifting to the floor, accompanied by laughter and the shriek of birds.

These images come to me often. Sometimes they explode into my consciousness, other times they slowly burrow, revealing themselves in stages. Fragments of pictures and scents and noises. At first they were blurred, dreamlike; now the details are sharper in all of my senses. But they remain squares of an unfinished patchwork. No matter how hard I try, I can't quite sew them into something meaningful. At least not yet. A strange old lady with apple-green eyes visits me in my dreams. She tries to help, whispering about journeys, a far-off land.

"Are you OK, Vi?" Katie asks.

"Yeah," I say—an obvious lie. My friends take an arm each, their body warmth closing around me, and we half-walk, half-skid across the parking lot toward the main entrance of the hospital. I can't help staring at the winter sky. It's this amazing pale-blue color. It almost looks like a sheet of glass suspended above us, reflecting the soft, muted colors of frostbitten London. For the briefest of moments, it really reminds me of something, or more precisely, someone. Though I can't place who.

We jog up the steps, grateful for the warm blast of air awaiting us in the hospital foyer, and I wonder if that smell—medicinal and unnatural—leaves my friends feeling uneasy, too. We break apart to pull off our hats and smooth down our hair. I smile at our collective vanity while nurses in shower caps and patients in brittle-with-starch hospital gowns move around us.

The receptionist sees me and waves. I know all of the admin staff not by their names, but by sound bites of descriptions in my head—a sign that I am becoming a true writer, perhaps. So this one is *The lady with eyes that always look tired, but with hair that never sleeps.* I return her wave and she smiles, but it looks kind of forced—like she can see the crushing, invisible weight I carry but doesn't know how to acknowledge it or take it away. Or perhaps she knows it should be me lying in that hospital bed instead of Nate, tubes snaking into my mouth. Perhaps she can see the black aura of guilt that surrounds me, entombs me—the crippling feeling I get from knowing Nate would have woken up, too, if only I'd been smarter, stronger, faster . . . better. It makes no sense, I know.

I head down the main corridor, my rubber soles squeaking against the vinyl floor. Alice, Katie, and I always walk this stretch fast, an unspoken agreement. Like me, they don't like seeing the medical staff—nothing personal, it's just easier to avoid eye contact with someone who may have changed your catheter.

"So, what did you bring him today?" Katie asks as we finally reach the lift. "The usual selection of fairy tales?"

"Not today." I punch the UP button, my finger cast in a jade light. "Today we've brought him something a bit more personal."

We watch the numbers flash sequentially above our heads, the lift descending its concrete tube toward us.

"Ooh, curious," Katie says.

Alice grins. "Something a bit more futuristic, something a bit more dystopian—"

"Oh my God," Katie shrieks, "don't tell me you've finished it."

The elevator arrives and we step into the little metal box. It lurches upward and I realize I no longer think about the mechanism whirring above us, pulling us higher and higher, farther from the safety of the ground. Pre-coma, I would have sung Abba in my head to block out the panic. But something about that coma changed me. Guilt aside, it's made me more confident, more self-assured. You'd think it would do the opposite, having dragged me so close to oblivion. I don't pretend to understand, but it's kind of nice, not shitting my pants every time I do a presentation.

Alice pulls her Kindle from her handbag. "Well, we've finished the first draft, haven't we, Violet?"

I nod. "Yeah, but I'm sure our editor will want to make changes."

"Oh yes, darling, our *editor*." Katie forces her voice into an over-the-top posh squeak, so she sounds more like the Queen than a Liverpudlian.

"Piss off," Alice says, laughing.

"No, really, it's great," Katie says. "I'm so pleased for you both. A proper book deal. And not just any book—the sequel to *The Gallows Dance*."

Alice looks coy for a moment. "Well, we had a little help." She means Russell Jones. After he posted that photo back in May, Alice's popularity as a fanfic writer soared. Getting a book deal, even with her unknown bestie as co-author, was pretty easy. But it was my idea to write the sequel, not Alice's. An idea that the old lady with apple-green eyes gave me soon after I regained consciousness, though I remember that dream as though it were last night.

I was standing in this orchard filled with birdsong and sunshine and the scent of fruit.

Then the old lady appeared and pushed something into my fist. Her barely-there lips parted and she spoke in a familiar voice. "It was no accident you came to our world with Alice. I brought you. The president had his plan, and I had mine."

I didn't really know what she meant, but I felt I should ask anyway. "What was your plan?"

"Saving the Imps does not end with the falling of the gallows, my child."

"What does it end with?"

She smiled. "There's no place like home, Little Flower."

I uncurled my palm and saw the tiniest viola flower nestled between the cracks in my skin. And suddenly, it all made sense. "You brought me into your world so I would become a true Imp. You want *me* to write the sequel?"

She nodded. "You and Alice. You write a pro-Imp sequel for the fandom to read. Break this loop, Little Flower. Set us free."

I woke that morning filled with an overwhelming urge to write a sequel with Alice. It felt like a matter of life or death—like the very future of the Imps depended on it. It took a jug of orange juice and several rounds of toast to remind myself the Imps are no more than characters from my favorite novel.

At first, I was nervous suggesting to Alice we write a sequel together; she's always been a bit protective of her writing. OK, I'll say it, a bit precious. But I think maybe the coma changed her, too. She's still Alice, but she just seems a bit ... *softer*. She leaves the house without makeup, she blushes when you compliment her, and the other day, she actually went to one of Katie's cello recitals with me, and the accompanying pianist wasn't even hot. Anyway, she threw her arms around me and said, "That's the best idea ever."

The process wasn't entirely smooth, but with Alice softening and me gaining confidence, we kind of met in the middle. There were a few spats. For example, she still has this ridiculous fangirl crush on Willow and wanted him to take center stage, whereas I was inclined to write him out completely. I don't know why, but his character really annoys me now; he seems so weak and selfish—I guess recent experiences have made me grow up and prioritize personality over abs. We eventually agreed that the protagonist would be a different character from *The Gallows Dance*. Someone with the potential for real growth. I knew immediately it had to be the puppy—Ash. Because a puppy can only get bigger.

But there was one character we agreed on one hundred percent from the get-go.

The lift doors open and the scent of medicine intensifies, causing my heart to flip. We walk down the corridor, reading the signs even though we've read them a thousand times, upping our pace as we approach the ward.

We reach the white doors and I pause so I can pump some alcohol rub on my hands. I take a moment to peer through the porthole windows. Nate lies on a bed, stretched out, his head elevated, so that at a glance he could be watching TV or listening to his iPod. This is my favorite bit of the hospital visit, watching him from behind a pane of glass, framed by a circular piece of wood. It's like he's in a whole other world, captured in a photo or a television screen. Floating in a bubble. Something about the surrealness, the distance, makes it feel like anything could happen—like he could just wake up.

"You ready?" Katie asks.

I respond by pushing through the doors into the ward. The tinny hospital sounds fill my head, the *pips* of the monitors, the wheeze of the ventilators, the smell of antiseptic and urine, and that sense of something magical, otherworldly, vanishes completely. Reality kicks in. Nate is in a coma. He hasn't woken up for six months. And with every day, every hour, every minute that passes, it becomes less likely he ever will. My vision clouds with tears and that black aura of guilt seems to cast the ward in shadow.

Alice sits in the chair beside him and rubs his hand. "Hey, squirt," she says.

I imagine him opening his eyes and telling her to get lost. He's fourteen. Then I remember he turned fifteen a few weeks back— I held his favorite homemade chocolate cake beneath his nose so he could smell it—and the tears begin to fall down my face.

Katie drags a comfy seat over so I can sit beside him, across the bed from Alice. "Dumb-ass hospital furniture," she mutters, battling it into position. I smile to myself; good old reliable Katie. No coma could change her.

Before I sit, I lean forward and kiss him on the forehead. He smells faintly of sweat and baby wipes, and I swear his golden eyelashes quiver slightly, stirring beneath my breath.

I still remember the first time I saw him like this. I'd only been awake for a short while, and even though the doctors assured me he was alive, was lying in the bed next to me, in fact, I could only make out the sandy spikes of his hair, and I just wouldn't believe it was him. I knew with such certainty he was dead, it was as if I'd watched him die.

So, as soon as the medical staff and the parents left the ward to have a private, "grown-up" chat, I pulled out my remaining tubes and stumbled to his bedside. Alice and Katie were pressing their buzzers like mad, trying to get the nurses to help, begging me in rasping voices to get back into bed before I fell. But I reached him all the same.

He looked like he was built from wax, all these wires and tubes and pieces of tape holding him together. But that little monitor was *pipping* away and I could finally see with my eyes what I could not believe with my heart.

The doctors were right.

He was alive.

Before the guilt and grief and anger arrived (and boy, did they arrive), I felt only relief. I wanted to kiss him and hold him and laugh all at once, but instead, I did an odd thing. I pulled back his covers and lifted his pajama top. And there it was, no bigger than the size of a penny; a red, circular scar on his abdomen. A healed bullet wound. And the strangest thing? It didn't surprise me, not in the least. I looked from Alice to Katie, and they didn't look surprised, either. And I knew we were all thinking the same thing—it was my responsibility to reach him, to wake him, to bring him home.

Later, Mum told me that Nate had died the day before I awoke, that he'd flatlined for three minutes before they'd managed to revive him. Three whole minutes. I can't even hold my breath for two. I remember Mum's face, draining of all color as she whispered the words: *I will never forget the sound of that flatline, Violet.* And I remember thinking: *Neither will I.*

Alice hands me her Kindle and I finally sink into the chair beside him. I rest one hand on his arm, which feels surprisingly warm, and with the other, I load up the first page of our manuscript. *The Sequel to* The Gallows Dance—*The Gallows Song.*

Alice peers over the bed at the screen. "No," she blurts out. "Go straight to the good bit, you know, the bit he'll really love."

"Yeah, don't make him listen to the setup," Katie says, perching on the bed. "The poor thing must be bored out of his tree as it is."

We never talk about it, my friends and I—why we fell into comas in the first place, why we woke within minutes of one another, Nate's mysterious bullet wound—but I sometimes wonder if they have strange post-coma dreams, too, if they're busy piecing together their own patchwork of disjointed memories. Because it's like they know Nate can really hear us, like they know there's something a bit different—a bit special—about the Comic-Con Four.

I drum my finger against the page-turner button, jumping through the electronic words until I find the right place. The entrance of the boy. The only character Alice and I could agree on one hundred percent from the get-go.

Then I squeeze Nate's warm flesh, and I begin to read.

Thorn circled the boy, looking him up and down. "And you think you can help us why?"

The boy smiled—his face all angles and mischief—and pushed his sandy hair from his forehead. "Because I may look like a dumb Imp kid, but I'm as clever as your average Gem. That makes me perfect spy material, don't you think?"

"OK, you think you're so clever . . . prove it."

"You're a Gem," the boy said.

Thorn scowled. "That's not so difficult to work out. I'm tall and I have symmetrical features."

"It wasn't that. Imps can be tall and attractive, too. Your voice gave you away—you try too hard to flatten your vowels."

Thorn adjusted his eye patch, pretending he wasn't rattled. "Well, you're certainly braver than the average Gem, I'll give you that. What's your name, Imp?"

The boy grinned his pixie grin. "Nate."

ACKNOWLEDGMENTS

First, to my wonderful parents. I grew up in a house filled with stories and love, sci-fi and music, laughter and kindness and freshly made cakes. I carry those things in my heart, always. You provide me with endless love and support. You've made me who I am.

To my fabulous readers: Lucy Fisher, Liam Gormley, Jenny Hargreaves, Steve Lee, Helen Spencer, Heather Thompson, Len and Gill Waterworth (Mum and Dad), Isobel Yates, and Helen Yates. You are some of my dearest family and friends; my cheerleading squad of wise Yodas. Thank you!

To my awesome friends. You've dried my tears, distracted me, and made me laugh. You've given me the strength I've needed during the past few years, and I love you all for it.

To the *Times* and Chicken House for holding the *Times/*Chicken House Children's Fiction Competition every year, which gives random, unknown writers (like me) the amazing opportunity to be published.

To everyone at Chicken House—what an amazingly supportive group of people. To Barry Cunningham and Rachel Leyshon for their generous encouragement, guidance, creativity, and their constant faith in me as a writer. To Jazz Bartlett for insisting Barry read my first manuscript, and for her brilliant publicity ideas. To Elinor Bagenal for doing such a fantastic job selling *The Fandom* all around the world. And of course, to my editor, Kesia Lupo, who has been a joy to work with. I honestly don't know how I ever wrote before I met you, Kesia. You provide endless ideas, clarity, and containment. And thank you for convincing me not to kill you-know-who!

To the Big Idea Competition, for recognizing the potential in Angela's idea, and of course to Angela McCann, for having such a big idea in the first place. The stars definitely fell into line the day you entered said competition. Thank you!

And finally, to Ajda Vucicevic, for all her help with my first manuscript, the novel that caught Chicken House's eye. Her encouragement and faith in me at the beginning of my writing adventure gave me the confidence to carry on, and I will always be eternally grateful to her.

Thanks again, guys. I couldn't wish for a better fandom!